JAMES CATHCART
SLAVE TO THE DEY OF ALGIERS
1785

ROBERT GAGE EVANS

THE SOJOURNER SERIES
BOOK FOUR

JAMES CATHCART—SLAVE TO THE DEY OF ALGIERS, 1785
by Robert Gage Evans

Book Four of the Sojourner Series

Copyright ©2017 by Robert Gage Evans

ISBN-10: 0998342513
ISBN-13: 9780998342511
LCCN: 2017944325

Edited by Jocelyne Thomas, Branwen Books Editing Services
Cover and interior layout by Ellie Searl, Publishista®

PINE FLAT EDITIONS
Sebastopol, CA

The Harbor of Algiers, 16th century

Extraordinary praise for this novel, previously titled
BARBARY SLAVE

"*BARBARY SLAVE* FOLLOWS THE ADVENTURES of American sailor James Cathcart as his ship is taken by Barbary pirates and he spends the following eleven years as a slave of the Dey of Algiers while American politicians refuse to pay ransom.

The book is largely set ashore as Cathcart works his way through the slave hierarchy and his character is used to explore the interaction between Christian slaves and their Muslim captors both at the local level and in international diplomacy. It also brings out the internal tensions in the region between the Turks and the various Arab factions.

The book had good characterizations and the various aspects of the plot were brought together in a well written and well-paced narrative that was good to read. Recommended." –David Hayes, editor, Historic Naval Fiction website:

"I FOUND *BARBARY SLAVE* A NOTABLE and plausible tale that provides a breath of fresh air from the usual pirate fare set in the Caribbean. Evans' research and ability to recreate the world in which [his protagonist] lives shine through." –Cindy Vallar, editor and reviewer, Pirates and Privateers website

"WELL-WRITTEN, RIVETING STORY. BEAUTIFUL historic details woven into an epic plot with unexpected twists and turns. Highly recommend it. Worth a read!" –J & M Valera, December 13, 2012

"THE HISTORICAL AND GEOGRAPHICAL RESEARCH are excellent. I have travelled through some of that area and many of the observations are strikingly accurate." –Flower, March 30, 2013

ALSO BY ROBERT GAGE EVANS

FICTION

OTHER BOOKS OF THE SOJOURNER SERIES

Book One
YOKUTS WARRIOR
SPRING
1792

Book Two
SUTTER'S FORT
ALTA CALIFORNIA
1838

Book Three
OMROD SMYTH
A COD FISHERMAN FROM BRISTOL TOWN
1579-1634

NONFICTION

PINE FLAT: A QUICKSILVER BOOMTOWN (2005)
PINE FLAT: FAMILIES OF THE MODINI PRESERVE (2016)

CHAPTER ONE

July 20, 1785

TODAY WAS THE SECOND DAY of aching, motionless heat. The first twelve days out of Plymouth Harbour were splendid, with a steady wind and sixteen men that quickly developed as a professional crew. There were the two new and awkward-natured sailors aboard, but they were trained to their proper duty within the first week. More than the swift progress of the ship and skill of the crew, I felt satisfied with my own competence on this, my first voyage as a deck officer. I must say, to myself anyway, that seventeen years old and second mate is not bad at all. Some might wink at the fact that my father was the owner of the merchant ship *Maria,* but not those who count. The crew and the investors of our cargo: timber, salt cod and beaver fur, were well-aware that I had served as cabin boy from my seventh birthday on this very ship. They were also confident that Captain Elrod Cathcart had demanded more from his son than any sailor aboard.

Now we were becalmed within smelling distance of the Portuguese coast. The smallest breeze would take the *Maria* to Cadiz in a single day, but nothing moved. Nothing shipboard, nothing on the sea around us. Toward the east there was a slight tickle, and then, in a sudden explosion, dawn boiled red along the horizon. At my first blink

I saw a line of small cumulus clouds march in file over the smooth ridge of Cape Vincent, but with my third blink, the simmering heat blotted clouds and coast from sight.

For all the good of it, I stood by the helm to feel sweat fall from my nose. The sloop sat like a dumpling in thick stew, and there was nothing left but to lick salt from my lips and dream of dark gravy over tender beef that only mothers could cook. Long delightful meals at home in Plymouth and father at the head of table conversing with men of wit and fortune. Laughter. The red wine of Portugal.

A single brown bird flew past, and I could hear Will Melman flailing about in the hidden depths of his galley. He dropped pots and muttered obscenities in a twittering stream. My old friend Will was in a mood, and he wanted all to understand that it wasn't good. The sun burned higher, and there were no more birds. The smell of coffee and biscuits drizzled into the shell of air surrounding the *Maria*. I licked sweat from the side crease of my lips and imagined eating one of Will's biscuits. They were his only success as a cook, always crisp and chewy, with a hint of burnt smoke. I thought of one now, slathered with honey and washed down with black, black coffee.

A ragged line of those familiar near-shore brown birds skimmed along the port side and suddenly veered north. They pierced through the thick, humid furnace in a lethargic flap-glide and then disappeared into the molten gray air. Will emerged from the galley, gave me a sour look, and walked up to the bow where Omrod Williams was assigned. Neither spoke. Will placed a tin cup and a flat brown biscuit on the deck next to the slowly moving holystone. He stood and watched Omrod work at scrubbing the deck until a large clean white spot emerged from the grime, and then turned on his bare heel and disappeared back into his galley-cave.

Perfect. Omrod, the less accomplished of the Williams brothers, on his knees for one stupid act or another, and Will treats him like an ill-treated victim. I'm the nigger's best friend—his only friend!—and what do I get? Hard looks and no coffee. Damn!

Heat pressed against my chest, and the shushing noise of Omrod stopped.

"What? What's that, Omrod?"

"Sail abeam," he repeated.

I looked, and through the shimmering will-o'-the-wisp was a ship. A strange ship, not like any that sailed the Atlantic.

"Captain!" I shouted.

Almost simultaneously, Captain Stevens and First Mate Vaughn arrived from their cabins and were at my shoulder. I noticed Sevillon Williams and Will at the bow, with the fool, Omrod Williams, still on his knees.

"Lateen-rigged," Captain Stevens muttered.

We all stared at the triangular-shaped sail hanging askew from the main mast. Suddenly, some outlandish combination of atmospheric conditions levitated the entire ship out of the ocean. Up, up out of the sea into the hot void. It was as if a giant puppeteer volunteered his model for our examination. Eight beetle-like legs flailed the ether in a slow steady pulse.

"Goddamn," Vaughn shouted. "She's a galley! A xebec!"

His job done, the puppeteer dropped the ship back into the steamy soup. Yet the strange image remained: one large slanted sail, huge oars in rhythmic cadence. A pirate ship—a Barbary pirate ship.

"Quiet now!" We were speechless even without Stevens's command. "Let's be sure of this. It could be anything—a Spanish prize, maybe. Not Barbary. Not Barbary. We've a treaty with the bastards, so we have no fear of the damn Barbary pirates."

Our tableau remained unchanged as the xebec inched closer. I stood at the useless helm, the captain and first mate rooted on either side. Omrod leaned his head against the amidships rail while his brother and Will gazed at the approaching ship.

The xebec's oar sweeps trailed swirling pools, and no one on the

Maria moved. When we were a few dozen rods from collision, each pirate's uniform of rags, head piece, and weapon stood in clear detail.

Captain Stevens turned his head toward me and whispered his final order. "James," he said, "lower the stars and stripes."

CHAPTER TWO

A GRAY-BEARDED MAN SAT ENTHRONED at the xebec's stern. I could see his eyes move about with catlike twitches, and each movement of the xebec's crew he directed with small gestures of his hand. He was close enough that I felt his eyes on mine for a brief moment, and my teeth were vivid points of pain.

The xebec eased along our port side, bow to our stern. Their oars were retracted in meticulous order, and the ships mashed together with a grinding jolt. The pirate captain, his white turban a beacon, directed a chaotic boarding of a swarm of small brown men, all screaming a torrent of hard, violent words. The pirates waved short, curved swords; all carried knives, and one pushed a blunderbuss in my face. A bramble-filled blanket of noise weighed me down, assaulted me more than the blows and shoves and kicks. One pirate yanked at my hair, while three others stripped off my shirt and shoes and pants. I did not struggle. The din of screams continued as they dragged me across the deck and forced me to scramble over heavy netting that connected our sloop to the xebec.

The heat beat my bare head and seared my feet to the deck. Pinches, shoves, and kicks continued through an interminable gauntlet of pirates that ended only upon reaching the dais of their captain. A flurry of blows forced me to crumple in a heap. When I attempted a small peek at the old man, red pain erupted through my entire skull, and I fainted.

Saltwater filled my nose and mouth. I flailed to the surface. Black eyes and smiling beards surrounded me. A high-pitched ringing in my head overwhelmed the slurp of passing waves. I looked up, and the pirate captain's eyes held mine again. He was smiling. The tranquil ruler of his world.

"Stand," he said.

I struggled to obey. Five of the *Maria's* crew lay battered, heads down on the blackened, greasy deck. "Get up, mates," I mumbled.

All except Sevillon began moving, and when he remained inert, a bucket of water flashed to set him in jerky, uncoordinated motion. We finally stood before the pirate captain, naked, our blood frying into instant scabs.

"I am Rais Mawlud-Qadir." He spoke the Spanish language, and after a brief visual inventory of our crew began to shake his head very slowly, an apparent sign of deep sympathy for our plight. "Christians, be consoled." He stopped his head movement but maintained a grim expression. "This world is full of vicissitudes, for such is the will of Allah. I have been a slave myself and know the pain and indignities that you now feel."

Rais Mawlud-Qadir spoke in a slow, precise parade of words, and my father's shipboard Spanish lessons allowed an adequate translation. "English, Spanish, and Latin," my father had demanded. "A merchant ship's captain must master at least these three languages."

"With Allah as my witness, you will be treated much better than I was by the infidels of Spain. I will give you bread and honey and a dish of coffee, and you must take heart. Possibly Allah will redeem you from captivity, as he has done twice to me." The old man stopped speaking, lowered his eyes, and studied each of us in turn.

I knew better than to speak. My father had often grabbed the tendon below my neck during his teaching lessons. He was an expert at putting me on the tips of my toes in a merry dance of pain. Even on long, cold watches, when we battled ice and fog more than British frigates, he'd grab me and sing the refrain: "Listen, my son; always listen to your betters. Keep your mouth shut and listen!" Mostly I obeyed him, but it was a burden that I refused at the most unfortunate times.

"Honored Rais," I began, thinking "Rais" meant captain—surely that was correct—yet immediately, as the salutation slipped from my tongue, a blow from behind crushed me back to the deck.

I lay convulsing, spinning in and out of consciousness, until someone pulled me to my feet and cuffed me repeatedly on the head. My eyes focused. The gray beard was twisted into a benevolent smile.

"Infidel, you must learn to speak only with permission. I am in the service of Ibn Hudaij, and you are his slave. If your impudence continues, you will die. Such is Allah's will."

Rais Mawlud-Qadir turned from me and slowly examined each of his newly acquired slaves. "Is the captain in attendance, or is he still on his ship with the remaining fools?" he asked.

Only a distant gull dared answer.

After a few moments he looked directly at me, and I noticed a milky film over his left eye. He nodded.

"Your Honor, please, his apologies, for my captain speaks only English." I drew my head down like a turtle and waited for the blow.

"Idiot! Dog! Can you point to your captain?"

Captain Stevens stood at my left. His body shook with palsy, and he covered his nakedness with both hands. Without looking up from the deck, I pointed my left thumb at him.

The pirate captain chuckled, and those around him joined with dutiful laughter. One of the young pirates walked over to Stevens and pulled him backward onto the deck. The entire crew of pirates howled.

Stevens flopped about like a tired fish, his tiny penis distended nearly out of sight, his arms helpless against the foot on his chest. The young pirate spit on Stevens's face, and the laughter became louder.

Mawlud-Qadir raised one hand and silence returned. He smiled. "Inform your esteemed captain that he has been captured by authority of the dey of Algiers. We are cruising the Atlantic under recent agreement with Portugal and with express encouragement from the British consul."

He began fiddling with his prayer beads, and the respectful silence continued.

The sun hammered at my head. My worst nightmare was a pleasant option to this sensation of doom that I felt. The *Maria* captured, the entire crew enslaved. What mistakes could I have avoided to prevent this disaster?

Suddenly, he waved an arm and in a high, thin voice yelled, "Take them below!"

<hr/>

The pirate gang pulled loose two stout bars and threw a thick door open. A putrid haze eased from the blackness and encased us in a woolly shroud. My lungs emptied of air, and my throat filled with vomit. I gagged and tried to retreat from the stench.

Our guards fell back as if attacked by a hoard of fleas. Distant groans of "Water, water," bubbled from the void. The Algerian pirates unsheathed swords and beat us with the flat sides. They screamed at us until we stumbled into the void, and the door slammed shut.

I could not breathe. Hands slithered about my body. Moans for water continued until a voice yelled in the Spanish language, "Silence!" and the moans stopped. "How many are you?"

"Six," I replied.

"Thank God, only six." A murmur of agreement trickled through the pitch-black hold. "What nation?"

"Americans, out of Plymouth."

Silence drifted for a long moment, then from the void, "Make yourselves comfortable, Americans."

I could no longer stand, and collapsed against a complaining lump of slime. It pushed me away, and I fell into a chowder of excrement and urine to grope about on my hands and knees.

"James! Is that you, Jimbo?" A hand grasped my shoulder and hauled me back to my feet. "We've got to get our backs against the hull."

Will Melman's muscles bulged through soft skin as I grasped with both my hands around his upper arm. We struggled through the slime to slither over bodies until rough timbers finally marked the end of our journey. The light was so dim that I perceived faceless shades who squawked protests, but we ignored them and cleared space for two. I sat with my vomit-clogged chest. "Out!" I screamed. "I've got to get out of this place!"

Will took me in a tight bear hug; water sloshed, and I shivered for a long time. Finally, I said, "Okay. It is okay, Will."

My stomach felt pinched off in the middle. The black smell pushed against me and invaded every orifice of my body. It trickled along my arms, like a massive, putrid leech.

Will nudged an elbow into my ribs. "Us slaves got to stick together." He gave me another tap. "You hear me, white boy? If we're going to see another day, we got to stick together."

"Tell me if I have another choice, nigger."

"Nigger, indeed." Will turned away from me, chuckled in a strange fashion, and then went silent.

Another clot of vomit stuck in my throat. The clean, soft option of death beckoned with seductive persistence. I moved toward the wavering flame of my mind's invention. I could even smell the delicate vapours of burning wax. In the far distance of this dream, just beyond my reach, the soft freshness of newly cut balsam branches beckoned. The entire universe became quiet and dark, with an oh-so-sweet smell.

CHAPTER THREE

THE SHARP CHOP THAT INEVITABLY follows a wind shift punished the xebec. I took a ragged step back into mindfulness and tried to speak. "Will?" The first effort was a lisping hiss. The second managed to get his attention.

"Yup, wind's up, and we're under weigh." He nudged closer and whispered in my ear. "I've got a little present for you. Give me your hand."

He took my hand in his and gently pulled in a manner that forced me to turn around and face the hull. With both his hand and mine touching the rough wood, Will whispered again. "Run your nose over to your hand."

I shifted full around, splashed slop over my legs, and sniffed once, then again. Such a gift! Small tendrils of fresh air seeped through a poorly chalked seam in the timbers. I breathed the rare perfume in gasping gulps. Slowly I stopped the frantic panting and leaned against the hull, nose to nose with Will Melman.

No whisper now; instead, a deep rumbling voice. "We're in deep shit, James, deep, deep shit."

"May we ignore the obvious for a moment," I said

Deep, deep, deep shit," he said.

"Maybe we can get the *Maria* back and escape."

"Dream on, my friend. With the Williams brothers as crew and Stevens still captain, maybe we can get these pirates to laugh themselves to death."

"You don't think you and me and Vaughn can lick the lot of them?"

"We'd give 'um a run of maybe six seconds."

The puke and shit and salt water through a leaky-hull sloshed about for a while. Will finally gave some more news. "From what I got from our neighbors, here-about, it appears that *Maria* got picked up by another xebec, so that leaves us six slaves are on our own, my friend."

"What in hell happened to the rest of our crew?"

"My bet is that a passel of drunks are going were very surprised when they woke up during the boarding by the pirates."

I went back to the air hole for a good long while and then returned to his shoulder. "Look here, Will, I want you to know that whatever it was that you cooked for me and Vaughn was just fine. Neither one of us was sick for a minute."

"Sure my cooking was good. Nobody on board ever thought otherwise."

"I saw with my own eyes, Will, after the fourth day at sea most of the crew was flopping around like sick fish with puking and shitting all day and night."

"You should have asked a few questions, my Second Mate. If you'd of asked me or Vaughn what was going on, you'd of found there was a bunch of drunks aboard, including our esteemed captain as the biggest pickle of the lot."

"I can't believe what you say, Will."

Will didn't answer and I ran my mind over the past two weeks. The first week was just what you'd expect with a new crew and captain. Good enough as far as I could see. The seventh day…mmm. Sick call was two men, both complaining of suffering from what they ate. Next day another sick soul and then an epidemic forced Me and Vaughn, two of the reliable able seamen and the Williams brothers to keep the *Maria* under weigh.

Where did they get the damn booze?"

"Can you list the freight we're carrying in the hold?'

"Lumber, fur, and salt cod."

"About a third of the cod boxes have a red slash along the top, and if you open one of those marked boxes, you'll find half dried cod and half bottles of Boston rum."

"Damn!"

"Not too bad, I'm told; salty cod, sweet rum, and some of my burned biscuits."

Will didn't go on and rant about my stupidity, he just kept quiet and let me work through the puzzel. Now that I think about it, all the crew on sick-call were hired by Captain Stevens."

"Mmmm," is what Will answered.

"So most of the crew got to feeling that there was no good reason to work up a sweat up on deck. Rum and cod all night and sleep through the day."

"Yup."

"And Stevens knew what was going on."

"Yup, he was part of the nigh-time party and he's the one that had those boxes marked with the red slashes. Our captain and most of his crew were all on the same diet."

"If my father ever shows up alive, Isaac Stevens is shark bait."

"Now, now, you can't be too hard on the man; he was just trying to earn a little extra gold from the Portuguese with his own consignment of rum. Every captain that I know takes the same route around the investors." Will went quiet for a while. "The difference between Stevens and your father is in choosing a partner for the operation."

"Are you accusing my father of profiteering? Carrying illegal rum?"

"Listen, my white nigger friend, our fathers always gave the investors their intended profit, but that didn't stop them from adding some cargo of their own on each voyage."

"Like some barrels of rum?"

"Sure, rum—or whatever they could manage to sell at a profit."

"My father never told me about that little arrangement. How come?"

"I'd guess that your father gave you the option to work out your own way of running a ship." There was a smile hidden in Will's voice. "If you ever made it to that esteemed rating, that is."

"Still, I feel stupid for not figuring out where my father and your father got enough money to own two ships and two fancy houses in Plymouth."

"The problem on this voyage was that Isaac's partner couldn't keep his mouth shut, and by our seventh night at sea, those marked cod boxes were up for grabs."

"How is it that you've waited until now to share this information with me? Not only about Captain Stevens and his friends but the deal that our fathers apparently held?"

"Well, my friend, for most of your life you were too young and foolish for any serious discussion of finances and the equations of risk and benefit for any business, and for this trip, you were too damn busy playing commander of the fleet to deal with mundane matters like a mutiny."

"I was that bad?"

"My biscuits weren't much better."

I settled into the rhythm of waves and smells for a long spell. Finally I blurted, "Look, we've got nothing better to do, so go ahead and tell me about our fathers."

Will didn't hesitate a beat. "First of all, they were good

businessmen and good friends. That is, they were clearheaded businessmen and sober friends. There was never an investor that had the slightest complaint."

"Tell me something about our fathers that I don't already know."

Will Melman waited until the xebec started a new downwind reach. "You know how he is, Jim. You've heard him plenty of times."

"Sure, Alex is hard to start talking and hard to stop—both."

"Right, but for all he's told you, I bet you've never heard him go on about the great Malinke nation, right?"

"Never heard of any such people."

"When the two of us were off someplace alone—on a watch together or loading sugar—he'd brag on how important our family was to the Malinke king. He'd give me that little smile of his. You know the one, Jimbo—the one with the tiny twist on the left side and both eyes squinty slits."

"Yeah, I know his smile. Your pa has a real nice smile when he allows it."

"'The Malinke,'" he'd say, "'all tribes along the Jaliba River knelt before the Malinke, and I remember that my people owned slaves without number, that gold spilled unnoticed onto the streets, and the Malinke always had grain stored for seven years of drought.'"

Will settled a little closer to me and put his voice in the storytelling mode. "Pa always started off the same way—the exact same way: 'The Malinke—all tribes along the mighty Jaliba River knelt before the Malinke, and all the Malinke knelt before Allah.' Then, when we were shoulder to shoulder under a blanket, I'd hear about his pilgrimage to Mecca."

I leaned my head on Will's shoulder and shut my eyes. "Tell me about Mecca."

"The part about Mecca was more a whispered song than a story. First he told about the unending deserts. Then Cairo, where the Malinke spent gold so freely that prices doubled within a week.

Finally, the Red Sea to Jeddah and then Mecca!"

I whispered, "He never told me about any trip to Mecca."

"Sure, I know exactly what he told you and what he didn't tell you." Will settled his bones against the timbers. "With me he'd always spend a long time on the important-stuff, like the victories over one tribe or another, and all the beautiful slave women he captured. The mighty Malinke did this and they did that. On and on, until he got to the Arabs."

The xebec was sailing fairly well now, on a long port reach that shifted the slop away from our feet. A nannering chop beat against the ship in a steady, sharp rhythm. I couldn't see Will, not even a shadowed outline, but his speaking blew small currents against my cheek. In my mind I watched his wide-set eyes drift out of sight. Will spoke of his father, who was also my ally, for Alex Melman was as much father to me as my own, and I listened with my fond memories.

"Jimbo, did my father ever tell you his Malinke name?"

"Nope, mostly I only heard him called Alex. A few times my dad called him Mr. Melman, but nothing else."

"During our private times he always called himself Gaosson Koita."

"That's nice—better than Alex Melman."

"'Gaosson Koita,' he'd say, 'had the best pirogue on the Jaliba River. Gaosson Koita could haul more grain to Mopti than any other man.'"

I joined with Will's quiet laugh, but it was hard to imagine that any nigger could brag about his old life. Especially to brag about some ridiculous nigger river or some no-account nigger town.

The laughing and talking stopped, and I could feel his brittle mood through the darkness.

"Listen up, white boy. I'm going to tell you something important."

"Sure, Will. Go ahead."

"Alex could forgive your father for being a slaver. Hard to believe, isn't it? I mean, my pa working with a white man in the slave business, but he never talked against Captain Cathcart or any other Christian slaver."

"Just a job to get done, I guess."

We were quiet for a long while, and then Will assumed Alex's thin, high-pitched voice, with the same nigger accents and the same slurring of one word into the next. I shut my eyes and listened.

CHAPTER FOUR

1757

WILL SPOKE, AS IF IN prayer: "Allah is the One God; Mohammed is the last prophet."

Then he was quiet for a bit. I could hear loud voices topside. There were also gulls squealing nearby, which indicated that the Xebec was close to some shore or other. Maybe Gibraltar or the coast of Spain. Of course there was the perpetual sloshing of shit at our ankles. I was five years younger than Will, but our competition aboard ship or the rare time we had ashore, was always as equals. Aside from Will's advantage in physical strength, we were always toe to toe in shipboard lessons of language, navigation, or sailing skills. This self-proclaimed role of teacher was new for Will and most emphatically not to my liking.

"What is this nonsense about Allah and prophets that you're muttering about?" I spit some phlegm into the muck at our feet. "You aren't going creepy on me, are you?"

"Dammit, Jimbo, I'm just trying to tell you what my father told me. I admit that his story was pretty weird the first couple of times I heard it, and at first I didn't realize that it wasn't Alex Melman talking about the old days—it was Gaosson Koita."

"Not exactly a name he could make up out of thin air, I guess."

"True enough. But what hit me hard in the belly was the way my father acted when he told his story. Even with thirty years past, he trembled and bugged his eyes when he told me how the bastards took him down with nets. It seemed that Alex Melman still couldn't believe that men who bowed to Mecca and prayed to Allah, just as the Malinke people prayed to Allah, could take him into slavery. He told me his story at least a dozen times, and each time there were tears when he told me that it was Arabs who took him down with nets."

"Will, I'm real confused with what you're telling me."

"I don't blame you one bit—it's a messy story."

"Can I ask a question or three?"

"Sure, Jimbo, ask away."

"Alex Melman was Gaosson Koita in the old days."

"Correct."

"Gaosson Koita was a big-shot warrior with a tribe called the Malinke, and all the Malinke believed that Allah, not Jesus, was the prophet of God."

"Right as rain, my boy."

"Then some other folks called Arabs, who were also true believers in Allah, came along to net Gaosson Koita and drag him off to slavery. Is that it, so far?"

Will coughed and joined his spit to the swill. "Just last summer we were in the warehouse with an inventory list to check, and my father started up again with his Gaosson Koita story. There was the usual bit about wooden collars and whips that spit blood." Will put his nose on mine. "You sure you haven't heard this before, Jimbo?"

"Not a whisper about collars and whips. I've heard both Alex and my father tell me how he got his Melman name, but never anything about Arabs and such."

"Yeah, well, there's a whole lot more before the Melman-name part." Will pitched his voice again to mimic his father. "Gaosson

Koita saw Timbouctou, brown and dusty, with bearded mullahs who never looked into my eyes. The Arabs bid us follow their tracks in the desert and left us without water. We followed the spoor of their camels until the wind came, and then many people from the Jaliba River died. Gaosson Koita endured until the oasis of Bidon Cing, where the Arabs sold him to tall men wrapped in blue robes, and they, in turn, sold him to Arabs in the city of Ghardia.'"

"Stop! You lost me again, Will. I haven't the foggiest notion of the places you name."

"That's two of us, white boy; I'm just giving what I heard."

"Are we near the end?"

"We're getting close to the part you've heard before. The rest of the secret story is about Gaosson Koita getting hauled from town to town, up over some damned-cold mountains, and finally to the auction at Oren."

"Oren? That's where our fathers first met, right? Close to Algiers, if I recall my map."

"Oren is west of Algiers, and both are on the Barbary Coast. Also, the story goes, that after the auction, Gaosson Koita was chained to a bunch of black folks in the hold of a ship with no food, water, or much air."

"Now this is a fact that sounds all too familiar, my black friend."

"Well, my white friend, I doubt if Captain Elrod Cathcart and my Mr. Gaosson Koita had similar memories of their first encounter."

"The only story I have starts with the good ship *Maria* leaving Oren and into smack-into seven days and seven nights of bad weather."

"Check, and also a bunch of white sailors dead from some kind of fever that always ended with bloated tongues and bad cramps." Will made his voice louder and more emphatic. "It was sixteen dead white sailors, with only Captain Elrod Cathcart and First Mate Vaughn to keep the damn ship under weigh."

"Right," I said. "That's the part where everything begins."

"I want you to know, Jimbo, that my father, Gaosson Koita, didn't give a good shit about any white-man problem, because he was just trying to keep his nose above the same stuff that we currently have slopping around our feet."

"Okay, so don't get huffy with me. The only thing I know for fact is that my father told me about the fever killing all the crew, and him going down into the hold, where he picked one slave from the heap of slaves chained below."

"I beg to inform you that your father picked the only man who was able to return his stare, and that is what I know for a fact."

"Gaosson Koita."

"Correct. So now we're on the same page. Our fathers and Roger Vaughn brought the *Maria* with a cargo of seventy-eight half-dead niggers and a half-ton of cork bark into Kingston Harbor."

"Those three were tough sons-a-bitches."

Will's voice was church quiet. "Well, they were tough old turkeys, and that's no lie. They also had the luck of decent weather and just one small sail to manage."

Will shut up and left me to end the story in my own mind. He let me imagine the three weeks it took to sell the cargo and reload with barrels of molasses for Boston. The three weeks it took to have a court approve the manumission deed—the freedom deed for the slave that helped two white men bring seventy-seven black men to market. "Alex," the deed said, because Alex was the first name Captain Cathcart yelled at him. "Alex! Hard-a-lee," he yelled, and the Malinke warrior ducked to avoid the swinging boom. Then, at the desk in Kingston Harbor it was "Melman" after the Jew banker who held a mortgage on the *Maria*. Alex Melman, alive, and a free nigger.

No one had ever explained the name beyond that to me, but Alex Melman shipped as cook, sailor, and particular friend to my father for twenty-six years. Alex came ashore one month in twelve, bought a cottage in Plymouth, purchased a wife in Kingston, and brought her home to keep him company. I never met Will's mother; she died a year before I was born, and Will Melman was always on board the *Maria* as the son of both Alex Melman and Captain Elrod Cathcart.

———

There were no shouts above and no gulls complaining. From the rhythm of waves on the Xebec, it felt as if we were in blue water again, out of sight from any landfall. "What do you really think, Will? Are they dead?"

"It's more likely than not," he said

"It was that damn General Washington who sent them on a damn fool's mission."

Will took on his smart-aleky tone of voice. "Well, your damn general was just trying to save the Bahama Islands from slavers. Of course it was Loyalist slavers he was trying to stop, not Virginia slavers."

I joined in, full steam. "The damn hypocrites from Virginia sent a Yankee ship from Plymouth to chase a few British loyalists from a bunch of no-account islands that couldn't grow anything but a bunch of pirates."

"Amen," Will whispered.

"And a damn good ship to boot. The whole Cathcart family went in hock to buy their second sloop, and now the *Maria's* captured, and the *Seagull* is lost at sea. How's that for luck," I said.

The smile came back into Will's voice. "Consistently bad, I'd say."

"Three's not been a single word from friend or foe about our fathers."

"Better than a year now," Will said.

"And here we are, sucking air from a tiny hole. Damn!"

I dozed to dream of white flannel sheets and sweet watery syrup from sugar maple trees. There was a nice young woman in the dream, dressed all in black, who warmed the syrup and drizzled it over clean snow. She smiled and kissed me on the forehead and handed over the plate of sugared snow.

The xebec tacked to starboard, and sewer slop moved above my ankles. The dream changed to scratchy wool and black medicine from a big kettle. An old lady filled a spoon with the evil-smelling mess and crammed it down my throat. I gagged and woke up.

"James?"

"What?" I wasn't much interested in more discussion or story telling from Will.

"Maybe this old pirate captain is correct—the vicissitude part, anyway. I mean, things just happen to people, and there's not much you can do but watch."

"What are you getting at?"

"Let's stop worrying about something we can't control and nuzzle up to enjoy the fresh air we've got. We can talk and laugh and get mad, and nothing we do will make any difference. Worry is like pissing in the wind."

"A body can choose to piss upwind or downwind," I said.

"The wind keeps changing, Jim, my boy. First thing you know, pee starts running down your face, and there's nothing you can do about it."

"Not much wind down here," I said.

"Go back to sleep," Will said.

<hr />

Somewhere toward the end of my dream about eating fish chowder, the hold door rattled and swung open. Fresh air washed over our bodies, and immediately heaps of slime began moaning. "Water; water."

A pirate stood in silhouette for a moment, coughed, gagged, and backed out of sight. The clamor for water grew apace, but none of the slaves moved. In a short while the man returned, but this time with a rag wrapped over his nose and mouth. He placed three buckets and some tall stacks of wooden bowls just inside the hold. The pirate stood still for a long time to survey the dim cavern. Finally, he pointed to a small group of men huddled to his left.

"You!" he yelled in the Spanish language.

The group of four men scuttled through the slop and waited for the next command.

"One dipper, one bowl—now!"

In a blink the men surrounded the buckets, lifted dippers, and slowly let the water dribble over their lips and tongue. I could feel my Adam's apple move and my throat constrict. The slaves gently dropped the dippers back into the bucket, picked up a bowl, and returned to a spot against the bulkhead.

The men from the *Maria* were chosen last.

Will, Omrod, and I were the last of the last, and we scraped the bottom for partial dips and swallowed quickly. I began to dip again for my full quota of water, but without any warning that I could detect, the pirate guard struck his bare foot full in my chest and sent me sprawling— backside first—into the cesspool. I sat up. The water buckets were gone, and one bowl remained by the open door. Without looking at the contents, I grabbed the bowl and waddled back to safety. The door slammed, and there was only the black smell.

For the next four days our guards repeated this ritual of buckets and bowls. I learned how to tip the water bucket for the fullest possible dipper. I became proficient at sucking rancid oil through my teeth and chewing black olives with calm deliberation. Six olives was what filled the bowls and made do for each watch. On the fifth day we dropped anchor. The light and fresh air returned in a heavenly gush, but the coffee, bread, and honey never appeared.

One of the Spanish sailors of our putrid cave turned toward us and spoke. "You are home now, my American brethren. This is Algiers, and in all likelihood you will spend the rest of your miserable lives here."

CHAPTER FIVE

August 1785

T HE XEBEC HAD BEEN MOORED in the City of Algiers harbor for a day and a half, and this was our first hour out from the black hole of shit and piss. My eyes could barely function as the sharp sunlight glared from two- and three-story white buildings. Hot! Hot! Hot! It was midday, and Rais Mawlud-Qadir moved his weight to the left and yelled, "Stop!" The pole dug into my shoulder as I struggled to maintain his throne on a level keel.

A tall man in white robes stood apart from the mob of screaming Algerians. He gave one nod to the pirate captain, and our caravan of ragamuffin slaves lurched forward again. The cobblestones were poorly set, and when Omrod stumbled, he forced Sevillon, Will, and me to strain every muscle to prevent our rais from ending on the rocks. During the next dozen paces a guard walked alongside Omrod and flailed him with a short leather crop.

Men and boys screamed obscenities at us. Children hit our legs with sticks and spit little showers into our faces. Men laughed at each attack and tucked small coins into the hands of brave youngsters. Images of white robes and turbans of many colors burned through the sweat in my eyes. Sharp, bright sunlight followed short respites of blessed cool shadows. One hill succeeded another until finally the journey ended and Rais Mawlud-Qadir dismounted from his chair. He waved for us to sit with our backs to a high white wall, and when he was assured that his slaves were settled in the shade and the guards were attentive to their duty, he entered through a large gate and disappeared.

A small breeze whispered fragrant scents; a serene quiet enveloped slave and guards alike. Servants appeared to tiptoe about and serve cups of water to the attendant Turks. The smallest noise from a slave brought murderous looks from the guards.

"Silence!" a guard hissed. "This is the home of Ibn Hudaij. Silence!"

I could see ten-foot-high walls topped with sharp metal spikes and shards of glass, and was thankful for the shady refuge they provided. Silence covered slave and captor, and a gentle whirlpool grabbed my mind. Sparrows twittered in mindless repetition. Time passed.

"Pssst!"

I opened my eyes, and a guard waved us toward the forming line. We stood for a while longer, and then captives and guards alike followed after our pirate captain to pass through first the large gate and then a narrow gate that forced most of us to bend under the portal. It was after the first step past the portal that we were transported into a land beautiful beyond imagination. Rose trees lined the meandering path; red bracts on green vines climbed white walls, and a white marble fountain bubbled water into increasingly larger bowls. Citrus trees, heavy with oranges and lemons, stood guard behind the roses. The few rooms I could see through open doors and windows had little furniture but were filled with countless rugs of intricate patterns and muted dark colors.

In truth, I could barely walk or think. Beauty and fragrance were dissolved into a fog of exhaustion.

The guard hissed again and motioned for us to sit down. Will and I sprawled on the bare bricks of a courtyard, our legs and arms akimbo, and stared into the pale blue sky.

I whispered, "Forty—is that correct?"

"That's my count: six from the *Maria*, eighteen or so Spanish fishermen, and the rest I can't figure."

A group of eight slaves spoke a few words, one to the other, but ignored all others.

"Sounds like French," I said.

Will shrugged his shoulders and crab-walked over to the group. I watched his hands wave and his head shake. He listened for a while, and then crabbed back to me. "It's like this—the first ship captured was Dutch, but most of the crew is Flemish. They total sixteen. The rest, except us, are Spanish fishermen from two separate ships. One Spaniard died the day before we were captured, so we sit here with forty men."

"What comes next? Do they have any idea?"

"Galleys for us, I imagine. But the Dutch are confident that a ransom will come for them."

"What do you think?"

"I think my stomach and backbone are tired of rubbing up against each other. I've also noticed that those Dutch fellows have been treated far better than the rest of us. They get real clothes, and we get venomous rags. We get rancid olives, and they get soup with vegetables."

My tongue stopped working. My mind was stuffed with straw. Olives or soup were remote notions that had no substance. House and street noises trickled through walls and leaves. Shadows lengthened, and a cluster of crested brown birds scooted rapidly about in a far corner of the courtyard to argue over scattered seeds and crumbs. Two house slaves entered the courtyard and placed a large kettle over an open fireplace. They traipsed back and forth with buckets, and sloshed water into the black pot. Next, they built a fire and set the water to boiling.

Every slave that I could see sat up to watch huge slabs of red bloody meat enter the bubbling water, and soon, odors of melting fat glided through the courtyard.

I felt the drool ease over my jaw, and scratched scabs from my body.

A curtain parted and a tall, handsome man appeared on a balcony overlooking the courtyard.

"Christians, listen to me, your owner, Ibn Hudaij."

We were silent.

"That I am a kind and good owner of slaves is evidenced by your fair treatment by me and my captains." He smiled at us as if we should reward such an announcement with our vigorous applause. When our silence continued, he gestured toward the pot. "You must prepare for your audience with potential buyers by showing them your finest attributes." Again with the pompous smile and nod of his head. "I have ordered this banquet about to be served to you as a step to put your mind at rest, for all of your potential owners are honest and patient men." The smile disappeared. "I have gone to great expense in purchasing a camel—"

Immediately a small cloud of whispers erupted, with those who understood Hudaij's Spanish translating to the rest. Scattered, harsh coughs introduced an increasingly loud staccato: "No! No!"

Captain Stevens grabbed my arm. "What are they saying? What's wrong?"

"Our owner is serving us camel, not beef."

Hunger departed from the European slaves, and any vestige of good sense left them. For reasons that remained a mystery to me, the European slaves gained a strength of their convictions with their collective cadence. "No! No! No!"

"Tell him, 'Yes! Yes!'" hissed Stevens.

The elegant grandee raised both hands and commanded, "Quiet!" His voice was sharp but well modulated. He looked at each slave until, once again, only the camel shimmering in bubbling water could be heard.

"Never again!" he said. "Never again will I let my kindness show to Christian slaves. You will not eat camel? Fine, that is your prerogative. Instead"—and for the first time his voice mounted an octave and nearly cracked—"eat your lice."

He turned and disappeared through the curtained door. Seconds later, two slaves jogged into the courtyard, inserted poles through the pot handles, and lugged it from the room. Trails of rich, gamy steam followed our banquet through the door. Ghosts of fat camel coursed through the silent room.

I stared at the line of Spanish and Dutch sailors. What insane conviction made them reject the meat of camel? Meat is meat, and the damn camel smelled better than any beef or pig that I'd ever encountered. Damn idiots. We all sat on the hard bricks and listened to our empty bellies. The damn idiots!

———

The sun fell into a pit beneath the walls, and darkness extinguished any noise. I curled between Omrod and Will, demanding sleep as relief from pain. Dreams with brilliant colors forced me to row a heavy barge through barriers of sand. Red sweat streamed over my body, but I could not move the huge beached vessel. Green clouds spit yellow slime over my face.

Omrod flailed about in his own dream and kicked me awake. Mosquitoes whirled in raucous clouds to sting every source of my blood. Centipedes, with armored backs and black putrid blood, competed for my drowsy attention. A chill eased up through the bricks, and I moved belly to back against Will and Omrod.

At daylight, guards marched us back to the docks and aboard the xebec. We removed sails, hauled goods onto the wharf, and swabbed our former prison. At high noon, oil and olives provided our only sustenance. During the afternoon, we unloaded bundles of fur and boxes of smoked cod from the *Maria*, and the crates of clocks, looms, and metal-sheathed plows from the larger Dutch ship. I never saw another one of the *Maria's* sailors, except our lot from the Barbary Xebec. After sunset, we marched back to our master's house and received a single bowl of boiled vegetables as repast. The house slaves also slipped us some fruit, and we made out tolerably well. Thus ended our first day as slaves.

Except for snores and insects humming in intimate chorus, a dull quiet covered the room. "Is this it, Will? Is this what slavery is all about?"

"Can't say, my white friend. We both start from the same spot, as far as any practical experience goes."

"You know damn well, my black friend, that you and I served the same ship under the same captain, and that my father never sent a negative word in your direction. Never! But he had me on extra duty if I blinked at the wrong time. I was closer to being a damn slave than you ever were, and that's no lie."

"Of course Captain Cathcart preferred me to you. I could best the captain in both chess and morabala. Plus, I'm five years older than you."

"That's what I'm saying. You were mate or cook, while I was always hauling at some rope or reefing a sail at the far end of a spar, like a damn slave."

Will worked a small smile for me and shrugged. "Look," he said, "given the reality of my intelligence, please explain the recent past for me. I've recently had Isaac Stevens as my captain and a dumb white kid for second mate. So tell me, idiot boy, how come is that?"

"Hard to say. I haven't got any good answer to the actual question of why a smart nigger can't be trusted to command an American ship." I tried to get back on the good side of my friend. "Let's just blame Washington and that damn Jefferson and all those Virginia smart-ass Southerners for your troubles."

"How about blaming all those fools who believe that the Old Testament is the word of God?"

"You're getting creepy on me again, Will. Please don't throw any of the Allah nonsense at me."

He turned his back to me and curled up to feign sleep and mutter. It took about ten repetitions before I caught the drift.

"Uppity whites," he kept repeating. "Damn uppity whites."

CHAPTER SIX

August 1785

A T DAYLIGHT, AND FOR THE two days following, the six slaves removed from the *Maria* were marched from our master's home to the bedistan—the slave market. Algerians gawked and pointed in our direction but seemed disinterested in actually considering the purchase of Ibn Hudaij's property. They were curious to see Americans, as most had ideas about what we looked like from the paintings commonly used to decorate their maps and charts of North America. The Algerins were surprised at my fair complexion, and some few seemed especially interested in my potential as a sodomite.

"Your teeth," they shouted. "Show us your teeth, and smile sweetly for your masters." I was unconcerned by their bluster and stared each heckler down with my best "second mate" scowl. Spanish was the language of preference in the market, and of course I pretended ignorance of their requests.

Two men approached, the elder slightly stooped, gray-bearded, and supported by a shiny black cane, while the younger man sported a trimmed moustache and a greased pointed beard. Both stood within three feet of me and stared as if I were a heifer for sale.

"May Allah save me," the older man said. "He has a pleasant

profile, with delicate curves in all the right places." He coughed. "Many years would melt from my cock with his diligent attention."

"Too stringy and bony for me," the younger man said. "These Franks need a young start, I vow. They are nothing but trouble unless you get them before eight years old. This one must be at least eighteen."

"An interesting challenge," the older man said.

"Nonsense. Just look at his eyes and the size of his head. He has the looks of a crude bumpkin to me. I guarantee he has no sense of poetry about him. None!" The younger man shook his head. "Not for me, thank you."

"Ah, you young men can never understand that the wild colt gives the best ride. Go ahead, take your soft mares and children, but give me the challenge of breaking one such as this." The old man stopped talking, looked more intently into my eyes, and gestured for me to bend closer.

The slave platform was approximately two feet above the ground, so I moved to the edge, bent at the waist, and in firm, precise Spanish said, "Move on, you doddering old pervert!"

His face lit with a smile. His beard jarred with small convulsions of laughter. A tear trickled from one eye, and then the old man turned away from the platform to walk through the crowd in a stiff, jerky gait.

The younger man remained, glared at me for a moment, and then began screaming. "Carrion pig of no faith! Infidel!"

His continuous stream of invective drew the attention of many interested spectators, who quickly joined with the yelling. I ignored them all.

Shortly, very shortly, the old man returned, escorted by a huge Turk. This mountain-of-a-man stepped up onto the platform. My eyes looked directly at his throat. I watched sweat erupt in bubbles along his collarbone and dribble in tiny rivulets between his massive breasts. Slowly, he extended both hands as if he were going to smash a mosquito in midflight, and in a mindless flash, he crashed his hands onto my ears.

I screamed at the pain, and screamed again as the monster twisted both of my ears and threw me down to smash my face onto the wooden floor. I kicked at him as he yanked my raggedy pants off, and then the giant kicked me about my ribs and head until I was lying at the edge of the platform, parallel to the crowd. I could hear loud cheers and laughter, and finally opened my eyes.

The old man obscured my line of sight. He smiled and moved even closer. He touched my head, nose, and lips and moved down my naked body until he fondled my genitals. The crowd cheered even louder. After a time, the old man left off stroking and returned to face me, almost nose to nose. He smiled, gently, kindly, and turned to gimp away.

The crowd grew bored with my inert posture and drifted away. Will helped me stand but remained silent. That he was angry with me was obvious, and he held himself from offering either advice or caution. What did he expect of me? Did he imagine that I would surrender to the demands of this heathen crowd and smile at the ancient pervert? Never. My father would certainly not tolerate any display of weakness in this situation.

The painful ringing in my ears continued through the next day, and my so-called friend, Will Melman, continued his silence. In fact, none of my fellow slaves would speak with me, and I was isolated in every conceivable manner, as if I were a leper or a Jew. But a Cathcart will never be humiliated to the vile manners of a slave. Never.

Late on the fifth day after our arrival in Algiers, we slaves were taken from the bedistan to the dey's palace. Our guards impressed upon us that the dey of Algiers could end our miserable lives with a twitch of his smallest finger. In their ranking of mortals, they placed the dey second only to the gran porte of Turkey, ruler of the Ottoman Empire.

"One small noise, one uncalled-for twitch, and you will die a very painful death," the sergeant of guards said.

Upon entering a huge hall, we slaves flung ourselves upon the cool marble floor. I focused my eyes on small cracks and remained frozen, to await the proper command. At a whispered instruction, we stood, but with eyes still on the small cracks. Another whisper and we moved, shoulders hunched, heads down, careful not to trip on the ragged slave shuffling two steps in front. We were all unconscious of the great creatures watching us and making small decisions about our fate. After three rotations around the hall, we were halted by a third, soft command.

Our owner, Ibn Hudaij, stepped into my restricted line of sight. He muttered, "Him," and moved on. A guard pushed me forward, steered me into a new line of slaves, and then, ever so softly said, "Forward, slaves."

"He bought us," one of the Spanish sailors said to his fellow slaves.

"You all belong to the dey of Algiers," one of the guards confirmed. "The rais offered all of his slaves to the dey, and all were rejected except the seven in this line."

Except for me and six of the Spanish fishermen, all the rest, including Will Melman, disappeared as we straggled out through interminable halls and arches. There was never an opportunity to send a word or signal to my friend; the only sounds uttered were the silent slaps of bare feet on tile floor. In the end, we were led into a hot cavernous room almost totally filled with water.

"Put all of your clothes into that wicker basket," the sergeant yelled.

After we were all naked, the same guard pointed to the steaming-hot pool. "Into the water," the guard yelled.

We descended down a series of small steps into the gigantic pool. "Jeeezus!" I said.

"Dios!" shouted a Spanish fisherman.

We waded down until immersed to our shoulders. "No human being can survive this cauldron," I mumbled.

"Deeper, filthy infidels! Scrub the lice from your hair." The guard's voice echoed from the ornate columns, driving each of us deeper into the bath until only our noses remained above the steaming water line.

I floated about the pool to discover eruptions of extraordinarily hot water and found, in the corners, limp eddies with a more tolerable temperature. My mind seemed to drizzle away into a formless reverie, and I passed Spanish fishermen as if they were floating logs. Nothing changed until an incomprehensible vision emerged from the vapors. At first I took the person for some exotic African albino. Then it spoke.

"Your turn, mate. Get on up for your shave."

Of all indignities suffered thus far as a slave, this was the worst. Two barbers lathered me with huge brushes as if I were a whitewashed fence. One shoved me down onto the stool and began scraping my head and face free of hair. The other began at my left ankle and moved up and down each leg. He grabbed my penis and threatened immediate castration if I moved or flinched, then deftly shaved between my legs—even the sacred scrotum and the crack of my ass. When the laughing insults and dull pain seemed interminable, they finished.

"Sweep up your mess," one of the barbers ordered. He nodded toward a broom and dustpan. When the pan was full, he pushed me toward a fire burning in the outer courtyard, and I dumped the sodden mess into the stinking flames.

The sergeant in charge reviewed each slave and then yelled, "Back into the water, lice-bait. Get your bare asses back into the water."

One by one, men who had been transformed into embarrassed infants sought solitude in the misty depths of the blue-tiled room. I felt diminished and vulnerable, small enough to crawl into an obscure hole. Tiny waves tickled my neck, and all slaves remained silent until we were finally herded out of the pool and given towels to dry our smooth, slippery bodies. Two house slaves arrived with piles of neatly folded clothes, and one of the guards yelled, "Put them on, Christian pigs."

Each item was made in the Turkish fashion: cotton trousers, loose and floppy, and shirts with wide open sleeves and the hem falling below our hips. The shoes were formed from yellow leather and the caps for our head of red cotton.

I tried, unsuccessfully, to swallow, but ended with a tortured, gulping croak that followed with a barking laugh. Spontaneously, every slave—even each Turk and Moor watching—began to howl with laughter. We pointed fingers, slapped knees, and rolled on the damp floor. We laughed and laughed until the sound rolled in echoed waves off the blue tile, then dribbled to a tentative halt. Finally we were quiet and began to fidget with our new clothes. We waited for some new instruction. We waited for whatever we were told to do, for we were slaves of the mighty dey of Algiers.

CHAPTER SEVEN

September 1785

CIDDI MAHAOMED WAS CHAMBERLAIN OF the dey's palace; that is, he was captain of the palace and ruled as he would a large ship at sea. No questions allowed—about the status of Will, for instance— and with instant obedience in every matter. I judged Ciddi and Isaac Stevens as peas in the same pod on the ignorance scale. Stevens was naught but a runt who was forced to stare upward to meet my eyes, while Ciddi Mahaomed was a vile, grotesque monster who towered over me.

In those first days and weeks spent with Ciddi, I invented a fantasy figure from odd bits of his strutting posture and my own daydreams. I made him into a shadow with no substance, a dolt who was the intellectual equivalent of Omrod. I tested the limits of my imagined independence against his bumbling quest for absolute authority. It was a contest that pitted my wit against his stupidity. A simple matter, or so I thought.

After the first month the routine of the new seven slaves was firmly established: up at dawn to work in the orchard or vineyard until noon with weeding and pruning and clearing debris, then over to the zoo until sunset. A bell rang to move us from one job to the next, and Ciddi maintained a constant shadow over us, even while we mucked shit from the stalls of large animals or carried the appropriate food to birds, animals, and a few large lizards. During most evenings we were left to talk among ourselves or sleep in our communal room. There were no tables or chairs, so when food was delivered, we sat on haunches to dip only right hands into each concoction. Often we used flat pieces of unleavened bread as spoons, but just as frequently the fastest fingers won the prized tidbits. Sleeping mats were unrolled at our leisure and scattered randomly through the room.

My duties as palace slave were simple, predictable, and no more onerous than those assigned by Captain Stevens aboard the *Maria*. In fact, there was only one oddity, one deviation from a totally witless life, and that was the easy access to dozens and dozens of books. They were arranged in a three-tiered bookcase and all apparently from a single seafarer's collection. There were many accounts of perilous adventures, and all were written in or had been translated into Spanish, including one to the northern seas by Vitus Bering. Some were tracts that described systems for navigation, and many were filled with maps. It was a treasure trove that I couldn't ignore.

One of the Spanish fishermen called Carlos—a small, slender soul with one brown eye and the other blue—was interested in learning how to read his own language. I desired a greater knowledge of his language, so my strategy in teaching accommodated both our needs. I first read aloud from the chosen text, and Carlos followed my finger from one word to the next. At the end of each page we agreed upon the Spanish pronunciation of every word, and followed that negotiation with a discussion of the subject matter of what had been read. The process was slow at first, but my student was quick-witted, and we made admirable progress.

Ciddi, the quiet monster, observed our conclaves during his perpetual rounds. Early in our initial sessions, when I was struggling with teaching duties and the substance of the texts, he was a fleeting shadow, an ephemeral silhouette in the doorway. Once I looked up from the book to see Ciddi with both hands on a stiff leather walking stick and staring malevolently at us. I admit to smiling once or twice at Ciddi and waving in recognition of his presence, but the excitement of learning and teaching overcame any uneasiness that percolated from my stomach.

The fisherman met with me every evening. We were as two lovers, alone among the many, and content in our small world. When the end finally came, I was more indignant than surprised by the interruption.

"False priest." Ciddi Mahaomed stood over us and yelled in a thunder-loud voice. "You are preaching lies to an innocent fisherman!"

I stared at the chamberlain and then glanced quickly over my shoulder to catch a glimpse of some offensive cleric. There was no ragged and bearded outlander who had inadvertently stumbled into the room—none but the lucky seven slaves, all of us quiet and attentive.

Ciddi switched from Turkish to Spanish and stormed at the fisherman. "Infidel dog, do you follow this false priest in his lies? Tell me the truth, or I'll shorten your legs!"

"Honored chamberlain," the fisherman choked, "the American sailor shows me the wisdom of the books. It is nothing more."

"There is only one Book; the rest are lies!"

Ciddi moved to face me, and in a lower, more deadly tone, said, "Tell me, infidel, do you believe what is written in these books?"

"Honored sir, they are but navigation books, written to help sailors move from one place in the world to another."

In a lower voice yet, he asked, "Do you believe what is written in these books?"

"Honored sir, they tell honestly of stars and tools that help sailors."

"Do you tell this poor fisherman what is written in this book?"

"Yes, your Honor. I try to teach him words that tell the apparent truth."

Ciddi's entire body seemed to engorge with disgust. His eyes bulged, and he screamed at his audience of fishermen, "Slaves! Seize this devil!"

With only a brief hesitation, three of my companions threw me to the floor and held my arms and legs. Ciddi took his walking stick and beat the soles of my feet. Each of the fourteen thumps sent lightning bolts from toes to ears. During the first six eruptions of scalding pain, I suppressed my tears, but for the rest, I blubbered for mercy. At brief intervals, Ciddi Mahaomed screamed, "No books! No talking! No preaching! No books! No talking! No preaching!"

———◆———

I was isolated from the other slaves after my beating. There were no books or paper for writing, or conversation with anyone other than Ciddi. If I whispered a brief question to one of the Spanish fishermen, he sought favor with the chamberlain by informing on me.

"No books! No talking! No preaching."

My toes became oozing stumps. No one slept near me or allowed my hand in the communal food pot. No leper suffered a worse lot.

The most degrading tasks were always given to me. I spent sunrise to sunset shovelling manure and discovered that lion excrement provided a most soothing balm to my feet. It was my only medication. Rotten cabbage and turnips I stole from the giraffe. At night I wrapped myself in self-pity. Everything in life seemed diminished in size and pace. Each day became a tiny replica of the previous one, with yesterday and tomorrow blurred into the ever-present gray fog of today. I prayed to Jesus Christ and to Mary for their mercy and gained no advantage in comfort from the effort. Once I prayed to Allah and asked for his forgiveness of my heathenish behavior, and he also declined to intervene on my behalf.

———◆———

"Look at me, fool."

Ciddi clapped his hands under my nose, and I focused on a spot beneath the line of his turban.

"It is Allah's will to place you in my service."

"Praise be to Allah," I mumbled.

"Yes, yes, and to his divine will may you yet survive the Devil's lust."

I remained silent, eyes unfocused.

Ciddi moved closer and lowered his voice to a hissing whisper. "Even now, after my best efforts, you remain the Devil's tool."

"Please help me, Allah," I said.

"You are nothing but a miserable toad." Ciddi composed himself. "The Devil is part of Allah's plan, and you are part of Allah's plan. No one escapes his benevolent design. Do you understand, you turd on a pig's ass?"

I nodded my head in vacant agreement and received a blow from his cane to my shoulder. His entire face came into focus, and I could see the angry eyes buzzing over his smile.

I shouted, "Yes sir. Yes, Your Honor, I understand!"

"That is good; it seems that even a worm can occasionally understand his purpose in life."

"Allah be praised," I said.

"Tonight, after the evening meal, we will begin with your new duty."

CHAPTER EIGHT

October 1785

E ACH DAY CONTINUED AS BEFORE. The animals gave me constant pleasure, and the entire expanse of the zoo was both calming to the spirit and exciting in its variety of creatures. This creation and toy of the dey offered huge animals I'd seen only in books. The aviary was a huge series of nets, with fist-size holes and a huge expanse for the large birds, and thumbnail-size holes in their net for the remaining flock of bizarrely formed and multicolored fowl. Often I was the only human in the zoo. Rarely did visitors attend the collections, and neither the dey nor his associates made an appearance while I was on duty.

Ciddi gave me my beatings. I had no friends, no conversations, and no books. At each sunrise Ciddi and his cane ruled my every moment. Pain and fear of pain drove me in mindless panic through the hours of light.

When my master first started off our evenings of exploration, he pulled me by hand into his small cave-like room. I was as blind as any mole, and stood quietly until Ciddi raised the wick of a large brass lantern, and light filled the room. He motioned toward a small stool. "Sit here and we will talk."

I lowered myself in stiff increments while Ciddi squatted before me and waited until I could breathe an even pattern. "The fisherman with eyes of two colors claims you for an alchemist. Does he speak the truth?"

"A thousand pardons, effendi. Carlos is mistaken. I can navigate a ship at sea and—"

"Silence! What any infidel says is of little consequence. You can read the Devil's scripture, is that not true?"

"Yes, effendi, I—"

"Good. The truth is out. It is proper for you to always tell me the truth. I know when you tell lies, and you must always tell the truth." Ciddi wriggled closer to me until we were but inches apart. "An angel whispered into my ear." He remained silent until my eyes registered the importance of the sacred event. "The angel suggested that good and evil can combine to serve Allah." Again he waited for my dense brain to accept celestial wisdom. "Together we can solve mysteries that have defied explanation. I will call upon the strength of righteousness, and you will plumb the depths of evil. Together we will turn base metals into gold. Together we can reveal machines whose gears will turn until Allah calls the faithful to heaven."

"Praise be to Allah," I said.

"Angels do not lie," Ciddi said.

"Is it alchemy, effendi? Do you want us to practice alchemy?"

"Yes," Ciddi said.

"Effendi! Please! I know nothing of alchemy."

"Silence!" Ciddi twisted the left portion of his face into a grotesque smile. "Have patience, my child. You are an ignorant infidel. You know nothing of faith, nothing of the magical powers that the Almighty grants to his faithful servants."

"I am an ignorant infidel," I said.

Ciddi nodded his agreement. "Try to understand the magnitude of my gift, ignorant child. Into my very ear an angel whispered of your destiny. The angel said that you will assist me in my discoveries. Together, the angel said—you and me."

"Praise be to Allah," I said. Doomed forever, I thought. Ciddi and his angel, partners for my painful and inevitable death

"We will begin this very night."

Our equipment was a mortar and pestle, a small oil-burning furnace, and a few tools available from the palace carpenter. The tools were placed on a single bench in a room as long as Ciddi with his arms extended, and as wide as me in the same posture. Each evening the chamberlain presented some odd assortment of medicines, spices, and metals for me to grind and cook. I made the best possible show of the project and, after the first week or so, added some random bits of Latin phrases to my performance.

Ciddi watched carefully as I brewed each mess. "Speak with the Devil, my child," he repeated over and over through the evening hours. Noxious fumes often drove us into the still night, but through every failed experiment at producing gold or rare gems, Ciddi was considerate in every manner of my well-being. He brought me fruit and honey-sweetened pastries as snacks, and made available for my refreshment one carafe filled with water and another with wine. I drank an occasional sip of water but dared not touch the other proffered gifts. In my mind Ciddi was a large bomb attached to a burning fuse, and any action on my part that could possibly shorten the taper was not worth the reward.

During the first weeks of our partnership, we talked in stiff lurches about the task at hand. But slowly Ciddi began sharing bits of palace gossip with me. He whined of competitors who made paltry efforts to undermine his power and bragged of small triumphs over my fellow slaves. I began answering his questions in a less guarded fashion and to dream again of small boats with white sails.

When a winter storm dumped fitful torrents of rain onto the city and port of Algiers, our little retreat became cold and damp. Ciddi placed a small rug over my shoulders.

"Would you drink some hot tea, my child?"

"No, effendi."

"Some warm gloves for your hands?"

"No, effendi."

Ciddi gave me his left-sided smile. "Tell me, child of the Devil. When will you reveal your secrets to me?"

I pushed the mortar and pestle away from me and spoke to the wall. "I am ignorant of any secrets, effendi. I know nothing of alchemy."

The awkward grimace faded. "No more of your lies, my little piglet."

I turned to face him. "Tell me, effendi. Would you have me surmount the Emperor Caligula and turn arsenic into gold?"

"You must be very careful with your tongue, infidel."

I mimicked his crude smile. "With all due deference to Your Honor's superior judgement, many have attempted a machine with perpetual motion, and gold from loose minerals, but all have failed. I am but a turd on a hog's ass and can never hope to achieve an alchemist's dream."

When we were busy in our laboratory, in either clement or cold weather, Ciddi always removed his yellow turban and revealed a cleanly shaven head. He lowered this bald head, as if in prayer, and the flickering lantern revealed odd concavities and bold scars over the entire right side of his skull. One evening, after a long moment, he looked up and met my eyes.

"You are in fact the Devil's servant," he said. "You have the power to use his evil words for your magic. No more of your lies. Perform the Devil's magic."

"I'm sorry, effendi. I cannot help you."

Ciddi reached over and opened a small chest that lay at his feet. He carefully lifted out a battered book and held it toward me. "Take it," he said.

The title page was printed in Spanish.

Almería
Investigation into claims of alchemy, and other Devil schemes,
Perpetuated by infidel Jews of this city.

During the next three nights, Ciddi sat close by my side, just outside the lantern's light, as I translated and digested the ancient account of three Jews brought to trial by their Moslem masters in the city of Almería. In the end, all three chose death by flame instead of dangling from hooks above the city gate for many days. Their payment for the quicker death was made in the form of recipes that they produced, guaranteed to generate gold from lead, and life from death.

When I finished the last page, Ciddi said, "Speak, child of the Devil. What does it say?"

"These are desperate lies, effendi. There is nothing here of any use to you."

He appeared more incredulous than bombastic. "How can this be? I paid five gold doubloons for our answers."

I turned on my stool and looked at him for a long moment. "Is it reasonable," I asked, "to take a few forlorn lies from dead Jews, two or three crucibles, and a small portable furnace, and perform magic where so many others have failed? I am sorry, effendi—you have given me an impossible task."

"I have you, my infidel, and the angel. Remember the angel. You now have the book, and always you have the Devil." His lips curled. "Shall I shorten your legs a bit more, or will you favor us with your endowments?"

"My lord," I said, "I believe that you can charm me into a man of the one faith easier than I can convert crude metal into pure gold."

We stared for a long moment before he dropped his eyes. Ciddi sat cross-legged, shoulders forward. After the beat of a small eternity, he stood and kicked the crucible into a clattering, smoky jumble that scattered across the room.

I remained still and silent.

Ciddi poked at me with his walking stick. "So be it. What else should I expect from a false priest?" His crooked smile returned. "We both know you are destined to eternal hell, where the flames will curl your skin and provoke constant pain in every part of your body." His eyes were thin slits. "Maybe I can help you attain the warmer climate a little faster."

A few days after Ciddi's declaration of my inevitable descent into hell, two vessels, one a Russian and the other a Leghornese, were captured by the cruisers of Algiers. On board the first were several handsome youth who were taken immediately into the palace. My chamberlain focused on alchemy of a different sort, and I was left unattended and ignored. My daily tasks reverted to the mundane chores of garden and zoo, and in the evening I began reading again. First in stolen spurts, then, when no one asked for my instruction and Ciddi ignored me, I enjoyed the safe solitude of reading.

As I look back on my experience at the dey's palace, I can guess that my services were originally intended to be other than shovelling lion manure. A sodomite or some such evil creature was my likely end. Nothing made much sense at the time, and I drifted through each inconvenience without thought or design

In early May of 1786, within a month after the arrival of the fair-haired Russian boys, two palace guards pulled me from my work in the vineyard and delivered me to the slave prison—the prison called Baegnio Bezique by the Algerians.

CHAPTER NINE

May 1786

"I AM IBRAM RAISANI, THE warden of this prison." He bent at the waist to examine each small detail of my face. "Ahhh," he said, "such a pretty young man." He stood straight, hands behind his back. "It's finished, my lad. No more fancy clothes and easy living such as you enjoyed over at the palace."

I understood his Spanish dialect well enough, but turned away from the warden with an impatient twist. I could see nothing but a mass of prisoners, moaning and moving about like a bucket of slimy worms.

Raisani pushed me to the floor and delivered a sharp kick to my ribs. "Pig! You must never move or speak without my permission."

I held my ribs and stared at my latest tormentor. He was a handsome brute, full of bluster and comfortable in his vocation. Raisani turned toward a guard standing a few feet from his shoulder and shouted, as if across a wide valley, "Sbirro! Bring some stout rings for this gentleman. Report!"

One of the guards clamped antique bracelets around my ankles. They seemed designed for someone of Herculean stature rather than for my average dimensions. I stumbled with awkward movements to stand before the prison warden again. "Sir, I'm an American! We have—"

With his brief nod, four guards threw me back onto the floor and pinioned my arms and legs. A fifth guard beat my bare feet with a wooden cudgel. After ten blows they hauled me upright yet again, and Ibram Raisani raised his right hand to my cheek, as might a wealthy woman. "Now, my little puppy, you may show your respect by kissing my hand."

Pain flashed from my toes to the pointed teeth in my mouth. I was disposed to bite the entire hand from his damned arm, but instead I kissed his meaty paw. Ibram Raisani laughed huge rolling guffaws until he finally sputtered, "My little piglet, my dear little infidel. Allah has sent you for my special entertainment, a comfort to my older age." He continued with his laughter as he turned and disappeared into the maggot heap of prisoners.

———◆———

"Capi Capar! Capi Capar! Capi Capar!"

The crier walked slowly about the perimeter of Baegnio Bezique with his falsetto message that the prison gates would soon be shut and locked for the night. For the past few hours I had waddled around, impaired by the rigs and chain connected to both legs, inspecting my home. Even in the perpetual murk, the prison design was clear: it was a three-storied hollow rectangle of carved black stone. The massive hulk of a building contained a tavern under nearly every first-floor arch. A few of the hostelries had a primitive sense of order, with four legs on most chairs and tables. But most were congeries of filth, with crude boards settled across empty barrels and garbage in every corner. My initial judgement was that all the taverns sold food, liquor, and merchandise, but the whirling morass of slaves and guards and visiting patrons prevented a coherent speculation on my part.

The "Capi Capar" shouts were clear warning to those patrons of taverns in the prison who were not incarcerated that they must depart. From whispered exchanges with other shackled prisoners, I gathered that those visitors to the prison were customers of certain goods and services available only in a prison. These virtuous Moslems had to leave before sunset, and I observed gangs of Turks and Moors leave the taverns scattered throughout the prison, and move toward the prison gates shortly after the crier began circulating. There were a few bare-footed Jews who scuttled through the shadows, chased by Turks flailing after them with curved swords. But most of the Moslems were content to laugh and sing military songs as they marched toward the exits.

When the last customers of prison services disappeared into the gathering gloom, the gates of the prison were shut, and a heavy chain clanked through six massive metal eyes and was secured at either end with two wraps around a large bolt. I found no one from the *Maria* in my roaming, so I was alone among hundreds, chin on my knees and hands grasping the heavy metal bracelet around each ankle, when two guards approached. One held a small copper ankle bracelet; the other guard, a leather strap. The short, dark guard stooped and said, "Well, well, well, and what do we have but the new prisoner promised by Ibram Raisani." He caressed my ears and nose and spoke with clear diction to his partner. "Here, my brother," the guard said, "we have a gift from Allah."

The taller and even darker guard also touched my nose and eyes. "Yes, my brother, a certain beauty."

The short guard tapped me on the shoulder with a long wooden switch. "Roll over, my little girl. Let us check those beautiful cheeks."

I sat before them in stubborn resistance to their request.

They roared with laughter, kicked at my legs in a tentative fashion, then squatted down on their haunches.

The larger man spoke. "Sit up and listen, my beauty. We are corporals of the guard—Christian corporals, we are called." The two looked at each other to laugh like the mules they so resembled. "Christian corporals!" They giggled a moment longer and then crouched even lower, their faces a few inches from my nose. "When the prison gates close, we are in charge, and there is no appeal to higher authority. When the gates open, Captain Raisani is boss. Ibram rules the day, while we rule the night. Do you understand, little one?"

"Yes sir." I supposed that at this stage of their interview with me that I should have felt some degree of fear for the fools, but they were such stupid geese I could barely restrain myself from laughing in their faces.

"The captain was appointed by Allah to his post, but we were picked by the first Christian secretary to our position. Do you understand, piglet? The Christain secretary picked us over many applicants, and therefore we are called the Christian corporals."

"You are Christian corporals but retain the True faith, is that the way of your postion, honoured corporal?"

"Good, you understand my first detail, but you must also know that this Christian devil, for reasons that I cannot fathom, also has the ear of our beloved dey."

The short corporal gave me a demented smile. "Do you now have a clear understanding of why we are called the Christian corporals?"

"Yes sir."

"Good."

They moved closer still "We don't want any trouble in the Baegnio tonight," the smaller and older of the two whispered, "Are you trouble, my lad?"

"No sir."

"Good. Now look carefully at this bracelet." He waved a set of handcuffs in front of my face. "For the small price of one sequin to Ibram Raisani in the morning and twelve masoons to us tonight, this tiny ring will replace the anchor you now wear."

"I haven't a penny."

"No money? Now, that's too bad." The older corporal shook his head in sympathy with my poverty.

"Yes, too bad," echoed the younger corporal.

A smile of hope lit his partner's face. "Possibly the young infidel could work in our tavern. I imagine that within a short month or so he could pay for his new bracelets."

"There's also the interest on his debt that he would inevitably accrue, my dear colleague."

"Six weeks would serve. I'm sure Ibram would agree." Again they roared with laughter and exhibited great pleasure with their unique solution to my poverty.

It was a surprise to me, and equally so for the corporals, when an elegantly dressed man stepped before us. He stood silently until the corporals recognized him and untangled from their frolic with me to stand almost at attention. No smiles showed, and the ears of both corporals gleamed red.

"Honored corporals, may I have a word with you?"

"Certainly, your Honor." The older corporal ducked his head slightly, like a stork greeting a possible mate, and clasped both hands by his belt.

"This new slave"—the man nodded toward me—"he comes from the palace?"

"Yes, First Secretary. It seems he has a glib tongue and brought no pleasure to Ciddi Mahaomed."

"Ah, Ciddi . . . And you have instructed this miserable one on his responsibilities?"

"Yes, your Honor."

"I've noticed lately, my corporal, that customers are forsaking your tavern to find comfort with unworthy competitors. Is this not true?"

"You have an eye for everything, Señor Gaston."

Without begging leave from the all-powerful corporals, the stranger spoke to me in passable English. "Do you remember me from your time with royal court?"

I shook my head.

"No? Well, sir, it is my pleasure to serve the dey as his first Christian secretary."

I sat up in a more hopeful posture. "Sir, how is it that such an esteemed personage remains in this locked prison?"

He gave a glum smile. "You must learn to pay more attention to your surroundings, Mr. Cathcart. You were a stupid young man in the court and must learn much more quickly if you wish to survive this prison to your next birthday."

"You are a slave?"

"Certainly I'm a slave, and therefore a resident of this prison." He raised his voice. "Sit up with a straight back and listen."

Señor Alphonse Gaston stood tall and straight before the corporals. "Have you determined a particular reason for the recent flight of customers from your tavern?"

"Somehow our grog has developed the taste of pepper."

"Ahhh, pepper. So I've heard."

"You are always well informed, señor."

"As it happens, Corporal, through an accident of fate, I have acquired a barrel of English whiskey, but unfortunately, my own patrons detest this crude beverage. They prefer French wine or cognac."

The senior corporal studied his shoe. "How tragic, your Honor. Do these customers prefer donkey piss?" Both corporals laughed sharply, and then quickly fell silent.

"Yes, my friends, a very good joke, this donkey piss remark." Señor Gaston remained quiet until both corporals finished settling their weight on one foot rather than the other. "Now, good sirs, it would be a great service to me if you could take this superfluous English whiskey from me and put it to some productive use."

The three men held their silence. Both corporals studied their shoes, and the first Christian secretary quietly observed the flow of slaves through the baegnio.

The older corporal cleared his throat. "Could it be, Eminence, that you have not replaced your recently deceased servant?"

"I am still searching for a likely candidate, Corporal."

Smiles burst from the Christian corporals, but the older man spoke with obvious relief of mind. "Ahhh! Such is the will of Allah! We would forever be in your debt, effendi, if you could take from us this miserable untrained pig for your own use. Could we hope for such a favor?"

Señor Gaston gave a nod in my direction. "Remove that weight from his ankle. You will receive the whiskey tomorrow afternoon."

The first secretary watched as I was released. "Follow me," he said.

———

Señor Gaston bulled his way through the maze of bodies on the ground floor of the prison. He led me up stone stairs to the second floor and down a corridor made nearly impassable by the jumble of chained slaves. A stout door at the south end of the aisle blocked our passage, but my guardian pulled a large key from his robe and worked the lock. He led me up another flight of stairs and onto the prison roof. The early evening stars forced us to stop our furious pace. We both listened and stared into the night. From minarets scattered around the city came the muezzins' lilting, caressing reminder of duty; Allah's lovely chorus drifted through hot air and seemed to generate the first breeze of evening.

"This way," Alphonse said.

I followed my protector, aware the dream must end, that my phantom angel would soon explode into his devil's mold. I kept very still, listened, and never said a word.

The dey's first Christian secretary opened a door into a room that smelled of sweet grass and incense; there was not the least stench from the prison. He pointed to a corner in the kitchen. "There, young man— that's for you." He took my hand and pulled me toward a tiny closet, where he unrolled a mat and pushed me to the floor.

"Sleep," he said.

I collapsed into a deep abyss with neither light nor dreams. During the cool hour before dawn I discovered the blanket over my body, and had a niggling memory of a soft kiss to my lips.

CHAPTER TEN

May 1786

A MUFFLED SHOUT DRIBBLED THROUGH my empty dream. "Arise!" the distant phantom murmured. "All who sleep, the day approaches! Arise!" Alphonse Gaston shook me, took my hand, and led me from a nest of sweet warmth down the pitch-dark stairs into the turmoil of Hades. We reached the ground floor as the Sbirro shouted, "Depart, slaves! Depart to your daily labor."

I stumbled along in mindless obedience, one hand holding his robe and the other fending off numerous supplicants who were seeking attention from the first Christian secretary to the dey of Algiers. Most of the slaves seemed able to converse in the Spanish language, but some few used Turkish or Arabic, and on that first tumultuous morning I threw an elbow into the ribs of an evil-looking Genovese who was petitioning Alphonse in Latin for a position in his tavern. The man kicked back at me, but the crowd swallowed him, and he disappeared from view.

Every able-bodied slave was forced from the prison gates down the twisting, narrow streets, and simultaneously the city gates were opened. The influx of laborers, farmers, camels, and asses was so great that the two opposing currents brought each other to a near standstill. Great explosions of curses erupted as the farmers and tradesmen joined with our Moor guards to condemn us as thieves and infidel pigs. Most of the donkeys and camels were loaded with fruit and vegetables, and slaves broke their fast with swift attacks on whatever was close at hand.

As the prison mob moved forward, Alphonse Gaston whispered into my ear. "I keep my eye on each pirate ship that comes into the harbor." He looked at me for a brief moment. "There are very few slaves that can read and write well enough to work for me." He pulled me around to stare into my eyes. "I knew about you and that African on your first day."

"Oh." I quickly imagined a job as first assistant Christian secretary to the dey of Algiers. No lion shit to shovel—merely ledgers and ink to move about.

He snagged two oranges from a donkey's pannier and shared one with me. "When Ciddi showed some interest in you, I had to back off." Alphonse chuckled. "Ciddi's a decent person, but you must never cross him or make him look as foolish as he is. "

Gaston cut the top from his orange with a knife that appeared miraculously from the left sleeve of his robe. He bent forward, squeezed the orange, and slurped at the opening. Only a small trickle disappeared into his beard. He dropped the pulped orange underfoot, took my orange back to cut a similar pattern, and then returned it. Most of the heavenly juice I consumed, but some dribbled down my chin and onto my hands. Orange juice and ink pens—maybe my luck was changing in this godforsaken place.

My protector spoke to me with a more emphatic voice. "You are a stupid young man."

"Yes, effendi," I whispered.

"You must learn to discern the needs of those who are superior in rank to you, and then you must make them successful through your diligent efforts." He paused briefly to look at me. "So, my very stupid young man, if you can develop the skills of patience and insight and compassion, then possibly you will be of some use to me in the future."

"I will try, effendi. Truly. I will—"

"Listen, stupid boy—no talking." Alphonse Gaston walked a dozen paces before speaking with an even louder and more brittle voice. "Here is my simple promise: if you continue with your petulant, selfish behavior, I will give you back to the corporals."

I listened to the gallimaufry of sounds that flowed around us. We turned a bend, and the road opened to a broader avenue, and wads of slaves began to slough off from the main core and disappear into a tangle of dark alleys.

Alphonse put his arm over my shoulder and continued with our conversation. "I will watch your progress for the next year or two. As a first step, I will apprentice you to a carpenter." He stopped us and turned my chin with his hand until our eyes met. "Your new mentor listens to others and does them no harm when armed with their weaknesses." He leaned closer to my ear. "When I bring you before the captain of the port, the vikilharche, tell him that you were a carpenter in that distant land of infidels. Further, that you were both a navigator and carpenter on the ship *Maria*."

"Yes sir," I answered.

"There is no hope of freedom for you. Those petty dreams of escape that pulled you through the past months are gone. There is only slavery, and you must look at new possibilities and new dreams. The old fantasies will only draw you to a slow and unpleasant death."

We walked at the crowd's pace until I could smell the sea. I tried to visualize how my father would plan the escape. Certainly something that involved a ship and small crew. He would council patience, certainly, but I must always be ready for any opportunity for escape that materialized. Forever a slave? Not a Cathcart, and most assuredly not me.

"Another thing, my young friend. You will also serve as my servant and live in my quarters. This last gift you will begin to appreciate as time passes."

"Yes, your Honor." Who was this benefactor of mine, I wondered? The one bearing mysterious gifts of oranges and a soft bed? Captain Elrod Cathcart whispered warnings into my ear. I started to see Alphonso Gaston as an unwitting tool for my escape to freedom, not the tool for my perpetual slavery.

At the harbor gate a large group of slaves waited until the dey's representatives arrived. The guard hissed at us to stand, uncover our heads, and lower our eyes. We all followed his instructions, even the first Christian secretary. After a moment, I peeked, and Alphonse smiled and nudged me toward an elegant officer.

The dey's captain of the port for the city of Algiers was seated upon huge cushions and sipped coffee from a tiny cup. The man, protected from the first rays of sun by a white bat-winged tent, was served by two slaves.

I followed Alphonse's lead and fell to my knees, face in the dust. I heard Alphonse and the vikilharche speaking in near-whispered tones but maintained my frozen posture.

"Sit up, my young infidel." He was a handsome man, with dark pock-free skin and a bold nose. Random patches of gray in his beard served as an interesting distraction for eyes that were afraid to meet his.

"You were captured by Rais Mawlud-Qadir, is that not correct?"

"Yes, your Honor," I answered.

"Your rank?"

"Esteemed sir, I was second mate on the merchant sloop *Maria*."

"Yes, and your duties?"

"Honored sir, I was the navigator and carpenter of the *Maria*."

The harbormaster turned to the dey's first Christian secretary. "Can you attest to this infidel's character?"

"Most respected Vikilharche, he is a young man of three languages, and I guarantee that he will serve you loyally."

"Good, First Christian secretary, then you may take him directly to the carpenter's shop."

The Harbourmaster took a sip of coffee, then turned to speak directly to me. "You will learn your craft from José Garcia, young man. He is one who has accepted his fate, and you, young slave, will do well to emulate him in every manner of industry and decorum."

"Yes, your Honor."

His left eyebrow moved upward into an arch. "I will ignore previous rumors." The eyebrow dropped. "You must take this opportunity to begin your service to Allah, and you must serve him with both your hands and mind." The vikilharche stopped his lecture, waved us off, and turned to the next man in line.

We crabbed backward a few paces, stood to a half crouch, and scuttled away from the tent and small coffee cups. Alphonse Gaston led me on a leisurely and circuitous route through the magnificent harbor. Here and there he pointed with his chin or arm to explain some point of history or engineering.

"Those boulders over there are mined in a quarry four miles from the harbor and carried here with only the effort of industrious slaves and no mechanical help of any sort." Alphonse pointed toward a cache of large rocks piled near the western terminus of the breakwater and then continued at his same pace.

I could barely hear him, as the sights were louder than his words. High above the starkly blue Mediterranean, a Turkish fort huddled on a promontory, seemingly ready to leap on any enemy. White buildings spilled down from the airy fort to merge in a jumbled sprawl near a towering wall of thick chiselled rock. This resolute edifice of a fort was interspersed by four connected fortresses and one fortified gate. A causeway led from the single gate to another series of three forts, all squatting on land stolen from the sea. This artificial peninsula curled to the east, thereby creating the harbor for the city and regency of Algiers. All in all, a very impressive scene.

Ships with flags from many nations lay at anchor within the protected nest. As I walked with Alphonse along the causeway road, a breeze freshened, and two small terns flitted among the breakers rolling at our feet. On the seaward side, rocks tumbled in a sharp declivity, while a gentle sandy beach marked the harbor side of the mole. There were small boats lolling here and there—ships' dinghies and fishing vessels, most with oars and small mast to hoist a scrap of sail. Two or three experienced sailors could manage most of the options that I saw, to good advantage.

A cloudless pale-blue sky shimmered in a canopy over ships and men. Alphonse waved toward a line of ships that were beached and tumbled, as if an unfortunate covey of sea monsters had made an errant turn. "It seems that the cruisers of Algiers loaf on the sand with greater frequency than one would expect."

"What do you mean?"

"Simple enough. The dey of all Algerians has neither sailors nor shipwrights to keep a substantial navy afloat. He survives by his wits and uses ancient history and a few European slaves to maintain his status."

"I must say, Señor Gaston, that none of the cutthroats who came rolling over the *Maria's* side looked either ancient or European."

Alphonse smiled a big toothy grin that pulled his shiny black moustache nearly to his nose. "Well, the dey does have a few old-timers around, like Rais Mawlud-Qadir, but they're survivors from another age with their tiny xebecs. Nowadays those old-timers are reduced to capturing slaves for a few of the rich grandees, and then they must suffer the payment of exorbitant taxes to the dey." He waved at the hulks. "There's the Algerian Navy resting on the mud."

I counted ten ancient ships careened on the beach. Tar pots bubbled beside each carcass while a crew of disorganized shipwrights beat and sawed upon their comatose victims. Farther along the wide inside curve of the harbor, past the dry-docked navy, another shipyard was marked by two partially completed hulls. At this site a disturbed anthill of organized activity seethed about the incipient ships, and a few rods higher on the beach, dozens of ramshackle sheds also served as a focus of energy. The entire mess of sheds and ships was patched onto the lowest level of a massive three-tiered octagon-shaped castle.

Turks in butterfly-bright costumes strutted in circles around their defined territory. Great planks of lumber were hauled up into the air by means of ropes and pulleys and fragile-appearing beams. The trembling arms swung into position and, in an either witless or incompetent manner, dropped each load of timber—as if a bomb—onto the open-ribbed ship's embryo. Immense scrambling cheers erupted from the carpenters with each thunderclap of fractured boards. The hammering and shouting continued through each crashing interruption and was moderated only by the whimsical collusion of wind and surf. I could only imagine what a small influx of Yankee shipwrights and sailors could do to bring order to this comedy of errors that offered witness to my eyes. I'd have bet that a dozen of my cousins and neighbors from back in Plymouth could bring this lot of bunglers into shipshape form in a month or two.

Alphonse shook himself, like a dog wet with water. "Come, enough of this idle and useless chitchat. I'll introduce you to your new master."

◆

On that first day in his shop, within the first minute after my introduction by Alphonse, I was assigned the task of building a small wooden box with a hinged top. In one fluid motion Alphonse was dismissed, and I was directed toward a neatly stacked pile of cut cedar boards. "A small box about this size." José Garcia opened his hands to a distance of about two feet. He dropped his arms, turned, and resumed work on an ornate door. His mallet and chisel nicked and tapped small curls of wood until leaves and clusters of grapes revealed themselves from the blank board.

I glanced at the tools hanging from wall pegs. The ripsaw I knew, and some of the other implements were of distant memory. A dull ache spread from my groin down the inside calf of each leg. What was that first step in the process? Which tool did the job?

"It's like this, lad." José brushed past me and picked up two cedar planks. Quickly, deftly, without speaking or providing any specific instruction, he measured, squared, cut with three different saws, drilled, and pegged the box together, then hinged the top. "Now," he said, "take this one apart and build me another slightly larger."

I labored until sunset, when Alphonse retrieved me, and through the next day until afternoon tea. José glanced briefly at my project before tossing it into the scrap heap. "Watch," he said, and fashioned another box. It seemed that each step was at a more leisurely pace than before, and I carefully studied his practiced movements and the response of each tool to the wood. I noticed how the vise served as a third arm, and the infinite care of each measurement and aiming of the drill.

"Take this one apart and build me another, somewhat smaller," he said. This time I felt a small degree of comfort in handling each tool and with the forward movement of the task. The second box was not accepted and neither was the third or fourth, but the fifth brought smiles as he noted the sharp corners and tight lid. Each subsequent job at the shop progressed in the same inevitable fashion: José Garcia gave me the perfect model of his intention, and I practiced until I too became master of that small task.

I kept my eyes on available dinghies and fishing boats, but I must say that I found myself becoming more and more intent upon pleasing this saintly man. He smiled at my successes and seemed blind to my mistakes. I chatted with my tools, with the craftsmen from neighboring sheds, with Turks touring through the premises, but rarely with José Garcia. He gave me clear, precise instructions and set the pace for each day's activities but rarely spoke without purpose. He worked hard and well, as did I.

CHAPTER ELEVEN

February 1787

WHILE SERVING ON THE *MARIA*, my father had forced me to learn French, Latin, and Spanish. He had drilled me on conjugations and vocabulary and declination during every possible moment. On watch or off, it made no difference to Captain Elrod Cathcart. It was always drill and practice, drill, drill, drill, and often interspersed with remarks comparing my progress with that made by the young Will Melman.

Alphonse provided lessons in Portuguese when we sat in his tavern to partake of a late evening meal or as we walked to our morning employment. He introduced new words in his normal flood of conversation and then quizzed my competence in both vocabulary and grammar when I responded to his seemingly innocent queries. He was gentle and humorous and unpredictable in his guidance of my instruction. I added Turkish and Arabic words to my vocabulary as customers drifted in and out of José Garcia's shop.

The rhythm of Algiers unfolded to me in stiff lurches, and slowly it revealed a composition that became less alien, more comfortable, and, finally, even friendly. I became part of the city, not a bizarre stranger with no rights or privileges. At least once during each week,

José Garcia packed his wooden tool box and led me through the streets of Algiers to the home of a wealthy merchant or important government official. Even though the box weighed over fifty pounds, and despite my offered assistance, José always carried his own tools.

Often his job was merely repairing an ill-fitting door or replacing a worn step, but occasionally a larger task required of us a daily early evening scurry to our second job. The shipyard tasks we always completed first, for there was never short change from José. He gave full measure for the dey of Algiers before we adjourned to work amid the smells of lemon, exotic spices, and perfume of women.

The sun was our master, a sneaky ruler capable of subterfuge and erratic movement. On one memorable occasion, the sun jumped unceremoniously into the sea while we were buried in a complicated repair of a floor joist. Our race to enter the prison gate before nightfall was lost, and our profit from replacing a termite-infested timber went to the Christian corporal on duty. He accepted José's small gold coin and murmured, "It is double next time, effendi."

With each completed task, however small, José Garcia recited the expenses for materials, the cost of necessary bribes, and then counted out my wages. In this fashion I learned the custom and powers of my city, and I also put money into my pocket. There was money for clothes, food, and tools, and money that could purchase the small pleasures available to a Christian slave. Any surplus coins I put into a small box of my own construction, and hid the box behind a loose brick in the kitchen.

Had my duties been confined to the carpentry shop, there would be no reason to complain of hard usage. José Garcia was the perfect tutor, and I grew to enjoy the quiet pleasures of my avocation. Other obligations, however, underscored the truth of my bondage. For instance, whenever the port captain, Hassan Bashaw, observed that work on a particular project was moving at a slower-than-normal pace, or whenever a ship docked with heavy, awkward, or numerous loads to be carried, I was frequently added to the gangs of slaves who were so used every day. The tradition of this harbor was to unload, in total, every friendly ship that brought presents to the dey—that is, every gun, all ammunition, and even the ballast were removed from ship to shore, all in an effort to clean and fumigate the vessel. Of course this onerous task always fell to the Christian slaves, and we apprentices in all the shops of the harbor were so used.

The largest project, however, that pulled me away from the carpentry shop was the construction of a huge military fortification at Bebal Wed. Slaves were pulled from many diverse jobs and joined together for two full months on this single project. The structure, about one mile from the harbor, was designed to shelter the entire navy of the Algerian regency as a combination fort and drydock. It was perceived by the Algerians as an emergency project, and therefore all other tasks were subverted by this one.

I heard constant rumors of different commercial nations sending an attack force upon us, and we slaves shared with the Moors and Turks the delightful fear of imminent invasion. On serious contemplation, however, it was difficult to imagine which nation posed a realistic threat to the Algerians, and what could motivate an attack. Spain, Portugal, and the Neapolitan states regularly paid ransom for their citizens to the dey of Algiers and were thus considered faithful patrons. The Hanseatic states enlisted private subscriptions for ransom as a means to free their captured merchants and sailors and never showed a hint of malice toward the Algerians. Britain and the northern states paid an annual tribute and were therefore unmolested by the pirates. Only the United States was represented as a threat to the Barbary States, and my country was neither united nor state enough to raise fifty thousand dollars to free twenty-six citizens. I was one of those twenty-six, of course, and we all had an intimate understanding of our predicament. Every detail of any contact between our country of citizenship and the country that held us as slaves was filtered to us, quickly and reliably, from my patron, the first Christian secretary to the dey of Algiers. All of us could attest to the fact that our country could not protect their merchants from predators, and the babbling envoys sent by the United States government did a fine job of entertaining the dey and his court with grotesque demonstrations of incompetence. But the sum total of the couriers from General Washington did nothing to relieve our bondage.

"Whom," I asked Alphonse, "should the dey of Algiers fear?"

"Whom, indeed?" my master answered.

In any event, every day, including even Friday, the Moslem Sabbath, we slaves worked from sunrise to six o'clock. There were more than one thousand of us, half naked, with no hats or shoes in the blazing summer heat. We carried earth in baskets from one point to another. Our perspiration flowed in tiny rivulets, and the guards beat those who fell. Even those such as José Garcia, and once for a full day, Alphonse Gaston, were enlisted in our marathon effort.

We did our jobs as instructed by Demetrius, a Greek master mason. He was a free man, a hireling of the dey, who was recommended for the job by the grand sultan of Turkey. Three times during construction of this project, major portions of the building collapsed with many injured and a few killed outright. When finally declared finished, even Hassan Bashaw hinted that a common shed would have served more effectively, especially a shed on the beach near the harbor.

It was an evening after a fatal accident that Hassan was our guest at the tavern. I observed while he and Alphonse smoked, drank coffee, and belittled the efforts of Greek masons.

"Ignore for a moment the distance we must drag each heavy gunboat to this grand monument of Greek ingenuity," said Alphonse.

Hassan chuckled. "As you are well aware, these are not common fishing boats but the finest forty-two gunships of the Algerian Navy."

"Still, there are the beautiful arches, so artfully designed in the Grecian manner."

"We must turn these huge ships several times, stand them stern down, and then shove them by brute force, with no levers, rollers, or assisting mechanical engines, into the storage area."

Alphonse smiled. "Sir, you must recognize as fact that when our ships are finally locked in their Greek palace, they will be free of depredation from the navies of Liechtenstein or Lilliput."

"Equally so, I'm sure, from the far weaker nations of Haiti and the United States of America." Hassan's sarcasm was a stronger statement than Alphonso's ridicule of my country.

◆

Shortly after the Greek mason's mess, Alphonse led me to the bath for the first time. Up to that point, he and I had little to do with each other. Each night I slept on my mat in the kitchen, and he had his air-washed bedroom. It was certainly true that Alphonse's intervention secured my job with José Garcia, and it is certainly true that he provided my lessons in Portuguese and in court protocol, but still, in spite of these and many other favors, my master made very few demands upon me. As his house servant, my duties were limited to cleaning his quarters, contracting with slaves from the lower levels to wash the laundry, and bringing him food from his tavern when it was ordered.

Alphonse's important position with the court often kept him at the palace through the night, and on those occasions I stood on his terrace to watch stars move in old comfortable patterns, or simply wandered silently from terrace to bedroom—back and forth—in a hopeless effort at capturing each tranquil moment.

The pleasant tedium of work with José Garcia and my refuge in Alphonse's sanctuary liberated me from the drama of prison life. Brief squalls of cholera or plague blew past my consciousness with scant concern. The mean prison life blurred into a distant inconvenience as

I worked, ate my evening meal in Alphonse Gaston's tavern, and slept in his seldom-used kitchen. It was a simple life—a sheltered, useful life.

Alphonse's tavern comprised three large rooms combined into one enterprise. In the fetid pit of the baegnio, his tavern was an oasis of cleanliness. Two Turks guarded the tavern's entrance and admitted only sober and substantial Algerians during the day. After the gates were locked, the corporals and various Christian clerks who were granted freedom to roam the prison by Ibram Raisani—for a standard fee, of course—could find good food and drink, served at tables maintained by attentive slaves. After my duties to Alphonse were finished, I frequently found a seat in a dark recess near the bustling kitchen and studied the behavior of my fellow slaves.

I came to understand the normal rituals of eating and drinking, and the studied insults that occupied the interests of customers in the first two rooms of the tavern. They were the normal actions of men in every port and on every ship. The third room of the tavern was beyond my experience. I heard the words of pleasure used to describe a sojourn into the third room, but in spite of the words, the smiles, and the obscene gestures, I was not prepared for Alphonse's invitation. "James," he said, "come with me to the bath."

We passed through a heavy cloth curtain, to a divan and a couch, both covered by soft blankets of the same deep-blue color. Here, with the help of an attendant, I discarded my clothes. On that first occasion, Alphonse stood naked at the second curtained door and smiled at me. He turned, stooped under the low lintel, and disappeared behind the heavy canvas. I sat quietly on the soft couch and let the image of Alphonse stand in my mind. Our disrobing by the pirates on board the *Maria* and the de-lousing swim in the dey's pool were aberrations without memory. Alphonse was the first adult—man or woman—to stand naked before my eyes. He was a handsome man and well proportioned. There was no hair on his chest, and with his flat stomach and firm legs he could easily stand as a model for any Roman artist.

His head popped from between the gray folds. "Come," he whispered, and I followed. Immediately I was struck by a roiling cloud of suffocating heat. In panic I moved back toward the door, but Alphonse held my arm and led me to a wooden bench, where we sat hip to hip. Three young men appeared and began to pour warm water over our bodies. One gave me a large cup filled with crushed lemon, sugar, and ice from Mount Lalla Khadija.

Water streamed over me, and I began to breathe more easily. Shortly, the naked and shaved bald men swaddled us in cotton towels and placed wooden clogs on our feet. I clopped awkwardly after the entourage, inhaling thicker steam, and was guided to a long pine table about a foot from the ground. Through the gloaming I could see Alphonse settle on a similar table.

I lay facedown, breathing through a padded hole in the bench, while the mosaby—that is the title for young men trained in those arts guaranteed to please men—began kneading my body. He caressed each toe and moved with calm deliberation along each foot and leg. He slowly pressed, pulled, and twisted every muscle and appendage in a process that began with pain and ended with a soft caress.

At first I was apprehensive, and each painfully inserted thumb caused me to jerk away and disrupt his rhythm. The mosaby murmured apologies, then continued with the same stroke until all pain evaporated. Soon my entire body settled into a soft, moist cloud. I relaxed and became lost in the joyous wonder of my body. After a final, vigorous titillation of my neck, ears, and scalp, the mosaby rolled me gently from stomach to back, and again began to massage my toes and feet. As he applied oil to his hands and began to swoop up my shin, knee, and calf, it seemed, by accident, that a feathery movement touched my penis. That appendage could well have been the target of Doctor Franklin's lightning-storm experiment. In uncontrolled response, the heedless rod filled and lengthened to its fullest. The mosaby's ministrations were now centered on this quivering pole. He kissed and licked the straining tip and recklessly rubbed my inner thigh. With a gentle caress he fondled my scrotum. I looked in Alphonse's direction, but could only detect shadows. With a sigh I gave myself over to these heathen ways. Red flares pulsed through my tightly closed eyes as the mosaby moved his hands and mouth to the rapid pace of my craving.

Later, after he finished kneading my flesh and cracking each joint, the handsome young man donned haircloth mittens to lather my entire body with soapsuds. He then took a large razor and scraped my face, neck, and chest free of hair. When he judged my body sufficiently clean, he began rinsing me. First he doused me with a bucket of hot water, then with a frigid blast of cold water. He giggled with the first toss from the iced bucket and kissed me flush on the lips. "Call me Abu," he said, and I gasped more at the kiss than the dash of cold water.

Abu helped me stand; covered me with clean, dry towels; and led me through the gray mist, back into the foyer of the third apartment, where I slumped onto the divan. Soon Alphonse was escorted into the room by his mosaby, and he also reclined upon a couch. The mosaby brought us sweet coffee and a pipe for Alphonse. We didn't speak, and I fled in and out of dreams that embraced ships in good weather and chased images of the bath from my mind.

I pulled the hood of my burnoose over my head, and we stepped through the final canvas door, back into the sight of many men seated in chairs. They were eating and drinking and telling lies; none paid us the slightest attention. None saw the red flush of my cheeks or the smile on my lips.

CHAPTER TWELVE

March 1787

MY DUTIES CHANGED AFTER THE bath. Work continued as before, but now Alphonse and I raced each dusk to reach our sanctuary. We giggled while eating from the same plate and drinking from one cup. The kitchen mat saw less service, and I dismissed the need for sleep as the sweet, lovely room of Alphonse also became mine. At first I stumbled through dreams filled with itchy shame and intently watched my feet while walking through the baegnio. At first, that is, for very quickly I came to welcome the joyous greeting of each sunrise and the warm silky anticipation of waking in the arms of my sweet joy, Alphonse Gaston. The ships of my dreams disappeared, and in their stead stood the image of my patron.

The change happened, no matter, and I welcomed this new freedom. Alphonse and I began sharing small secrets, and our world diminished until others became shadowy intrusions of remote consequence. Every task was magically successful; odious oppressors became benefactors, and each day was clement. Even José Garcia noticed my sunny disposition and assigned increasingly important jobs to me. Our small shop nearly doubled production, and our evening appointments became increasingly lucrative. The dey charged

Alphonse with conducting all European negotiations, and as a direct consequence of this new duty, money quickly flowed into the Algerian treasury. Life held more delight than pain, and the pain quickly disappeared. Our immense pleasure came from pleasing the other.

———

"Do you think much of gaining your freedom?" I cast the question across the darkness of our room. Alphonse lay reclined on the raised platform of mats and pillows, while I leaned, shoulder against the wall, watching the stars through the open window and listening to the night sounds.

"No," he replied. We were silent for a long moment. "Whenever I go down that path of confusion, I lose more freedom than I gain, and you, my young friend, would be wise to give up such fantasies."

"My natural right is freedom." Anger stirred my stomach. "In my country we fight for our freedom. I can't speak for what others might believe."

"What do you make of the stars tonight, James?"

"The stars?"

"Yes, tell me what you make of the stars at this moment."

I glanced over my shoulder and quickly surveyed the quadrant visible through the window. "Jupiter is still chasing Venus to the horizon, and there is no difference from last night and very little difference from every night in this heathen city." A hint of annoyance sparked my voice; Alphonse was embarked on his mission as Oriental philosopher.

"Pick a star that pales in comparison with others, my friend. Study it intently, and report what you observe."

I dropped to my hands and knees, as quiet as any Mohegan Indian, and inched across the bedroom floor. With a ferocious roar, I launched myself onto the bed to encounter nothing but silk sheets and pillows.

As quick as any viper, musk-perfumed muscle locked my arms against the connecting stem of my neck and head, and every kick and twist was a futile effort for freedom. Alphonse restrained and directed, by virtue of his headlock on me, and gently placed us on the resilient mats. I relaxed, his weight upon me, his sweat merging with mine.

He untangled his arms from mine and began kneading the muscles of my shoulders, rubbing and gently scratching at my back. His weight upon me increased as he kissed and nipped at my ear. I shuddered in delicious anticipation. Alphonse whispered, "Your star, my friend. Does your star shine brighter now, or less so? Tell me what you see."

◆

My star was brighter, and life was good. Our routine jobs became simple and enormously productive. Alphonse reported that the dey smiled and tapped him on the shoulder after the Venetians agreed to an increase in their annual tax. I completed a large chest, replete with secret locks and drawers, and José Garcia smiled and tapped me on the shoulder. At night, over dinner and wine, Alphonse and I challenged the other with strategies to implement our dreams and fantasies.

One example of an impossible task that we accepted was the goal to moderate the life of my compatriots. As a first step, we met with Swedish Consul Peter Eric Skjoldebrand during the late afternoon at the tavern of Alphonse, to develop a plan that would provide a monthly allowance for all American slaves.

"Could we arrange for the Swedes to sell a brace of cannon to the Americans?" I asked.

"We certainly have the best thirty-six-pounders in the world," said Peter.

"What if your county were to sell a few of your marvelous weapons to my county at a very handsome profit?"

"Swedes and profit make a good match, but what is the advantage to Captain Stevens and the others?" said Peter.

I leaned forward on the tavern table. "If the senators from Massachusetts could educate their colleagues of the special technology that might be stolen from Swedish cannon, Congress might pass an appropriate bit of legislation to purchase them."

"Again, I must ask, how does the poor American sailor of this baenio benefit from such diplomacy?" said the Swedish Counsel. "Pleae describe to me the path from the sale of cannon to an extra bottle of rum for Captain Stevens."

"It is a simple exchange, my friends. I'n certain that the Americans will pay an excessive price for the cannon; then the generous Swedes will deliver the surplus compensation to Peter Eric, who in turn delivers an annual donation of Spanish doubloons to the dey's treasury, and *voila*—life for American prisoners is improved."

"Impossible," said Peter Eric.

"Impossible," said Alphonse.

All in all, the plan evolved as an exchange of United States tax money for some interesting Swedish technology. Alphonse always had access to European and American newspapers, and we laughed as various editors of Boston and Montreal newspapers discussed the possibility that these Swedish weapons could serve as an archetype for replication in an American armory. Two factories, were in fact created: an armory in Virginia and another located near Boston. The two senators representing investors of New England and the two senators eager to help Southern financiers, received near unanimous support from their colleagues for this meritorious project. The required money, dubbed ruinous by American senators who were not elected by citzens from Virginia or Massechuetts, and fair by the swedes, was sent to Sweden as a contractual obligation. However, the unfortunate vagaries of weather prevented delivery of the cannon by the Swedes, and the entire matter was quickly forgotten by all senators and most of the American taxpayers.

Peter Eric, Alphose and the dey of Algeria met for tea and discussion of irrelevant issues on a blustery March afternoon, and all three smiled at one-another from beginning to end.

"How did it go?" I queried of Alhonse at our evening meal.

"Fine," answered my patron. "Pass along the wine bottle, if you please."

"The details, good sir, if you please."

"Six cents per day is allocated for maintenance of the eighteen surviving American sailors and mates." Alphone paused to give me a toothy smile. "Captain Stevens and the two other American ship captains will get one dollar per day and also their legitimate privilege due their rank, which is freedom from the baegnio."

"My goodness. Well done, I'm sure that the Americans will be pleased with their new blessings."

"There is even more for your compatriots, Jim Cathcart. Mr. Skjoldebrand has graciously provided a small cottage for the three officers on his own estate."

"No!"

"Yes, indeed, my friend."

Over the next few weeks I made the effort to observe how the mates and men spent their six cents, and saw them purchase either an extra cup of rum or an extra ration of watery stew from one of the lesser taverns. No recognition came to me from the mates and sailors that they appreciated the new stipend. Whenever I saw one or another in passing, it appeared to me that the small improvement in their lot caused them to grumble and complain with greater frequency than before, and I came to see them as mean-spirited men who had no backbone and no spirit of industry. They seemed content to isolate themselves from all social intercourse with prisoners of other nations, to wallow in a sea of self-pity, and to constantly complain of their lot. There were certainly never any whispers about plans to escape or find employment from this lot of slaves.

I also became increasingly upset with their verbal abuse directed toward me by all of my former shipmates aboard the *Maria*. Granted, my prosperity stood in sharp contrast to their depraved level of existence, for I had my job and extra income with José. Their jibes and rough hints at my relationship with Alphonse, however, eliminated any temptation to relinquish my advantages to satisfy their demented squawks. It seemed to me that nothing improved their demeanor—not the Swedish cannon money, not the comfortable dwelling for the captains, and certainly not the small favors that I could grant them.

◆

Alphonse taught me the pleasure of giving gifts. Nearly every day he made some bestowal of favor or substance—often in surprising circumstances—for my use. On one sunlit morning, a new suit of clothes covered my pillow. I was given the gift of exotic fruit or handsomely prepared foods on many evenings. Alphonse took me on visits to the homes of influential grandees, and they came to view me as a possible agent for their political and commercial machinations. The bath, of course, offered unlimited opportunities for Alphonse to indulge my pleasure.

I lacked the necessary resources to reciprocate his kindness, but spent much of my daydream time devising strategies to return his generosity. Certain efforts were possible; for instance, I managed to build a cedar bookshelf for his apartment and a sleigh headboard for his bed. I pilfered the book of Vitas Bering's adventures from the library of a termite-ravaged house, with the foreknowledge that the illiterate owner would never miss it and that Alphonse would smile through every page.

We were both pleased by the scramble of good deeds heaped one on the other, and slowly I learned how to accept his dotage. In one instance, however, his gift was far beyond my ability to reciprocate. On my third celebration of Ramadan, the month of fasting and contemplation of Mohammed's words from Allah, Alphonse promised our participation in a very special event: a review of the dey of Algiers' janissary troops.

CHAPTER THIRTEEN

March 1788

During the sweet moments we spent on our tiny island above the prison, Alphonse often entertained me with his ripping enactment of palace gossip. It was his pleasure to make me laugh over the antics of Ciddi or one of the European ambassadors at court. His words painted pictures of fat Frenchmen crawling facedown to beg a favor of the dey, or of Ciddi managing a harem filled with bored and ignored women. At some point in his soliloquy, he always sat up straight against the pastel cushions and said, "Enough! Enough of my blathering woman's talk. Now it is time for you to tell me your secrets, James. Tell me about your family and your life among the red savages of America."

I could frequently outwait his request; given a few moments of silence, Alphonse usually filled the void with his own voice. I always offered him the comfort of a sympathetic ear, but on those rare occasions when I could not avoid a contribution to the conversation, I usually gave him some wildly absurd descriptions of Will Melman's exploits. I made my friend Will into a great hero at the Battle of Saratoga and an uncanny navigator aboard the *Maria*. The Will Melman of my stories was a deadly marksman with rifle or cannon, and equally proficient at annihilating red men or Englishmen.

Alphonse eventually formulated a standard and bemused request. "Come, now, James, tell me more about the infamous Will Melman."

Alphonse smiled without pause as he led me through the now familiar streets. We admired the sprawling estates of wealthy men, clucked with pleasure over the multitudinous mists of pink and white blossoms covering most every building, and threw small coins to trailing beggar boys. The sweet perfume of flowers combined with sewer stench, spices, and sea scent into a brew that identified Algiers. We passed through the gates of the dey's palace, saluted the posted sentry, and were directed to a large tent. The symbol of a fish billowed on two sides of the stretched canvas. I was somewhat giddy with anticipation at seeing the famous janissary, but thoroughly confused by the scene before my eyes.

Even Alphonse's steady smile changed into a painful gash as we entered the huge structure. There was first a huge kitchen that sported large work tables and well-vented fireplaces. The remaining space in the tent showed dining tables in orderly rows. Scattered groups of soldiers wandered throughout the tent, and none paid us the least attention. Some were playing stringed instruments and singing, and others were talking in the animated fashion of confident men. All wore the striking uniforms of the Turkish sultan's army.

After an interminable wait, a dark-skinned soldier with a heavy beard detached himself from a group of four men. His billowing black pantaloons were secured with a wide red and white belt, and into the belt was sheathed a large white-handled dagger. Over the man's black vest, a heavy brown cloak trailed to the top of his black leather slippers. With the pantaloons flagging and the cloak billowing, he mimicked a small ship approaching in a light breeze. His turban comprised three parts: a red cap centered on a cleanly shaven head; a white crane feather drooping in a loop toward his nose; and, at the rear of this bonnet, a long flap of gray cloth was secured to the cap by means of a stiff leather strap.

It was only when this audacious vision held out his hand and smiled that I recognized my friend and dear companion. I stared. This was not the nigger Will of my memory. I extended my hand. "Will?"

His smile flashed ancient memories of shared holidays and frozen watches. The smile closed and disappeared. "Jim," he said, "after three years, and you look in better health than the last time we were together."

We clasped hands, and I looked carefully into his eyes. "Can we sit and talk for a while?" I asked.

"Certainly. We have a few minutes before the parade begins. Follow me."

We made our way through the clusters of brilliantly uniformed janissaries and sat at the first dining table. It was a clean, well-maintained table.

"Have you met Alphonse Gaston? He's the dey's first Christian secretary."

"Yes, Jim, we've met several times." He looked directly at Alphonse. "I want to thank you for interceding on my behalf. You have truly been an instrument for Allah, contriving my freedom from slavery and enlistment with the gran porte of Turkey. Both events have emerged as special gifts from you, and I hope to vindicate your confidence in me."

It was a carefully memorized speech, yet sincerely delivered. Alphonse dropped his eyes and murmured, "It is my pleasure to serve Allah in this matter."

Will gazed directly at me. "My name is Ahmed al-Koita."

When I didn't respond, he continued. "I am a follower of Islam and testify that there is no god but Allah; Mohammed is the prophet of Allah." Ahmed al-Koita struggled on with this second practiced speech. "I have sworn loyalty to the gran porte of Turkey and to the 58th Corps of Janissary. These men you see around you here today—they are my comrades to death."

He would have continued, but I interrupted. "Wait, let me speak." The small ears, patrician nose, green eyes of a rare cat, and black skin that soaked the light of any candle—all the same. "Gaosson Koita is smiling at the very sound of your name, I'm sure. Congratulations, Ahmed al-Koita."

I switched from speaking Turkish to English. "Is it okay for you to speak to an infidel? Can you tell me more about what is with your life, Ahmed?"

His shoulders relaxed a little, but still no smile. He continued in English, and Alphonse stood and left the table. "It's all true, Jim-boy. I'm a Moslem, and as you see, a janissary." My friend looked past me into the blank nothingness of white canvas. He spoke to himself, allowing me to eavesdrop. "They respect me, Jim." There was little inflection to his voice. Each isolated comment slipped past his tongue, accompanied by a small hand gesture or twist of his lips. "They think that I know a lot about cannon. The men of the janissary like me, and I'm certain that I can make something of myself here." Ahmed paused and lifted his left hand with dramatic vigor. "I'm not a nigger; I'm a subaltern." He lowered his hand and sat with quiet dignity. "I can protect each of my brothers in battle, and they will protect me. This is it, Jim-boy. Nobody is going to call me 'nigger' again, not even in jest. I'm a free man. I've chosen Allah as the One God and the janissary as my expression of loyalty to Mohammed."

After a few moments, I tried to string my thoughts into a response that would not affront my old friend. "You are certainly correct, Ahmed al-Koita—you've found a home." He returned a faint smile, and then we talked about my life, in scratchy bits, until the soldiers began drifting away.

"I've got to go now, Jim, but listen—stay and watch the parade, and then meet me at the coffeehouse near the Swordsmith Guild. Señor Gaston will know the place." He stood. "I want you to see all my comrades on parade, and later to share a pipe and coffee with a few who are willing to sit with you." He turned and disappeared into the crowd.

I sat at the table for a while longer, until Alphonse tapped my shoulder. "Come," he said, "you will enjoy the parade."

◆

The parade grounds adjoined the dey's palace and the janissary barracks, and it was sheep-cropped smooth to an even green carpet. The late afternoon shadows from the palace protected the dey of Algiers, who was seated on a cushioned settee and elevated even further on a six-foot-high podium. A sprinkling of foreign consuls and merchants, plus a large group of the dey's military officers, stood, all jumbled together on a slightly elevated reviewing stand.

Alphonse assumed his teacher's pose. "You must understand, my young friend, that these janissaries have a negligible loyalty to the dey of Algiers. They follow an absolute commitment to Allah, and their next level of loyalty is to the Turkish sultan. Every janissary believes that Mohammed will lead them to heaven, but it is the sultan who directs their temporal affairs."

A snappish annoyance bubbled in my stomach. "Isn't that the dey of Algiers elevated above everyone else? Over there, at the center of the reviewing stand?"

"Quiet!" Alphonse leaned over to my ear and hissed. "Save your display of stupidity for tonight." He took two steps away from me and assumed his First-Christian-secretary smile and studied the swarm of janissaries as they formed into clumpy patterns. After a suitable interval he moved closer and whispered, "These soldiers before you choose service to the dey of Algiers because he is from their own ranks. The dey of Algiers is a Turkish janissary, and he too has total allegiance to the Turkish sultan, both as a soldier and as an indebted politician. You must understand that the dey is a loyal servant to the Turkish sultan in the same manner that your friend Ahmed al-Koita is a loyal servant to the sultan."

I nudged at a small pebble with my toe. "I didn't know how it all worked with the Turks and Algerians." The pebble joined a row of three brethren. "I'm sorry for my stupidity." The apology was genuine, and when Alphonse started speaking again, his pleasantly pompous words again held affection for me.

"Listen, James, in the world conceived by those who populate the Ottoman Empire, there is a very strict and consistent order of power. Are you ready to learn the order?"

"Yes."

He held up his thumb from a closed fist. "First, and in every moment of existence, is the One God, Allah. Allah is all. Allah is everything. Allah is nothing."

"Yes," I said.

Now the first finger joined with the thumb. "His prophet Mohammed bears the responsibility of giving the word of Allah to all mortals." The second finger popped up. "In the shift of power from heaven to earth, the Turkish sultan serves as chosen spokesman for Mohammed." Now the third finger, "And on the distant horizon from the omnipotence of Allah sits the dey of Algiers. He must serve Allah and Mohammed and the sultan as a dutiful captain. The dey's rank falls to the third order of power."

I turned to Alphonse. "Bravo! I finally understand, my lord."

He ignored my interruption. "It may seem an odd covenant, James, yet these few soldiers parading before us today rule all the Moors and Arabs of Algeria for the sultan of Turkey. They are closely held subjects of the sultan and Allah. You must always remember that the janissary corps serves only Allah and the Turkish sultan. The dey of Algiers and these few janissaries rule the multitudinous Arabs and

Moors of Algiers for Allah and the gran porte of Turkey."

"For goodness sake, Alphonse, I really do understand your message; these janissaries are similar to the Hessian mercenaries used by the British in their wars."

"No, no, no! Not at all. The corps of janissaries provides the sultan with everything that he needs. They are his army, police, tax collector, and loyal comrades. The janissaries are paid by the sultan, and they serve him for life." He smiled and looked directly at me. "Your old foe, the Hessians, would appear as undisciplined children if matched against the janissaries. These men in their absurd costumes go to war as to a favorite brother's wedding: with love and joy. They die willingly for the sultan and for Allah."

The ranks stood ready. Eight Bektashi dervishes, all dressed in green, stood in the vanguard. Their leader called in a voice that silenced all and penetrated into the palace walls. *"Allah kermis"*— God is beautiful. The other seven replied with a long, drawn-out, sonorous *"Huuuuuuu, Heeee,"* and the parade in celebration of the dey of Algiers' loyalty to the sultan of Turkey began.

Each squad of the infantry regiment displayed a different uniform, and each man ambled at his own pace down the parade grounds. They vied with the other to cast the surliest of glances at the audience, and they fingered a variety of sabres, scimitars, and short yataghans with undisguised pleasure. No one seemed willing to take issue with their lack of cadence or bellicose attitude. The cloaks, vests, and belts of the infantry ranged in color from black to vivid orange.

Next came the cavalry, all mounted on small Arabian geldings that pranced about in total disarray across the neat and expansive parade ground. From either side of every saddlebow hung an armory of hatchets and maces and small spears, and all the while the cavalrymen waved long-barreled rifles in one hand and a pistol in the other. The movement of their horses directed with subtle movements from knee and heel. Only one squad of the calvary served as the exception, and they rode in rank order, maintained a dignified eyes-front posture, and in their right hands each held a new Austrian carbine.

Finally, with Ahmed al-Koita walking in attendance, came four battery of cannon mounted on large-wheeled carts and hauled by teams of black mules. Each group—infantry, cavalry and artillery—constantly echoed the lead dervish's *"Allah kermis"* with their *"Huuuuuu,"* until the entire regiment seemed transported in a mass that combined them as one and dismissed all others as irrelevant.

The sights! Their turbans! One was of peach color, wound in circular fashion to a height of three feet, with a small brass bell ensconced on top. Others sported vertical leather straps, feathers of every size and color, long flaps of cloth flowing behind, and even giraffe tails dangling from turban to dust.

There was no avoiding the obvious differences marking each soldier, but I was struck by their similarities—especially the eyes, capable of tearing through any obstruction with the ease of a sharp knife into a woman's stomach. The guns and swords and cannon were powerful tools, but the burning eyes told me the truth of Ahmed al-Koita's janissary.

Chapter Fourteen

THE COFFEEHOUSE WAS CRAMMED WITH short-legged tables, cushions, and a swirling mass of men, all under three arches of an open arcade. Bougainvillea vines rambled around support columns and flashed purple bracts. A storyteller sat on a small raised platform, a scarf and wand before him, and as Alphonse and I entered into the space, he started a chant of poetry while accompanying himself on a one-stringed fiddle.

Ahmed waved for us to join him, and we sat on cushions, crowded shoulder to shoulder with his compatriots. A light-skinned slave served us thimbles of coffee and a bowl of raisins, and we turned our attention to the storyteller.

The scraping movement of bow on string slowed briefly, burst into a rapid crescendo, and suddenly stopped. Of an instant, conversation began rumbling in all corners; two of the janissaries in our company pulled short pipes from their sleeves, tapped in shreds of tobacco, and waited silently until the attentive slave brought a burning taper and ignited each pipe.

"We are celebrating," Ahmed said.

"Ah, yes," I said. "The end of Ramadan?"

"No. Well certainly, Ramadan, but tomorrow our company leaves for M'Sila with orders to convince a reluctant chief to pay his due taxes."

Alphonse wrinkled his brow. "South? To the Atlas Mountains?"

"Not so far as the mountains," Ahmed responded. "In the lee of the Atlas, above a dry lake and into some hills that may offer an ambush or two. Nothing to worry about, but nonetheless, we will finally see some action!"

We three sat with our thoughts until Ahmed began again. "I can't introduce my comrades to you since you are Christian slaves and we are loyal janissaries. They would berate and insult you if I brought you to their attention."

"We understand," said Alphonse.

Ahmed glanced around the tables. "Most of my friends have been in the janissary corps from the time they were children and are stuck with one note, one way of perceiving life." He smiled at me with a hint at our previous camaraderie. "Not unlike the storyteller's fiddle: one note, play fast or slow, it is still the one note."

"Not much different from most of our folks," I said. "Just think about the likes of Omrod or Sevillon or even most Americans: one note played fast or slow."

Ahmed sipped from his cup. "What do you hear about those two idiots?"

"I understand from one of the Christian corporals that they're both in bad shape."

Ahmed took a deep pull from the nargileh and then flicked his chin toward the seated janissary troops. "These men are smarter than most Americans I've ever met. They are tougher and certainly more loyal to God and king."

Alphonse moved his body between us and gazed directly into my eyes. "James, you must count yourself privileged to be called friend by a representative of the janissary."

"I do, most assuredly."

Alphonse leaned forward as my confidante. "Your friend Ahmed will ascend the ranks, and he will certainly lead his men to many victories."

I nodded and smiled. "He led troops at Saratoga to glory; I'm certain he'll do even better with the janissary."

"You must help him achieve his goals."

"Is this another of your Oriental games?" I was more irritated than surprised.

Now Alphonse leaned back to include Ahmed in his conversation. "The two of you must listen carefully to what I say."

We nodded. "Of course."

"First of all, we must never embarrass Ahmed again with our company. He is a subaltern and responsible for the honor of his corps. It is beneath his dignity to hold lengthy conversations with slaves, and his superiors will begin to doubt his commitment to Allah and to the gran porte if such unwholesome behavior continues."

I moved uneasily on the cushion. "Pardon me, Alphonse, but wasn't this meeting your idea?"

"Indeed, my young friends, and if I may be so bold, I must take some credit for the initial meeting between a person with the foolish Christian name of Will Melman and the chief imam of the janissary."

"He's right, Jim. This is the last time for us. The Christian way, the nigger way, is done and gone. I've been chosen for this life, and there's no room for you." Ahmed al-Koita gave me his best janissary stare. "In fact, you are now the archenemy of my life, the prime reminder of my life as a slave. We've been parted by Allah." Ahmed dropped his head in prayer. "Praise be to Allah."

I stood to leave, hot in the head, with an empty belly.

Alphonse pulled me back to the cushion. "Listen, both of you roosters." He looked first at Ahmed. "Your friend Jim Cathcart talks about you constantly, about your deeds together and about your family. He never tells of his family—always yours, and most frequently about your father."

Alphonse waved us to silence. "It seems that fate, possibly the will of Allah, has returned you to Africa. It was within my power to provide some small assistance to advance your cause, which I did, not for you but for James. Pay attention, now! Accept my wisdom. Listen."

Ahmed looked at me, and I shrugged my shoulders in agreement for a truce. We both turned our shoulders toward Alphonse. We sat straight on our cushions.

"You will find, Ahmed, that money is essential for promotion within the corps of janissaries. It is necessary to compensate your superiors for their loyalty to the gran porte. His Eminence has much to do and often forgets to reward his commanders in this remote outpost. There are other inconveniences created by the dey that can only be smoothed with gold. As the difficulties of the gran porte increase—may Allah show his support for the great sultan—you, my young subaltern, will find a greater need for grease. Life holds many rough edges, and there is often a need for lubrication to ease one's passage through difficult constraints."

Alphonse reached for his coffee, drank a small sip, waited for us to digest his wisdom, and then continued. "And where will this gift of power come from, this shower of gold to advance the cause of Ahmed al-Koita?" Alphonse paused and looked directly at me. "It will come from your friend, James Cathcart."

We stared at the madman spouting such foolishness, and again Alphonse held his right hand, palm out, as a gesture for our further silence.

"I have said enough for now, but we three will meet again in some less conspicuous place, on your return from showing the sultan's colors." Alphonse pointed with his chin. "Look, it appears that our storyteller is rested and ready to continue."

I glanced to the raised platform as the storyteller tapped the table with his wand. The rumbling of many conversations dissipated to attentive quiet, and with an astounding assortment of voices, the storyteller recounted a tale of Nasreddin Hoje, a teacher and philosopher of ancient Turkey. From what I could make of the poem, it seemed that Hoje awakened one night to the shouts of two men quarrelling in front of his house. The storyteller mimicked the angry cries and forceful groans from the combatants, and each of us seated in the coffeehouse could only be wholly sympathetic with Hoje as he wrapped himself in his quilt and ran outside to separate the battling men. Unfortunately, the disputants were not easily placated; in fact, the ruffians resented Nasreddin's interference, turned on him, and beat him unmercifully. Into the gutter fell Nasreddin, quivering and moaning with pain, and the two men picked up his quilt and ran into the darkness. Bruised and aching, Nasreddin Hoje stumbled back to his room.

His wife, only partially awake, asked, "What were the men quarrelling about?"

"About my quilt, apparently, because they've got it and they've stopped quarrelling."

We all burst into laughter with the final nasal rendering of the story, and a slave moved quickly through the audience to collect coins in an inverted half drum. The coffee cups were again filled, tobacco was again flamed to life, and the diverse conversations were rekindled.

"It's time for us to leave," Alphonse said. "Please stay seated, Ahmed al-Koita; stay with your comrades and fight bravely. May Allah be with you, ever-more."

I struggled to my feet, resisted the temptation to shake the hand of Ahmed al-Koita, to embrace my friend Will Melman, and followed Alphonse into the street. We barely managed the first turn of the crowded alley, when Alphonse stopped and pointed to a small wooden booth. "It's time for your fortune to be told, my friend. I have premonitions of good tidings for you and seek their confirmation."

He ushered me to the booth, and I sat before a very young boy. Without looking at me, and glancing only briefly at the six masoons that Alphonse placed in his keeping, the boy slowly poured a pool of black ink into his cupped left hand. The young fortune-teller gazed raptly at the black puddle and, after a long wait, began speaking in a wavering high-pitched voice.

> *Into Allah's hands you have fallen.*
> *Despair and grief in shadows long,*
> *Shorten with the new saint's song.*
>
> *Though not of the chosen few,*
> *Through you the mysteries cling*
> *To guess where fortunes fling.*

He paused, and in a voice pitched higher yet said:

> *The sea, yet not the sea. There is the danger. Twice.*
> *The sea, yet not the sea.*

The boy dumped the ink back into a small clay pot, wiped his hand with a dirty rag, and shuddered into a trance. The session was over, and the world seemed to be getting too difficult for a second mate to understand. Here I was, abandoned by my one and only best friend—not counting Alphonse, of course—and then dragged by the same unmentionable Alphonse to the company of a catatonic fortune-teller. A child who earned six masons for merely reciting a silly rhyme.

We walked back to the baegnio without comment or discussion of the day's events. The gates would soon close, and our Sabbath was nearly over. "The sea, yet not the sea."

Chapter Fifteen

July 1788

IF MY LIFE WERE FILLED with parades, storytellers, and grape leaves filled with lamb, one might reasonably describe the slave business as something less than burdensome, but such was not reality. In fact, immediately after my reunion with Ahmed al-Koita (the new name was a perfect fit for the image of my friend), one hideous job trailed the next through the spring and summer. First, Hassan Bashaw assigned all slaves to the task of dredging the harbor. Then, José Garcia received an assignment to completely remodel the cabin of a captured frigate—and at the very same time it seemed that every grandee in Algiers demanded his immediate service for large and complicated jobs. Each Friday blurred without pause into the monotony of Monday.

Just as the possibility of a holiday appeared on the horizon, the Swedish consul sent an urgent message requesting the construction and installation of a door. An attached drawing, with measurements and a roughly drawn design, was included.

"You take the job, lad," José Garcia said.

Alphonse gave me permission to stay overnight in the wood shop, and I worked until pitch dark for the next five evenings. With the routing and joining of English elm and native cedar from the high Atlas Mountains, I achieved a lovely balance of color and pattern. But it was the leaf and grape design, chiseled at eye level and slightly left of center, that in my opinion, gave the door a solid richness. I sanded and lacquered the surface four times and thereby completed my first work of art—all without José Garcia's help or consultation. On a Friday afternoon it was hung without a single complication and with high praise from Consul Peter Eric.

I knew from Alphonse that the dey was most pleased with serving as a conduit for funds to sustain his American prisoners since nearly half the American cannon money went into his private treasury. "Can we harvest a bit more of their ripe fruit?" asked the dey of his first Christian secretary.

"Not likely; they are a parsimonious tribe of infidels, Your Liege."

"They are children with dreams of glory as their natural right. Infidels with no resources for honor or integrity."

"Do I detect an assignment for your unworthy Christian secretary?"

"Try another round of letters to those American senators of yours. Pet their soft fur, and fill their empty brains with dreams of wealth and power."

Unbelievably—to me, at any rate—the government of Sweden received an additional payment on the two undelivered cannon as a second good-faith response from the United States government. The result was an additional payment of ten cents per day for the maintenance of American sailors, and two dollars per day for the three captains who were enslaved by the Barbary pirates. This sum went to the Americans after the dey's commission, of course.

The first Christian secretary to the dey of Algiers barely smiled when an anonymous gift was delivered to his tavern long after the gates were locked. The messenger dropped a small silk bag at our table, next to the chicken bones from our meal and away from the wine glasses half-filled from a green bottle. Alphonse spilled the small gold coins into my cupped hands until they were full.

"Save these for Ahmad al-Koita," he said.

"This is from the dey to me?" I was perplexed, of course, because I had done nothing to earn such a reward."

"Hush," said, Alphonse. "The small handful of gold nothing, it is merely a tiny signal that the dey is aware of your existence, and will continue watching you to determine how you may best serve his interests."

"Where will I store this gold?"

"Soon, I will show you the proper place to place the gold."

"The dey, what has he in mind as a position for me?"

"Zero. You are nothing to the dey." Alphone emptied his glass of wine and banged it on the table. "Why on earth would the dey of Algiers think that a thoughtless slave named James Cathcart could have any use for him at all?"

"Will I eventually learn of my fate here in Algiers?"

"Maybe, but not at all likely."

Alphonse poured his glass full of red wine, and sat contemplating a singular spot on the wall of his tavern until it was empty once again.

"Off to bed," he said. "Quiet. No talking. No questions. Quiet."

I approached the small cottage that Peter Eric had made available to the American ship captains. They were engrossed at cards, with scattered empty bottles on the floor and one nearly empty on their table. My stomach shuttered. Bitter gorge entered my throat. This was the life of American ship captain. Slaves of the dey of Algiers, yet ensconced with some degree of comfort in the tiny cottage on the comfortable grounds of the Swedish Embassy. They were ordered by Iban Raisani to remain in or near their assigned quarters and do nothing. Nothing. No work carrying rocks, no ledgers to copy—nothing. And so the four officers obeyed the Harbour Master's orders, and limited their puny lives to cards and drinking whatever whiskey or wine that they could surreptitiously purchase from one servant or another who worked at the embassy.

"Ah, James." My uncle glanced at me with narrowed eyes, looked back at his cards, compressed them together, and placed them on the table. "Working on the Sabbath, I see."

"Yes sir. A small job for Consul Skjoldebrand. He has a reception for his new assistant this week and was in a bit of a hurry."

"Ha! I expect we'll have a bunch of niggers crawling all over this place any day now." He gave me a shuddering stare—not into my eyes but toward different spots above my head. "What's the matter, James? Have you no pride?" He emptied the remaining contents of the bottle into his glass, and the other three captains got up from the table and disappeared toward their shared bedrooms. "Go ahead, James—admit to the fact that you enjoy working for niggers."

"Excuse me, Uncle Stevens. I'm merely doing my duty. I'm a slave, sir, and must do as I'm told."

"Well, young man, you don't see me toad-eating, do you?" Captain Stevens bugged his

eyes at me. "Even if I were still in that miserable prison, I'd rather starve next to some American swab than lick the spittle of a nigger!"

Again I tried to excuse myself. "Begging your pardon, sir, but the Swedes have negotiated

an increase to four dollars per day for each American captain."

"Ha! Take your bloody money back to your bloody mosaby and that uppity first Christian secretary; we don't want anything from you. If I ever get the chance, my boy, I'll throw you overboard, tied to a heavy anchor." He shook his head like a tired old horse. "Your father was a whoremonger, and it seems that there's nothing I could do to protect your mother from the likes of father or son."

"My father will not waste an anchor on your miserable soul. He'll merely touch his finger to your chest and flip your miserable, lying hide into a nice stretch of the very cold Atlantic ocean." I turned and walked rapidly away from my captain, my uncle.

He called to my back, "Bastard! Whore for niggers!"

<hr>

Later that evening I sat on the roof to stare at bats as they carved sharp-edged pictures in the purple dusk. Allah received his final prayers for the day, and the sounds of Algiers frittered away to a faint murmur.

Alphonse let me mope for a decent time, then spoke. "What's wrong? You didn't eat; you haven't said a word all night."

"Nothing is wrong," I said. After a few minutes, Alphonse came over to my side and began a gentle massage of my shoulders.

"You're a better man than he is," Alphonse whispered. "Ignore that mean-spirited and stupid person. You are a good man, James. A good man."

<hr>

Alphonse suffered indignities of a different sort.

The old dey died in his bed after contracting brain fever, and the curious situation of a peaceful death so confused the grandees and ship captains and janissary officers that they shrugged their shoulders and bowed their way through the smooth transfer of title to the old dey's favorite nephew. The wonders of Allah's patience never ceased to amaze the faithful, and only the sudden death of the new dey's two younger brothers and the disappearance of an elderly uncle brought knowing smiles from the citizens of substance.

The gran porte of Turkey recognized the new dey of Algiers and also demanded double the annual tribute. The tribute was due immediately, of course, and Alphonse was assigned the task of designing a more profitable relationship with the Christian nations to thus satisfy this new and crushing financial obligation. The new dey made a pointed suggestion that this silly new upstart, the United States, should be brought to heel.

"Enough of their impertinence, my first Christian secretary; we must squeeze the infidel bastards. We have twenty-six of their sailors, so tell me the true worth of these twenty-six miserable infidels."

"Truly, most illustrious prince," Alphonse said. "It is eighteen sailors now, for plague, my prince, still haunts the prison."

"Twenty-six, you stupid infidel; we captured twenty-six, so they must pay for twenty-six! It is not my fault that their weak constitutions are unable to survive this interminable bargaining. We must have fifty thousand Spanish dollars from the dogs. Fifty thousand dollars and a twenty-six-gun frigate—one gun for each miserable dog. Write down my demands and send it to the pig-lovers. Now! Now!"

Alphonse told me of the exchange with the new dey, of course, and we both agreed that the following days and months would be increasingly difficult for the American captives.

"If I lose favor with this dey, you can be assured that the current pastoral life of you and your compatriots will be replaced by very ugly nightmares.

Our lives continued in this unremitting fashion until mid-July, three years after the date of my capture. On that anniversary, with our first free day since Ahmed's parade, Alphonse took me on a picnic.

Cool air trickled down the hills as we passed through Bebazoon Gate. Our mules coughed and sighed as we rode slowly up the first rise until the rising sun exploded over mountains to glare directly into our eyes. When we reached the river La Haratch, a sturdily built bridge straddled the center of a nearly dry river, but the causeway on either side lay in tangled ruin. We followed a well-worn trail through the water and back onto the road.

"Hadrian built this bridge; what's that—fourteen centuries ago?" Alphonse looked over his shoulder at me and smiled. "The Romans kept the roads passable and the wells full for eight hundred years or so—especially the wells full." He waved at the sharp-pointed weeds and gray scrub that dominated the rolling plain. "This was a bountiful region when the legionnaires ruled, and those ancient men lived by a splendid compact with their masters."

"I'm ignorant of Romans and Hadrian here in Algeria. Tell me what you know of the history."

"First of all, you must understand that those Roman soldiers who survived twenty years of road building and ambushes, were rewarded in their retirement with twenty acres for their service. These hard-working men used their ingenuity and strength to plant and irrigate, and the families that they created continued to flourish even after Rome died."

"What happened to their farms and roads?"

"Allah sent his Arabs to this bountiful land."

I looked around and saw little evidence of Roman diligence. A few crumpled foundations of houses and barns. Spiked green weeds guarding the remnants of a single well. "I'd say a few good farmers could quickly bring this area back into production; what about you?"

"Not likely." He looked up toward some thin cirrus clouds. "Oh, maybe in the next millennium the Algerians will learn some effective farming techniques for this place, but not in the foreseeable future."

"The soil looks good, and there seems at least the potential for an adequate supply of water. I would think the dey could emulate those old-time Romans without much effort."

"Ha! Only after the Christians control Algiers again, only then will the desert bloom again."

"Now we have the Turks and their Arabs where Hadrian

flourished. How can you pretend such omniscient power, my lord? Christians in Algeria, indeed!"

"Fie with your ignorance, James. I speak of common knowledge, nothing else." Alphonse plodded along for a short while before returning to his lecture. "The Arabs abhor all farmers, and of course Allah loves the Arabs above all others. Even though the Turks pretend control of this land, it is the Arab priest who determines which ideas flourish and which fade to dust." He gave me his tutor's wink. "A simple syllogism explains the lonely bridge and weeds. Allah loves the desert. Farmers hate the desert. Arabs love the desert. Allah hates all farmers and loves all Arabs."

"Love or hate, people still need to eat. Are you telling me that no one grows food around here? That the Arabs must import all the food they require?"

"Again, my young student, when the Roman farmers departed this region hundreds of years ago, the irrigation system quickly failed. The previously cultivated and productive land became vacant of all farmers. Desert weeds replaced wheat. However, and this is important for you to understand, my friend, the Arabs do in fact manage a few slaves in each tiny island of the desert that has a permanent water supply. It is these slave-farmers who produce date and citrus trees of some worth, but otherwise there is only wind and weeds."

My eyes supported the account recited by Alphonse, so I gave him due credit. There was a slight goad to my words. "Thank you, sir," I said. "I shall treasure such golden nuggets forever."

We rode silently through a small swamp and up a tolerably good road. The river meandered under our feet again and led us along the edge of a marsh. July heat had drained any standing water from the expansive marsh, and a multitude of brown brittle rushes stood available for harvesting. Several mountaineers were loading donkeys with those reeds, but the rough-hewn men ignored our greeting.

The mules clopped side by side, parallel to the river, and we were now nearly to Cape Temendefust. "James, we must have a conversation about your future."

"I'm listening, Alphonse."

"A Jew of my acquaintance has sold me some important information." He hesitated for a few moments. "I'm to be ransomed in the near future. A month—three at the most."

I looked at him and quickly away. Through the shimmering light appeared a family of Arabs; they sat on their heels, washing clothes at a spring of fresh water. As we approached, all five got up and walked over to the road. Without speaking to us, the two youngest children gave us some prickly pears and unripe pomegranates. I dug into my purse and satisfied them with two masoons, then we continued with our silent progress.

I thought, isn't it strange how life responds to the brief moments of happiness? A little joy collects along fingertips and earlobes, and then a thousand thunderstorms confront those few dewdrops, and life falls again into the black abyss. I mistakenly held the easy banter about religion, the beauty of hills and river, and Alphonse's affection as ordained gifts. Now sweat coursed down my back. Alphonse was leaving.

At the next level course of road, he continued as if there had been no interruption. "You must survive this heathen place." He gave a vacant smile in my direction. "You need to survive, and I need something more complicated: I need respect for my family." He looked down the road like a blind man. "Do you remember Rais Mawlud-Qadir?"

"Certainly," I said. "He was captain of the xebec that captured the *Maria*."

"Did you know that the captain is famous for always giving the same speech to his new captives?"

"The one about life's vicissitudes?"

"Yes, and in my mind he is correct in his summary. We must

enjoy pleasure when it appears, endure through most of the hateful hours, and cultivate those few good people who become our friends."

I didn't respond to his pompous gibberish.

"You're a good person, James, and you are my friend." He halted his mule. "I believe that we've given each other some moments of happiness—am I correct?"

I looked at the ground without speaking.

"Well, in any event, we have a final choice to make."

I found his eyes. "You're sure? You will leave in a month—three at the most?"

"Yes, I'm positive that my information is accurate."

"But you have a choice in the matter, don't you? You have power and prestige here in Algiers; why not stay?" I stared at the ground again.

"I must leave, James." He blinked his gray eyes. "Before that final day, I want to give you a final gift."

The gorge in my throat denied any response.

"The gift may kill us both, but you must listen to the offer and tell me what you think."

"I think you should stay."

"That's impossible," Alphonse said.

"Then keep your gift; go, but leave me alone!"

CHAPTER SIXTEEN

August 1789

T
HE MULES PLODDED A SMOOTH, somnolent rhythm along the old
Roman road. A bird with a yellow breast sat on a low bush,
trilling a repetitive series of ascending notes. I nurtured the
smoldering rage that I held for Alphonse the deserter. My gut churned
with memories of our comfortable retreat atop the prison, so full of
laughter and love.

"My grandfather was a large landowner," Alphonse began.

"I'm not listening to you anymore," I said.

"In all of Portugal there was no land as rich in beauty as that of
my family. There were mountains to the north and the Atlantic Ocean
at the southern margin of our land. It was rich, well-watered soil, and
all around Albufeina the Gaston name was respected. Our tenants
were well treated, and we paid our full taxes to king and church."

The bird followed from one bush to another, and I sat taller in my
saddle, confident that the bird twitted a more important message than
of Alphonse.

"When the local priest became a bishop, he came as a guest to my
grandfather and described the new cathedral that the Pope in Rome
required. My grandfather proclaimed the old church adequate and

stood as the only grandee in Albufeina who did not contribute an oblation. When the local priest received his red hat, our tenants seemed unable to produce at their previous level, and our taxes doubled and then doubled again."

"Not much different from my father," I said. "Except he owed taxes to the king of England, and exorbitant interest to every Boston banker in sight. He fought the war of rebellion to clear his taxes from the king and debts to the bankers, and now my father is gone. He is likely dead, but the bankers still hold out their hands to his ghost."

Alphonse waited until he was confident that my short speech was finished. "Shortly after my father married, my grandfather died, and very soon the debts were beyond any value that could be attached to our land. The cardinal consecrated the land of my ancestors for the church, and our land became God's domain. My father became a tenant on his own land, with one third of his grapes promised to the church."

"The Church of Rome?"

"Certainly."

"The church has such power?"

"The holy church is all-powerful."

I studied the sharp rocks and pointed thistles for a bit. The bothersome bird had disappeared. "What about you, Alphonse? How did you end in slavery?"

"The Gaston name earned me a commission in the army, and my life in the army led me to slavery and eventually to you." He swung his mule off the road and into the shade of three scrubby pomegranate trees. We dismounted, secured the mules to separate trees, and walked back and forth within the brief limits of shade: two ducks in a line. Alphonse stopped, turned to face me, and put his right hand on my shoulder. "Your people are not able or not willing to meet the dey's ransom demands, and you will soon be on your own. Do you understand the depth of your predicament?"

"Yes. I understand that you will leave me and I will be on my own. I understand that you and I will never laugh at our jokes or express our love for the other."

"I am over forty years old, James, and must return to my family." Alphonse put his face close to mine, and I could see the tiny flecks of gold in his eyes. "I must return to Portugal as a wealthy man, and I must gather around me all of my family who still live. I want my brothers and uncles and cousins to watch as I piss on the grave of a dead cardinal."

I placed my hands on his shoulders and my forehead on his. "I would enjoy such a sight myself."

"We have separate paths to travel, James." He pushed away to look me in the eyes again. "But maybe we can help each other arrive safely at our chosen destinations." He looked over my shoulder for a moment, then back. "I want to propose a game of chance that if successful will make us wealthy. So entirely wealthy that I can buy the land of my father from the Church of Rome and you can to buy your freedom, and return to your country as the owner and captain of a fine ship."

"If my mother is still alive, she would appreciate the ship at least as much as our reunion."

"You admit that your father is dead?"

"He disappeared toward the end of our war."

"He was lost at sea?"

"General Washington dispatched him to the Bahamas. He never arrived at his destination, and Loyalist troops from the Carolinas captured every island of the Bahamas chain."

"I see."

"We know a hurricane struck South Florida about the time he was to reach the Bahamas—nothing else."

"What about Ahmed's father?"

"They always sailed together, without exception." I studied the craggy face of my dear friend for a moment. "Tell me—does Ahmed have some role in this grand scheme of yours?"

"Indeed, and his reward will be to serve Allah as a captain of the janissary."

Alphonse dropped his arms to dangle at his side. "We will hurt no one in this game of chance, but we three may die a very painful death."

I made no comment, and after a long moment he said, "Come, let us move on."

We untied our mules and continued side by side down the road. I hid in the deep folds of my hood until my eyes and throat and stomach were steadfast. "Alphonse, I'm ready to listen to your proposition."

"Good," he said. "In the very near future I will introduce you to Miciah Coan Baccri. All the profits that I have saved from my tavern, and from many other endeavors, have been nurtured by this man. He is an honest man, and his family owns the largest bank in Barcelona."

"He's a Jew?"

"Of course he is—what else?"

"A Jew-moneylender, and you trust him?"

"We need capital for our enterprise and a safe place to store our profit if we are successful. Can you describe alternative choices, my dear friend?"

"We can stay here in Algiers. You have power and wealth and me. We'll both forget the pissing and fine ship."

Alphonse pursed his lips and shook his head. "No, I have no choice in the matter, so I must move forward with my plan. You are welcome to join with me, but in any event, I will move toward my destiny."

I sighed. "Tell me what I must know."

"You must know that Allah forbids charging or giving interest, so that single fact of theology eliminates one large chunk of humanity from the effective management of money."

"Certainly."

"Truthfully now, which Christian friend or relative would you trust with your money?"

"No one comes to mind. Certainly none here in Algiers."

"It is my experience that relatives take your money as their rightful due and spend it on themselves. And as for friends? Ha! Give me a staunch enemy as banker, then both your money and your welfare will be better off."

"I'm insulted."

"Good, but listen anyway." Alphonse squeezed his right eye nearly shut. "The Jews are another matter altogether, for the manipulation of money is their profession and their art. Money allows them to live where they are hated, and they are hated everywhere because they know the secrets of money."

Alphonse unhinged his squint and gave me his sad smile. "Here is a puzzle for your resolution. How is it that a single grain of wheat returns the farmer many more, and a single masoon returns a Jew many more, yet the farmer is respected and the Jew hated?" Alphonse shrugged his shoulders. "The Jew is simply a farmer of money. The Jews have studied the vagaries of weather that lead to disaster, and they know the proper mix of water and fertilizer that lead to bountiful profit."

"And therefore you trust the Jews with your money?"

"Certainly I trust them; they are far and away the best choice available, and they work the magic of interest both ways."

"Both ways?"

"Three years ago I gave Miciah five hundred Spanish doubloons, and now I can go to his uncle in Barcelona and claim nearly eight hundred. Isn't that transaction a much better return than from a sack of doubloons under my mattress?"

"And what would you owe this benevolent farmer of money if you had borrowed five hundred doubloons three years ago? What would friend Miciah shove in your face today?"

Alphonse waved his hand in the hot air. "Well, certainly more than eight hundred. But you must understand that any farmer must be paid for his efforts. The important question that must be answered is, how does it happen that when it comes time to pay for risk taken, the Jew is condemned as a usurer?"

"But, Alphonse, a Christian would not lend one hundred to collect two hundred within the year, and your fictional farmer does not expect seed thrown at the ground to bounce back a hundredfold and to jump unaided into waiting baskets. It is not the service rendered; it is the charge for the service that turns people against the Jews. More, it is their obsequious manner in lending and their rapacious behavior in collecting that sets them apart."

"You speak as a blind innocent. Why don't you venture a loan from your loving Christian corporals and notice how blandly they collect their interest and how quickly they forgive a delinquent payment."

"Two wrongs don't make a right," I said.

"You are a very stupid innocent, my friend." He brought his mule close to mine. "I look forward to introducing you to Miciah and to his family. I want you to know that he is one who can walk into a cave of vipers and emerge unscathed. I want you to gain his friendship; in fact, you must gain his friendship, for our enterprise is doomed otherwise."

Insects began stealing the day, with cicadas in their high-pitched drone and bees and flies adding their own vibrations to the hot, still atmosphere. The incline of the road increased until a dull battered terrain dominated my vision. A few scattered wild fig, date, and pomegranate trees grew among clumps of mint and sage, but the sum of those disparate parts provided small relief from the drab landscape. A stone-filled wadi dribbled from between two hills; boulders as big as small houses lay scattered many yards beyond the dry streambed.

"Over here," Alphonse said. "It's time for our picnic." We guided our mules around the wind-eroded rocks and clattered up the increasingly narrow canyon until we were immersed in cool shade. We stopped and dismounted, leaving the reins on the ground. The mules immediately began chopping scattered dry herbs.

"Here, help me."

I joined with Alphonse to untie a wicker basket from the rear of his saddle. Then he carried the basket a few paces to a flat rock that formed a right angle with a granitic escarpment. We shook out the blue cloth, smoothed the edges, and placed pots of food near the center. The tavern cook had prepared a simple meal of bread, chicken, and rice. There were garnishes of leeks, onions, turnip, and yoghurt available for the bread, and a Spanish red wine diluted with clean well water served as our beverage.

We dined in the Algerian fashion, using our right hands to transfer food from the bowls to our mouth. Habit forced us to eat quickly and silently, even though we had ample food and much to discuss. Finally, after repacking the picnic hamper, Alphonse began to explain his plan.

"After three years of honest service, you must know that our dey survives only at the behest of others."

"After three years I understand that my neck survives only with permission from our dey."

"James, please resist the temptation to parade your rough Yankee humor. You must understand the larger picture before you can see the merit of small details."

"I'm listening, Señor Gaston." What other option did I have?

Alphonse nodded. "The dey of Algiers survives because the British and most of the sea-faring nations of the world, pay an annual tribute to the dey. He survive because his pirates punish those nations who refuse the pay tribute to the dey. And finally, the dey of Algiers survives because the janissaries serve as his sword arm. Each and every force that gives sanction for his survival, including the gran porte of Turkey, is perfectly capable of cutting the dey's little neck or starving him of gold."

Brown rough-winged swallows swooped and darted in crisscross patterns along the horizon of the small canyon. Sharp clicks announced the capture of each insect, and I kept quiet for a change.

"Now, with that preamble, let me explain the part that will make our fortune." Alphonse slid backward until we were separated by a distance of three paces. "You know, of course, that our dey's navy is a joke. He has a few pitiful ships at sea and a few others on the beach, but what you may not know is the extent of his naval supplies."

"Well, it happens that last year when I was on a job with José, I saw a huge warehouse full of Norwegian timber—beautiful spars and beams for a ship of any size. When I asked Jose what purpose the wood served, he merely shrugged his shoulders and kept his mouth shut."

"Yes, I know the one you entered; it is east of the dockyard." Alphonse gave me both a wink and his lovely smile. "That shed holds a small beginning of the total inventory, for the dey maintains a stock of navel supplies that is the envy of both the British and French. He has barrels of powder and shot stacked in countless neat piles, plus rope and tar in large quantities. Much of this bounty was captured from the Spanish in 1775, and the rest was received as tribute from many different nations."

I didn't move or speak.

"I propose that we blow the dust off a tiny quantity of the dey's powder and shot. They are the most portable items of his inventory, and I have in mind some orphan munitions that can easily be transferred to a small barge."

"That's the plan, Alphonse? You and me and a small barge?"

"It happens that a Genovese captain of my acquaintance is willing to transfer the goods from barge to his ship."

"Ahhh, silly me. I was worried for a moment."

"This trusted captain will sell our goods in his home port and then deposit our share of the profits in the Baccri Bank of Genova. Then a courier of the Baccri family will carry our gold in a ship owned by the Baccri family to their bank in Barcelona."

"Nothing could be easier, my teacher. We are already rich beyond my comprehension."

"As I said at the beginning, it is a very dangerous enterprise, but I'm confident that the warring powers of Europe will pay exorbitant prices for any manner of munitions."

I looked at Alphonse's face. For the first time, I noticed that his left eyelid drooped slightly and recalled that Uncle Stevens had often warned me of men with droopy eyelids. "Why don't we just light your powder and blow ourselves away? The idea of a quick end, rather than a meat hook through my shoulder blade, sounds very appealing."

"Still with the annoying banter, I see." Alphonse shrugged and gave me insincere smile. "Come, James, let us return to the prison."

I maintained a pained silence as we stowed our basket, mounted the mules, and returned by the same road. At the swamp, men were loading donkeys with bundled reed and helping those just emerging from the muck to pull off leeches.

A furlong past the swamp we took the seaward fork of the road through barren sandy hills, and nothing stood worthy of notice until Cape Temendefust bore a mile or so directly to our right. A ridge of quicksand, possibly five hundred feet in height, continued for about a mile and completely blocked passage from the sea to the back country. Between this natural barrier and the cape, a wind-blasted castle emerged.

"There is a large Turkish garrison of five hundred men on active alert in this bedraggled facility that you see before our eyes."

"For what reason are they so stupidly isolated from any commerce?" I asked.

"I agree, the castle has no strategic importance that anyone can discern. I merely direct your attention to the fact of the matter."

I could see Alphonse spinning his web for my capture. Maybe it was appropriate to remember the warmth of his embrace, and to give serious thought to the possible advantages won by both of us with the deed of his victory. The itch on my left shoulder disappeared and my stomach relaxed a bit.

We traveled in silence for two miles from the quicksand, and toward the city of Algiers where we stopped and observed a complex formation of eroded entrenchments with large cannon akimbo along the ditch. Alphonse waved his arm toward the rusted and useless weapons. "This is where the Spanish landed both infantry and cavalry in 1775. They had supply ships as numerous as water bugs anchored offshore, and the entire operation was under the command of their brilliant Irish pet, Count-General O'Reily."

"But the Spanish were defeated, as I recall."

"The results seem improbable, don't they? How could the Christian Spanish forces fail to subdue the heathen Moors? The Spanish Army had ample weapons and cadres of priests, and they had God on their side. How could they fail, indeed? "

His eyes glistened, and I listened as he gave a long explanation of the military tactics that demanded a charge of the holy Spanish forces up hills of quicksand. He rationalized their panic-driven retreat when attacked by a herd of riderless camels and minimized the impact of those who died of thirst on the beaches.

It was a story that diminished any confidence I might have in Spanish planning, or with possible success in outwitting the dey of Algiers. When Alphonse emptied of words, we sat quietly to watch the surf line break smoothly along the beach, then we moved farther along the road until the crest of a large hill exposed a splendid view of the city. I felt a kinship that surprised me. There! I could see the baegnio, my home with Alphonse, and scattered about the hillsides were the estates of grandees who were now customers or acquaintances. There also, the quarry road. Yes, certainly, painful places, but they seemed lost, diminished by the flickering memories of José Garcia's calm goodness and Alphonse's secrets. "It's beautiful," I murmured.

I felt a dangerous excitement that sharpened the city's splendor. At our feet were the three forts surrounding the tiny bay; minarets spiked the azure sky. Red-tile-capped white buildings spilled down hillsides, and five furlongs or so from the main gate of Algiers, along the shore and toward the city, was a fortification called the Star Castle. It was composed of five acute angles, and commanded a westward view.

"My goodness," I said. "Here is a fortress very was capable of giving great annoyance to any enemy that might attempt a landing."

"Nothing like the paultry fort stuck in the midst of nowhere, is it."

"If I were considering an invasion of Algiers, I'd avoid the Star Castle."

"Can you guess the strength of troops manning the Star Castle?" Alphonse asked.

"Ask me something simple, like how many baskets of sand have I carried past the miserable place."

Alphonse maintained a bruised silence for a dozen paces.

"Okay," I said, "let me guess: four hundred janissaries and another four hundred servants for the guards."

"Please, James, this fort is essential to the defence of Algiers, and it is known to hold a wondrous supply of powder and shot." He turned and smiled for the second time that afternoon. "The Star Castle is manned by one family, my friend. One very small Turkish family."

"Ahh," I said. "The disparate elements have come together in my miserable mind: the moneylender, the friendly ship owner, and a huge supply of munitions."

"Guarded by one family," Alphonse said.

"And this one family—are they somehow friends with the first Christian secretary to the dey of Algiers?"

Alphonse patted his mule on the right shoulder, and the beast increased his rate of speed in a forthright fashion.

CHAPTER SEVENTEEN

IT WAS ONLY ONE WEEK after my guided tour of the back country, on the seventeenth of July 1789, that the entire Algerian Navy disappeared toward Constantinople. War had been declared between the Ottoman porte and the empress of Russia, so the dey was required to exhume one xebec of thirty guns, four saeltia of twenty guns or so, and one fourteen-gun javeque, all to serve in this new jihad.

With the navy successfully dispatched, the confusion normally rampant among Algerian government functionaries reached a high-water mark of ineptitude. There was much talk of Allah's guiding hand, and rolling of eyes at every Christian nation, but little else. Every government activity in and around the harbor fell into lethargic decline. Even the perpetual dredging and repair of the seawall was ignored. Every clerk waited for his superior to assign a task, and every officer of the court waited for word of Allah's smashing victory over the Russian infidels.

◆

We were together on the large bed in the apartment over the prison. Alphonse studied the ceiling for a prolonged time; suffered an attack of coughing, and finally turned toward me, with his posture very erect, and using very precise diction, he said, "You must serve on the burial detail."

I stared at him for a long moment. "You want me to leave this safe-haven and wander through Baegnio Bezique searching for dead bodies?"

Alphonse nodded his head three or four time before responding. "Yes, it is the only way."

"The plague is common these past weeks. Most of the bodies that I find will be victims of the plague." When Alphonse remained silent, I continued. You want me to pile the plague victims in a two-wheeled car and take them for burial in the Christian cemetary?"

"Yes, it is the only way."

Between the gate of Bebal Wed and the dey's garden of citrus trees, is the large burying ground where the Moors and Turks mark the memories of their famous leaders with cupolas and sepulchres, but below this holy ground and next to the sea was the Christian cemetery. We Christians were required to bury our dead in the soft sand with no markers and no public services. During the best of times, the prison provided a daily quota of six Christian bodies, but during the summer of 1789, outbreaks of both cholera and plague delivered thirty or more bodies on each and every day to the beach.

Alphonse arranged for me to collect the Christian dead on our chosen day and transport them to the sand. It was a task normally assigned to punish miscreants, and the prison captain marked my service as evidence of gross insubordination toward the first Christian secretary. Ibram Raisani smiled through his white beard as I approach the gate, pushing my two-wheeled cart, filled with dead bodies. I had a Spanish slave to help with the pushing and two Portugese slaves to pull the cart, but Ibram spoke only to me.

"Ahhh, James, my boy, you are so young, and still, after these many years, so beautifully dressed." He spit at my feet. "The Christian corporals have their eyes on you, my lad. One more slip with Señor

Gaston and they'll have a long line at their tavern, all will be ready for your services."

"Excuse me sir, these bodies are oozing excrement of the floor of your prison. Please allow me to prceed with my assigned duty."

"These men who wait for you, my little piglet, they will pay for your services during the morning and night both, I believe."

I gave him my most contrite expression and said, "Please, esteemed sir, may I hire these slaves of yours to help me move the cart?"

The captain shrugged his shoulders. "Certainly—twenty masoons and they are yours for this trip and this single trip only."

I studiously placed the coins, one by one, into the hands of Captain Ibram Raisani. A vision of fresh sheets and the smell of a hot Plymouth chowder dropped unasked into my mind, and the fear of death from cholera diminished by a very small degree.

Two Christian corporals inspected each body for possible gold teeth, and then pushed open the left-hand side of the prison gate for us. My hired slaves and I carried the rigid offal-dripping dead men for nearly twenty blocks before we met the waiting donkey cart. The driver sat quietly on the cobbles, and watched with idle concern as we filled his vehicle to overflowing. We walked ahead of the donkey cart, through the harbour gate, along a walk of small stones for two hundred paces, and down onto the sand until the mule could pull his load no further.

The Spaniards shoveled, while the rest of us shouldered dead into their shallow pit. As acting chaplain, I gave the service. "Please, Lord, give them peace in heaven for they had none on earth. Amen."

It was Friday and Sabbath-quiet in the city and harbor of Algiers. The second call to prayer whispered lovely echoes into Allah's ear and heart. No one seemed about. A naked sun burned with an incandescent fervor, and I found our barge exactly where Alphonse had told me. Tied with two ancient ropes to a bole on a pier of no descernable use.

I took the tiller, my crew pushed of, settled their oars, and pulled the barge slowly toward the Star Castle. As we nudged the pier, a Turk of middle-age, but grey hair, bowed from the waist, helped to secure our barge, and then walked silently down the short stone wharf. We followed through a large wooden gate, descended two three-step stairwells, and entered the armory.

Stacked in rows from floor to ceiling were barrels of powder. In an adjoining cell, shot was arranged by weight. Grapeshot in stout wooden boxes and four-pound balls packaged in groups of six in sisal nets, while twelve-pound balls were piled in stacks along the wall and held in place by heavy rough-sawn planks.

"Quickly, now. I want two men on each barrel." One of the Spaniish sailors teamed with me and the other comprised two more teams. We wrestled gunpowder up the stairs and rolled barrels along stone corridors. "Put the powder amidships," I directed. We all worked together to stow cargo in the center of the barge with muttered curses in three languages as fingers cracked and backs strained.

Each team made nine more trips for powder before I ordered, "Grape now, fore 'n' aft on either side of the powder. Keep her trim, now." The light shot went to the stubbed bow, and every loose spot we filled with twelve-pounders.

The armory seemed barely dented, yet our barge sat in the water with but a few inches of freeboard showing. All sat at an oar, pinched by munitions, and none laughed when I said the obvious. "Careful now—we've powder to sink a fleet of frigates."

The family of Turks stood in rank file, with the youngest son, a boy of five or so, first in line and the father last. "Here." I pointed to a box of grape shot. "Sit here and there." The family settled like cormorants on pilings, and I moved to the tiller. In two months' time the Turk would be a petty grandee, with two fishing boats and a small plot of land outside Aynalik—or so Alphonse had promised. Everyone would profit and none would suffer—or so Alphonse had promised.

Barely a ripple disturbed the harbor. The sun battered us with surly intensity, and we paddled slowly toward a Genovese javeque. It was anchored somewhat apart from its nearest neighbor and half a mile abeam of the Star Castle.

Cargo nets and pulleys were waiting, and the Genovese captain gave short cursory orders to the crews of both vessels. It was a nimble operation and gave further evidence of Alphonse's good planning. We left the family aboard the javeque and returned twice more to Star Castle. Twice more we loaded the barge to capacity and suffered through the hot sun during each round trip.

My mind was a useless shell when we finally returned the barge to the mole where we had started our voyage earlier in the day. I saw no Turk or lounging Algerian that seemed to observe us as we moved away from the barge. My crew followed through the wharf's jumbled litter to José Garcia's carpenter shop. The shop was empty and I bolted the door from any stranger catching us by surprise. I pulled a large leather bag from beneath a loose board and paid each Spanish or Portuguese sailor the agreed-upon fifty Spanish doubloons. It was an amount sufficient to keep a slave well fed and clothed for a year or more.

"Don't forget," I said. "You must return the two-wheeled cart."

"What shall we tell the corporals of your absence?"

"Tell them that I fell sick at the cemetary. Describe the black pus uder my arms and the constant vomiting on the sand."

"Yes, we will tell the corporals we ran from you in fear of our lives."

"Good, very good." I added an added an additional handful of masoons for each sailor, and the five Iberians left in an elated mood.

I waited until past midnight to approach the gate of Baegnio Bezique and found a rock to beat the entry door. "Help," I cried. "I'm dying."

"Go away," said a voice. "Go down the street to die."

I heard two men laughed at the joke.

"Ten masoons if you let me enter," I called.

"What is your name?" one of the men responded.

"I am the servant to Alphonse Gaston, First Secretary to the dey of Algiers."

Silence, for a bit. "You are dead, we were told."

"I am very sick, but not yet dead." I waited a moment: "Fifteen masoons to open the gate, my corporals."

"Fifteen for each of us," came the response.

"Open the door," I called.

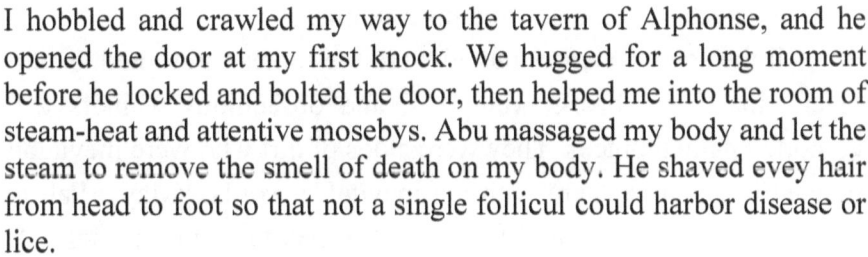

I hobbled and crawled my way to the tavern of Alphonse, and he opened the door at my first knock. We hugged for a long moment before he locked and bolted the door, then helped me into the room of steam-heat and attentive mosebys. Abu massaged my body and let the steam to remove the smell of death on my body. He shaved evey hair from head to foot so that not a single follicul could harbor disease or lice.

Alphonse made a bed for me in his tavern, and kept all custamers from entering. I slept like a child; ate exotic meals prepared by the tavern cook and we both spent so many hours in the steam room that my fingers and toes were puckered and pink. On the second day as an invalid, the doctor who serviced the European population of Algiers, came to the prison, examined me and proclaimed that I was still of a contagious phase of the Black Death, and that all should avoid contact with me. The respected doctor whispered to Iban Raisany that he did not expect me to survive the day.

On the next two succeeding days, holy doctors spilled holy water on my body and mumbeled holy words into my ears and told the Captain of Baegnio Beaique that I was destined for Hell, and would arrive in the next day or two. On the seventh day my recovery was announced by the prison crier, the best tavern in the prison re-opened to favoured customers only, and in the mid-afternoon of the propitious day, I put a comfortable brown robe on my body, and departed from the prison under the care of the First Christian secretary to the dey of Algiers.

◆

For an hour or more we wandered through narrow and dark streets approaching the Mellah, the Jews' quarter, always asking questions designed to hide our identity. Many people were anxious to help, yet few were helpful. I let Alphonse do all the talking and let my mind descend into a black pit. It was a fool's errand, and we were two enormous fools to trust Jews. Two fools to believe our armory caper went undetected by the dey and his minions.

All the Jews we encountered were the same: barefooted, clad in black cloaks and black skull caps, and obsequious whiners with contorted pathetic faces. They were clods of dirt who were inevitably greeted by each Moslem with the inevitable words: "May Allah let you finish your miserable life." Now I observed a curious sight. As each Jew entered the gate to the Mellah, he slipped shoes or sandals on his feet. Animated expressions suddenly lit each face, smiles cracked through grimaces, and calls of concern to friends echoed in a euphonious roundelay. Right before my eyes, these Jews of their own quarter acquired human qualities. It was a miracle! I nudged Alphonse to exclaim my discovery, but he shushed me quiet and led me through the bustling pedestrians.

Then, as one lightning strike follows another, a second magical event occurred. First I heard them—laughing and calling to one another over torrents of moving bodies. Then! For the first time in nearly four years, I saw a woman. She displayed brilliantly colored skirts and a small velvet waistcoat, all embroidered in gold. A silk scarf covered her head, and her bold eyes dropped mine to the dust. Suddenly there were many women, and I stared with insolent rudeness. Alphonse kept muttering, "Eyes down. Eyes down." They went about their business, and I tried to recall mine.

Miciah Coan Baccri was a large man with a dark complexion, oiled moustache, and pointed beard. His eyes were brighter than any lamp in the house. His wife was beautiful, with mounds of black, black hair that tumbled in waves around her neck and shoulders, and bright white teeth that kept me from staring overly long at her large nose and abundant breasts. She welcomed us into her home and disappeared into the maelstrom of women that bustled through the large kitchen area. Miciah's mother sat by the hearth and tilted her head against a large camel-like hump as she sang a faint welcome to me. Gray hair curled from her nose, and she was beautiful. Miciah's infant daughter crawled on my feet, struggled to pull herself up to my knees, and slobbered a constant stream of gibberish to me. Her eyes crossed and her hair seemed chewed by moths, and she was beautiful.

All the women—cousins, sisters, aunts—were laughing, yelling, arguing, and moving through the house as if my eyes were not glued to their bottoms and legs and breasts. They were fat and skinny, old and young, and all were beautiful.

"Mr. Cathcart!" Miciah Baccri was not smiling. "Mr. Cathcart, for how long now have you been a slave?"

"More than three years, sir."

"And how old are you, Mr. Cathcart?"

"Twenty, sir."

"Yes, twenty." He smiled with his mouth. "Come, we will work in my office."

Alphonse and I followed down halls of polished marble and through a spacious courtyard that engaged flowing water, fragrant citrus trees, and huge blooming rosebushes in lovely equilibrium. His office held no windows and one stout door.

In my travels as a carpenter I frequently observed government offices, and Miciah's room was a miniature tax collector's domain. There were strong steel storage boxes stacked along one wall; a tall, western-style desk holding a leather-bound account book. Fronting another wall, from floor to ceiling, were shelves with additional account books coded with numbers and letters of European design. As an additional component to the complex system, one shelf held books of blue leather, while smaller sections on different shelves included books bond in black, orange, red, and white leather. An aura of order and competence filled the space.

Miciah gestured for us to sit on cushions placed around a low table, and as we settled, a Negro slave entered with a coffee urn and three cups. He quickly filled the small cups, served them, and stood waiting as we sipped the sweet black Yemeni brew. Alphonse finished his cup first, placed the empty cup on the table, reached beneath the folds of his burnoose, and, magician-like, with drew a clenched hand full of coins. Without drawing undue attention to himself, Alphonse filled the servants' empty coffee cup with coins and turned toward me with a gentle smile. I sipped the last drops and followed my mentor's example, although with less practiced facility.

The slave withdrew with two cups filled with gold coins, and Miciah Coan Baccri opened shop.

"The goods were loaded safely, and the ship has cleared the harbor. If everything goes well, the captain will make Genoa within a few days, and two weeks later we can settle our accounts." He paused briefly. "In any event, there is a good likelihood that the total due will be approximately twelve thousand Spanish doubloons." He leaned forward but kept his voice in an even, moderate tone. "Half of the gross income will come to me, while you two split the other half as you mutually agree." He looked carefully at each of us to catch any possible objection.

Alphonse murmured, "The arrangement seems more than fair, Miciah. I can guess that expenses will greatly diminish your profit in this complicated venture."

Miciah stared at Alphonse, judged the comment not overly

sarcastic, and continued. "Tonight I must understand the parameters of your partnership and how you want the funds held."

Alphonse finished chewing a raisin and then described our agreement. "First," he said, "James and I begin with a fifty-fifty partnership. Next, one quarter of Mr. Cathcart's net profit is transferred to me in exchange for my ownership in the baegnio tavern." He paused while Miciah completed transcribing the instructions. "Half of my total funds should be deposited in an interest-bearing account at your relative's bank in Alicante, and the remaining half in a bank of your choice in Lisbon." He stopped talking and pulled a large sealed envelope from his burnoose. "If, for some reason, I am unable to withdraw my funds, this letter gives instructions for notifying my father, who lives in Albufeina, of the accounts, and authorizing his withdrawal of all principal and accumulated interest." Alphonse handed the letter to Miciah and sat back on the large cushion.

"Yes, well designed, Alphonse. I would only add another beneficiary in the event your father dies before you. If there are no claimants to the account, the money reverts to the Baccri family, and in this case, to me."

"Deserving as you may be, Miciah, I will add my partner, James L. Cathcart, as second in line for these funds. Need I draw a second deed?"

"Don't bother. I'll have my secretary add a codicil to this letter and have you sign it within the next few days." He turned to me. "And you, Mr. Cathcart—how will you have your funds allotted?"

"Put half in the Alicante bank and half here in Algiers. Is interest available here in Algiers?"

"Yes. You can collect two percent per annum on accounts here with me and three percent in Alicante if the funds are not diminished over the next year. The money at my disposal is available at your request, with one month advance notice." He anticipated my next question. "Each year, in the week following Ramadan, you will receive an accounting of principal and interest for both accounts."

We were all silent for a few moments, then Miciah broke the reverie by lifting a small silver bell and giving a small shake. The faint high notes quickly brought the Negro slave back into our attendance.

"We will eat now," said Miciah to his slave.

Within moments bowls and pots filled the table. Glasses with red wine were filled after each sip. Tender young grape leaves filled with rice and nuts, lamb baked with honey and raisins, kuskussu seasoned with saffron, and vegetables loaded the table. Fruit, cooked or fresh, came in profusion. Never had I attended such a feast. Never had I consumed so much food in a single sitting. Finally, after long minutes of silent, intense eating, the slave presented a thinly wafered pastry and large, plump figs—both immersed in honey. Large bowls of water and huge towels for our hands and lips were presented. I could barely move. My eyelids drifted shut and screwed open only with great difficulty. The ritual of drinking coffee and tipping the slaves was repeated.

Miciah faced me and began talking. "Mr. Cathcart, I have been watching you for the past few years, and I believe that you will make your mark here in Algiers."

I popped fully awake. Miciah Coan Baccri was a Jew, yes. But he also had unlimited access to the dey, and he had my fortune in his possession.

"You've done well with learning the important languages, and you've also learned the customs and priorities of our city." He looked at Alphonse and received a nod in return. "You are ready to move up in the hierarchy."

I scrambled to understand what the baker was telling me. What was this about promotion to a new job in Algiers? Where was my promised ship and freedom?

Alphonse put his finger up to silence my questions.

Miciah sipped his wine and then continued. "Hassan Bashaw is now treasurer of the regency. You know this, I'm sure; what you do not know is that he will be the next dey of Algiers. Hassan is a favorite of both janissary officers and ship captains. He is not overly greedy and shares his profits with those who would give him support. If you are close to Hassan Bashaw, you will also profit from his generosity."

Alphonse leaned forward to speak, but something was wrong. I interrupted Miciah. "Alphonse, are you feeling unwell?" Sweat popped in exuberant beads on his forehead. He flushed a deep-red color.

"A bit tired. Perhaps the excellent wine and rich food is too much for my constitution." He smiled wanly and continued. "James, I must tell a secret about my friend Miciah. The secret is simply that once Miciah was poor and now he is rich." Alphonse chuckled weakly. "In fact, he was not so very rich when I first met him in 1782—merely a simple shopkeeper hustling greens and melons to kitchens of the grandee."

Alphonse gagged and stared at his knee. Now his skin was gray. He shivered from toe to nose.

"My friend!" Miciah exclaimed.

"'Tis nothing," Alphonse whispered. "Indigestion." He sat up and waved his hand. Alphonse coughed, as if to clear his throat, and then continued. "It seems that Miciah Coan Baccri knew for a fact that a favored wife of the bey of Turkey desired a particular diamond brooch. It was an heirloom of an ancient French family, and further—Allah works in such wondrous ways—he, Miciah Coan Baccri, could secure this magnificent brooch for only sixty thousand francs!"

Our host beamed a smile toward the depleted Alphonse.

"So, my friend James, the deal was struck. The bey bought the brooch and paid in wheat delivered at his harbor, at a price of four francs per sack of one hundred pounds. Miciah shipped his wheat to

Marseilles, where it happened that the British were blockading the port. His captain slipped the blockade during a storm, a maneuver that you and your uncle have practiced many times, and sold the wheat at fifty francs for a sack."

Miciah laughed heartily and spoke to me. "I can see by the furrow of your eyebrows that you are attempting some simple multiplication. Let me save you the effort. The wheat sold for 3,750,000 francs, and one of my uncles purchased the brooch in Paris for thirty thousand francs!" Miciah laughed again and I stared at him.

"Of course," Miciah said, "there were significant expenses, but all in all, the venture realized a nice profit."

"What a wonder," I said.

"The lessons of that venture with the bey, I will underscore, Mr. Cathcart. First, a friend is someone who can facilitate a profit. Second, a friend makes certain that the profits are fair all around. Our powder-and-shot enterprise will make many people happy, and therefore they are my friends. In the future they will inform me of every opportunity that might turn a profit, and I will digest the sum total of all received information and weigh both cost and benefits. There are no political boundaries to consider. No constraints of religion or philosophy— only profit.

"Third, you are now my friend, Mr. Cathcart, and tomorrow you will give up your vocation as a carpenter and become Hassan Bashaw's coffeegee. You will listen carefully to every conversation and tell me everything, so that I can determine where the profits are located."

I glanced at Alphonse, and his chin was down against his throat; his normal olive complexion remained a greyish hue. Any further words from Baccri were superfluous.

"Alphonse? Alphonse?" I reached over to touch him, and he shuddered awake.

"Just the moment. I must rest the moment." His eyes shut and his head nodded down, only to come up again, eyes wide in a fearsome state. "But we must go. It will cost us three pipes of wine to get through the gate at this late hour."

"I'll send two slaves to assist you through the streets." Miciah tinkled the bell again, and shortly we were negotiating the narrow alleys of the Mellah.

Within a few paces it was obvious that Alphonse could not walk. I supported him on one side, and a dark Moor helped on the other. We did not encounter any of the night police patrols and were admitted through the small side door of the baegnio within thirty minutes after leaving Baccri's mansion.

Just inside the prison Alphonse began to vomit. At nearly every step through the moaning shackled men, he heaved black and green gall. His backside stank with foul diarrhea. He dripped death up every step to his rooftop aerie. I knew the plague. Six of my fellow Americans had died from the Black Death. I knew the rhythm of the dance, the certain steps that followed to the end. I stripped him of his clothes and threw them out the door onto the roof of the baegnio. I soaked a large towel and cleaned the vomit and excrement from my true friend. Already the swelling under each arm had erupted into purple boils. His face contorted into a new and ghastly mold. He was silent, shaking with chills. I covered him and attempted to place water in his mouth. The fluid dribbled over his lips and teeth, but Alphonse made no effort to swallow.

"Alphonse?" Only his fluttery breathing answered. I wiped the trickle of black phlegm from his lips. His skin looked like the underside of a dead fish. I felt no concern for my own welfare. I was immune to fear of possible contamination and conscious only of the suffering endured by my companion.

"Quiet, Alphonse."

Through the windows only stars cast sharp bright points of light
over the dark city. The muezzins' last call to prayer hung languidly in
the cool, comfortable apartment. Alphonse was dead. He would never
piss on the grave of a dead cardinal.

Chapter Eighteen

I BURIED ALPHONSE AND THIRTY-SIX other slaves. There he was, my Alphonse, asleep in a gaping hole full of twisted fly-encrusted bodies. He did not suddenly stand and climb through the jumbled litter of arms and legs to chortle over his finest joke. He did not survive the sand thudding down upon his sweet face, filling his nostrils and covering his eyes.

"Alphonse," I whispered. "Stop the charade; give me your smile. Come back to me."

There were no men from Portugal in the burial detail, for Alphonse's burial marked ransom day for two hundred twenty of the more than five hundred kinsmen living in the prison. Those whose names had been called at daylight wept in joy. The priests and Portuguese consul tried to calm those frantic slaves not marked for freedom.

"You must be patient," they insisted, "for your turn will come soon. The money for ransom is on the way."

Distraught slaves settled into the arms of friends and lovers who were leaving Algiers. They whispered of small villages, with the roads and landmarks needed to find families who tended vineyards or pulled fishing nets. The departing free men made gifts of money and clothes to those staying, and when the Sbirro called "Forward, infidels," the emancipated sailors walked in ragged file through the prison gate, down the cobbled streets, and to a waiting ship.

The baegnio surged with crashing waves of weeping. The deserted slaves felt abandoned to the plague and to cruel treatment. For them there was only a life of fearful waiting, a life with no purpose. For me there was a position as coffeegee to the treasurer of Algiers, Hassan Bashaw.

———

My new job offered a term of useful service. I was still a slave, certainly, but it offered an opportunity to receive compensation for work honestly completed. I saw the job as no less important than second mate aboard the *Maria*, and I cherished this final gift from Alphonse. I held it as a mark of his esteem for me. It also served as a memorial to his generosity and to our intimacy. I vowed that neither Hassan Bashaw nor Alphonse Gaston would be disappointed in my dedication to this job. Both would see merit in my efforts.

As coffeegee, I brewed the coffee and served it to the treasurer and to his visitors. If the guest ranked as an aghabasi or was a rich merchant, that personage accepted a large cup. If some humble petitioner appeared before Hassan Bashaw, he received the tiniest thimble of a cup. At the end of each audience, the empty cup was filled with coins, and this revenue flowed into a chest for which only I had the key. No one, great or weak, showed disrespect to Hassan Bashaw by leaving less than a full measure. No one, great or weak, received less than his full attention, and in my opinion, his decisions seemed wise and generous.

I witnessed a wealthy merchant complain of excessive tariff demanded on a load of Norwegian lumber that he had imported. "Effendi! My lumber is reserved for use by the Algerian Navy. If I must pay excessive tariff on my lumber, then I must raise the cost for the lumber to the navy." The merchant managed a heartfelt shrug of his shoulders. "If the navy must pay high prices for my products, the burden of taxes upon the citizens of Algiers must grow."

With no smile and no answering shrug, Hassan decreed, "You must pay the assessed tariff and must charge the navy their anticipated price for your lovely Norwegian wood."

A poor man who provided ferry service between moored ship and shore complained, "They promised one masoon for each passenger that I deposited on shore. When the last man pulled himself up onto the wharf, he threw one masoon at me for the ten passengers I carried." The poor man looked at his feet. "The single coin bounced into the sea."

"Why do you appear before me?" Hassan asked.

"I am a poor man and cannot feed my family."

"Is the client who robbed you still anchored in our harbor?"

"He departed yesterday, effendi, at sunset."

"Was the thief a true believer?"

"They were infidels from a northern land."

Hassan Bashaw, captain of the Port of Algiers, nodded a few times and then turned to stare at me. "Allah is great," he said, and then pointed a long skinny finger directly at me. "If Allah can make one infidel a thief, then Allah can certainly find a charitable heart in another infidel."

There was no reason to look at my employer, for I knew that he stared at me with the ravenous eyes of a sea hawk.

"Listen, my clumsy spiller of coffee, my lazy infidel who slops coffee onto my constituents—open that small chest at your side and remove ten masoon for the benefit of this honest citizen."

I paused for two heartbeats before moving, which was sufficient time for Hassan to utter a more urgent request. "Allah is truly moved by the plight of this poor man, my slow and stupid servant, so twenty masoon from your chest will serve as a gesture of our charity."

"Certainly," I said, and waved my hand for the ferryman to come forward and receive his reward from Allah.

Six days of every week Hassan held himself available to petitioners, and for each of those six days I filled more than one hundred cups for the supplicants.

On Thursday evenings I unlocked the small chest and distributed wages to the slaves working under my direction. A quarter to one-half I kept for myself, depending upon the favours or information given to me by my dependents. I rewarded fairly, and there were no complaints from a single one of them.

Friday mornings I devoted full attention to my tavern. There was a review of accounts with my manager, and that business often ended with our eating lunch together. After a short nap, I ordered food and wine for the week and collected rent from those slaves whom I permitted to sleep in the tavern after business hours.

It was just before the second Portuguese contingent departed, that I negotiated the purchase of my second tavern with a genial merchant on the list of homeward bound captives. He accepted my eight hundred sequins for his small but clean establishment. "Keep my chef and manager," he advised. "They are both from Spain and not likely to gain their freedom for at least a year."

"They are honest?"

"Honest enough," he replied.

"Any advice for me, before you leave?"

The small dark man gave me a huge smile. "Don't hire any Americans for service in your taverns," he said.

<hr />

The last part of each Friday afternoon I kept free for the inevitable summons from Miciah Coan Baccri. He asked questions, whose answers I supplied.

"Can you name the grandees or ship captains who have unpaid debts and may merit my attention?"

"Yes sir, there is—"

"Which nations have paid the dey his annual assessment to sail upon his sea?"

"The Dutch and Swedes are prompt in their payments. England and France make elegant promises but are in fact a few months late."

"What about the Russians and Americans?"

"Nothing at all, from them—at least not that I've heard."

At the end of each conversation, after the final sip of coffee, Miciah accepted the accumulated earnings from my service as coffeegee and profits generated by my taverns. He made a show of filling a large yellow card that indicated a deposit into my new savings account. He marked his initials next to amount received, and I placed my initials next to his.

"I will give you an accounting that includes the accumulated interest at the end of six months," he said.

"When can we talk of purchasing both a ship and my freedom?" I asked.

There was a painful silence before my banker answered. "Not in the foreseeable future, I'm afraid."

I leaned toward him. "Alphonse promised sufficient profit from our munitions venture to allow a quick resolution of this plan for a ship and freedom. I was, in fact, hoping to buy the freedom for all the American captives."

Again there was an extended bout of silence. "Many problems have developed," my banker said. "There are awkward difficulties in selling the munitions, and there are other considerations that my family must make."

"Can you give me an illustration of such difficulties?"

"Not yet."

At our third meeting since the death of Alphonse, I stood up from the cushion, about to leave, and Miciah said, "Wait a moment." He leaned toward me and spoke in his calm, efficient voice. "My family has found that Alphonse's father is dead." He paused for two heartbeats. "The Gaston account thereby reverts to our bank."

I returned to my seat and listened to my heart beat. There was no logic in making a plea for justice. What was the merit in repeating his promise to Alphonse? What was the use? He was a Jew—there was no benefit at all. Eventually I stood and remained still and silent until Miciah waved me away.

—◆—

On that first Saturday evening after burying Alphonse, Iban Raisani, still the prison captain, stayed in my tavern far past closing time. We negotiated the extent and nature of his compensations. I let him choose my first manager and guaranteed satisfaction for his every craving of food or drink or use of the bath. In the end he said, "The apartment shared by you and Senor Gaston these past months, now belongs to you and our new first Christian secretary to the dey of Algiers."

I nodded and maintained a neutral demeanour. "What do you perceive as the appropriate arrangement for the apartment?"

Raisani gave his well-lubricated smile. "You will negotiate a 'share and share alike' contract, of couse. Let me know what the final terms are in a week or so."

I had assumed that the tavern was mine through the right of inheritance from Alphonse, much in the manner that I had assumed Alphonses' wealth upon his death. In fact, the apartment was an honor granted by the dey of Algiers to his slave of highest rank. The middling position of coffeegee would normally warrant a mat in a tavern I might select, so it was that my childish notions were deflated by Miciah and Ibram.

I accepted Miciah's vision of my financial condition. I accepted the shared occupancy of the apartment with a smile. I also thanked the Ibran profusely for his generosity, knowing full well that he was merely acting at the direction of the dey of Algiers.

From the first moment of our meeting, Giovanni de la Cruz granted total authority for management of the apartment to me. I could only assume that Alphonse and Hassan had made some previous arrangements, so I took over the airy-clean room and gave Giovanni my mat in the kitchen. During the hot, still nights, when neither of us could sleep, we talked and became friends. There were moments of trust in our relationship, especially in situations involving business or professional problems, but there was little laughter, and there were no delicious surprises to share.

Each day the plague carried away upward of forty slaves. Conditions became so desperate that the prison gates were locked and daily conscriptions of labour suspended. Only we who directly served the Turks were allowed to fulfil our daily obligations, and often both Giovanni and I found it convenient to spend evenings in his office at the palace.

Through those frightful times my health remained robust, even though I spent many hours tending to the dying and took no precautions that others found essential. I made no special moment of my service to the sick; it was merely a duty that my father would expect of me as common courtesy. Yes, and Alphonse also would be pleased by my charity.

Finally, the rate of daily losses diminished, and the practiced routine of the baegnio returned. I left my apartment when the gates opened at daylight, and hurried to the harbor where the treasurer maintained his office. Hassan's seat had to be comfortably arranged and coffee ready upon his arrival. At five o'clock in the evening, my duties at the harbor were completed, and I quickly returned to managing my taverns.

I must admit that even without the plague and the erratic redemption of captives, my ability to secure honest managers and diligent employees remained a constant problem. The standards established by Alphonse became mine: cooks were Neapolitan or

Genovese, the best general managers were Spanish, while servers and cleaners were always Spanish or Portuguese. Alphonse never employed Americans, and I followed his lead in the matter. I always attended to the needs of my compatriots and often advised them of opportunities to improve their lot. My heartfelt suggestions to each American slave were rarely considered in a favourable manner, but they always accepted my donations of food and clothing with grudging ill humor.

One pleasure I did allow myself at the end of each evening—a leisurely retreat into the hot, steamy bath. It was my contention that clean pores and the thoughtful attention of a young man could contribute greatly to good health. My commitment to this routine, combined with a glass of fresh sweet goat milk taken before sleeping, served me well in enabling my survival.

CHAPTER NINETEEN

June 1790

DURING THE FOURTH MAY OF my captivity, in the Warlike City and Kingdom of Algiers (such was the formal protocol title of the city and country), one hundred fourteen Christian slaves died of the plague, and in June one hundred fifty-five died. My friend Giovanni de la Cruz lingered a few days, and on the eleventh of June, 1789, departed this life. He was greatly admired by all who knew him, Christian and Moslem alike, and during his illness I rendered to him every possible service and secured the medical attention of both the resident French surgeon and the Spanish Hospital doctor. All my efforts were to no avail, and the day after he died I was appointed chief secretary of the harbor.

My new position held power over a larger number of people than coffeegee, and the emoluments and information came from different sources. Miciah encouraged the move, while Hassan Bashaw demanded the change. "I need order where there is only chaos," Hassan said. "You must find the thieves who steal from me and eliminate them."

A witless Turkish fisherman became my superior. He was a Moslem who rose to his exalted and powerful position by virtue of his birthplace—for only Turks were eligible to control the kingdom's harbor, and he met this stringent standard. His resistance to the plague was vigorous, while that of his compatriots delicate. Allah in his wisdom decreed the fisherman as chief of customs of the port of Algiers, with me as his first Christian secretary.

This man had never been in any office before and was in rank only a sergeant. He was ignorant and without wealth or education. I saw him as stubbornly proud of his new position and morose in his insecurities.

"Infidel slave, what is the meaning of this record?"

"Honoured effendi, this is an account of the dey's receipts, and here, effendi, is the name of the ship from which the cargo was taken. Next on the account ledger is the declared cargo with the assigned value of each item. And finally, effendi, in this column at the extreme right side of the ledger, you will notice the sum-total of taxes due on the cargo."

"Ah! I understand," said the fisherman. His eyes glazed as they scrambled to decipher each scratch and column. Tears welled from the strain.

On each succeeding day of my tenure, I noted an increasing deficit from two separate sources; that income from customs receipts exceeded the amount transferred to the treasurer, Hassan Bashaw. Also, and equally obvious, that the listed inventory of goods held in warehouses awaiting tax judgements frequently lacked substance. Both tax money and stored goods disappeared at an unwholesome rate. As chief clerk of the port, it was my job to reconcile the account ledger with the taxes collected and to match the goods in storage with bills of lading. I was specifically charged with ferreting out possible thieves, but only Christian feet were subject to beating; only Christian necks were in jeopardy of hanging.

In my mind, I had no alternative. I had to confront the fisherman.

On the first Thursday of September 1788, mimosa perfume

trailed over city walls to blend sweetly with warm sea smells and acrid bubbling tar pots. The fisherman looked up at me from his spot of shade overlooking the harbor. There were no pillows or coffee or attendant slaves for the janissary sergeant. A quiet spot with a view of the sea, and his short pipe answered all needs.

"What now, infidel scribbler?"

"Effendi, there is a problem—"

"Dog of the Devil, why do you annoy me with problems? There are slaves smashing rocks with heavy hammers who have problems. Scratch in your books without bothering me." He waved his hand toward the alcove where my clerks worked. "Go!"

"Effendi, there is money missing from each day's taxes. It has been so for the past month. Hassan Bashaw will be making inquiries."

The fisherman looked at me. His right eye nearly closed with concentration while his left stared in wide disbelief. Finally he grunted, "Fix it so I am not bothered. My duties should not include correcting the stupidities of infidel clerks!"

"It is not possible to change the numbers, effendi. The money must be found."

"So, which Christian worm is stealing from the dey? Is it you, chief liar of all dogs? Yes! Yes!" The sergeant stood shake his arm at me. "I will have your soulless body in hell!" With that harangue, the fisherman began walking rapidly back and forth, waving arms and mumbling to his ancestors. He stopped, pointed his right hand at me, and said, "Now! This very afternoon I will seek an audience with Treasurer Hassan Bashaw." With both hands on his waist, and spittal streaming, he screamed: "I am certain that it is you stealing money each day. You! You! Therefore it is you who will die for your misdeeds!"

He turned from me and walked rapidly toward the harbor gate. I returned to my European desk and stood reviewing the accounts until my chief assistant began to clear his throat. I looked up, noticed the late hour, and dismissed the entire staff with a "Go now, and enjoy your leisure."

A star emerged from the sea, struggled to overcome the fleeing sun, and finally surmounted the red and green lanterns that marked each ship at anchor. The smells of greasy food and sewerage filth covered the harbor, seeping through the whispers of early evening calm. I tried to replay the drama that I had incited with the Turk, and to change the choices made over those ignored. A well of anxiety grew in my stomach. I had to pee and spit and put my head between my knees. Stupid! Stupid. Dumb! Dumb! I should have kept the sergeant quiet with his dreams and ignorant of any action that I contrived to satisfy Hassan Bashaw. Stupid! Dumb!

An hour after sunset a black slave, well dressed in white robes, entered my office, stood before me, and said, "Follow me."

My walk down the dark quay to the treasurer's office was blessedly short. The handsome slave held the door open for me, and I walked toward the lighted lantern shimmering in the far recesses of the building. Hassan Bashaw stared at me until I lowered my eyes. "You are a fool," he said, "and still a child." The treasurer turned from me and spoke to the only other person present. "Miciah, how far does this riddle extend? What manner of person might I be to even speak to such a fool?"

Hassan turned his gaze back to me. "Slave Cathcart, the penalty for stealing from my treasury is death. A Turk has testified to me that you are a thief, that you have embezzled money from the daily port tax receipts. The chief of my harbor claimed that you named a Turk as a robber, and therefore you are both thief and liar. Death by flame is your sentence. You will die quickly in this life and suffer eternal hell in the next."

The chancellor of Algiers held my eyes for a brief moment and then lifted himself in one fluid motion from his cushion. Without speaking further, he stepped from his office and walked into the dark night.

A minute or two passed before Miciah Baccri broke the silence. "Mr. Cathcart, you are indeed both a fool and a child to challenge a Turk. Hassan Bashaw has no choice but to give the death penalty for your audacity."

"It is the sergeant who is guilty of theft. I am guilty of abject stupidity."

"Slave Cathcart, do you imagine yourself in a nursery explaining some misdeed to your mother? You are a slave. You are nothing to your owners, and you are now facing immediate death."

For the first time since pirates came over the *Maria's* rail, I could not swallow. A buzzing sound behind my head increased in volume. My entire body shook in the hot night air.

"Here, Cathcart. Sit here." Miciah Baccri pointed to a pillow facing him.

"Listen carefully. I am about to save your foolish life."

I settled cross-legged on the pillow and leaned forward, looking intently at my saviour.

"Both Hassan Bashaw and I believe that you can serve us better alive than dead. When Hassan becomes dey of Algiers—which is inevitable—he has plans for you, therefore you must disappear for a year or so."

We listened to the night sounds of the harbor until a bell rang ten times, and Miciah started speaking again.

"While I am neither a fortune-teller nor a Sufi dervish, I predict that very soon your accuser will disappear from this life. Allah may have a similar fate for you. If not, then after an extended absence you may again serve your master."

"Miciah Baccri, you have me ready for execution, saved for your future use, and now thrown to my stars. Which is it? Am I dead or alive?"

He smiled with a tight curl to his lips. "For now, you live. Your friend Ahmed al-Koita has returned from a successful mission and will likely be promoted to Bolukbasi. He was able to convince a recalcitrant sheik that his annual levy of taxes was both fair and honourable, and Ahmed will be rewarded for his diligence to the dey and to Allah."

My stomach still claimed dominance over my mind, but I managed a perfunctory question to Miciah "I am certainly happy that Ahmed will achieve the rank of captain, but what does his achievement have to do with my survival?"

"Allah determines the course of all events, my friend!" Miciah's sardonic smile flashed and was quickly replaced by a more serious expression. "Another problem presents itself to the dey of Algiers, one that has no apparent solution. It seems that over a year past, a chief of the Tamanqhasset Tuareg escorted a caravan of slaves and gold—tribute to the dey of Algiers from the King of Bambara. Our agents verified the facts: nearly one hundred slaves and twelve camels loaded with gold left Tamanqhasset in April of 1787, yet the caravan never reached Ghardia, the first outpost of Turk authority."

"Yes, I have also heard the story of lost gold."

"This outrage is certainly the work of Tuareg bandits, for there can be no other explanation." Micciah shrugged his shoulders to verify the mystery. "How can a heavily guarded caravan disappear?"

We sat in silence until I finally asked, "What is next for me?"

"It is well known that nothing transpires in the desert without Tuareg indulgence, and therefore the dey has assigned Captain Ahmed al-Koita the task of finding his missing tribute."

"A suicide mission, I imagine."

"You, Mr. Cathcart, will join the janissary troop in retrieving both gold and slaves. You will serve as Hassan Bashaw's personal representative during this important mission."

"Is there no choice?" I said.

"Yes, there is hanging or burning. Either may seem preferable at some point in the future, but for now I recommend that we complete our arrangements and that you follow every task given to you as a preparation for your service to the dey of Algiers."

The plan was simple. I gave up everything: my position as clerk, both taverns, and all of my possessions, including my bank accounts. The sale of munitions disappeared into the world of dreams. In exchange for my return to beggary, it became my privilege to roam the desert and look for sand pirates. Miciah advised me of accounting practices for the mission, and he described emergency tactics that I must use to survive as an effective slave to the dey of Algiers.

"You must be prepared for the totally unexpected," he advised. "You will find that most emergencies can be ameliorated with gold. Guns are useless." Miciah said he would provide me with the gold needed for all expenses to manage the mission, but cautioned, "keep a large amount strapped to my body at all times. Do you understand what I am saying?"

Miciah talked far into the night, and he told me that if the Bambara gifts were retrieved, Ahmed and I would each receive a share. The reward to us remained dependent upon expenses incurred and the weight of gold placed before the dey of Algiers. Miciah also explained that my taverns would be reinstated and an important position under Hassan Bashaw confirmed, but only if the lost gold and slaves were brought to Algiers.

"If I survive, and bring the entire tribute to Algiers, then I may resume my life as a slave to the dey of Algiers. Am I correct in this brief summary of my situation?"

"Correct indeed; you will be a wealthy and powerful slave, and certainly alive enough to enjoys the bounties of your world."

I read the contract prepared by Miciah for a second time, and noted that my financial savings lapsed to the Baccri family if I did not return within two years. I signed the document. The sergeant seemed a wise and pious Turk to my newly opedes eyes. I remained a stupid Christian slave, however, and maybe there was a god in heaven who would chose to reward the faithful. Possibly God's name was Allah, and possibly I should mend my ways as a nonbeliever. More likely, to my deranged mind, that god's name was Lucky Chance or Unlucky Chance: take your pick.

CHAPTER TWENTY

November 1790

THE SELECTION AND BRIEFING OF troops by Bolukbasi Ahmed al-Koita took a fearfully long time. He and I had a few formal meetings to define my status within the squad under his command, but there were no opportunities for casual chatter. It was mid-November before the fifteen janissary troopers—each with a Negro slave—plus the half-dozen Kabyle muleteers, two cooks, and two Arab guides, departed from Algiers. My assignment as clerk and treasurer ranked me as an officer of the caravan, so I rated a donkey to ride and another to carry account books, writing equipment, and personal baggage. A third donkey managed panniers balanced with sacks of gold coins. Through each day two guards walked on either side of the valuable donkey, and at night I slept with books on one side, gold on the other, and a pistol at the ready.

Those first moments through the Babel gate were the best and the worst. I was alive—that was the best part! The blue sky arched over the beautiful city like a seamless dome. I could breathe the delightful aroma of wild herbs and sea salt, and my body felt the joy of release from confinement and the comfort of hard work. I do admit to constantly looking over my shoulder for the inevitable rush of searching soldiers. I grieved for the required loss of my foreskin, but the itching was over and the scabs departed. The worst part, however, was the fur ball of anxiety that roiled in my stomach, for I worried about the mistakes of style or substance that I might make and thereby embarrass Ahmed. I was a ship's officer or sailor for my early life, and now it seemed doubtful that I could survive riding my donkey through difficult terrain. I worried that I would I slow the column and delay the schedule set by Captain al-Koita? My mind created an unending list of disasters initiated by my ineptitude, but most flew into the thin mountain air before the first noon break, and the rest disappeared soon after.

A warm sun drew our caravan past leafless orchards and scraggly farms, up the first hills, away from the harbor and Alphonse's grave. Strong stone walls and white buildings dwindled to the rank of harmless toys as we moved up the rocky gouged road, upward through the hills. Day by day we moved to higher ground, often with precipitous undulations, and finally into the Grande Kabalie, where cold rain tucked the tails of each beast.

The first two weeks of travel up the Atlas Mountains were difficult but well within my ability to manage my duties. Three of the older janissaries complained of the rapid pace and blisters on their backsides, and one of the Kabyle fell farther and farther behind the column and failed to answer his name on the sixth morning. Others complained of this or that hardship, and I felt more and more confident of surviving any crisis submitted by mountains, mules, or Allah.

As we approached the final summit of the Grande Kabyle, my heavy wool burnoose moulded around my shoulders. I hid within my hood, trusting the donkey to choose earth over sky. I glanced briefly at the flashing, fathomless descent revealed through scudding clouds, and once we doubled around sharp rocky edges where the panniers mounted on our pack animals scraped in hollow shrieks. Men and animals leaned to catch the inward mountain pull. Occasionally, the curtain of clouds lifted to reveal a glimpse of the Mediterranean Sea: a blue smear of sky streaking to merge with a narrow slit of deep sapphire.

Toward the end of the second week, we ascended through the final pass and quickly dropped into a wilderness of dark cedar trees and ephemeral creatures called djinn. It seemed, at least from the behavior of our remaining Kabyle, that the djinn confirmed themselves as our constant and divisive companions, with their strange discreet noises and subtle movements. Our muleteers smiled a great deal, but everyone else spoke with brittle, fidgety words. Smoke drifted through the branches from hidden Kabyle villages, and on one occasion children screamed at the sight of us and disappeared into the silent shadows. Solitary mountaineers, more wild creatures than men, measured our strength, and in a blink became one with the twigs and brown limbs.

I felt burdened with the oppressive grandeur of the huge trees. Any hint of human habitation always came as a surprise, yet there it was: a tiny thatched hut of sticks and stones, a patch of newly tilled ground. Never did we receive a greeting of welcome during this section of our passage. Scolding jays followed us with raucous heraldry. There were trees in great variety, and the precipitous changes of elevation stunned me with the glory of both deciduous and conifer varieties. Still…. I missed the open freedom offered by the sea, and only after we struggled through the last high pass and down the winding road onto a scrubby barren plateau did I feel comfortable. On the distant horizon a tiny hamlet with a Turkish fort glimmered, and Captain Ahmed al-Koita inspected his men and animals for the befitting qualities of military orderliness that were expected for the janissary, and then we eagerly moved toward our first contact with civilization in over a month.

We stayed four days at Quasar Boukari. Captain al-Koita assigned his squad of Janissary to useless chores, guaranteed to keep them busy day and night. At the first sunset in this squalid, cold village, our commander called for his officers. "Follow me," he said. "We have an important assignment to complete."

The coffeehouse stood open to the sandy street. Cool air coiled about our legs; a solitary pine tree whispered from black-shadowed boughs. Stars, brighter than lanterns, outlined the scattered buildings. Bolukbasi Ahmed, Odabasi Ahmet Blibita Mumdi, and I entered with our captain, and we sat at the first vacant table. A young Arab filled coffee cups and then solicitously touched a burning taper to Ahmed's pipe.

Our neighbours were Arabs in hooded white burnooses, three blue-veiled Tuareg, and a few merchants and traders. We all sat upon mats around low tables; most were silent, yet a few spoke in quiet, distracted spurts. Two greybeards played chess while a handful of young men observed them.

"Over there," said Blib, nodding toward the Tuareg. "They are most assuredly our guides who will serve us from Laghouat and into the desert."

"What are they doing here?" I asked. "We've still three or four weeks before reaching Laghouat."

"Oh, don't make much of their attendance. They're just checking us out and practicing fierce looks on the Arabs!" Blib quipped.

"They are certainly impressive-looking men," I said. "Can you tell me anything about them?"

"My words will not give us much pleasure, and you'll get to know them soon enough." The janissary quartermaster sipped his sweet coffee and continued. "In general terms I will say that the Tuareg tribes control everything south of the Tazili Mountains, and probably south to Timbouctou. At least, they act like they own the lot."

Blib leaned forward until he was inches from my nose. "Those Shamba-Arabs over there, in the white outfits—they control everything north of Ghardia. Always remember that there are a whole lot more Arabs than Tuareg, and both need lots and lots of land. The Arab population increases with each blink of the eye, while the Tuareg remain stable in their numbers." When it was clear that I had no response to his lecture, he queried, "Do you understand what I am telling you, my friend?"

"Understand what?" I was still fumbling with how our friendship would unfold. More often than not, I found myself feeling more ignorant than Omrod Williams in Blib's company. He seemed given to making assumptions about my general fund of knowledge that were often mistaken. I felt myself responding to his demands with a growing feeling of anger by creating for his pleasure, a bumpkin who was dumber than dirt.

I wasn't the only one so affected by the quartermaster's demeanour. As we struggled through the mountains or stood with outstretched hands around a fire, I watched as Blib fabricated wild premises and spun sketchy facts into granite conclusions. He was glib and clever and witty, and most often likable. It seemed that we wanted a mutual friendship—there was no one else for either of us—but I was intimidated by his haughtiness.

"Look, my newly circumcised friend, it's very simple. Neither the Shamba nor the Tuareg need any excuse for a fight. Allah put them together on the desert so they could test each other in battle, and that's what Shamba and Tuareg do best: fight! But the blue-veiled ones can't survive the constant pressure from the larger Shamba tribes, and they're being pushed south into the mountains."

"Both are damn tough," said Ahmed.

Blib winked at his commander and lowered his voice to a near whisper. "But the Shamba are also smart, my captain. They are tough, smart, and cruel—a winning combination on land or sea. Don't you agree?"

Ahmed and I waited for him to continue.

"Beyond any other consideration is the bold fact that the Tuareg are not true believers. They strut around as if they were direct descendants of Mohammed and Fatima, and they clearly consider themselves better than Turks." Blib shrugged in the fashion of a Genovese sailor. "They want everyone, including the janissary, to kiss the dust they walk on and thank them for the privilege."

We all smiled, and Blib turned to look at the three Tuareg. They were covered completely in dark indigo blue. Only their eyes remained uncovered, and when one of the warriors peered toward us, Blib quickly returned his attention to us.

"Of course, it is well known that the Shamba will take up with any temporary ally as long as they can make a few masoon or cut a few throats in the process."

"How are they different from the Turks, Blib?"

Blib gave me his best janissary stare and then laughed. "Yes, my pretender to the faith, the Shamba are similar to the Turks. Not smart like us, but sneaky-clever. The Shamba have the foresight to make temporary alliances with other Arab tribes against the Tuareg." Blib smiled. "Make note of the ephemeral nature of life among the Shamba, for no agreement lasts long around here. If the Tuareg aren't available for a battle, any friend will do as well."

"Sounds like life in the baegnio to me. Where does the dey stand in all this?" I asked.

"Simple. The dey picks the strongest tribe—the Shamba in the north, the Tuareg in the south—and says to the chief or sheik or whoever is in charge: 'Here is your annual tax. Collect it any way you like, and pay me in gold coin!' The dey sends weapons and occasionally a troop of janissary to help the favoured tribes collect the assessed taxes from their neighbours. It's a great system, and seems to work for the dey."

"What is their avocation? How do the Shamba provide food for the table?"

"They raid remote villages and sell slaves. They collect camels from careless neighbours, and they drink tea."

Ahmed shook his head at the two old-maid gossips, stood from his mat, and walked over to the three Tuareg. We watched as he made a brief bow to them and commenced talking. His hands moved in equal parts with his mouth. After a few minutes he sat to smoke and drink coffee with the blue-veiled men.

I turned to our Quartermaster, and he was smiling insanely. His eyes seemed held open with small sticks. Every tooth, to his molars, was showing.

"What is it?" I asked.

"Watch! Listen! Enjoy!" He nodded toward a group of men taking their places on a platform at the rear of the coffeehouse.

The drab building suddenly bloomed into a glittering theatre. Men struggled with two-tiered benches and placed them in a manner that extended the boundaries of the coffeehouse out into the street. Lamps, elevated on posts, were lit. Wool-robed men materialized from the darkness and filled the benches. Some few dribbled toward a crude bar at the far end, located between the newly erected benches and the south wall of the mud-brick building. Here and there, conspicuous among the closely seated white-robed figures, were the bright red cloaks of important tribesmen. Most of the patrons drank coffee, but Blib and some of the tribesmen were served an evil-smelling alcoholic beverage.

At the far end of the outdoor hall, through smoke drifting from pipes and lanterns, I could dimly perceive a group of women. Each had a crown that was embellished with a large black feather and ringed with dazzling gold coins. They wore brightly coloured silk gowns, embossed and overlaid with gold medallions; all wore numerous arm bracelets, dozens of rings, and no veils!

I was excited by the prospect of some exotic entertainment and asked Blib, "Who are the women?"

"They are from a local tribe. Walid Nails they are called. Quiet! Later I will explain."

I listened and watched. On the platform, musicians were seated cross-legged. The oldest, a gray-bearded emaciated fellow, drummed a deep-toned beat on a large skin-covered barrel. Another, nearly as old as the first, pattered fingers alternately over two small drums, while three younger men blew upon reed pipes, and one who also clanged the cymbals on occasion. The five men all seemed of one family.

With a flare from the cymbals, an ululation of flutes, and rapid drumbeats, a dancer appeared on the platform. She began swaying and shaking her torso. A length of bright red silk twirled above her head, which she lowered to a level just below her flirtatious eyes. Rippling shivers surged through each stomach muscle, and she sang to a wild torrent of music in an ear-shattering falsetto.

"I saw him twice in Algiers," shouted Blib.

"Him! Are they all men?" I shouted back.

"No, just this one; the rest are most emphatically women." Blib's laugh carried above the instruments, the singing, and the cheering crowd.

As a dying flower in a gentle breeze, the impersonator slowly waved back and forth, sinking until his head touched the ground. Pivoting in this awkward, beautifully submissive posture, he made two complete turns. A spectator jumped from the crowd onto the dance floor, put a gold coin between his teeth, and leaned over until the two were nose to nose. The dancer snapped at the coin, like a cur at a bone, catching hold of it, and together both men slowly stood. Cheers, whistles, and drums sounded approval for the performance. The spectator withdrew his claim to the coin, and the dancer made his way through the audience of men, accepting small coins and stopping to drink and talk with his admiring customers. Blib applauded the entertainer with words of praise and a silver coin.

The music began again. A fat blond woman jiggled and swayed to the derisive laughter of a few and the insouciant neglect of most. Quickly—as if to correct a mistake—the blonde departed, and with barely a missed beat and everyone's rapt attention, a black-haired girl dressed in white began dancing. She held herself with confident grace, the centre of attention. Earrings, bracelets, a necklace of tiny gold coins—all flashed and tinkled with every movement. I studied her black slanting eyes darkened by kohl, her red mouth smiling. She seemed to hum a giddy invitation to every man present. There was no subtlety in her performance. She made a direct assault on each man present, an appeal in gestures, a yearning message: "Only you can satisfy me."

At the end of the dance, every man stood screaming for her attention. They held gold coins aloft and pushed neighbours to create a clear line of sight between the temptress and her victim. I clapped and cheered with every man and boy. Only Blib was silent. He stood with his hand raised, holding up four large gold coins. The dancer came through the mass of supplicants, studied me for a moment, and took Blib in hand. She and the quartermaster smiled broadly as they trailed through the jeering, yelling, pleading crowd.

"Don't feel bad."

I turned, and Captain Ahmed al-Koita was smiling at me.

"It happens all the time. Fifty men screaming and Blib gets the prize."

"Not his money, then?"

"Nope. There's lots of money out there, and she chose Blib over the others. I've seen the same conclusion three times now."

"Any theory that might explain this infatuation that women have for him?"

Well, he's not as ugly as you or as handsome as me, so the source of his power must be some apparent only to women."

"A hidden power?"

"From you and me, in any event."

We sat on our mats. The young Arab filled our cups. "What are Walid Nails?" I asked.

"From what I've heard, they are a local tribe—descendants of Berber and Arabs that mixed together over the past few hundred years. They call themselves the Walid Nails for some mysterious reason and have a most unusual attitude toward their women." Ahmed sipped his coffee and smoked his pipe. The musicians were quiet, and patrons carried on with their loud hand-waving conversations. A few of the women singers and dancers were clustered together near the empty platform, smoking and chatting with one another.

With some exasperation, I asked, "And just what is the unusual attitude?"

"Oh! It's fairly simple. When the girls are very young, they leave home to begin earning their marriage dower. At six or seven they act as servants to their older sisters. They watch and learn how to dress and dance and please men."

"Please men?"

"They're skilled prostitutes. When a young woman becomes rich enough, off she goes to her parents, and she is provided a husband and a life with servants. Her sons stay at home. Her daughters continue the tradition."

"I can't believe it! No parent would allow a daughter into whoredom. It can't be."

"Not only can it be, my friend, it is; just look around. Speak with the ultimate authority on the subject tomorrow morning. If he is sober, that is."

My commander tortured me with an extended bout of silence before continuing.

"The Walid Nails think that you're dumb and they are smart. As far as they are concerned, the entire scheme is a clever business transaction. Each woman makes lots of money, and most of it goes to her dower. I'm told that it is a sum greater than most men can earn in two lifetimes. This enormous wealth is split between the new husband and her parents. What more could any father expect from a useless daughter? What more could any husband hope for from a marriage?"

"I can't believe it," I said.

Ahmed continued to smile, drink his coffee, and smoke.

Soon the musicians returned. The dancing and the auction repeated again and again. I couldn't believe it, but I watched, and at the end of each performance, I held up two coins in each hand, as high as I could reach—but to no avail.

◆

After three days of duty for the troopers and important assignments for the officers, Ahmed ordered the caravan under way. We drifted ever further out onto the gnarled cold plateau. At dawn on the second day from Quasar Boukari, a damp, misty overcast sky lowered, and heavy rain began falling. We halted at mid-afternoon, set up camp, and crawled—chilled and wet—into our tents and under wool blankets.

For the next three days we slogged through mud and endured intermittent showers. Each day was colder than the last. Snow began falling—large gently falling flakes that piled quickly into knee-deep drifts. The wind increased, and snow raced past scrubby leafless trees, stinging and blinding man and beast. Ahmed pushed us toward Ain Wessara, but the storm was too ferocious.

Six days we lay in tents, wrapped in camel hides and wool blankets, emerging only to drink hot sweet tea, eat cold kuskussu, and expose our frosted buttocks to the elements. No one talked. We dozed as the wind screamed in wailing fits.

The days after the storm were cold and pleasant, but the tenacious mud impeded our progress. Dumpy hills and sharp crevasses crosshatched the plateau from east to west, forcing us to make uncomfortable detours away from our line of march to the south. The land was empty of people and, for the most part, covered with scattered clumps of grass and stunted shrubs. There was ample forage for the animals, but little that might encourage farmers or settlers.

I had probably never walked more than three miles when on shore with my father, and remember riding horses on a single visit to Boston. My view of the world had been from the deck of a ship prior to this journey. Now my mind was awash with visions of mountains and strange people. I recognized that the painful moments suffered in cold or mud were soon covered with dense fog, while those moments of strange birds singing and vistas exploding before my eyes and laughter with friends remained like indelible jots in my memory.

We stopped one night at Ain Wessara and two nights at Djelfa. In between the two barren and ugly outposts, we observed two large lakes that were filled with bitter water. Our guides told us that except during very wet winters, the lakes offered dust, quicksand traps, and a few mud holes. The final climb up the Saharan Atlas, through dense stands of pine, was cold and windy, but neither rain nor snow impeded our progress. We twisted down the lee side of the mountains, through fewer trees, encountering increasingly frequent scrubby thornbushes, until we reached Laghouat.

CHAPTER TWENTY-ONE

January 1791

ARABS CONTROLLED LAGHOUAT, AND THE few Turks who lived in this sea of Arabs survived by carefully manipulating the feuds and vendettas that drove each Arab. "Know this fact in both your stomach and mind: each and every family of Laghouat wages perpetual war against all others," said Blib.

We walked through dimly lit shops looking for non-existent bargains. Blib stopped, faced me nose to nose, and continued with an arm-waving discourse on the vile behavior of Laghouat Arabs. "I have been reliably told of one family that killed the barking dog of another. The dog has been dead sixty years, yet each month people die because of the insult. I'm told of eldest sons killed by jealous siblings, fathers killing whichever son threatens his authority. You may observe the obscene behavior of the Shamba but make no progress in understanding the mysteries of Allah's great plan!"

This deference to his creator was a rare admission of bewilderment for Blib. After a few steps through the crowd, he pulled me into a tiny three-table tavern and recouped his position as final authority on all matters. "You see, my ignorant Frank, you Europeans and Americans can never understand the Arab mind. Only we Turks can untangle such cunning mysteries."

"I thank Allah five times each day for your wisdom, Lieutenant."

"Only five? I'm insulted."

"Show mercy, effendi; my knees are near breaking."

"Weak knees are the least of your problems. You must understand that our survival depends upon the untangling of their wretched actions and twisting them for our own benefit. The venomous atmosphere of hatred created by the Shamba allows the few Turks—the outsiders—to step in as the arbitrators of Koranic justice. Only we can collect the taxes and maintain some semblance of peace. No Arab can give authority to another without losing face; therefore, we can give them the rare privilege of collectively hating the Turk while filling our treasury. It is the will of Allah, and it has been his benign will for almost three hundred years. Praise is to Allah."

I nodded to his benediction. His ranting was tedious, and I said, "Let's get going. We've agreed to join the captain and meet our Tuareg guides."

Blib was no teacher. Captain Cathcart and Alphonse and Jose Garcia were teachers, and it had been their goal to watch me benefit from their instruction. My learning was their reward, while Blib merely wanted to dominate me with the virtuosity of his information. He had no interest in my receiving profit from his monologue. The glory of his company was my assumed gain.

* * *

As the three Tuareg moved toward us through the crowded bazaar of Laghouat, the frothy sea of white-robed Arabs cleared away in smooth ripples. Salim was the prow, while Abu'l-Qasim and Tashmani served as hull for the five black slaves of their retinue. This same pattern had followed us from Quasar Boukari, and always in the same configuration. I watched the indigo garments whipping in the wind, a blue ship on the distant horizon. From a great distance I could see

Salim's eyes: black, unblinking, recessed deep in the veil that wrapped around and over his face, head, and neck. His twin black beacons cleared away the debris of lesser mortals. Captain Ahmed al-Koita walked a few steps to the front of our troop and ceremoniously announced to the Tuareg army, "I am the emissary of dey Muhammad Bashaw and the gran porte of Turkey."

As Ahmed began speaking, all of the Tuareg entourage stopped except Salim, and he continued until two paces from the janissary captain. The bazaar that had been a raucous cacophony of sound became quiet, and all listened.

"I am Salim Shushufi, brother to the Sultan Agg-Abba. I come at his request to bring you into his presence." He looked at each of us in turn and said, "We shall leave in four days."

According to Blib it was our responsibility, the quartermaster and I, to outfit the caravan for a three-month desert sojourn. I had the money, and he was expert at any task required. Our first undertaking was the most difficult and most important: Because only a camel can survive such a trip, Ahmed directed us to purchase approximately two hundred animals. In truth, Blib knew little more than I about the beast, so we embraced our ignorance with Turkish enthusiasm, maintained a haughty demeanor, and studiously ignored any gratuitous recommendation of excellence from each vendor. During the first hour of investigating the options available to us, our charade generated a few moments of humor, one ferocious bite to my shoulder, and no progress in consummating our task.

Our intensity for evaluating each animal was admirable. "Very interesting. What's that—our fifth color? Tell me, Blib—do camels with green teeth respond more admirably to orders than those with black? Certainly four legs are better than three, and two brown eyes seem superior to one of blue. But teeth, Blib—tell me about teeth!" I waved my arms and leaned forward to catch his attention. "Tell me, my esteemed Turk, which one—which two hundred—do I purchase?"

On this day of dung and dust and clouds of nostril-filling flies, Blib was silent. The owner of the camels yelled for attention—noises from the bazaar swelled to an ear-splitting level—but Blib was silent. "Gad-blast it!" I shouted. "What the bloody hell difference does it make? They're all miserable, rotten excuses for a good mule. Get a price for the lot, and let's get out of here."

"Do not buy camels from this man." Tashmani looked from us to the owner of the tethered camels. "He is a goatherd and knows only of goats." The Arab who owned the camel all around us, made a move toward Tashmani, but stopped, frozen in mid motion. Tashmani's dagger pressed gently on the peddler's throat, drawing a small bubble of blood. After a few seconds the dagger disappeared and Tashmani turned to us. "Follow me," he said.

For the next few days we swallowed our pride and trailed after our Tuareg guide as he inspected, bargained for, and purchased everything we needed to load upon our two hundred riding and pack camels. Dates in baskets and goatskin water bags—enough for our use, plus extras for gifts or trade. Flour and tea and honey sufficient for Ahmed's army and, I suspect, for many of Tashmani's friends and relatives as well. Blib smiled his conquering hero smile, and I simply paid the required gold, recorded the transactions, and consumed gallons of tea during the intervals.

Blib and I also got to know our savior. "You see," said Tashmani, "I have only one name because I am no longer a noble. I was born a noble and lived like a noble as a young man—then came the day that I ran from my enemy." He sipped his tiny cup of tea by turning his head, lifting a corner of the veil, and unobtrusively draining each drop. Immediately, as it touched the table, his cup was filled to brimming by his slave.

"It is as Allah wills," he said. "In my next battle, I will die a Tuareg noble." Again, he turned his head away from us, lifted his veil, and drank his tea. "You must pay close attention, my foreign friends, for I will teach you about the desert. Listen and watch with great care, because nothing is as it seems in the desert."

CHAPTER TWENTY-TWO

January 1791

THE SHEBKA WILL ALWAYS INCITE two images in my mind: a depressing labyrinth of hills void of vegetation, and a camel whose behavior perfectly matched the environment. Both were malevolent. Both were controlled by the unpredictable whims of mean-spirited djinni.

She complained with hisses and groans and jumped at every shadow with a violent twist. Six times she cast me from her great height onto the rocky terrain. My efforts to firmly grasp the large cross-shaped pommel failed. My dignity lay among the rocks and dust. Lurking djinni laughed at every bruise, tittered at every cut. After the sixth fall on that first day—at each rise of hill we could still glimpse Laghouat—Tashmani stood before me. I struggled painfully to my feet.

He held my eyes for a long moment and said, "Watch."

My camel reclined before us with majestic arrogance, placidly chewing a twig, four legs folded out of sight. The wooden saddle—the rahla—remained fastened to the beast's hump, and Tashmani quickly climbed up onto the seat. He avoided touching the beautifully carved crosspiece and settled with the pommel between his thighs and his naked feet crossed one over the other on the thickest part of the camel's neck. The blue-veiled warrior snapped his fingers at me while pointing to his feet.

I watched Tashmani trample, gently but firmly, on the squealing camel's neck. Suddenly, hind legs first, the camel began to surge. Our Tuareg guide shifted effortlessly with the forward pitch, one hand loosely holding the reins, the other a small switch. Then came the backward pitch as the camel rose to her forelegs, followed by a violent scramble on fully extended hind legs. With light foot pressure on her neck, Tashmani guided the animal around the patient janissary troop. Only Captain Ahmed al-Koita looked at me askance.

Some few hours after the lesson, a faint twinge of hope eased into my consciousness, for it seemed remotely possible—the fleeting image danced ghostlike in my mind—that eventually this evil beast would credit me with some power over our mutual destiny. The previous eight weeks of riding a smooth-gaited donkey had ruined me for the merciless roll and pitch of a camel. The small placid beast and the green mountains did not exist on the same planet with the camel and chalk wastes of Shebka. One dead valley led only to the next. A vision of lifeless rocks and hills stayed imprinted on my mind's eye into the dark. At night the silence screamed. The security of our caravan seemed evanescent. I felt lonely, vulnerable, and afraid.

The weeks of preparation at the janissary barracks faded. My Moslem facade became a nurturing comfort as I discovered that prayer helped translate the chaos—the emptiness—into a space with order. When the caravan failed to stop for the daylight supplications, I did my best to pay homage to Allah on my own initiative. I sought his guidance in understanding the mysteries of my life. Planted atop my camel, twisting through space as if seated in a wind-whipped crow's nest, I thought about my life as a series of inevitable acts carefully designed by the One God.

The desert and Allah seemed one. In this barren waste there could be no other option: only a single-minded and savage god would survive. Only Allah. Only the pitiless designer of this living hell could fathom rhyme or reason for the desert. I must admit, however, that in spite of my initial impressions and the very real pains to my body, two favorable conclusions emerged from our Laghouat to Ghardia journey.

A few miles past my camel-riding lesson, the landscape became a shimmering, lifeless, flat field of salt that lay unending, horizon to horizon, with no interruption of boulders or precipitous ditches or obstacles of any kind. For this terrain, our Tuareg guides set a slow pace for the caravan, and, held in combination—the terrain and the slow pace—, Allah devised a doubly bountiful gift for me. He gave me the privilege of riding a camel. I speak not of merely surviving atop a mountain that perpetually suffered from cataclysmic earthquakes— nothing so petty. He gave me the power of balance, the sense of belonging that unites a rider and animal into something greater than the two previously separate entities. By the time we reached Ghardia, riding became a joyous flight that occurred without thought or effort.

I observed that the Tuareg and Kabyle spoke graciously to their whining, cantankerous beasts, and that they rode gently with relaxed ease. During the first minutes and miles of each day's sojourn, almost every camel behaved in some perverse or petulant manner. The experienced riders, especially the Tuareg, responded to their camels with tough compassion—a buried affection. The men in blue treated the misdeeds of their animals as if perpetrated by some invading djinni and were ignored. Negligent beasts received repeated instruction in the sphere of weakness until absolute obedience became rote. I made every effort to emulate the Tuareg's exemplary behavior, and each day became more comfortable for me. My camel transformed itself from an ignorant, dark spirit into a personality with merit, virtues, and a sense of humor.

Time passed quickly. My camel and I entertained one another with tricks and games. The sun blazed swiftly across a dome whose expanse had previously seemed without limit or purpose. A comfortable leisure emerged from the security of companionship with my camel and the desert. My childish fears disappeared. Night became a time for contemplation of Alphonse's stars. The dim specks grew apace with my memories of his gentle love. Each long moment presented a treasure that emerged in flashes, or fashioned itself in slowly unraveled clues until a riddle's answer evolved before the question.

The important and significant question of fleas comes to mind, for it was only after days of not scratching and not being conscious of not scratching, that I suddenly realized the vermin were missing. Always in the past, fleas had provided a reminder to me that pleasure was ephemeral, while misery constant. But the desert took my fleas; they disappeared into the moistureless void. Their departure increased my list of gifts from Allah.

Each moment stood without distraction. The endless blue sky spilled in seamless compassion over the featureless desert. Our line of two hundred camels extended beyond vision, beyond care. All seemed a harmonious entity. The silence surged softly into my mind, creating an ease that was foreign to my experience. Time moved with less rigorous compulsion. It was "as the sea, but not the sea."

After five days of white, flat sand, the caravan moved onto the Hamada, a table of denuded, dusted, and varnished rock. Shades of red and black wove complex patterns that dimmed into the distant blur. We clomped over the hard surface for another four days, and just as sand again began collecting into small stable waves, we arrived at the oasis town of Ghardia.

CHAPTER TWENTY-THREE

THE TUAREG WERE CLEARLY UNCOMFORTABLE with the mood of Ghardia. Salim held that we merely stop long enough to refill our water bags and refresh the camels. "Two days and one night will meet our needs," he said.

Ahmed ruled against those wishes. "I am here as representative of the dey of Algiers," he told Salim. "I must maintain our protocol and meet with the leaders of this community."

"You will put us all in great danger with such frivolity." Salim closer to whiper in Ahmed's ear. "My informants say that the Shamba are preparing to kill us all. Turks and Tuareg both."

"If we do not bend our knee to the local Chief, we guarantee an attack. If I can arrange a meeting to discuss their grievences, and suggest possible solutions the dey of Algiers may approve, then we may keep them on a neutral footing."

Salim turned quickly, and stalked away from our commander.

After setting up camp at the edge of the oasis, Ahmad sent Blib and me to meet with the chief of the Ghardia-Shamba.

◆

We entered the walled town through a gate leading to a lively marketplace. It was a kaleidoscope of images moving slowly across the stage: Arabs in predominance, with Bedouin, pale M'zabites, and tall muscled Negroes in descending percentages. Robes, burnooses, and turbans of many colors swirled through the smells of dolmas, kuskussu, and kebabs. Dark little souks, displaying tiny inventories of silver brooches and bracelets, peered from beneath arches that led into the town.

The alleys were perhaps six to eight feet in width, with strong palm logs connecting most shops and homes across the way. Each structure was shoulder to shoulder, the sun-dried bricks of one adjoined to the next, with the logs over our heads to embrace the building across the way.

"Why the timbers?" I asked of Blib.

He shrugged and said, "Either the bricks are made from inferior parts, or they have an inordinate fear of earth tremors. Possibly both factors contribute to this novel architecture; I'm not sure."

If Blib didn't know, only Allah could provide the answer. We walked uphill using a tall minaret as our pole star, for the chief's palace adjoined the central mosque of this city. An Arab guide drifted along behind us, close enough to hear any request for information, but unobtrusive in his demeanor.

According to Ahmen, Bachaga Messaoud Ben Sheik Brahim, chief of the Shamba, protector of Ghardia, stood as our dey's loyal servant. He always paid his assessed taxes promptly, and four times in his life he had proclaimed homage to Allah by kneeling and praying before the holy Kaaba in Mecca. His fierce warriors always responded with their assistance when called to help in the defence of Algiers. Sheik Brahim was a loyal supplicant to the dey of Algiers, and Salim's forecast of doom aside, more likely a friend than foe.

The gift that I carried from Dey Muhammad Bashaw to his friend and close ally marked the importance of their relationship. It was an elaborately carved French clock with precious stones designating the minute intervals, and lapis lazuli studded in a design representing the constellation we called the Southern Cross.

The chief smiled benevolently at the European trinket, turned it once completely around, and handed it to a kneeling aide. His well-trimmed white beard and spiked moustache both smiled toward us. A bright-red felt shawl settled over the sheik's head and shoulders, marring the virtuous white that covered the rest of his body. I could only think of something inanimate: a mannequin or a Greek icon. His smile smelled of sulphur. Chief Brahim looked first at Blib and then at me. I felt a fish bone caught in my throat. He motioned for us to be seated.

Blib offered the ritual inquiries of health and well-being.

The Shamba leader rejected the ritual responses and spoke to us in the Arabic language—the language of poets and Mohammed. "My friends, you must return to Algiers. There is nothing for you in the desert. Only trees of thorns and empty wells."

"As Allah wills, my most gracious sheik," answered Quartermaster Mumdi, "but we must follow our instructions from the dey of Algiers." Blib waved his right arm toward the ceiling. "We will succeed in our assigned mission or we will die. Those are the only two options available to us."

"Admirable sentiments; the dey would expect no less from his janissary." The chief looked blandly at us and continued. "The tribute from the king of Bambara must be forgotten. Slaves, gold—forget them. Only the sand exists. Your small troop—ferocious as they may seem to you and the dey of Algiers—is nothing. A pebble that is quickly ground to dust."

"Your Honor," replied Blib, "the dey was very clear in his instructions. He stated that we were to find and return his tribute. He did not offer contingencies or the opportunity for excuses."

"Please excuse my rudeness." A spark of anger tinted the old sheik's eyes. "Twice over have I been in error. First for presuming to intercede between you and the dey of Algiers, and second for not providing you with proper refreshments. Please accept my apologies."

"It is nothing, Your Honor. We thank you for permitting an audience. Your wisdom and hospitality are renowned throughout the regency of Algiers."

The chief looked at us strangely. I couldn't decipher his intention, but there was a quick nod from the aide who had received the clock to our Arab guide. For no apparent reason, my skin dampened with cold sweat. The palace turned frigid. I suffered a sudden attack of tremors.

Our host moved his right hand slightly. Immediately a covey of slaves began serving sweet meats, dates, figs, and tea. As a former coffeegee, I appreciated their skill in tipping the steaming pots at shoulder level and unerringly filling the small cups placed at our knees. I reached for a fig, but Blib surreptitiously nudged me, and the fig remained untended. Every bit of noise disappeared from the audience hall. An argument escalated toward violence somewhere outside the open windows, but that intrusion also dropped quickly into the silence.

"The protector of Ghardia is too kind." Blib looked at his hands, then back at the chief. "The desert winds blow in many directions. Perhaps you have heard whispers about the gold or the tribute slaves stolen from the dey of Algiers? Any hint from any source could help us serve our dey."

"No, there is nothing that I can do or say that might assist your little band of intruders."

The silence in the room persisted. Blib stood, and I quickly followed his example. "We have imposed far too much on your hospitality, my lord." Blib paused, gave a slight nod, and continued, "We beg permission to purchase some meager supplies and then to continue with our orders from the dey of Algiers."

"Of course; it is nothing. May Allah protect you and guide you to success."

We both bowed deeply. Blib recited the parting formality and began backing toward the exit.

We turned to leave from the audience chamber, and I noticed that our Shamba guide stood, hesitated briefly, and then followed us through the series of arches and halls toward the exit of the palace.

The first two archways from the audience chamber led down long tunnellike halls, and at each intersection stood six fully armed Shamba. The remaining seven openings led to either living quarters or space for clerks and servants. I saw little furniture in any of the rooms except a surfeit of beautifully colored rugs, and the rich opulence of the rugs stood in sharp contrast to the simple straw-brick building. Finally we walked through the small barricaded front door into brilliant sunshine.

Blib spoke to me over his shoulder, yet he maintained a steady pace down the narrow street, "Beware! Speak in the Turkish language, for we have spies on every side."

"Certainly. What in hell was going on with that old man? I thought that he was the dey's true friend here about."

Even surrounded by spies and walking at a pace that we were unlikely to maintain much longer, Blib-the-teacher took the podium. "Well," he said, I hope that by now you can remember that Arabs hate towns. Especially do these Shamba hate towns and town people, and hate anyone who cannot show kinship to a Shamba nomad."

"There is a vague memory of a past lecture in the same vein," I said.

"Just add another fact to your porous mind, this tribe is tough and mean, and that the old lion back on his pile of rugs is the toughest and meanest Arab in the world."

"Of course."

Blib seemed unable to stop talking, and his mouth and eyes moved with equal velocity. "From what I understand, the Shamba left Yemen probably six or seven hundred years ago and wandered across the desert until they ended up here. The Berber and Tuareg, who were here first and who also thought they were the gilded rooster, have been pushed aside and crushed by these newcomers." He shouted above the crowd noises. "Just numbers. You see, the Shamba breed their women like camel, and the others don't." He looked around for a possible linguist and smiled. "Every other generation or so, these sons of the Prophet stop fighting each other. When they stop, that's when the trouble begins."

"Trouble?"

"Trouble for those who still control a little land that might better serve the Shamba."

We spewed out of the alley into the riotous market area. The clamor forced Blib to move closer and shout into my ear. "It all seems to work for the Shamba. They command the northern caravan routes, the best wells, and the richest oasis. Our dey of Algiers seeks the Shamba as allies." Blib stopped to look me in the eye. "The Shamba are richest tribe in the desert. Did you count those rugs in the palace?"

"Well," I said, "there were many beautiful rugs, but not much else. Empty rooms, from what I could see."

"The Shamba are nomads. Tomorrow they could be a hundred miles away—five hundred miles in a week. Towns are a hated convenience, a place to meet and trade, to pick up supplies, to sneak a drink of brandy or store valued but heavy items. The palace is just a shell, a town tent, a place to display wealth."

"When the chief moves his court, do the rugs also move?"

"Camels and rugs are easy to count and easy to move. They serve to instruct all observers of the pervasive power held by the Shamba."

"Given that equation, I'm impressed."

"Unfortunately, my informants tell me that the Shamba and their tame tribes are all loving comrades, and that's bad news for us." He turned from me and continued on at his rapid pace. As we approached an intersection, I turned to make an inquiry of directions and noticed that our guide had disappeared. After a few missed turns and our ending in dead-end alleys, we finally reached the town gate, quickly walked to our camp, and reported to Ahmed.

"We're in trouble, my noble leader," I said.

Blib nodded in agreement, but put a finger to his lips and then drew a finger across his neck.

I knew when to take a hint. We three sat down around a small fire and watched dust roil over our camels. A slave served tea, and Blib sang the praises of Sheik Brahim, counting him as a firm and loyal servant of the dey. After our third cup and a tiresome series of accolades to the Shamba, Ahmed suggested that we complete our inventory of supplies already purchased.

Ahmed told the trailing slaves to stay behind and for them to begin packing our cooking gear. After a few steps into the privacy of our camel herd, he said, "All of our Arabs have disappeared. A few of the slaves have also departed, so I don't need a fortune-teller to divine what's going on around here."

"Do you have a plan?" asked Blib.

"We need to get out of this town right now." He looked at me. "Jamie, find Tashmani and tell him that we now share his opinion of the Shamba. Tell him we must leave in two hours. There's a good moon tonight, so we'll make it to the first well before midnight."

"Blib, organize the troops and prepare for an imminent attack. From this moment, we are on constant alert"

Ahmed hissed our release, "Get going, both of you."

———◆———

The two of us were surrounded by camel but stood next to a docile white mare. Tashmani's eyes gleamed, and his eyebrows formed sharp peaks. He fingered the hilt of his dagger with soft, sensuous strokes. "You are a Frank, a new Moslem, therefore you cannot know the Arabs for what they are, my friend. They have no honor. They come like vile beasts to steal land. They pretend special knowledge of Allah to elevate themselves over all others. Bah!" Tashmani raised his veil and spit in the sand. "It will be my pleasure to send a few of those miserable dogs to their rightful place in hell. The Tuareg are ready." He turned and walked away.

The din of screeching, complaining camels celebrated the setting sun. Janissary troopers walked in groups of three or four, carbines held loosely in one hand, to patrol the perimeter of our camp. They advised the slaves to act with haste and counseled strangers from approaching too closely.

In the two hours between sunset and moonrise, the caravan traveled thirty miles, and we reached the well, Bir Hassi-Fahl, near midnight.

Salim and Ahmed drew the Tuareg and janissary squads around them to discuss our options.

"They will strike at sunrise and from the east; it is always so," said Salim.

Several troopers muttered their agreement, and Salim continued. "The Shamba are cowards, the Devil's own spawn; we may anticipate exactly ninety Arabs, all with guns, to match our thirty. We will need to prepare ourselves for the glory of death in the service of Allah."

I checked the holster on my right hip to feel the revolver stored at the ready. This was not the sea, of course, but my experience of preparing for battle on my father's ship had progressed in a similar fashion. I was not afraid of encountering enemy fire. In fact, I felt a confidence in this odd collection of Turks and Tuareg that mimicked my shipmates aboard the *Maria*.

Ahmed turned from the Tuareg leader to his men. "You must direct the slaves to gather camel dung and dig for the roots of any brush they can find. Then, an hour before sunrise, you must have them build large fires and prepare meals as normal."

The troopers mumbled sounds in approval of their commander's cunning.

"Also, you must issue carbines and swords to all slaves and to the Kabyle herdsmen."

A few of the janissary uttered negative comments, but the vast majority of his men continued to support Ahmed.

"How shall we establish our perimeter?" asked Blib.

"Entrench the slaves and herdsmen on the east side of the camp, and then give them the necessary instructions to use their weapons. Tell them to begin firing at first sight of the Shamba, and to aim for the camels. First hit the camels and then the men." He paused, made a swift calculation, and continued. "Blib, you take the eagle squad over the first dunes to the northeast. No camels for you, but pack all the ammunition that you can carry on your back. Establish your target line just east of the cooking fires. I'll take the other squad southeast and set up a cross fire. James, get a carbine from Blib and stay close to him."

Ahmed returned his attention to Salim. "Are your slaves also warriors?"

"They can kill with the lance and will die with bravery."

"That is good to hear. But for you, sir, I must order the most difficult and important task."

"We are ready, Captain."

"You and your men will mount camels and go at least one mile west of the well."

"West, my lord?"

"Yes, you must protect us if the Shamba circle to the rear; but if they attack only from the east, wait until all gunfire slows to sporadic bursts, and then charge through the center of our camp. Look for dismounted Arabs. Look for janissary that need help. Kill the Shamba on foot, and then give chase to the rest. We must not allow any survivors."

"You will find that the Tuareg are honorable warriors, Ahmed al-Koita, and therefore we use only the lance, sword, and knife. No guns. Our steel is sufficient to send them to Allah for their final judgement."

"As you will, Salim. May Allah protect his Tuareg warriors."

A near full moon dropped into the abyss of dawn. Fires flared. The barren well site suddenly burst into a disturbed ant heap of activity. Camels complained as they were moved from one foraging place to another. Free men yelled to slaves for food and water. Older slaves implored novices to move with greater alacrity. Jupiter became opalescent, and a magic wand created quiet over Bir Hassi. Cook fires blazed, and the first odors of boiled mimosa drifted through the surrounding dunes. Two desert partridge called, and faint echoes replied. A pale phosphorescent luster leaked over the eastern horizon. With a passionate eruption, the sun burst forth and the Shamba came thundering from the Helios.

Our slaves fired a wild first shot and burrowed out of sight. The Kabyle followed Blib's instructions and held their fire. Finally, with Blibs first shot, it seemed that our sharp explosions reached through small gray clouds to tumble camels and riders into uncontrolled derangement. The front line of the Shamba spontaneously regenerated as new attackers replaced those who had fallen. White camels, necks stretched parallel to the ground, loped through the sand. White-robed men brandished curved swords in quick probing slices. Animals and riders screamed in terrified ecstasy, always on the thin edge of balance, vulnerable to the first stumble or swerve.

Our volley of carbine fire from both flanks of the dunes collapsed the Arab charge. Camels and men dropped, causing the next line and the next to warp upon themselves, creating a seething mass of noise and blood.

I knew that our weapons were the newest invention of the Florentine gun maker Michele Loenzoni. They had been purchased from Venetians in exchange for a captured merchant ship. They were different from all other long guns in that the balls and powder were placed in separate tubes in the stock. It took but a single backward and forward motion of a lever to cause a revolving breech lock to select a both a ball and a charge from their respective magazines. This magical machine placed each bullet properly in the barrel, primed the flash pan, and set the gun at half cock. Aim. Fire! Seven rapid shots before reloading. I was practiced in using the weapon and comfortable in my ability to hold our position.

Corporal Tazakky, of the eagle squad, lounged next to me in the sand. He was a veteran of many wars, and his carbine joined the battle as his intimate comrade. After each explosion, Tazakky smiled, spoke gently to his piece, fondled the brightly polished wooden stock, and fired again. In his older age this new weapon gave him the virility of a much younger man. They were a happy pair. Tazakky smiled constantly at his potency.

After the first seven shots from my weapon, I reloaded ball and powder into the barrel and watched the chaos swirl around me. It made no sense to my startled mind. Noise and smoke obstructed everything. Strange phenomena appeared without reason. I stared at a surprising desert bloom: a corsage of brilliant crimson flowers erupted where moments before Tazakky talked and smiled and laughed in an intimate colloquy with his weapon.

A swarm of huge hornets buzzed all around me. Private Tuil Gassi yelled in great agony. He threw his arms up and down, as if at prayers, and slowly melted out of my sight. Suddenly—without explanation—I felt pounded into the sand by an intense pain in my upper leg. The sun crashed against my eyes. My bowels discharged, combining blood and excrement as one.

Blib yelled, "Reverse fire!" Someone pulled me in quick jerky movements over the ridge of the dune. I rolled once, listening to the silence and squeezing the pain from my leg. The hornets disappeared.

My mind immersed itself in the pain. I put both hands on my upper thigh, and a sticky foulness washed over my fingers. Scattered carbine shots began sounding around me again. I could hear someone frantically yelling my name.

I sat up. Blood pumped through my clenched fingers. In quick, awkward movements I released my leg and tore a large strip from the lower hem of the burnoose. The goatskin water bag was full, and I squandered the full ration in soaking the rag and cleaning my backside. Two more strips of burnoose served as a wrapping to stem the flow of blood. The pain diminished and trickled into a persistent flutter.

"Jamie! Jamie! Here! Quickly!"

I turned toward the yelling and crabbed up the dune. Three janissary were lying prone at the peak of the dune, firing as rapidly as they could insert ball and powder—aim and shoot.

Blib turned his grim stained face toward me. "Here!"

I crawled to him and looked over the crest. Less than ten feet down the slope lay the bodies of Tazakky, Tuil, and two other troopers. From the crest of the next dune surged dozens of Arabs. They slogged through the sand, occasionally dropping to their knees, taking aim with their long-barreled rifles, firing, and then arduously reloading before springing to the attack.

Slightly apart from the attacking Arabs, obscured by lumpy clouds of smoke, sat three men on white camels. They watched passively as their kinsmen flowed around them and down the steep slope. The red shawl identified Sheik Brahim; the two others did not matter.

Blib threw a carbine to me. "Begin firing!" he yelled, and then squinted down his barrel before pulling off a round.

Three belts of ammunition still looped from my shoulders, and in awkward, hesitant movements I began firing my weapon.

"Lower! Pick your target and squeeze the trigger." Blib's voice was sharp and insistent. "Now!"

After five shots I could decipher the relationship between the men who were wading upslope, ever closer to us, and the sight lines along the barrel of my carbine. The pain in my leg disappeared only to be replaced by the hammering concussion of constant gunfire.

Men appeared before me and then dropped in violent spasms to join my janissary friends in the sand. The trooper on my left suddenly threw up his arms and collapsed, head askew, with bloody pulp for a neck. Gray smoke settled in the depression between the dunes. I continued mindlessly loading and firing shot after shot until Blib shook me and yelled, "Stop!"

I looked at him, and then followed his gaze to the dune opposite us. Three white camels still stood in passive silhouette, yet something was different. My mind scrambled to decipher the strange signals. Blue! Blue, not white! The Tuareg!

I could see three Arabs prone in the sand. Each dead body was marked in almost vertical declension by a long, thin lance. Four men in blue rode along the horizon on their camels, stopped briefly to draw curved swords from leather scabbards, and began to move their mounts down the slope.

"Rapid near fire!" yelled Blib to his army of three. Those Arabs nearest to us dropped like ragged floppy dolls. In the middle depression between the dunes, confusion reigned. Men began moving in all directions. Some dropped their weapons and ran; others paired together and continued to fire in tandem. One rider in blue dropped, then, another.

Blib yelled "Charge!" and, followed closely by the remaining janissary trooper, mounted the crest. The two ran down the slope and began hacking in furious blows at the Arab mob. I watched the drama from my distant seat with passive astonishment.

Rifles and carbines were useless to the combatants. Steel reflected the red desert flowers that kept blooming in the now brilliant sun. The janissary and the Tuareg joined and then dispersed to shadow the fluttering rags of men. None made their escape over the sand. The Arabs all gleefully entered heaven, confident of a salacious welcome by countless compliant virgins.

Blib switched his sword to the left hand. His right arm hung limply. He looked directly at the sun and seemed to melt slowly into the hot sand.

I put my head down on my arms and closed my eyes. I mumbled to the ever-present Allah, to the djinni smiling behind his dune, "In a moment. Just a moment, Blib, and I will return to our duty; in a moment."

An annoying buzzing sound forced me to open my eyes. A growling, seething black mass covered Tazakky. I turned away from the apparition and studied the spectacle before me. Clouds of flies blurred the sleeping forms scattered between the dunes. Blib and the remaining trooper struggled in stumbling slow motion through the loose sand. I watched as three mounted Tuareg shambled past me and continued the hundred yards down toward the well.

Scattered shots continued to sound from the far dunes. A carpet of dead men and beasts sprawled in serene repose around the well. Three Kabyle herdsmen and six of our slaves wandered among the bodies, removing weapons and and gold from teeth. Four janissary mounted a dune on the far side of the camp and waved the Tuareg toward a plume of dust heading north, and our three remaining blue-robed cavalry turned and headed in pursuit.

It was an hour or more before Ahmed and three other troopers, all uninjured, reached us. They examined our wounds, rebound them in rags torn from robes, and fashioned a sling for Blib's arm.

The sun blazed overhead.

"Come," said Ahmed, "we must get you down to the tents." He helped me up, and with my arms over the shoulders of two troopers, I managed to stagger down the dune and into our ravaged camp. Slaves relieved the janissary and carried me into a tent. I immediately collapsed into a blank void.

◆

"Goddammit! Stop!" I opened my eyes.

Tashmani stopped pulling at my wound, squatted on his haunches, and looked at me. The shadows were long. "You have the honor of a wound from battle, my lord."

"It's not my first, I can tell you."

"There has been no such good fortune in my life." His eyes smiled from the blue veil. He leaned over me and again probed at my leg, with the same painful result. "This wound will heal in two or three days, but we must move tonight."

I protested. "Impossible, Tashmani. It will not heal in such a short time, nor will I move so quickly."

"Everything is as Allah requires. In the desert air all wounds heal quickly, but there is no cure for a scimitar across the throat."

"What are you talking about?"

"The Shamba are certain to look for their lost army. They will be upon us like flies upon their dead if we do not immediately leave this place."

I worked his words over in my poor excuse for a mind. "You win, Tashmani. When do we leave?"

"There is much confusion in the camp," he said, "Captain al-Koita and the One God will decide when we leave." The Tuareg warrior stared steadily at me. "There is a matter that I must put before you."

"Name it, Tashmani, and I will give you what I can."

"In today's battle a Tuareg noble joined Allah in heaven. To serve that hero in his celestial home, four of our brave slaves died—noble and slaves together. Salim Shushufi, as brother of the sultan, is still alive on this earth and must be served by more than one slave. For me, one is adequate." Tashmani put his nose to mine. "We need the transfer of two of the slaves that remain in the dey's service."

"For use by Salim?"

"Yes."

"How many slaves are left?" I paused and managed a small shrug. "Never mind. Take your pick. Whatever you need. They will die an honorable death in the ledgers of our master, the dey."

Tashmani gave a slight bow and quickly left the tent. I rolled to my right side, away from the throbbing wound, and fluttered once again into unconsciousness.

CHAPTER TWENTY-FOUR

February 1791

THE MOON CONTINUED HIDING IN the depths of Hades. The stars cast stark shadows from the dunes and gave guidance for our escape. Blib and Tashmani supervised four slaves as they carried me from the tent and lifted me atop a docile female camel. "Stop!" I groaned. "It's too much. Leave me. Go on without me." The pain jerked spasms from my body, causing more pain. "Leave me! Dammit! Dammit! Stop!"

"Here," Blib directed a slave, "put this pillow against the saddle."

"It's no good! Quit it! Leave me here in the sand!"

Tashmani tore strips of cloth and bound my leg to the pommel. "Quiet now," he admonished. "The djinni will jump into your open mouth if you keep on with your squalling."

A black slave tied a long rope to the camel's halter, talked softly to the beast for some moments, and stroked her muzzle, ears, and neck. Then, tapping gently, he urged the camel to stand. The explosion of pain quickly evaporated into a tiny closet of black silence. Small rays of light slowly, erratically poked at my mind. I opened one eye and saw a man walking across a tranquil sea, barely skimming the surface, leaving no ripples of progress. I opened my other eye. The apparition continued his toil, rope over shoulder, hauling some lightweight vehicle through the depths. "How very interesting," I observed, and fled back to my dim closet.

I woke to pain and small noises. The moon appeared, waned now to a turkey-egg shape and revealing all around us silhouettes of sculpted sandstone hills: ships and castles, animals and gods. The pace was slow and due east toward the empty, flat, and rocky land and away from the sand.

A tolerable position evolved for me. If I leaned on my elbows, using the cushion to support my back, and rolled my body in rhythm to the camel's gait, I prevented my injured leg from striking the pommel. Life became preferable to death. The wound stopped bleeding, and the pain diminished. Ahmed brought his camel around, matched our pace, and asked after my health. "Tolerably well," I answered. "What happened? What's our strength?"

"We're down to twenty: you, Blib and I, plus four troopers who can still fight and one who probably won't make the night. Tashmani, Salim . . ." He stopped his inventory and looked at me for a long moment. ". . . and the three slaves assigned to Salim!" He coughed and I remained silent. "Three Kabyle and four remaining slaves on the dey's inventory. Camels for all, plus six pack animals."

"The ledgers?" I asked. "The ledgers and the gold?"

"Both packed on one camel."

We rode silently until I finally asked again, "What happened?"

"The trap that we set for them became our trap."

"What do you mean?"

"They sent about half their force at our center. I expected their entire attack from the east, but Sheik Brahim looped a quarter of his men around to the north, and the remaining Arabs in a similar maneuver to the south. After the firing began and we revealed our position, he simply attacked our rear and broke our defence."

"Are you sure it was Sheik Brahim?"

"Yes, Salim and his Tuareg killed him first. The chief and two aides were directing the attack, when the Tuareg came along and saved our asses."

"I thought Arabs always attacked together. Out of the rising sun." The comment felt bitter in my mouth. My pain was Ahmed's fault. When he didn't answer my complaint, I dozed to the undulating sway of my camel and woke as he began speaking.

"You're right, Jamie. I made every dumb mistake possible. I lost men who trusted me. Tazakky was going to retire after this mission. Tuil . . . the rest." He stopped, slowly drew in the night, and then huffed into the silence. "General Arnold was the best, you know. He fought like the janissary, always in the lead, yelling, 'let's go, my brave boys. Let's go.' Always in the lead, covered with mud and blood, showing the way." Ahmed coughed loudly, scattering the night air, and continued. "I was more like General Gates and those other fat-generals at Saratoga, sitting on my butt on top of a hill. Out of the way. Way, way out of the way, just watching my troops get torn up. Sitting with a finger up my ass—that's what I was doing."

"You did the best you could, Captain."

"They drove Benedict Arnold out of the army, out of the country he loved." A note of passion came into Ahmed's voice. "He didn't abandon his troops. A few scabby vermin who couldn't fight and wouldn't leave Arnold alone: ass-kisser Wilkinson and that slink, John Brown, chased him out of the army with a ton of lies. Miserable sons-a-bitches—except maybe Morgan. He wasn't an old lady gossip, and he fought with his men. The liars said Arnold stole money. Said he was a coward. Those lying bastards even said he wasn't at Saratoga! God damn! Kicked out! The damn fools chased their best general right out of the army."

"You're probably right," I said. "Leastways, my father would agree with you."

"Those two were the only ones that I was proud to serve with. Your father and mine, plus General Arnold. They'd all make damn good janissary.

"Did you serve with General Arnold?"

"I was with him at Bemis Heights—him and that Polish engineer, Koz something. They had us digging trenches through the night, and carrying rocks all day. Hottest, most rotten place I've ever seen. It was no place for a fourteen-year-old nigger."

Captain al-Koita was silent for another long stretch. The quiet shush of my camel padding through the sand became accented by the occasional clicking of her hoof hitting pebbles. I dozed, then came back to attention when he continued.

"The man was bold and didn't sit back like I did. When Burgoyne finally attacked, Gates refused Arnold's plan to counterattack. Arnold told Gates to take his 'bloody damned orders to hell,' and rode into battle. I was with Larned's brigade, and I'll tell you we were catching hell. A few of the ol' boys were ready to skedaddle, and the rest were on the edge. Just when Major Larned looked like he was calling it a day, along came Arnold shouting, 'Come on, boys. Hurry up, my brave boys!'"

"What happened?"

"We turned and followed the man. We charged right at those redcoats and broke them. Five times we ran up against their bayonets. Five times they crammed cannon down our throats. Toward the end General Arnold had Morgan's troops mixed up with Larned's and Poor's, and we all followed him like we were one. 'Come on, boys. Hurry up, my brave boys.' I'll never forget that day."

"Both our fathers said the battle at Bemis Heights broke the British."

"Yup, no Washington to fuss and dottle and get in the way, just Arnold covered with mud and blood to win our only victory of the war."

"What about the last battle of the war?"

"That was a French victory over the red coats. The French navy sunk the British navy and the French army forced the King to surrender his colonies. Washington wasn't anywhere in sight."

"Our fathers and most people I know have the same memory of General Washington and his friends."

"Here's my problem, Jamie. I sat on my dumb ass and let the Shamba run the show. It was their battle, not mine. Salim was General Arnold, and I was Gates."

Another long spell of silence stretched between us before Ahmed finished his self-flagellation. "I got greedy. I didn't think through the possibilities. 'What if?' General Arnold used to say, and then 'What if?' again and again."

Ahmed was finally quiet. The moon coursed toward the western horizon, and the click of stone on the camel's feet became increasingly frequent.

"We're on the run, Captain; where are we headed?"

Ahmed turned slightly toward me. "We're almost full on the stone-filled section of the desert now. Another hour and we'll head south, a bit southeast, to give wide berth to El Golia. That's the last of the Shamba towns. South until we get to Tuareg country and some help, maybe, some help and maybe some information from the Tuareg."

"They took some heavy loses, I hope we still have some friends out hear in this damned desert."

"The city of Amguid. That's where Salim says his brother will be—somewhere near Amguid, anyway. That's where we're heading. I have no contingencies. No plans. We're just running."

The moon disappeared as the false dawn spread its evanescent light. Our Tuareg guides turned the bedraggled caravan south, and the three remaining Kabyle tribesmen held themselves apart from the rest.

They waited until Ahmed and I were abreast of them.

"Effendi. A word with you."

"What is it?" Ahmed answered the Kabyle man with obvious weariness.

"We are leaving now, effendi. You are going south, and we will go north. North to our people, not to those of the veil."

"Yes, I understand what you are telling me." Ahmed raised a hand as if in benediction and said, "May Allah go with you and protect you."

"Our lives are assuredly in Allah's hands, effendi. In his wisdom he may help us find food and water. He may also help us find a quick death."

"You may each take one camel and whatever supplies you need," said Ahmed.

"Praise Allah! Captain al-Koita, and may Allah grant you have many wives and many sons."

Our tiny caravan halted as Blib supervised the redistribution of supplies. We all watched as the Kabyle gently guided their mounts over the pebbled terrain, then quickly disappeared into the shadowy predawn light.

Blib and Ahmed checked the injured trooper and then consulted with the two Tuareg guides. After some discussion, Ahmed announced, "Everyone, except the two injured: off your camels. Tie lead ropes and walk."

We started again. Ahmed drifted back to my side. "Another mistake," he said.

"How so?"

"Those Kabyle. We should have killed them. They'll do their best to avoid the Arabs, but they will fail. The Arabs will torture them, get the information, and kill them, or they will buy the information and kill them. Either way, the Kabyle are dead and the Arabs know where we are going."

"Maybe not, Ahmed. Maybe they'll slip around the Shamba and get away. Maybe they'll get home." I leaned back against the pillow and thought about my leg. It didn't hurt very much now—only when I changed positions.

The sun spewed above the horizon, and we struggled along in the full light. Warming rocks muttered and sang as they expanded. "The djinni are speaking," Tashmani explained. He smiled, embracing the comfort and reality of tiny angels speaking to the privileged Tuareg.

Early morning mirages mirrored the distant dunes. We trudged over bleak rocky desert, yet our dream shape ahead showed strings of deep-blue lakes with mountainous dunes standing on their mirrored reflections.

"A beautiful vista," I commented.

"Yes, and useful also. Judging from the mirage and the direction of the wind, we'll be out of these rocks and into sand by noon." Without further comment, Tashmani picked up his pace and relieved Salim at the head of our paltry column.

The wind began to stir in petulant gasps and then slowly increased in velocity until sand streamed over the dark-colored gravel. Lakes and dunes disappeared. Endless barren waste—no vegetation, animals, or water—spread like an unending bad dream.

"How are you feeling?" Ahmed asked.

I squirmed around on my perch, peeled off two layers of robe, removed the wrapping, and examined my wound. The bullet had entered my upper left thigh and departed with a near miss of my manhood. The bones seemed intact, and now the wound was a mass of pinkish-purple proud flesh.

"Amazing! Ahmed, look at this. In one day the wound is healing over." I wiggled the injured leg, and he gave a cursory glance at the lesion. After readjusting my robe, I settled back on the wooden saddle. "Amazing. I'll probably walk tomorrow."

"This desert air must be a curative," said Ahmed, "I've had men recover from broken arms and bad stab wounds in just a few days. The same wound took months after Saratoga. Months, hell! Most of the poor buggers nicked at Saratoga died. Green pus, the sweats, and into the cold, cold ground.

"Lucky you, Jamie. An admirable battle scar to brag about. You're a hero now." He looked up at me and smiled. It was the first grin from him in weeks. Months. A captain of the janissary has no time for frivolity. "One thing, though. How will you explain this wound? The bullet appears to have entered from the rear. How will you explain any act of gallantry?"

"Simple, my illustrious general. I followed your lead in attacking to the rear!"

He smiled again. "Yes, that will do. All grandchildren and drunks will admire such a tale."

Ahmed adjusted his turban ends more tightly around his face and neck, waved to me, and walked rapidly to join Tashmani.

Visibility diminished. Our world became glossed with red as the blowing dust and sand increased. We struggled into the gale. Piles of sand slowly replaced the rocks; wind stung our eyes and filled our nostrils with sand. Heaps grew into mounds. Midday offered sizeable dunes and the first sparse clusters of driun—a ropy grass with a huge root system. My fatigue was such that I could barely retain my saddle.

Our guides turned into the lee of a substantial dune and halted. The wind stopped. Slaves unloaded, then hobbled and released the camels to forage. The dromedaries quickly scattered to muzzle driun and clumps of small thorny bushes. Tiny green leaves hid among very long abundant white thorns. Yet even with muzzle and tongue exuding thorns, like needles in a pincushion, the camels continued to prune in calm deliberation.

The surviving Tuareg slave, with his two new assistants in tow, found a vague depression—a remnant of an ancient wadi—and began to scoop away a hole with a brass bowl. He continued down for possibly three feet until a damp layer of sand appeared. The three men widened and deepened the hole until it was about four feet deep and six feet in diameter, and then they left for other duties.

Tashmani spoke from behind my shoulder. "The djinni do not like to be observed doing good work. After all, how could they maintain their honor by doing good deeds? Only the weak or holy provide charity. The strong take as they will, and the djinni cause even the Tuareg to tremble."

I turned to check his eyes. Was that a hint of wiggery from this desert knight? A jest? "C'mon now, Tashmani—you're teasing me."

"No, my friend, there are no jokes in the desert. Only the djinni. Allah is of the oasis. Leisure and humor are of the oasis. Here are the djinni and death."

Water appeared in the hole. Cool and clear water slowly filled the hole. I lazily watched the cooks as they gathered twigs and started a fire. One man squatted, naked to the waist; rippling muscles showed through his dark-brown skin. He took flour from a linen sack, put it into a large wooden bowl, and mixed it with water. As the consistency thickened, he crushed two pieces of rock salt, one on the other, and sprinkled it onto the gray mass. He squeezed and kneaded the batter with his unwashed hands, pushed aside the glowing embers of fire, and laid the flat dough on the hot sand. Without further preparation, he pushed the embers back in place and sat on his haunches, adding twigs to the burning fire.

I napped, lulled by the wind's ululation. Within ten minutes, the aroma from desert bread gathered everyone around the fire. The dune protected us with shade and sheltered us from the omnipresent wind. We ate the hot bread and drank steaming sweet peppermint tea out of small wooden cups. The bread reeked of ammonia, and the tea seemed brewed from tanner's bark. Altogether, it was a Thanksgiving feast.

The Tuareg drifted away to eat. Even then, thirty feet from the fire, they turned their heads as they ate or drank. Whenever we were together in tents, they inevitably covered their heads with a cloth. No exception: no Tuareg can allow a witness to his eating. If a human, a mere human, could observe an opening in a blue veil, how easy would it be for a djinn? A quick dive through a gaping mouth or up flaring nostrils, and the spirit of life is plucked from a careless Tuareg. Vigilance is everything in the desert. Constant vigilance.

When we finished our meal, the slaves cleaned the utensils with sand, carefully scraping the soot from the bottom of the tea kettle. Salim and Tashmani attended to their own feet, pulling thorns and small sharp pebbles from the tough skin. The wind continued to howl. My eyes fluttered and sweet sleep returned.

CHAPTER TWENTY-FIVE

March 1791

SHIP-SIZED BOULDERS LITTERED THE wadi as we moved ever south. A seesaw shift between shade and blinding sunlight brought the black-and-white bird in and out of focus as it followed us in a tail-bobbing dance from tree to shrub. A single raven croaked raucous complaint at our trespass, and as his echo died, a man leading a camel emerged at the next bend. He appeared as if a magical phantasm; at first I saw only pink-and-brown sandstone pillars and turrets gouged in rough canyon walls. Then the man materialized with the camel on a long tether. Atop the camel sat a woman with a small child in her arms.

Tashmani adjusted the remaining rags in a tight weave over his nose and above his eyes. He braced shoulders and tucked his chin nearly to his chest. My Tuareg friend held himself as one who marched before legions of fierce warriors; he moved toward the waiting family.

"Metulem, metulem," said Tashmani.

The stranger replied to his greeting in the same way. The men solemnly rubbed their palms together, placed both hands on their hearts, and concluded the ritual by putting two fingers to their lips.

My ability to speak and understand the Arabic language had progressed from adequate to excellent during our sojourn over the mountains and onto the desert. Since meeting the Tuareg guides, especially Tashmani, my talent with their Berber language moved from zero to barely adequate.

"How is your father?" Tashmani began.

"He is well," the man replied.

"And your grandfather—how is he?"

"He is well."

So it went. I was able to put together the sequence of relatives as Tashmani inquired after sons and daughters but never about the man's wife. She suffered the exchange of inquirers about health, but most of the time the woman stared boldly at me and Will. Tashmani completed his obligation down to second cousins once removed, and then the stranger took his turn.

Ahmed al-Koita and I sought shade beneath a shelf of rock and waited. We sat shoulder to shoulder and didn't speak. The wagtail watched us with head-tilting intensity and suddenly flew away in an awkward windmilling of wings. A small scorpion moved in reluctant spurts over my foot, paused in the shade of my leg, and scurried into a small hole.

"Tell me, cousin," said Tashmani to the stranger, "is our sultan now leading a caravan in the south?"

"It has been but four days since I left Sultan Agg-Abba and fifty of his warriors."

Tashmani digested the small piece of information and pressed for additional details. "Tell me, cousin, where did you leave our honored chief and his warriors?"

"Allah, the mighty and all-knowing, allowed rain to fall on the eastern slopes of Mt. Iftesene, and now the sultan's camels grow fat on the green grass."

"You were with the sultan?"

"Yes, cousin. I repaired swords and lances for our noble warriors."

"How many days will it take me to reach our mighty lord Sultan Agg-Abba?"

"Three days mounted on a camel, eight days on foot."

"Cousin," said Tashmani, "we are without food, water, or camel."

Both Tuareg looked away from the other.

The woman spoke with an intensity that failed the man. "Please excuse my lack of hospitality," she said. "Would you take the time for tea with us?"

Tashmani demurred that he would, and the travelers signaled their camel to kneel. Minutes later we sat silently around a small fire, drinking tea and eating cold kuskussu. Our fingers blurred as we rolled balls from the bowl and wolfed them down. We three raced one another in a flailing of right hands, and in ten heartbeats the bottom of the wooden bowl gleamed with empty lustre. I looked up to study the Tuareg woman.

She was young, in her early twenties, I judged, with bright smiling teeth and European features—that is, a small nose, high forehead, and thin lips. Her honey-colored skin shimmered with a nacreous gloss, and she wore large looping silver earrings in both ears and silver bracelets on each arm. The sum of flesh and costume created an exotic tang that brought saliva rushing to my mouth. She posed, left hand on her chin, and returned my stare with an uninhibited smile.

Ahmed nudged me, and in English whispered, "Mind your damn manners! Take the bloody dumb smile off your face."

I sat cross-legged in the sand, alternately staring at the small cooking fire and at the beautiful woman. "Ahmed, you're a tried and true Moslem. You've studied the Koran with an imam. So tell me how is it that the women of Algiers and the M'zabite towns remain hidden from a man's sight, yet here with the Tuareg, who claim the same faith, my eyes burn from the stare of a beautiful woman. Please explain this mystery to me, my pious friend."

"It's a mystery of man, not of Allah, you idiot infidel." He seemed complete with his answer and disappeared back into a black reverie. He coughed, paused, coughed again, and continued with the exchange in our native language. "There is nothing in the Koran that diminishes women. Mohammed taught that Allah recognizes men and women as equal in his eyes." He sighed and watched as she bent and stretched while loading the camel. "Scratch any Arab, and he will claim his blood runs directly from Mohammed, but the power of women is merely an old family tradition. For Arabs, quiet and out of sight is the inevitable rule; the Tuareg are different. Their tradition holds that a queen of ancient time made the first rules, and therefore it seems that these Tuareg just got used to uppity women. Either way, it is all the will of Allah, so don't worry your petty infidel mind about unnecessary details."

"Worry? I'm just trying to figure out what happens if I have a word or two with the lady. Will her husband poke me with his lance if I look cross-eyed at his wife, or what?"

"You'd better ask Tashmani for the protocol. In the meantime, keep your eyes on the scenery."

Ahmed got up and walked to the shade of another boulder, and we both watched Tashmani converse with the woman. She spoke with her hands and lips and looked directly into the Tuareg warrior's eyes. Her husband stood in the hot sun checking equipment attached to the camel's saddle.

Tashmani turned from the woman, walked over to me, sat on his haunches, and began trickling sand through his fingers. He stared at me from the shreds of tattered blue cloth. "She thinks that you are very ugly." He moved his face closer to mine. "She asked if you had a neck at all and why you walked like a pregnant donkey and had eyes of a camel in heat. I am requested to ask your thoughts of her observations."

I sat in the silence, sorting each insult for its purpose. Maybe there was no offense intended. Maybe she merely relayed her perception of the truth to Tashmani. If her ideal man were Tashmani, then assuredly there could be no disrespect from the lady. Hell! Compared with Tashmani or any Tuareg I'd seen, no one could charge her with insolence. No indeed. She was just a lovely, truthful woman.

"Who is she, Tashmani?"

"She is the eldest daughter of a queen, oh ugly one." A spark of humor spit at me from his black eyes.

"Very clever," I said.

Her husband studied distant rock formations, while the princess waved flies away from the child's face. A small black halo formed over the boy, held briefly, and collapsed in clusters at the moisture seeping from his eyes and nose. The woman looked at her child and then over at me, holding her eyes on mine.

I searched for interesting vistas along the wadi. "What is her name?"

"Dakadeit."

"Is that her husband?"

"For now, he serves as her only husband."

"For now?"

"She has given notice that with the new moon they will be divorced."

"How is that possible, Tashmani? Doesn't the Koran give only men that privilege?"

"You are in a separate land, effendi, with unique laws. It is women who give our names, and a queen that gave the Tuareg first breath. With us, men will always listen to women, as Allah planned. In His wisdom, Allah gave the Tuareg people noble women to produce noble children." He made a small shrug of his shoulders. "Does a lioness deliver a jackal? Honored men can arrive only from honored women, and both praise the other."

I watched Dakadeit pick up her sleeping child, lift him over her head, and with a practiced motion ease him into a soft cloth sack strapped to her back. Her breasts raised and lowered with the task, and I barely noticed as Dakadeit smiled at me. She turned and called to her husband for help in mounting the camel, and in a few minutes the wagtail and raven provided our only companionship.

CHAPTER TWENTY-SIX

W E STRUGGLED UP THE WATER-ruined walls of the small canyon to a barren stony plain. Pitted black boulders forced us to walk erratically in a generally southern direction, and near midafternoon we descended into another wadi. Perhaps it was the same one, and we were simply wandering in a mindless detour. I didn't care. Nothing mattered except putting one foot in front of the other. It seemed to my poor excuse for a mind that I would never see Plymouth Harbor again or stand at the helm of a ship at sea. The logic of serving the dey of Algiers as a strategy to gain ultimate freedom for me and my shipmates was another imaginary mirage so common in this place. It was only the rapidly fading memory of some bits of kuskussu passing down my throat that gave me the necessary strength to take another step followed by yet another step.

The sky gradually darkened to a purple-black hue. A beard of gray rain hung from the clouds, and eruptions pulsed within each thunderhead as the Lightning-Djinn coursed about seeking liars and adulterers. One bright streak emerged in jagged flight toward us, followed by a thunderous explosion that deafened our ears and rolled rocks into the canyon.

Large raindrops hissed as they struck rocks and evaporated. Fractures of blue tore at the clouds in bold, swift strokes. Wispy shreds fluttered along the horizon, and then there was nothing but a brassy sun buried in the empty blue sky.

We descended the precipitous gorge into a herd of thirty or so goats, tended by a girl of possibly twelve years. They all stood stock-still near a thornbush to watch us stumble along the rocky terrain. She wore a white robe and over her shoulders a blue scarf. In one hand she held a spindle of black goat's hair.

As Tashmani spoke, the girl's glistening white teeth welcomed us. "Your mother's tent is near, my little cousin?"

She pointed up the wadi. "Not far; you will arrive before dark."

I noticed her eyes always on the goats: watching them eat, smiling at the antics of two kids, frowning when one nanny moved temporarily out of sight. The girl offered us water from her small kidskin, and we each sipped sparingly. A young goat rubbed against her leg and bounced off mine in mock terror. We started walking again, and when I looked back over my shoulder, there were only rocks and scraggly trees.

Small clumps of clouds ranked in orderly file along the western horizon. They reflected pink shadows from the sun as we approached a cluster of crude shelters. Tashmani stopped and removed his veil. His skin appeared lighter than mine, his skull shaved to short stubble except for a long tress down the back of his head. His sparse beard surprised me. A man of such virility! I imagined something other than the patchy tufts that he revealed.

After vigorously shaking the tattered blue veil, he wrapped the remains of the twelve-foot-long cloth around his head and neck until a mere slit for his eyes showed. Ahmed and I slapped dust from our rags and finger-raked our hair and beards, all with little effect.

Four women in blue garments sat in the sand as a riot of naked children scurried in and about—all curious and slightly afraid of strangers.

"*Metulem,*" said Tashmani.

"Metulem," the women answered in chorus. Three continued with repairing sandals and saddlebags, but the eldest woman stood, walked over to a nearby goat, and began milking it. A thin blue stream hissed into a wooden vessel as the Tuareg woman pulled the teats with slow grace. "Where are your camels and slaves?" she asked.

"The camels were stolen and the slaves killed by the Shamba Arabs."

The woman stopped pulling at the nanny for a moment and looked directly at Tashmani with bold eyes. "Were there other Tuareg warriors that also left the battle?"

"Salim Shushufi and Abu'l-Qasim both died a hero's death. They are with Allah."

Tashmani held the woman's stare until she leaned her head against the goat and continued the milking. Tears now seasoned the milk.

When the bowl filled and eyes dry, the woman stood before Tashmani. "These other two"—she nodded in our direction—"they also ran from the Shamba and left my brother dead?"

"They are honored representatives from the dey of Algiers. The Frank is a collector of taxes and an adequate warrior, but the black man is a fierce soldier for the dey."

Moving without haste, the woman carried the bowl full of milk over to Tashmani and held it up to him.

He waited, silent, hands at his side.

"Tell me, cousin, it is well known that warriors die in battle; how is it that you three are here and not my brother, Abu'l-Qasim?"

"Allah moves each man according to his will, my cousin. We mortals can only observe life passing and pray for guidance. When the Arabs attacked on the first occasion at Bir Hassi-Fahl, we sent ninety of the dogs to their death. Your brother, Abu'l-Qasim, died a glorious death in that battle. Four of our slaves died at his side during the battle, and they will continue their service to him in heaven."

The woman continued to hold the bowl and maintained her silence.

Tashmani inhaled a deep breath of desert air. "The second battle I cannot describe. These two here before you, the Frank and the black Turk, made known their desire to witness the paintings bestowed by our ancestors." He cleared his parched throat. "You know the holy site, cousin, in the caves below the red mountain with three peaks. Upon our return from this pilgrimage, the desert was littered with bodies of Shamba, but our all our slaves and camel were dead or stolen. The Turks who had survived the first battle were also dead, and Salim Shushufi was in heaven. Allah denied me the opportunity to die in that battle."

After a long moment, Tashmani took the bowl and drank the milk. In turn she offered the milk to Ahmed and then to me. I took a deep draught and gagged from the sharp, rank taste. Only a male goat mounting this nanny could produce such an offensive flavor. I took two additional sips of the vile brew and returned the bowl. She studied my features, and I felt her glare as it covered my face and then descended slowly down to my groin. With a click of her tongue she finally turned from me and rejoined the circle of women and children.

Ahmed motioned for both Tashmani and me to follow, and we walked a dozen rods from the camp, past jumbled piles of rock and a few scrubby tamarisk.

"What's next, Tashmani?" said Ahmed.

"You both come as mendicants and therefore have no rank that is likely to yield any protection from the Tuareg." Tashmani paused for a long moment. "I am now perceived by my people as twice a coward, and my fate is likely either death or slavery. I will certainly choose death as the preferred option."

"Tashmani," said Ahmed, "how can we help you in this matter? There was never a hint of cowardice in your behavior. You are considered a brave warrior even with the janissary."

"Allah and my sultan will decide my fate. You must maintain complete silence in this matter."

I joined the discussion. "Tell us what can we do to get help against the Shamba?"

"Nothing."

"But, Tashmani," I argued, "when we were at Ghardia, you said that your sultan would be our great ally, that his warriors would help retrieve the lost gold. What has changed?"

"In Ghardia you had many camels and slaves and a gift worthy of my sultan. Also, Salim Shushufi, the sultan's brother, was alive, and Abu, his kinsman, was alive. Now they are dead, and you have nothing to give. We three are nothing to the Tuareg."

I moved a few steps into the shade of a boulder and reached into my ragged burnoose. The book was still securely wedged into my thieves' belt, the parting gift from Miciah. I called from the deep shade. "Tashmani, in what manner can we impress the Sultan Agg-Abba with our importance?"

He coughed, hesitated, and then answered. "If we could show him twenty camel and ten warriors with slaves to serve, plus a gift of gold suitable for a sultan, then perhaps he would offer his hospitality."

I stepped forward into the light, pulled my account book from the folds of my robe, and assumed the tone and posture of a shrewd Jewish banker. "And how much might that be in silver coins, my faithless friends?"

Ahmed recovered first. "What in hell, Jamie? I thought the Arabs stole everything. What's going on?"

"You must remember, Bolukbasi, that Miciah Baccri required a close record of every transaction and for this account book never to leave my side." I opened the book to the first blank page and again asked Tashmani, "How much do we need for everything that you need?"

The Tuareg's eyes narrowed to tiny slits. He looked up at the twilight sky, stared at me for another minute, and then blurted an extravagant number. "Forty of the dey's silver coins."

I didn't respond.

"In addition, you must pay ten gold coins for the sultan."

With a dramatic flourish, I opened my robe to reveal the money belt, and their expressions gave me abundant pleasure. I accepted the moment as a small repayment for the cost of carrying the damn anchor over the past four months. "I am violating Baccri's advice in showing this secret, but it seems that we are at the end of our line."

Both Ahmed and Tashmani gaped as I first counted out forty silver sequins, and from another compartment of the soft leather belt ten Spanish gold doubloons.

Ahmed was the first to speak. "You bloody-lubber-headed thief! All this time I've pegged you as just another feeble white man, you son of a bitch!" He kept shaking his head at me, smiling in a weak skewed manner.

Tashmani simply stared at the coins piled on the flat red rock for a long moment, then he took one silver coin from the pile, then walked around a man-high pile of boulders and over to the four women. He spoke to the group with firm, sharp words. They twittered among themselves until the eldest held out her hand and received the silver coin. Tashmani turned and walked back to us. He held his head and shoulders with noble grandeur.

We three separated from one another and sat staring at nothing. The drama of revealing the fortune faded into the abyss of our hunger. We waited with mindless patience. The shadows lengthened. Sounds and smells erupted from the kitchen lean-to. We endured the thud of a large mortar crushing millet grains. Then I watched a young woman grind flour between two heavy, smooth rocks, and finally smoke from ethal branches carried the aroma of cooking bread into the soft darkness. Every hidden djinn was tantalized beyond control. Children and dogs scampered within inches of my frozen form. Movement and sights swirled in abundant profusion, but nothing served to distract my eyes and nose from the goat simmering in slow turns above hot coals. The first stars mocked us, certain that we would perish of starvation, and a young woman approached our scattered clique with two large bowls.

"I am Kitra, your slave." She smiled to include all three of her new owners, placed the bowls before us, and turned back to the cooking fire. She made three additional trips, with bread, cups, tea, and yogurt, all in an effort to fuel our empty bodies. Balls of kuskussu, shreds of meat torn from the goat's charred hindquarters, and hunks of bread dropped into our gullets.

Tashmani sat and twisted away from us to lift his veil and eat, never permitting propriety to impede his rate of consumption.

I licked the astringent yogurt from my fingers, slowly sipped a small cup of sweet tea, and observed a young boy lead a brown camel to within a dozen paces from our circle. Tashmani stood, walked over to the boy, and took two small soft leather bags and the camel's bridle from him. Man, boy, and camel moved to a small bush, where Tashmani secured the bridle to a bare branch. Both Tuareg warriors walked around the animal to examine legs, feet, and eyes. Tashmani checked the saddle and then returned to our circle.

"When the moon is near full, I shall return. In the interval, rest and have your clothes repaired." Tashmani walked over to the red rock bearing the shining piles of coins and filled one leather sack with silver and the other with gold. He tied both bags around his neck and dropped them down beneath the folds of his burnoose. With no further comment, Tashmani mounted the camel and disappeared into the dark night.

◆

I belched twice and emitted a series of magnificent farts, but neither Kitra nor Captain al-Koita made a single comment. My mind said I was still famished, but my eyelids flopped shut. I woke to piss while the sun was still evident, and then returned quickly to my nest in the sand.

It appeared to be just past sunset when Ahmed shook me awake. "How much is left?" he asked.

My mind drifted with the camp noises and the first tentative hoots and whistles of night birds. "Fifty silver and thirty gold."

"How in hell did you manage it?"

"It was Baccri's idea. He said that I must carry a full load of coins and never tell anyone, not even you."

"Look, James, if I'd known about the coins, it is possible that some of my troopers would still be alive." Ahmed rinsed his fingers in a wooden bucket filled with water and shook them dry. "I'm commander, and I get to decide what to do, based upon all the available options. What if that bullet had nicked you a bit higher, you nincompoop? Then where would we be?"

"I'd be dead, Agha. So stony cold dead that I wouldn't care a fig for you or Baccri or this entire sand pile!"

"Look, I'm sorry; it's such a shock. It's great. You're a hero." Ahmed shrugged.

"If I'm so admirable, how come you're so damned angry with me?"

"Angry? Allah rains silver and gold upon me, and I should be angry? Ha! You and Baccri are angels of mercy."

An edge of irritation remained between us. "I'm sorry; it probably was a mistake not to let you know about the coins. I mean, after all, you're the commander and my friend, not Baccri."

Silence trickled over our brittle shadows until the gushing splatter of a camel urinating disturbed our reverie. We started laughing with the first trickle, and rolled on the ground, bellowing, long after the camel ceased pissing.

"There's not a river in this country with more water," I croaked.

"Hell, make that all of Barbary," added Ahmed.

The quiet rhythm of the dusk returned. "Where did Tashmani go?" I asked.

"Only Allah knows. To buy an army, I suppose. We've got near a month before we have an answer, so I guess there's no sense worrying about it."

"We'll just find a berth around here. We can dream about good old gunnies and bean duff on board the *Maria*."

I finished smoothing my sandy depression and looked up to see Kitra with two large blankets. She gave one to each of us and disappeared back toward the camp of women and children.

The moon moved not an inch before I was asleep. There was food in my belly and warm comfort for the first time in over a month. I woke only once, when a fox coughed sharply, and the camp dogs answered with petulant advice.

CHAPTER TWENTY-SEVEN

April 1791

NAKED CHILDREN TAUGHT US THE only sensible language. They were beautiful youngsters, bold in their investigations of me, shy about themselves. With the first dim light of dawn, they ranged before our sleeping forms, studying the strange beings now available for their pleasure. As I opened my eyes, they smiled in chorus and took three steps backward. I shut my eyes and counted silently to ten. This time when I opened my eyes they were four steps closer, and two of the girls giggled in anticipation of a new game. We exchanged our names, and they quickly resolved to teach us the names of every desert treasure within the domain of their seasonal campsite. Only my intellectual limitations prevented the immediate achievement of such an admirable goal. We laughed together at my ludicrous errors at pronouncing their Berber words, and the children demanded sufficient repetitions of each word or phrase until it became acceptable to their ears.

The camp dogs began to accept our smell and gave us a begrudging status in the pack. I noticed that slave and Tuareg children joined together to play chase games and gobble odd bits of food on the run. They taught the janissary captain and the ugly Frank how to ride a stick camel and how to properly ambush Arabs.

During the second day of our hiatus from hunger and fear, four Tuareg women, along with Kitra, erected a tent for us. I leaned against a shadowed rock and watched as they moved—bending, lifting, laughing, as the wind tugged trailing edges of ragged and royal garments. They placed beautifully carved and decorated tamarisk tent pegs into excavated holes and then backfilled with sand. Long poles tied at each quadrant provided a sturdy frame for the red goatskin roof. The women brought armloads of woven reed mats to cover the ground and to provide walls for each side of the tent. An entrance mat was rigged with rope so that it could be raised or lowered.

Ahmed and I moved into our new home before sun blasted the day into lethargy. A broad roof gave pleasant shade, and as the heat became oppressive, we rolled up the side mats to let the wind blow in under the roof. On our first evening in the red tent, Ahmed and I sat and watched the sun slide toward the horizon. Mountains swam in burgundy haze; sand shimmered with a greenish hue.

"Ahmed? Look at how the red tents curve among the rocks. They look like a string of bright jewels sheltered in a secret haven."

"A poet. Now I've got a damn poet on my hands."

We both chuckled and watched the young children straggle into camp. Some of our compatriots were loaded with thorny brushwood for the evening fire; others were surrounded by goats. The near hills turned mauve and then a deep purple, while two women milked nannies, and another stood at the big wooden mortar to ram millet with a heavy pestle. The hollow boom created a comforting cadence to the evening. A tea kettle screamed. Bread came steaming from ashes, and Kitra served our meal.

My life assumed an unconventional pattern of comfort and ease. Food and water appeared without my concern or effort. Children laughed without fear of reprimand. Ahmed fell in love. I observed his decline from haughty commanding officer to blathering idiot, and must admit that some jealousy emerged during the process. At first Kitra served us with equal delight; bits of honey-soaked fruit and savory olives often accompanied our cups of sweet tea. Her smile flowed over us in a warm bath. I began to feel an abiding irritation when I noticed that my portions of food and her doting indulgences paled beside those received by Captain al-Koita.

On our fifth evening, the stars were still faint, and only Venus shone bright on the eastern horizon. Children carried bundles of twigs and thorns and placed them in a pile before our tent. Kitra dropped an ember into the wood, kneeled, and blew gently on the hot coal. Soon she offered a blazing fire for a crowd of females and children and two foreign guests. Three Tuareg women began singing. Children milled about in dust-raising riot until the hypnotic chant settled them into an attentive audience. A teenage boy covered the mortar with a wet goatskin and fluttered trilling rhythms. He nourished the clapping and spontaneous explosions of dancing with a loud emphatic beat, and an old woman spiced the concert with high wailing swoops of soprano solos and led verses in endless permutations. The youngest children fell asleep; mothers picked up the limp forms and drifted away toward their tents. The drum thumped on and on, hypnotically, in minor tones that entered my body as a djinn might steal into that of a negligent Tuareg warrior.

When the ashes of the fire were near cold, I lay on my back with fingers entwined under my head and studied the Milky Way. The distant misty trail teased me with the lure of increasingly remote stars; each far-off speck registered on my eyes like a new vision. I studied very carefully. There! Another faint sparkle emerged for census, drawing me ever further into the domain of Allah, away from sand and wind and rank goat milk. Alphonse whispered into my ear. "Look at the stars, my friend. Tell me what you see? Look carefully."

"I see you, Alphonse. I see you."

The drum stopped. Only night sounds and Kitra speaking softly disturbed the tranquil scene. Ahmed whispered a mélange of languages as she massaged his shoulders and arms and lowered her ear to catch every word. They spoke of a river and kings, of rain that watered large fields of grain. I heard sharp complaints of masters and slaves, and when the words stopped I got up and went into the red tent. Only the complaining fox and chattering owl intruded briefly into my sleep.

When I opened my eyes to the dim light of early dawn, Kitra stood naked before Ahmed's sleeping form. Her lustrous beauty denied the need of sunlight. She and Ahmed were the same shade of deep velvety black. Her sturdy hips and shoulders stood in contrast to her slim waist. As she turned to pick up her robe, Kitra saw me watching and smiled. Her full lips balanced large eyes and a prominent nose. They were calm, harmonious features. Her breasts jiggled in a pear-shaped dance as she slipped the blue cloth over her shoulders. I shut my eyes and quickly opened them, only to find the tent empty of her warmth. The vision and smell of Kitra, however, remained engraved into my mind.

<hr />

The children explained to me that the Tuareg rarely pitched their tents near water holes. Even a stupid Frank must realize that lions used the rare places where water existed as an ambuscade, and that Arabs looked for victims in the same manner. Each morning, long before dawn, I lay on my mat and listened as Ahmed and Kitra joined their quiet snores. Her gentle rumbling stopped when the camp water-carrier began stumbling through the dark. The boy always whispered loud curses and served as camp rooster while loading two donkeys with empty water bags. Kitra left our tent when the boy left the encampment. He returned a short while past dawn, snapping a wooden switch at the trailing animal, sloshing into camp with the water required by our small universe.

Two weeks of idleness spurred Ahmed to remedy my slothful life. He ordered me on the water pilgrimage with a lad of ten. So it was that the lad and I followed a maze of gullies filled with sharp stones and thornbushes to find a spring on the flank of a tall mountain. We studied the area carefully before descending to the tiny oasis, and returned to camp with the sharp heat of early morning sun. The lad complained loudly of the stupid Frank's astonishing inability to move fast enough to make the round trip without leaving children and women to suffer dehydration. After his harangue to one and all about my burdensome behavior, he grabbed some bread and quickly joined an army of child warriors.

I returned to my sleeping mat. One trip was enough. My burden as protector of the dey's resources gave me the mood of an old man. I was almost twenty-three, for goodness' sake. My dignity was certainly depleted with the fact of a ten-year-old child heralding the list of my deficiencies, but there was also the truth of Kitra's inevitable dawn departure that I was reluctant to miss. The glorious vision of a black Venus was, I admit, a growing delight of mine. I don't think that I was actually jealous of my captain's concubine, but there was indeed the pleasure of considering the palpable beauty of her neck and breasts and hip every single morning, for goodness' sake.

Shortly after dawn, nearly four weeks after our arrival, the camp did indeed suffer an invasion. The first indication of trouble was a steady dull roaring sound, followed almost immediately by musket shots. Neither Ahmed nor I were armed, so I quickly scuttled toward a complex of large boulders a few yards from the tent. Too late! As I dove for the security of a small cave, three men on camels fired their weapons into the sky. I stopped and raised my hands in surrender.

Squealing camels and cheering riders filled the camp of red tents with dust and noise.

"Drop your hands, oh ugly Frank."

My mind scrambled to understand the command. I looked carefully at my conquerors and became even more disorientated. Two of the warriors were Negro, yet decked out in Tuareg regalia, complete with the blue veil showing fierce brown eyes. The third warrior was a beautiful smiling woman. Dakadeit!

"Put down your hands," repeated Dakadeit.

I slowly lowered my hands. "What is this?"

"This is the army that will do your bidding. The army that will destroy the Shamba pigs!"

Ahmed appeared at my side to ask, "Where is Tashmani?"

"I am here."

We both turned, and there was Tashmani on a handsome camel, his deep-blue robe and veil a vivid contrast with the white dromedary. Our friend carried a long matchlock rifle in his right hand, an inward curving sword at the belt, and a sheathed dagger on his left arm. I was astonished by his magnificent bearing. A confused jumble of fear and trust rumbled in my stomach. His camel knelt and Tashmani dismounted. A slave led the camel away, and Tashmani signalled for Ahmed, Dakadeit, and me to follow him.

Kitra served us sweet tea, and I noted that Dakadeit received tea first, followed by Ahmed. We consumed two cups of the syrupy beverage before Kitra left us and Tashmani began to speak.

"My friends, you must understand that our army is a gift of Dakadeit." Tashmani paused and nodded toward the beautiful woman. She gave not the slightest response to his declaration, and he continued. "My sultan, Agg-Abba, threatened to throw my offering of gold coins into the sand and me into the fire, but Dakadeit intervened and saved our mission."

I was certain that both Ahmed and I appeared like gaping fools to our Tuareg mentors.

"Let me explain." Dakadeit spoke slowly and expressed herself with a flute-clear voice and graphic gestures of her hands. "With the Tuareg, it is always the women who determine the order of power. A man takes a woman's name and her status upon marriage. A man moves into the woman's home and listens carefully to her wisdom." She looked directly at me, and the sun was diminished by her smile. "A woman chooses her husband. She decides when the marriage should begin and when it is finished. For instance, with this new moon, Taher is no longer my husband, and neither Taher nor his son may share my tent."

Tashmani waited until the silence was complete and continued the explanation. "A new mullah is among the Tuareg, and you will meet him soon enough." Tashmani's eyes gave special meaning to that future meeting. "Imam Bu Guttaya is Allah's voice, his very breath, and he will explain the Koran for us. Iman Bu Guttaya says that Mohammed admonishes all women to wear the veil and to remain hidden from all men. Bu Guttaya preaches that men must dominate women in every moment of life. It is his word that women must be obedient to their masters in the same manner that slaves must be obedient to their masters. Further, he claims that it is blasphemy to act against the word of Allah, to change one word or one intention of the Koran. So speaks Imam Bu Guttaya."

Dakadeit could contain herself no longer. "My mother is blood descendant of Queen Tin Hanan. It was our beloved queen who told her daughter and her daughter's daughter, on and on through the ancient times, to maintain the Tuareg code, and now my mother serves as queen. It is her duty, and eventually will be mine, to carry on with our traditions, but this interloper, this Devil incarnate, would change the natural order of Tuareg life. This mullah strives for the power of Satan, and most assuredly, Bu Guttaya uses the sultan, my father, as his witless fool. I will fight them both by helping you."

Ahmed stared at Dakadeit to listen and study her every gesture.

When the silence became heavy, he turned to Tashmani. "Who are these troops? What is their training?"

"They are free slaves. Most have served the Tuareg as farmers at an oasis, or as leaders of caravans trading salt for grain. They are all owners of property and are held in some small esteem by their Tuareg masters. They are free of slavery but not yet free in spirit. These farmers and merchants who have enlisted in our army want to prove themselves worthy of the blue veil." Tashmani gestured expansively to include the entire militia that had followed him to the camp in the desert.

"You both must understand that these black men have never seen battle. Maybe they have defended land and tents against Arab attacks, yes, but they have never been warriors. They are free slaves who want to be Tuareg. They are black slaves who lust for the blue veil and their freedom."

Tashmani hesitated, but no one intruded with divergent thoughts. "It is well known that for the Arabs a slave is less than a goat and that slaves must serve their Arab masters with invisible silence. Slaves are nothing to the Arabs. Even in death there are no rewards for slaves. Only pain in this life and fire in the next."

Ahmed held up his hand. "Slower, my friend. We are treading on dangerous ground."

"Listen carefully to us," said Dakadeit, "and you will understand our words."

Ahmed nodded and she continued.

"In the past, slaves among the Tuareg could be seen as men. Some few achieved freedom, and all accepted the Prophet as their guide in life and savior in death." The Tuareg princess spread her hands in a palms-up gesture. "This imam, Bu Guttaya, will destroy our traditions and offer the Shamba our land."

Ahmed nodded in slow repetition. "Let me see if I understand our situation."

"Continue," Dakadeit said.

"We now have in our service a group of farmers and merchants acting as Yeni—that is, novice warriors."

"Yes," said Tashmani.

Ahmed smiled strangely. "Well, the likes of them won a war against the British, so maybe we can do the same against the Shamba." He got up from the sand. "I think that I will go and review the troops. Maybe, just maybe, we have the same core of courage that General Washington found in his farmers and merchants."

The two military minds departed, and Kitra appeared with more tea, honey-covered dates, and large ripe olives. She fussed about, serving us, removing pits from the serving tray, until Dakadeit dismissed her. A large overhanging rock provided bountiful shade for us, and tendrils of gently moving air caressed us in friendly embrace. The sweet tea and dates complemented the astringent olives and Dakadeit's beauty. With each sip of tea, I covertly devoured her face and breasts. My tentative glances were met by her direct stare, thereby disabling any ability that I had to speak.

With a smile she said, "Are you rich in your country?"

If Dakadeit wanted me rich, so be it. "In the mighty kingdom of Algiers, I have many responsibilities with the all-powerful dey. Both slaves and gold I hold in abundance—so, yes, I am wealthy." I sat with a more erect posture and stared directly into her eyes. "Understand also that Ahmed is a captain of the janissary, a vanquisher of both Frank and Arab. If Allah wills, he will one day command many armies for the dey of Algiers and therefore will rank with the highest Turks and have great wealth."

Dakadeit gave me a brief nod. "All well and good, Ja Mai Ne, but for now, you are the olive pit and I am the meat. We are one, and Allah will protect us from those who would eat me and spit you into the dust."

She spoke slowly, and I understood every word. Even the

invention of my name I understood. Ja Mai Ne. Yes, much more dignified than the childish Jamie. Ja Mai Ne. It had the ring of Tuareg manliness about it. I nodded vigorously in support of her brilliant mind.

"You and I have zealous enemies," she said. "With Allah's help, they can be defeated, therefore our thoughts must always be strong." Her smile churned my stomach. "You must understand the power and possible flaws of my enemies, because my opponents are also yours."

"Tell me."

"We have two independent enemies at our throat. There is this Imam Bu Guttaya, who would turn the Tuareg into Arabs." Dakadeit inched closer and smiled at me with her teeth showing sharp two sharp incissors of impressive length. "My father, the sultan Agg-Abba is the Iman's partner in this attack upon the Tuareg people. Together the two fools believe that wisdom leaks into a man's brain through a perpetually erect cock."

I nodded in agreement to her assertion, but turned from her sharp teeth.

"It bears repeating, Ja Mai Ne, but you must fully understand that my father rules only through my mother, and that when she dies, I am queen and must choose a new sultan. I will not make the mistake of my mother. My next husband will serve only me and the Tuareg."

"I am very clear on the facts of royal succession for the Tuareg," I said.

"Good, for you must also know that my father, in collusion with the imam, would change that tradition. These two servants of the Devil would demolish the Tuareg by destroying me."

It was some time before I noticed that she was no longer spking. I looked at her eyes and then quickly up into the tamarisk tree that provided us with delicately laced shade. A dead leaf dangled from a spider's web, unable to fall. What would Hassan Bashaw have me do? What profit would Baccri have me find? How could she look at me without pause, turning each of my arms and legs into prison gruel?

"All my resources will be spent in your protection, my lady."

"Finally, you have a tongue."

"Yes, my lady."

"I will tell you of my aspirations, and you will show me how a Frank can anticipate the plan of Allah. Speak at your turn, and we will begin with our negotiations."

My mind was still full of fluff, so I nodded to my princess.

"The dey's gold, Ja Mai Ne, was stolen by the Shamba." She waited until my expression revealed comprehension of her assertion. "The djinni have whispered into my ears. They tell me of gold promised by the king of the Bambara to your mighty dey of Algiers, and how the gold and slaves and camels have gone poof! Into the sands."

"Do the djinni whisper directions for the discovery of the dey's gold?"

"Our land of mountains and desert is truly magical, my ugly friend. The djinni are everywhere, and it should not surprise a wise Frank that both my sultan Agg-Abba and the chief of Ghardia Shamba sold many slaves and many camels in Beni-Abbes this past season. Together, my lord—Tuareg and Shamba together, buying slaves of one and selling camel to the other. Is that not a magical event?"

"The dey of Algiers might better consider the occasion as traitorous of both his vassals, my lady."

"Even more mysterious, at least to my simple mind: the Shamba have stopped stealing from the Tuareg. Truly. Allah and his angels are now one with the Tuareg."

As Dakadeit bent at the waist to retrieve her cup, I studied her breasts. They were carelessly revealed, nearly to the nipple; each was a soft melon. The sight caused saliva to well in my mouth and a strange tingle to deaden my fingers. She straightened, ordered her robe, sipped tea in thoughtful meditation, and continued. "The gold and slaves stolen from the King of the Bambara is in Ghardia and held by Sheik El Monem."

"Ahh," I said, "that name is familiar to me as a prince who mourns the death of his father, Sheik Brahim."

She smiled in sympathy for the grieving son.

"I know the palace," I said. "It is on a hill in the center of the city and guarded by the very army that attacked our caravan at Bir Hassi-Fahl. It was the Shamba from Ghardia who killed Salim Shushufi and Abu'l-Qasim."

"I spit on the Shamba! I spit on all Arabs." Dakadeit drew moisture into her mouth and spit into the sand. "We must visit the viper in his den and kill them all." She took a few moments to compose herself before completing our negotiations. "The gold is your problem. You, Ahmed, and Tashmani must use my troops and your great ingenuity to retrieve the gold, and when you count the bags of gold coin, eight will go on to your master, while two bags will stay with me."

"One after each batch of eight bags are counted," I automatically responded.

"Two." Her black eyes ended the debate. "Two bags in ten, and I will provide escort for you and the janissary from the ashes of Ghardia all the way to Laghouat."

"Agreed," I said.

"Understand, Ja Mai Ne, that our goal is not merely to slap a Shamba prince in the face, and then for you to disappear back to your nest in Algiers. No, no, no. We are not planning some pointless manly feat of prowess. We are planning a war of extermination against those who would destroy the Tuareg life. I need gold to fight the imam, and gold to fight Agg-Abba." Dakadeit paused; her body shuddered as she smiled at me. "I also need you, my lord."

"Me?"

"You are of the true faith?"

"Yes," I lowered my eyes.

She studied my features for an interminable time. "It doesn't matter," she said. "Tonight we shall have an ahal, and it will please me if you attend."

"Certainly I will attend the ahal, but give me some description of the activity."

"The young people, Ja Mai Ne, the unmarried men and women, meet to sing and talk. An ahal is a very pleasant affair, so do not concern yourself with any false apprehension. There will be no demands made upon you for making long speeches." Dakadeit stood over me. "I must leave. When you see flames that reach toward the stars, come to the ahal." She turned and walked away from me.

For a short interval after our conversation, I wandered a barren stretch of moor to watch Ahmed and Tashmani work with their merchants and farmers. The dust and shouting roiled my mind, so I returned to my tent until the cool evening breeze stirred me. Kitra served the meal, and I listened quietly as Ahmed and Tashmani debated the appropriate strategy for transforming slaves into Tuareg warriors. The stars marked familiar patterns before I was able to ask Tashmani the meaning of ahal.

He asked a question in return. "Who invited you to an ahal?"

"Dakadeit," I answered.

"Ahhh." His eyes grew large. "So you are the one." He adjusted his veil a bit more securely. "You must wear clean robes and appear as a handsome warrior."

His long pause before continuing made it clear that there were insurmountable obstacles in his list of assigned tasks. "Well, a clean robe, in any event." Tashmani moved closer to speak in a husky whisper. "You must go to the big fire"—he pointed toward the flames that were now showing through a grove of tamarisk trees—"and sit.

You must watch the women as they watch you."

"Tashmani," I asked, "will you go with me?"

"No, no, my friend. It is not proper for me to attend an ahal. Remember, I have but one name, and I am therefore a coward. When my cousins died gloriously in battle, I remained unscarred. When my fellow Tuareg warriors sought heaven in combat with the Shamba, I hid in the caves of our ancients. No woman would invite me to an ahal, for they all know of my disgrace. You must go alone, as Dakadeit wishes."

In my mind Tashmani was a handsome and strong and ferocious warrior, but not a person with whom to confide secrets or display signs of weak character. In most matters, and certainly in his assessment of my duties at the ahal, he must be trusted as a worthy advisor.

———◆———

By my quick count, there were Forty Tuareg gathered around the fire. I took the first spot in the circle that was vacant and carefully observed the sights. Blue cloaks and black shadows swirled among the yellow sparks as they talked and drank tea served by slave girls. Firelight and moonlight reflected from silver bangles of each woman. Red henna flashed through hair of the women and drew the eye to red dabs on cheeks, arms, and nails.

I found the entire setting very peculiar. During the past month our small outpost of red tents rendered only a few women and children. Dogs and goats and camels wandered about the camp in great profusion, but men were rare and ephemeral. As I sat before the bonfire, twenty or young warriors strutted about with virile poses and menacing expressions. They were all strangers to me. An equal number of beautiful women had materialized from the ether, and other than Dakedeit, they were also strangers to my eye. The teacups disappeared, and a young woman with long hair and long arms began to sing and play a one-stringed guitar. The forty men and women of the circle matched her beat with clapping hands, while in the shadows a boy drummed on his stretched goatskin.

My eyes followed each scene as they shifted effortlessly from one to the next. The initial maiden twirled and sang and played until everyone joined in the frolicsome spirit she created. Then another lass followed, and yet another, until in turn a young man sought the fire-warmed stage. He used a high falsetto voice to create a sense of urgent attention. The audience joined in a fast, vibrant exchange of verses, with the chorus beginning before the young man ended his portion of the song. A swirling mass of people started to move about the fire, singing, sitting, and staring at neighbors with unabashed interest. I made a brief effort to join the ritual parade of beautiful women and handsome men; but quickly felt inadequate to emulating their vivid courtship manners, and dropped to sit at the edge of the circle.

The evening stars grew brighter and the fire less vigorous. Partners joined under cloaks to whisper teasing jests. My ear slowly tuned to the words, and I deciphered a common theme from the songs: men sang in praise of lovely women, and women described visions of the ideal warrior. Both characterized Arabs as cowardly dogs—pigs who were pretenders of the true religion, hypocrites who truly lacked Allah's guidance.

As the fire smoldered, with red eyes blinking, Dakadeit moved to sit beside me and pulled my cloak over her shoulders. Without speaking, she moved closer to me. I immersed myself in the perfume of her sweat.

A man and woman stopped singing, and for a long while there was only the crackling of ethal branches. I was sitting beside a beautiful woman—and a princess, for Allah's sake! Alphonse had always moved with a patient understanding of my anxiety. His gentle hints moved slowly to grand adventures. Every step we had taken onto unfamiliar ground was cushioned by his concern for me.

My queen stood and glided to the center of the ring to sing in a fine contralto. She claimed high status for me in the land of Franks, and the beat of drum and hands increased. Dakadeit's voice, now a reedy soprano, elevated me to an exalted position with the all-powerful dey of Algiers—his confidante and advisor, in fact. With ever faster tempo, Dakadeit shifted to a wild higher pitch to describe my heroics in battle against the Shamba. She described a battle that destroyed the enemy and created a wandering desert wind destined to perpetually whisper the name of a great warrior: "Ja Mai Ne! Ja Mai Ne!"

The western mountains swallowed and gulped the moon in one bite. Embers barely whispered from the fire. We were the last couple, and Dakadeit took my arm. "Let us go," she said.

Her tent was no different from mine. As we lifted the reed mat and entered, she pulled away from under my cloak and in quick succession stripped off her heavy burnoose and inner robes. She stood naked in the cold shadows while I gaped like a frozen statue.

"Have you never been with a woman before, Ja Mai Ne?"

"No."

"Are you an Arab who loves boys?"

"No."

She stepped closer until her breasts touched my chest, and I reached to caress her. "You must be mad," she whispered. "A zealot, a dervish flying through life to seek answers before questions are asked." She undid my belt and dropped my robes. "It is unnatural for a man of your age to ignore women."

I took each soft breast in my hands.

"Tonight you shall lose your way to heaven." She kissed my chest and then looked up at me for the first time. "Allah gives men a small taste of happiness before death." I bent to her neck, kissed behind her ear, and we tripped in an awkward tangle of limbs onto her mat.

CHAPTER TWENTY-EIGHT

April 1791

A TARNISHED LIGHT LEAKED INTO the tent. I could hear the water boy cursing his donkey, bidding him to hold still while he secured the goat skins. A pack of jackals complained in the distance, and Dakadeit's warm body pulled me closer. My left hand moved in feathery strokes over her breasts and stomach, and my erect penis squirmed against her lower back. Dakadeit shuddered in pleasurable recollection of my prowess, and turned to embrace me.

"*Metulem, metulem,*" came a cheery greeting from the shadows.

"What in hell?" I rose up on my elbows to chase away the phantom. On his haunches at the entrance of the tent sat a Tuareg. I could only see his outline.

"How is your father?" the shadow crowed.

"My father be damned! What in hell are you doing here?" I shouted.

Dakadeit sat up in the chill dawn, and with calm, measured tones said, "Honored imam, please excuse the Frank for his rudeness. Metulem, metulem."

The holy man moved closer to our bed. I could see that his veil fit loosely, revealing both nose and mouth.

"Ah! Dakadeit! How is your mother?"

"She is well, Imam Bu Guttaya, as are my aunt and younger sister. I must say, however, that I am not pleased with your early morning visit."

"Rude or not, Dakadeit, this particular Frank is an envoy from the dey of Algiers, and as I can see, currently is ensconsed in your bed." He pulled the blue veil below his chin. "Your father directed me to determine if this Frank, this very ugly Frank, is likely your next husband."

Dakadeit clapped her hands twice, and Kitra appeared as the echo sounded. "Bring tea for our esteemed guest." Naked as a Greek goddess, she stood, crossed the room, and picked up her robe from the floor. Her breasts pointed at the imam as she dressed. "Tell me, Imam, what have you and my father cooked-up as the purpose of your visit?"

"There are many reasons, noble lady, but the favor of your company is Allah's sufficient reward for my devotion. No excuse is needed for my presence, for only Allah decides, and we mortals must respond to his path." The mullah pressed his hands together and bowed in the direction of Mecca. "I do, however, admit to simple curiosity concerning this representative of our mighty dey of Algiers. Judging from the color of his complexion, I assume that this stranger among us is not a janissary officer."

He stared intently at me. As the first sharp streaks of light filtered through the wall mats, I could focus my indignation on his ugly face. I adjusted the blanket around my waist, leaned forward, and prepared for a siege.

The imam ignored me after a brief exchange of severe expressions, then returned his attention to Dakadeit. "Does he believe in Allah as the One God, and Mohammed as the last Prophet?"

My patience was terminated! I stood, dropped the blanket, posed briefly, and paraded past the imam to gather my robe. The scabs from my circumcision had long since healed, and my limp penis flopped in mute evidence of dedication to the true faith.

Dakadeit waited until I was dressed and sipping my tea before she answered our visitor. "Both Ja Mai Ne and Ahmed al-Koita, the janissary Bolukbasi, will join you in prayer and discussion if you wish. I believe that you will find them excellent scholars of the Koran—much more aware of Allah's message than our distracted Tuareg men."

"Ahh," said the iman, "I am encouraged by your thoughtful permission to promote my mission to God." He bowed with three short nods of his head and shoulders. "I look forward to teaching the young Frank the subtle glory of the True Word."

Dakadeit moved to the open door, turned to smile briefly in my direction, and left me alone with Iman Bu Guttaya.

◆

The sun evaporated all early morning vapors. The mullah was a Tuareg, in his outward attire, in any event. He wore the blue robes and veil, but held the veil in Arab fashion to reveal the black skin, thick lips, and broad nose of the south. His face mimicked that of the male gorilla in the dey of Algiers' zoo. It seemed to me that he came from the region of Goa or possibly even Timbouctou.

"A Niger River Nigger," my father would say to me and Will. "They're best sold to the southern plantations," Captain Cathcart always advised us. "Put the bastards where there's hot weather and an owner not afraid to use his whip." Alex Melman usually added a note of his own for us to consider. "Those Niger River tribes," he'd tell us, "they're as brutal as any white-man's tribe. To my certain knowledge, they just as comfortable using a whip on reticent slaves as some ignorant white man on a Georgia rice plantation."

I was fascinated by the chain of prayer beads around his neck, in combination with an extensive collection of amulets. I'd already noticed that every Tuareg wore prayer beads and amulets of some sort or other. "To fend-off evil spirits, you know," Tashmani told me. But Iman Bu Guttaya revealed a collection of amulets of such a vast array, that he seemed more typical of a successful merchant then a Tuareg cleric. So it was that my eyes revealed one set of images for my mind to digest, but my stomach shouted a warning of another sort all-together; for even though it was likely that Imam Guttaya sold amulets now and again, he was most emphatically a devoted servant of Allah. I gathered my wits for the coming battle and smiled at my new teacher of the True Faith.

◆

We sat quietly, sipping tea and listening to the diverse sounds of women talking and working. In far distance there were shouts from the excited men of Ahmed's army as they prepared reluctant camels for their day of training. In a practiced move, the mullah flashed a tiny carefully sharpened stone axe before my eyes. I knew it to be a good-luck charm of the highest order.

"This is for you, effendi," said the imam. "Please accept a gift that will protect you for the duration of your visit among the Tuareg people."

'I've been told by a person of high authority, good sir, that the angels throw these little amulets down from heaven to warn blasphemers and perjurers that they must reform."

"Ahh, Princess Dakadeit, of course."

"This wise person of my acquaintance, warned me that the little ax cuts both ways: good fortune to the faithful, misadventure to the doubter."

"It is so, as Dakadeit can certainly attest; luck comes only to the true believers." The imam turned his eyes to me and shook the axe under my chin. "Take it as a gift fro me, my true believer."

The odd little toy felt light in my hand. The edges were rough-hewn and could serve no practical purpose; Indian arrowheads revealed finer workmanship and clearer intention. I was now obligated to reciprocate with a gift in return for this useless trinket.

"Imam Bu Guttaya," I said, "as the the dey of Algiers' representative, I would like to thank you for such an auspicious gift, and in like manner, to give you these five masoons to promote your holy work."

The imam took the brass coins, turned them over in his hand, and returned them to me. "I could not accept this gift," he said.

I was unsettled by his refusal, but good sense prevailed and I simply dug again into my robe to extract a small silver coin. "My apologies, Imam; I inadvertently presented the wrong gift. Please accept this silver coin."

Again he carefully examined the coin, scratched it lightly with a nail that he pulled from a bag hanging at his neck, and the coin disappeared. Without further reference to the exchange of gifts, the holy merchant broached a new subject: "It is clear from the evidence I have collected, that you are now the husband of Princess Dakadeit."

I could not restrain my small smile. "Yes, Imam, she is the consummated wife of the noble Frank, Ja Mai Ne."

The imam's eyes were yellow where most Tuareg people had white. His impassive gaze showed neither surprise nor pleasure at the announcement, and he suddenly stood in front of me, and I quickly followed his act. My mind felt stuffed with straw. My stomach moved up and down in mindless repetition, in the same fashion as a toy called the bandelure.

After a few dozen paces, the iman stopped, turned me, and said, "Come, Ja Mai Ne. It gives me no pleasure to watch slaves playing at warrior games; nor you, I presume." Imam Bu Guttaya gave no pause for an answer. "My joy is with Allah, the One God, always present, always guiding the righteous in triumph over evil. Is that not so, my friend from the land of Franks? Is it not so?"

I murmured assent. This desert mullah had the same smell as the janissary imam of Algiers. Both had fetid breath and the greasy smell of unmitigated arrogance. Both held Allah as an omnipotent, and of course they were the all-knowing extension of of Allah—a very neat and useful equation. The janissary chaplain had given me a mnemonic device that rapidly advanced my reputation as a scholar of the Koran. Once imprinted with the orderly details of the holy book, I found that even Miciah was impressed with my conversion to the true religion. Bu Guttaya seemed ready for a combat of faith, and I expected no mercy from him. I was also willing to tell him exactly what he wanted to hear.

"Let us move into the shade and away from children and goats." Imam Bu Guttaya led the way for a short walk until we settled into the sand and only an arm's length from the other. He stared directly into my eyes. This was a game Will Melman and I had practiced for hours, and the imam soon saved face by asking his first question: "Do you believe that Allah is the One God and Mohammed is the last and greatest prophet?"

"Yes," I answered.

"Is the Koran the literal work of Allah?"

This was an easy question. Both this imam and the janissary chaplain were certainly literalists for the revealed word and merely wanted the standard references and the acceptable names to support their belief.

"Honored imam," I began, "the great al-Ashari would make no compromise with the words of the Koran. His guidance is sufficient for me. The Koran says exactly what it means. God holds all knowledge, will, power, sight—all as real and distinct qualities. He sits upon a throne and judges the merits of every living person." I hesitated, confident that by substituting Thomas Aquinas for al-Ashari my answer would have pleased a good Catholic in the same fashion.

Bu Guttaya waved me to silence. "A safe answer, my foreign friend. Now, for my comfort and yours, I would hear your confession of faith."

With the precise motion of long practice, the imam followed my lead as I knelt to the sand and prepared for prayer. I purified my hands and face in the sand. Standing, facing toward holy Mecca, we bowed from the waist, repeating, "There is no God but the One God, and Mohammed is his prophet." Continuing with the declaration of faith, we lay prostrate and touched our heads on the sand. After completing a silent prayer, we again sat facing each other, and my inquisition continued.

"Describe your silent prayers to me, and when you finish I will tell you how it is with me. You may begin."

"At the beginning I asked God to find me, to be present with me. As I lay in the sand, the images of Jesus and Mohammed whirled around one another, like the vortex of a dust storm, replacing my invocation with a blur of mystery. I became frightened, until those two angels restrained their fury and stopped. Then, to my surprise, Jesus and Mohammed turned to face each other with postures of supplication and prayer." I paused until the iman twitched a single finger. "Eventually the angel, Jesus, flew away, and then there was only Mohammed."

Bu Guttaya's face softened. He didn't smile. It was as if his features were made of wax and had been left a bit too long in the sun. We sat studying the other, and Kitra unobtrusively poured tea and left small cups spewing fragrant mint odors at our side.

"I live to attain union with God," began the imam. "I now accept you as a true believer and as a fellow seeker of enlightenment." He stared directly at my forehead and continued with his confession of faith. "You will remember from the Koran, Ja Mai Ne, that the One God is always near; that his presence is everywhere. Think back on Mohammed's night journey when he communed with God, face-to-face."

Bu Guttaya's eyes remained locked upon mine. At first I could distinguish the large black pupil from his brown iris. At the next blink, the comforting noises of people and animals disappeared. Two sparks of light drew life from the silence of his words, and I listened to my teacher with unreserved concentration.

"I also have met God," said the imam. "Face-to-face, and once, we talked, as did the Prophet. He gave my life a loving emptiness that can only be expressed through my subjugation to his word. The Prophet and I have both seen God's face; therefore, we are one—an extension of the same mind and the same body, the Prophet and I."

Bu Guttaya frowned at me as if I had just asked an impertinent question. "Of course I must live the humble and austere life of Mohammed! Of course I must diminish my attainments; my miracles of sickness to health are nothing, as were his. The word of God is everything; the word of God is nothing. Such is the message given to Mohammed and to me."

"Amen," I said.

He sat straight, eyes peering into the nothing of his dreams. He placed his fingers lightly on the knee joint opposite from the hand, thereby crossing his left arm over the right, and began again. "Kill them wheresoever ye find them, and expel them from out of which they have expelled you."

I recognized the lines from the Koran. They had been cause for uneasiness when I first repeated them aloud for the janissary chaplain. Now, watching the imam chant the admonition, first with his head straight, then with left ear on his left shoulder followed by right ear on his right shoulder in unchanging sequence or modulation of voice, I became frightened that my feigned belief was turning to mush. That my scholarly repetition of Koranic scripture was slowly drifting toward a certain trust of the True Word.

His trance oozed into my mind. Minutes passed. I watched him move and speak, and as one metal bell vibrating from a well-struck blow can cause another bell, sitting passively and untouched, to begin an answering note, so I responded. First with mimicked movements, then, with lips barely moving. "Kill them wheresoever ye find them . . ."

Sunlight invaded our refuge under the rock shelf. My vision of this world returned. Imam Bu Guttaya emerged like a giant toad hungry for a fresh morsel. I steadied myself and returned his stare.

"It is time for the noon prayer," he said. We both began the cleansing process, wiping sand on our hands and feet, and stood facing Mecca. I recognized a change in my disposition. In the past all prayers had been wooden rituals: endured and repeated. "There is no God but the One God, and Mohammed is His Prophet" was baggage to be released while perpetuating the necessary facade. They were alien words that frequently prompted resentment and lengthy silent rebuttal. Now, bowing from the waist in tandem with the imam, I thoughtlessly repeated the Koranic message: "God misleadeth whom He will, and guideth whom He will" Over and over—prostrate, head touching the hot sand I said, "No vision taketh in Him, but He taketh in all vision. He is the subtle, the all-informed. He has created man, in order that they worship Him."

Over and over and over.

We ended our prayer with "There is no God but the One God, and Mohammed is His Prophet," I swallowed freely. I straightened my posture and sat, erect, to face my imam.

"The people of Mecca were Mohammed's enemies," said Bu Guttaya. "Idols and sloth and sin they loved more than the One God. These swine caused the Prophet to leave the holy city, while the people of Yathrib accepted the family and teaching of the Prophet.

From Yathrib came the power of Allah. From Mecca came the power of the Devil!"

"This I understand, my teacher."

"Good, then you know that in the battle that followed, good conquered evil, and the wealthy idolaters of Mecca were crushed, and Allah commanded the true believers to turn their prayers from Jerusalem to the Koaba—the holy black rock of Mecca."

"What was next, my teacher?"

"The forces of good sharpened their swords on the necks of those who would not accept the word. Many Jews, Christians, and heathens of every stripe crumpled to the onslaught of Mohammed's army. Our True Believers gave testimony to Allah from beyond the desert, and then the Prophet died."

I could feel tears course down the crease of my nose. "Tell me, my teacher, who took the Prophet's place? Who became the second caliph?"

Bu Guttaya's visage ground itself inward in a convulsion of hatred. His eyes disappeared into their sockets as a turtle's head escapes danger, while his beard expanded in a brittle thicket of thorns. "A dog of Mecca, Abu Bakr, with lies and duplicitous actions, stole the title of Prophet."

"How could such deceit survive, my teacher?"

"The Koran tells the truth, Ja Mai Ne. The Koran explicitly demands that leadership of the faithful belongs to the family of the Prophet. But Abu Bakr was not of the holy family, and when death took Abu Bakr, the Sunni pigs heaped Umar, and after him, Uthman, onto the groaning backs of the faithful."

"Yes, my teacher."

He droned on and on with references to Ali ibn Abi Talib and cousins and a son-in-law and three caliphs, but nothing registered on my memory tree until I heard an extended silence and said, "I understand, my teacher."

"Ali and the line of his descendants are called imams because they bear Allah's divine wisdom and guidance. The rule of law, the rule of wisdom, belongs to the imam of this here and now. Listen well, true believer, because I am the imam of this age."

We studied each other as the shadows dimmed, and the sharp hills to the west turned, in succession, to orange, mauve and deep purple. I dimly remembered the motion of afternoon prayer, and now, at sunset, the routine of supplication was a comfort that gave further credit to Bu Guttaya's message.

His voice was a whisper into my ear. "Allah spoke to me in a chorus of sounds. Each bright tone washed over me as an essence of truth. He said that I must lead a war against unbelievers until all opposition has ceased. Now, Ja Mai Ne, I look to you as my seventh disciple to aid me in this jihad, this holy war against the Devil's forces."

Dark shadows swarmed over us, and for the first time that day I began to feel weary. The soft curve of Dakadeit's breast flashed in brief memory. I was hungry, and my bladder pressed for attention.

"What service can I render to you? I am a Frank bound to Dey Muhammad Bashaw of Algiers."

"The Tuareg are like those from Mecca of old. They express the words of Allah for their temporal benefit. They twist meanings to suit their idiotic traditions. Allah demands an immediate end to their subversions of his perfect design. Women must always humble themselves to men. They must be chaste and not tempt men in their natural urges. The Koran names veil and harem as mandatory for women, and all are compelled to follow this direct word from God. I am his messenger and must enforce his will."

"I understand, my teacher."

"You as my disciple, Ja Mai Ne, and I ask of you: will prove your loyalty to me and your faith in Allah by killing Dakadeit. She is a witch who tempts every man and subverts the true meaning of the

Koran. She must die, and you are the chosen spear of Allah."

I walked away from the imam and his tedious day. It had been a long day, and well spent, for now my understanding of the participants in the looming battle was clear. My wife was my only chance for survival in this remote pile of stone and sand. Bu Guttaya would drive a spear into my chest with not a blink of his eye, for he had a warrant from Allah to kill all who would interfere with the spread of his word. Guttaya's word, of course.

The evening meal was spilling an attractive odor over the sand and pulling me through the long shadows toward my red tent. Tashmani and Ahmed would have tales to tell about their newly fledged warriors, and possibly Dakadeit would appear to share her perfume with me. A long day finished and a full night of promise just beginning.

CHAPTER TWENTY-NINE

April 1791

A TINY OWL CELEBRATED THE capture of another scorpion with twittered chirps. I tossed about on my sleeping mat, moving through the nether world of dreams with fitful lurches of wakefulness. I did not hear Dakadeit enter our tent. Her soft warmth slowed my restless surges, and I moved closer to receive her gentle strokes to my back and shoulders.

"Are you one of his seven assassins, my lover?"

"No," I muttered, and then added, "He does not know what I will do."

"He knows a great deal, but not everything." My wife whispered into my ear. "I have my family and the spirit of Queen Tin Hanan to speak for me. What do you have, Ja Mai Ne? Can a brave Frank protect himself from an evil witch? Bu Guttaya is indeed the evil witch, and he will destroy you. He has the ability to destroy you, but not me."

The night air grew hotter. Dakadeit's whisper was unrelenting as she moved her hands to the small of my back, then down over my buttocks and thighs. I rolled over to press my nose on hers, to kiss her eyes, and explain that I held no fear of witches or sellers of amulets, but my words melted in a maze of slippery arms and gentle moans. A violent discharge pulsed through me into Dakadeit, and we lay silent in our sweet smell. Even as I made to relieve her of my weight, she tightened the grip of her legs about my waist and began again to move in gentle rippling movements of her hips. I held myself above Dakadeit, watching her squirm in delicious contortions, and restrained myself from impetuous behavior. My joy evolved from her pleasure as we moved to her rhythm and studied the other until she exploded in a flailing tangle of arms and legs and kisses. We indulged the other with slippery reminders of pleasure until the tiny owl announced dawn.

"They want to be Tuareg—not like Tuareg, but the true-blue, authentic entity." Ahmed looked into the crackling flames of ethal branches. "They want to stab Arabs with lances and hack off arms and ride their camels across the sand."

"What do you want, Ahmed al-Koita?"

"I want an army, not forty dead heroes. As it stands of this moment, they are nothing but bloody imbeciles for me." He flicked a pebble with his thumb into the fire, and a tiny explosion of sparks erupted into the night sky.

"These sellers of salt, these date farmers—they want to walk as if they owned the earth, to melt strangers with a stare. How many years, for I don't know how many generations, these black slaves have they served the noble Tuareg. During that eternity, they have felt shame for looking at the sand when listening to a Tuareg speak." Ahmed pointed his finger at me and shouted, "Now, when I say to them: 'you must fight like the Turks, not the Tuareg,' they shake their heads at my stupidity."

My friend and commander shook his head in sympathy with his charges. "Do you have any suggestions, Je Mai Ne?"

"None."

"These black slaves are ready to die for me, Jamie. Ha! They are more than ready to die—they relish the idea. Think, my friend, what I am offering to them if they die in battle wearing blue robes."

"What?"

"Allah will summon them to heaven as Tuareg."

I noticed more than sadness in Ahmed's voice. There was the tension of an angry officer of the janissary apparent. "Any advice from Tasmani on the topic?"

"He is silent on all matters in this training of black slaves to serve as warriors dressed in Tuareg regalia." Ahmed turned his head aslant, as if listening to a singing thrush. "Now that you mention my aide in this adventure, I note that he never offers advice to me or to the slaves. He doesn't seem vindictive toward them, but simply acts as an interested observer of their progress in achieving some small degree of military skill."

"Are you concerned in any way about Tashmani's lack of commitment to your venture?"

"No! Not for an instant. He is a loyal servant to me and to Dakadeit, and I have no concern at all when we finally go into battle."

"Well, these recruits of yours are slaves," I offered. "I mean to say that they are free men only in a very restricted fashion. The Tuareg toss them a crumb or two, but they can't squat in the sand without permission from someone wearing a blue veil. I would think that dying in battle would get Allah's attention, and in heaven they can squat anywhere they want."

"You're still an idiot, my friend." He gave me his older-brother smile. "You don't know anything about these troopers or about the deserts of Africa."

We were both quiet for a bit and then he continued. "It's all a joke in my mind, and my troopers have no sense of humor. They can't appreciate the absurdity of the situation and laugh at themselves, and they certainly can't laugh at me."

"I doubt that Tashmani has your view of humor, or farce, for that matter."

"Does no one appreciate my delimma? Are there no allies for me in serving the dey of Algiers? Where can I find a sympathetic Christian, rational Moor or cleaver Jew in this world of sand and wind?"

"Ahh, now the true notes of self-pity sound resplendent into my ears."

"Infidel pig-eater—that's exactly what you Christian slavers want all blacks to believe. You want us to believe that it is our fault if we wear chains. The Prophet has dismissed all that nonsense. He says that we must simply declare—"

"Save your breath. Please. My cock has already been snipped. Your problem is to convert forty slaves into forty Tuareg in the next month or so; not to tell strange jokes to your old shipmate."

We sat quietly for a long while before Ahmed resumed his discourse. "You're correct, lubber-butt. I need to create a mythology that will keep them safe for the rest of their lives. Maybe that's what every army offers every man: a safe place to hide his mind. The enemy is always wrong, so just throw in a little rape and pillage now and again and a friend who will listen to your troubles, and you've got heaven on earth."

I shook my head in fond disagreement but could think of nothing to say. Ahmed was under full sail.

"The angels, holy rocks, and burning bushes—all those tricks that people show as proof of God's power—they all serve a purpose. Maybe even God's purpose."

"Hallelujah and amen."

"Most likely though, they're just good stories, and people love to hear good stories. Everybody loves stories with great heroes, terrible villains, and heavenly endings, so maybe that's my job with these troopers. I'll tell stories they believe, and soon enough, my black Tuareg will see themselves as heroes. Ahmed and Allah together, we'll turn my boys into the truest of true believers."

Ahmed al-Koita—janissary captain, pretender to faultless knowledge—stood and stretched. "True believers in themselves."

Ahmed walked around the perimeter of the fire, stretched again, and sat closer to me than before. He spoke in a softer voice. "Don't be confused by what I say about my mission. I'm still a Moslem. Truly a true believer. The Prophet still serves as my messenger to Allah. I like taking time each day to pray, to think about my fears and seek guidance to overcome my weaknesses. I like being with others doing the same thing at the same time. I feel at one with a family that gives the comfort of their caring guidance. My religion is a fort that gives me great security."

"Ahmed. You do roll on at the mouth. First you give me the fairy tale theory: just stories to enjoy. Then you tell me to ignore the inventions of storytellers and note that one fable is, after all, better than another. I'm confused again. I wouldn't want you to be consistent or logical in your ramblings, but tell me again about Moslems selling Moslems into slavery."

"Look, I've thought about my father a great deal, and my conclusion is that he just ran into some bad luck."

"Bad luck! Sweet Jesus!"

"I'm serious," said Ahmed. "It's the vicissitudes thing again. The wrong place with a few renegade Arab slavers. The right place with your father. Vicissitudes—your old friend Rais Mawlud-Qadir had one thing right."

"So if life is a roll of the dice, where does that put Allah in the grand design?"

Ahmed was silent for a bit and then continued. "Joining a religion is like joining a club. Membership gives rights and privileges, but there are dues to pay. In exchange for the comradeship and guidance, you have to play the game of believing. The charade works as long as the benefits are greater than the costs."

"Where do you and I stand in this game?"

"For some reason, you and I get to choose which club we want to join. Most folks take what they are born with and wiggle through any small opening that their club might offer. I choose to be a Moslem because membership in the Christian Club doesn't do me much good. Back in Plymouth, a Christian nigger is still a nigger, and I'm not willing to abide by those rules any longer.

"What about here in this desert?" I smiled. "This is all some sort of cosmic joke for us to appreciate?"

"Look at us now, white man. We were both slaves, equal, and in just a few years I became an important janissary captain and you're a rich power behind the throne. It's possible, even likely, that we could run this country someday. I mean, I could become the dey of Algiers and you my First Christian secretary. Think on that joke for a moment or so."

"So where is the choice, Ahmed? It doesn't appear to me that we are doing much choosing. I'm not. If Hassan Bashaw says cut some scraps off my cock, off it comes. Bu Guttaya says join his little club of assassins and I get the choice killing Dakadeit or to wake up some fine morning dead to this world. I think I'll take the Vicissitude Club. Where do I sign up for that one?"

"You do have mighty big troubles, my friend," said Ahmed.

"Ha! Suddenly we get to keep our own troubles. Some friend!"

He shoved me over into the sand, and we both laughed. A golden glow whispered through the dunes and wiped the sky clean of stars. A silent djinn kept filling our cups with hot, sweet tea and leaving honey-soaked titbits at our fingertips. We spoke that night in our English language, and neither the spirits of the omnipresent Queen Tin Hanan nor the Prophet's emissary could make sense of the squawks and barks that passed between us that night.

In the end Ahmed and I formulated a plan. It was clear that our only hope for survival was with Dakadeit. Her strength was our strength. Her survival was ours, and my job was to serve as husband to our benefactress as long as she deemed fit, and that condition of servitude was just fine with me. When she eventually saw her father and his mullah dead, I'd probably get a final kiss on the cheek from my queen and a gentle push down the road. Not a bad bargain in my mind. She would save the Tuareg traditions, and I would remember a few precious moments with the ruling queen of all Tuareg. Ahmed's duty was simple enough: train his army of true believers, retrieve the dey's gold, and then help me carry it back to Algiers.

CHAPTER THIRTY

June 1791

I NEVER SPOKE THE NAME of Dakadeit's mother. She was always "honored descendant of the queen" or "celebrated mother of my wife." Her camp and tents were similar to every Tuareg encampment: red tents with mat siding, and most certainly, women working and children playing naked in the dust. The men attached by marriage or birth to women of the Queen's domaine were always off on a sojourn, raiding, guiding a merchant's caravan, or seeking good forage.

We now had three tiny encampments scattered along a mountain trail, each separated from the other for reasons of privacy and sanitation. Ahmed and Kitra and I were attached to the original clump of tents, while Dakadeit's entourage was uphill and her mother's larger group were downhill from us. The valley below the cascade of red tents shimmered green with flashes of yellow and red flowers, marking the benevolence of recent rains. Goats and hobbled camels trailed attendant children through every verdant gully.

The initial meeting with my mother-in-law-to-be went well. After the requisite inquiries into the health of all living and dead relations and many cups of tea, I finally posed the question: "May I have your support in taking your daughter, Dakadeit, as my wife?"

Her demeanor in answering my question matched the quiet assurance of my father. Both were masters of their ship. I liked her, yet she gave no evidence of returning my esteem.

"You must understand, my son, that it is not my decision to make. Dakadeit has a plan that includes you, and she will not honor me with the substance of her plot. I doubt that Allah has the same design, so in such matters a mother can only watch and pray."

I sat with quiet patience.

"My answer is a very tentative yes. I will ask Allah and my loving ancestor, the good Queen Tin Hanan, for mercy." She leaned forward at the waist and examined me as she might some albino goat or horned pig. "We know little of you." She gave two toad-like blinks. "Dakadeit was correct in one detail. You are exceedingly ugly. I will pray for a bout of temporary blindness when you are in my company."

With that invocation, I was dismissed. It was clear to one and all that royal in-laws must be forgiven both sins and insults.

My assigned tent hung between two goat-pruned trees. Their lacy shade combined with that from an adjacent cliff combined to hide me in cool solitude. Two young boys, cousins they claimed, fetched water, wood, and extra mats. Kitra appeared like an apparition, a smiling djinn, and began preparing dough for bread. She served me tea and hovered nearby, waiting for my next request and any glimpse of Ahmed. A small plain brown bird sat huddled at the edge of a thornbush. It stared at me without apparent fear, issued two high-pitched *peep-peeps*, and disappeared deeper into the bush.

Dusk was my favorite time of day. Light and shade sought a perfect balance, as if placating each other before the inevitable triumph of night. The wind generally renounced its reign of excoriation and coos in mock defeat. Each harmonious sound of beast and man calmed the blood and tilted the mind toward a consideration of abstract inventions. Dusk deepened into night. The first planets appeared, and now a flare of firelight surmounted all trees.

A faint tremor of thunder seeped into my consciousness. I was most certainly annoyed as the rumble intruded upon my meditation of life and death. The clamor tumbled over the hill that protected my tent and erupted into a rush of yells and rifle shots. I stepped from my tent, sabre in hand, and Ahmed al-Koita's army absorbed me with their violent affection. Camels milled small dust storms, screamed more loudly than their riders, and kneeled with grumbles and curled lips.

Tashmani and Ahmed sauntered up to me, smiling through their blue veils. "We have come to join the celebration of your wedding," said Ahmed.

"All of you?" I looked around at my quiet retreat. Camels hobbled from bush to small tree, seeking leaves among the thorns, dropping dung in random piles and gushes of urine upon the pegs of my tent. Fires belched new smoke, and sleeping mats dropped free in sheltered bowers. My mindless meditation disappeared into the cacophony of a military camp.

"Come," Tashmani said.

I relinquished my own commitment to self-pity and followed along the path leading to the queen's tent. "Now," said my Tuareg friend, "the sun has set, and we will begin the celebration of your wedding."

◆

Our noisy procession moved past boulders and through sharp thornbushes. There were forty soldiers in attendance, dressed in the blue robes of their dreams. Also, Tashmani, the great janissary Bolukbasi Ahmed al-Koita, and me, the bridegroom. Abutting the queen's tent burned a great fire. It seethed with brilliant illumination and heat sufficient to roast six goats. Troopers and officers received cups of milk from smiling slaves, and we scattered around the fire.

Without discussion, the serious business of eating began. Bowls of spicy baked lentils and joints of goat meat ranked beside mounds of kuskussu. Interspersed among the crushed and steamed grain were onions and herbs of such sharp mordancy that gobs of sweat dripped from the end of my nose. Each salty drop stimulated my appetite to greater devotion, and I managed to maintain the pace established by my silent companions.

Unending portions appeared among the men. No one spoke. Varied groups of four or five sat together, with representatives from Ahmed's army joining members of Dakadeit's family. All dipped into the bowls, and, one after the other, the wooden vessels were mopped with hunks of bread until the right hand of each banqueter fell limp and content. Dark, shadowed djinni flew in constant swoops through the entire meal, but the black Tuareg protected their lips and nostrils with the magic of their blue veils.

As the men sat drinking sweet mint tea and talking with neighbors in short declarations, the women began to eat. They finished quickly and stood in a circle around the fire. Small boys kindled the fire higher, sparks scattered, and a young woman began to sing. A drummer scored the beat, and soon a chorus joined in melodious harmony. Verse and refrain recounted countless Tuareg victories and portrayed Arabs as evil exceptions to Allah's good judgement. The fire burned with even greater intensity as stories of love and heroism surged through the smoke in clear falsetto voices. Dancers hurtled in twisting gyrations, casting monster shadows on rock walls. The celebration continued until bright Jupiter's arrival sent all to their sleeping mats.

The subsequent seven nights followed in the same pattern, yet each had a novel twist. The neighbors, at almost every moment of feasting and firelight, differed in their songs and the manner in which they danced. I felt immersed in a swirl of oneness that brushed over the chasm of our differences. I learned some songs and danced without regard to the inevitable howling laughs and jeers. The storytelling became more intimate and I less ignorant in the ministrations of love. On the seventh night, a yearling camel roasted in the coals.

On the eighth day, I was truly and officially married.

There was no ceremony or declaration of vows—only an infinite gauntlet of women shaking tambourines, yelling wedding night instructions, and singing ironic songs of bravery. All laughed and pointed, but the lewd cackles from old hens overwhelmed the titters of envy from young girls. Matching the twin files of women, but separated further by ten paces, stood Ahmed's mounted army. I assumed Dakadeit waited for me in the tent: the reward for negotiating this endless stretch of dust and noise.

The men cheered and waved their lances; women struck tambourines on their elbows and knees and closed my escape route as I edged closer to the tent. In a final, staggering, stumbling burst of speed, I reached the tent, lifted the mat, and entered.

The noise stopped.

I looked around at our wedding gifts: the sleeping mats, metal pots, wooden bowls, and metal-bound chest. Everything neat and orderly, and lacking only Dakadeit.

I sat on the floor mats, noticed my breathing slow to a reasonable rate, and wondered what form the next discomfit would take. This heathen ritual violated every memory of Christian weddings that I could recall: a Baptist ceremony for two cousins; and a long, depressing Quaker meeting that lacked food, conversation, or purpose. I don't remember any smiles or jokes at either Christian rite, and I'm certain that no one told the groom which position of intercourse best pleases a new wife. My memory failed. Did any of the Quaker dowagers grab the groom's penis and threaten everlasting hell if her sexual needs were ignored? Probably not, but then, I had been a child and oblivious to the subtleties of sex and religion.

I thought about my marriage and could admit that for the greater part of the last three weeks I was terrified of entering a contract that reversed every sensible convention taught to me by my father. Here I was, under a contract of marriage, that gave every right and prerogative to the female participant, not the man. The laws of all civilized countries were scraped. I held the dancing and singing as a random joy, but food passed through my throat with a curious difficulty. I peed more often than usual.

Nothing moved outside the tent. Quiet replaced pandemonium. I waited patiently, mindlessly, until my wife entered our tent in the company of her mother and a dozen or so female relations, one after the other. The young women did not giggle or laugh as Dakadeit took her place beside me. We sat cross-legged with hands on our knees. Food and candles appeared at our side; four cousins stood near the entrance, smiling, and Dakadeit's mother eased herself to the floor. She finally smiled and spoke in a fashion that included us both.

"My lady, the Queen Tin Hanan gives you her blessings. Allah gives no blessings, and upon him depends your fate. He will also decide what portion of happiness can be yours and intercede on your behalf as he wishes. So it is written."

Silence returned to the tent. I studied the strips of palm shreds crossing one over the other to form our floor mat.

In a voice weary from disappointment, looking first at Dakadeit and then at me, the living queen continued. "This is not a union of my choice. My daughter, you have a vision of our Tuareg ancestry that comes from ancient times. You have dreams that are not mine, fears that are not mine. Tonight we celebrate a marriage that I protest. Once again you have married a man without my countenance. In my love for you, I grieve. In my love for the Tuareg of Allah and all our ancient ancestors, I grieve."

She shook her head slowly back and forth. "Today I feel an old woman. Tomorrow I may feel young again and celebrate your happiness."

Both women smiled at tomorrow's promise, and Dakadeit's mother sat straighter.

"Who knows, my strange and lovely daughter—you may be closer to the great queen than I. Your outlandish ways and bold plans appal me, but who am I to judge? Only Allah knows the truth, and his plans are secret from mere mortals."

Dakadeit gave her mother a wan smile but no verbal response. I watched both women very carefully, and neither seemed willing to continue down familiar roads.

My mother-in-law unscrambled her limbs and held an arm for assistance in standing. The eldest cousin stepped forward to help the reigning descendant of an ancient queen. She stood, nodded very briefly at me, turned, and led her attendants through the opening of our tent.

Dakadeit served me cold kuskussu and lukewarm tea. I was not hungry and consumed small portions of each. Shadows from the distant campfire fluttered through the trees and over our tent. Desultory singing and laughter continued long after we consummated our marriage with a short hug and rapid descent to sleep. The water boys shouted their alarm at the impending dawn. I dozed awhile longer and woke to feel my wife looking at me.

"We must talk," she said.

I nodded into the darkness, and she continued.

"This marriage suits us both at this moment, and will end when you return to your master, the dey of Algiers." She stopped, lingering for any possible response from me.

I watched the candle cast shadows as both my stomach and mind settled into a regulated thump. My predictions of our relationship was on target, but still, there was the exciting possibilities of Dakadeit as my partner for life that sent small jots of exuberance down the sinews of my back. There would never be another person in my life with such vitality. We exchanged expressions of eyes and lips that needed no further analysis, and my wife continued her recitation of mundane instructions to me.

"Tomorrow my father, the sultan Agg-Abba, will honor our marriage with his presence. You must understand that he is an angry man who has given one part of his soul to Bu Guttaya and a lesser part to my mother. Make no mistake, my husband—he is a dangerous villain. He is sultan of our people, yet he would change our ways. He is husband to my mother, yet he would cause her pain. He is my father, yet he would have me dead." Her strident lecture stopped and was replaced by her smile of affection for me. "Tell me, Ja Mai Ne—in your land do children fear their father? Indeed, do they hate their father?"

I nodded. "It was not so with me and my father, but in my opinion, it is not uncommon in my land to hate one's father. Men often say otherwise, but they act the truth. It is in truth, a common aversion, father from son. Usually, again, in my opinion, that the conflict is resolved with the son disappearing from the domination of his father at the first opportunity."

It was my turn to endure a spate of silence, and finally I inched closer to ask, "What do you fear, Dakadeit? My terror is that I will replicate my father with his silent anger."

"No, my strange Frank. I have no such silly thoughts, for I am of queens, and no man or woman can destroy my spirit. I do fear the pain that my father can inflict upon me and on my people, but he is nothing to me. I watch when that stupid mullah whispers into his left ear. I listen as my mother chews his right ear and warns him of discomfort if he turns on his queen. I hate him for his weakness and lack of pride in the Tuareg traditions."

"Tell me, Wife, what comes next?"

"Tomorrow I will give my father a small present. A gift designed to return the pain he so generously bestows. A gift, my husband, which you and Captain Ahmed al-Koita will deliver."

She outlined her plan through the next hour, allowed me a few hours rest, and then together we went into the chill, dark morning. A black Tuareg sentry led us to Ahmed's tent, and we three roused Tashmani. Ahmed and I stirred the fire to life, and in the time it took Kitra to prepare our cup of tea, Ahmed and Tashmani listened to their instructions from my wife. With teacups empty and a handful each of cold kuskussu devoured, the military officers of my queen's army disappeared into the night.

With the first light of the day that would celebrate the giving of gifts, I noticed fewer cook fires spread through the encampment. Many of the visiting Tuareg relatives had departed during the night, using stars as beacons for their return home. This ninth day was the last of our wedding, and the remaining guests made their final visits in the cool morning hours. They recommended the number of children we should produce, and a few left parting gifts. Dakadeit and I sat drinking tea with each well-wisher and accepted both advice and gifts with weary smiles.

Near noon I heard clanking weapons and groaning camels outside our tent. I summoned Kitra to open the mats on all sides so that Ahmed could display his troops to my wife. The warriors were impressively fitted with full battle gear. I looked again and counted only fifteen black cavalrymen on their mounts. Ahmed and Tashmani stood at our entrance.

Ahmed wore a janissary-style headpiece: a red scarf held erect with the shoulder bone of a goat, and a giraffe tail dangling down his back. His white robes were worn to reveal his face. Tashmani and the troopers all wore Tuareg blue robes and veils.

Dakadeit's mother appeared, smiled, and sat beside her daughter. Long minutes passed until an explosion of yells burst from the crest of a small rocky hill south of the tents. Blue-robed men on white camels cascaded down the hill and raced toward us with lances pointed and long curved swords slicing the air.

At a hand movement from Tashmani, the black Tuareg turned their camels, nose to tail, and signaled the mounts to kneel, then dismounted to aim long rifles at their brethren. The attacking force slowed as they approached the armed barricade. They stopped completely as squads of Ahmed's troops crested hills on three quadrants and then came toward us, all firing their ancient rifles into the air and whooping down the rocky slopes.

Sultan Agg-Abba and his nobles found themselves penned into a dusty corral of dun-colored camels and black Tuareg. Minutes later, from the north, the sultan's rear guard burst into view. They were oblivious to the tactical situation and were quickly cut off by the remaining squad of Ahmed's army.

On another cue from Tashmani, the dismounted troopers returned to their saddles, and, in an impressively disciplined manner, all the squads formed in rank behind their commander.

The sultan dismounted, threw his reins to a slave, and walked in bold fast strides to face Ahmed. Each returned the stare of the other in ferocious combat until Agg-Abba turned to face Tashmani.

"How did you leave my brother, Salim Shushufi?"

"Dead, my sultan, with Arabs in drifts around him," answered Tashmani. "Your brother is a hero sitting with Allah in heaven."

It was clear to all present the sultan was repeating a practiced litany to his subordinate. "And you, lowly vassal to me and also to my brother—I see that once again you live while noble Tuareg die bravely in battle." The volume of the sultan's voice increased, but his dignity was in tatters. "From this moment you must stay from my sight or I will sell you as a eunuch to the next Fez caravan."

"Sultan Agg-Abba." Ahmed al-Koita stepped between the Tuareg warriors.

Slowly the noble Tuareg looked down at his new adversary. The Tuareg was head and shoulders above my friend and took the condescending posture of a giant allowing a dwarf some few moments of his precious time.

"Tashmani is my lieutenant," said Captain al-Koita. "He is under my command. Hear now and believe what I say to you. First of all you must understand that Tashmani was far away from the battle that consumed your brother, Salim Shushufi. Tashmani was following my orders in showing me the great Tuareg rock paintings. He was not present when the Arabs attacked Salim Shushufi and my janissaries. Your brother died a hero's death, but Tashmani was many days' ride away when the Arab dogs attacked. Tashmani's bravery is unquestioned by me and all who serve me."

"Bah!" said the sultan, and turned to enter the tent of his daughter and her new husband.

Captain al-Koita spoke to the sultan's rear end. "I will continue our conversation at a more convenient time, my sultan Agg-Abba."

The sultan passed through the opening of the queen's red tent.

"Welcome, my husband," said Dakadeit's mother.

I was next to Dakadeit and close enough to notice that the sultan's hand trembled through the second cup of tea and well into the endless inquiries into his health. Eventually he turned to me.

"Many years ago, in Algiers, I saw and spoke to a Frank. Now one sits here as my son." He seemed to shudder as his shoulders turned to remove my form from his sight. He never spoke to me again. Once was enough for both of us.

Dakadeit clapped her hands twice, softly, and a slave entered our tent carrying a Moroccan leather saddle. The goat-skin seat was a soft cushion, and the twin pommel was tooled with many intricate designs. The dey of Algiers would lust for such a gift.

"This is for you, Father. It marks my marriage to the Frank, Ja Mai Ne, and other beginnings as well."

"Go on, Daughter," the sultan prompted. Anger edged each word. "You would sit with men, so stop your womanish banter."

Dakadeit waited even longer, until the sultan adjusted his posture on the mat and sipped from his teacup.

"The freemen outside this tent wish to prove their worth as Tuareg. They will multiply our power and bring wealth to our people. With the black Tuareg as kinsmen, the Arab will melt at our ferocity."

"Daughter"—the sultan spoke as to a child, an imbecile child—"look at their skin and tell me they are Tuareg. Smell them and tell me they are Tuareg. Look into their eyes, peering like owls from stolen veils, and tell me they are Tuareg. They are farmers! Sellers of salt! Slaves in every manner except for one! That one dispensation is granted by me. They come to their freedom through my kindness. Slaves they will become again, as I wish!"

Dakadeit's mother spoke. "Husband, you have been absent from our tent for many moons."

"It is the time for salt caravans, my wife." He spoke in a sulky, gruff manner. "I've led camels to Ghat for dates and figs. With the new moon we go to Tessalit for millet. The Adar Tuareg are worse than the Arab: robbers and thieves. It is a dangerous trip." He mumbled on, listing his strengths against each adversary, touching his beads. His eyes focused on distant responsibilities.

"A blanket is not sufficient for the cold nights, my husband. As memory of your virility diminishes, I see more clearly those men who would cater to my needs."

"I am here now. Your threats fall on deaf ears."

The sultan's wife picked up a bowl of dates and handed them to her husband. "Do you care for a date?" she asked. He took a few, then she returned the bowl to its former position. "I have studied the Koran many times, my husband, and see little argument with the wishes of our ancestor Queen Tin Hanan and Allah. Neither allows any distinction between men and women before the One God. Both admonish us to free our slaves; both teach us to accept them as equals if they but admit to the One God and his Prophet." She paused to emphasize her next point. "You, my sultan, can do no less than Mohammed in recognizing the merit and love of your free slaves."

"Nonsense," he said.

"You also demean women in bargaining for what is rightfully theirs. By the queen who first gave issue to the Tuareg, I swear: support my daughter in her venture or reclaim your status as my low-born vassal. Follow my bidding or relinquish your rule as sultan of the Tazili Tuareg!"

I think that I retained my aggrieved expression through her speech, but in truth I was cheering my mother-in-law and also beginning to understand the source of Dakadeit's strength.

Flies buzzed in lazy profusion as silence enveloped the tent. For the first time since leaving the Arab towns to the north, I heard a muezzin call the faithful to prayer. The clear, mellifluous chant filtered through the trees and echoed against the stone canyons. All men responded like true believers. All of the Tuareg men, host or guest, followed the path past boulders and thorn trees until we all stood before Imam Bu Guttaya.

An arched sandstone enclave served as the holy mosque. Trees grew to the entrance, and soft sand textured the surface. Bu Guttaya turned toward Mecca and began his prayer to Allah. The congregation ranged in orderly rows behind him and followed his lead. When his prayers were completed, the imam stood, turned to face the throng of faithful, and spoke to us.

"You who believe in the One God and his last Prophet, Mohammed, celebrate with me his unity. Look about us and observe the beauty of mountains and desert. See how they fit together in serving you. It is God's plan that works. He created the seeds that come to life with each bounteous rain, life that begets further life until those in God's image are sustained. It is God's plan.

"He has you before me as true believers—strange men from far lands, black and white who kneel before God as one. The power of

Islam speaks to those who listen. All who profess Allah as the One God will join him in heaven. All who profess Allah as the One God are the same before him: equal.

"Men of the blue veil, your wrath is known wherever men speak of bravery. Idolaters and atheists tremble in fear of your mission for Allah. His strength is yours. His strength increases as the Tuareg increase. It is his will that black and white Tuareg unite against the infidel."

Imam Bu Guttaya bowed with a slight nod to his parishioners and turned once again to face the east. We joined him in the sand, and then small clusters of men stood and slowly walked back toward the tents. Ahmed and I waited until the sultan left and followed ten paces behind him.

"Jamie, my boy, we have just observed a master politician in action. He reminds me of General Washington telling the troops that each defeat was a sterling victory. Of course, George only had old men and a boy like me to convince that black was white. All sensible folks were home taking care of the farm."

"What is our friend the imam up to?"

Ahmed's nose and brows puckered in thought. "Whatever it is, you can bet that the results will be painful for us!"

We walked through the verdant wadi speaking softly in English. "Maybe it's a white flag," I ventured. "Maybe he and Allah had a conversation, and now he's all for peace and tolerance."

"Don't be a crackbrain! The bastard is going to get us. I only hope that Dakadeit and her mother—especially her mother—can keep the old sultan in line." Ahmed tapped his hip to the tempo of our walking. "We need to speed our training. We've got to move faster. Tashmani says the sultan will leave with a big caravan in about two weeks and won't be back until early fall."

"The men seem to be improving," I said. "They were very impressive this morning."

"I agree, but they need lots of work in scouting, and fighting as a single unit. They continue with their belief that the first one to heaven receives a special reward from Allah." He wagged his head a few times with affectionate resignation. "Mostly they need to learn how to hit an enemy camel in the ass. The rifles are hopeless antiques, so maybe they'll get in one shot. One shot to get an Arab's attention, then they can follow with lance and sword. That's the drill we're working on."

"They're good men."

"Well, the training will continue, and I need you and Dakadeit to work on this supply list." He pulled a scrap of sun-bleached leather from the folds of his robe and handed it over to me. Without looking, I slipped it into my belt.

"One more task, white man. Tonight we begin your practice with pistol, knife, and short sword. You're in this army too, Ja Mai Ne!"

I think I smiled before we parted to our separate tasks: he had his army to train and I had my wife to love. The solitude of our tent seemed disconcerting as there was no one demanding our attention. Dakadeit was strangely quiet as she took tiny dabs of food from the bowl and turned each pinch over and over with the fingers of her right hand before slowly placing it into her mouth.

"Sit." She motioned toward a small rug next to a large cushion. "Listen very carefully," she said.

CHAPTER THIRTY-ONE

D AKADEIT WAS A GOOD TEACHER, and in most inquiries I was a gifted student. We pleasured each other through the nights and sent couriers for needed supplies by day. She proved with irreproachable logic how her people lived astride the center of existence. "Notice, Ja Mai Ne, that the pilgrims to Mecca who travel from the great rivers of the south must first pay homage to the Tuareg. Such is Allah's design. Merchants come from every direction of the stars, as do traders whose caravans carry absurd luxuries and many slaves under our nose. Such is Allah's design. False believers—Copts, Egyptians, Animists—they all rely upon the Tuareg for guidance and protection. There are no exceptions."

My wife could read some few words, and as days and weeks merged into one, I found joy in working with a willing student. Our text was the holy Koran, and we spent part of each day studying the words and directives from Allah. She learned and rewarded me for her progress with gifts of intimate affection.

Dakadeit entered all transactions of money and goods into the dey's account book, and her enthusiasm for learning the fundamentals of accounting matched my passion for gaining proficiency in each new sexual conjunction. Every pleasure we gave the other became heightened by the certainty of our parting. Women smiled when they saw us walking together. Children circled us in dust storms of ridicule and challenge. Our red tent became a comfortable island of serenity as I played Alphonse's game of giving, and Dakadeit quickly learned the rules.

The remaining wedding guests disappeared into oblivion. The black army, plus Tashmani, evaporated at daybreak and returned with the first faint star. Dakadeit, her mother, and all the other women softened and smiled when Sultan Agg-Abba and his entourage left for the south. He cited the dual threat of weather and infernal competition from the Hoggar Tuareg as cause to leave his wife, the queen. Bu Guttaya joined the djinni in their ephemeral travels through the land. Naked children formed straw camels and fought violent and always victorious battles against the evil Arab. Handsome women pounded grain into flour and gossiped about the nightly endurance of Dakadeit's Frank. The deeds were greater for the telling.

To all who studied our movements, we feigned a consistent message: "What is the hurry? We have nowhere to go. We have a ridiculous assortment of black slaves who pretend the status of warriors. All can clearly see that the two representatives from the dey of Algiers are fools and their token Tuareg is a coward. They will never move from the paltry village of red tents. Never."

The fourth full moon of my marriage was well above the horizon when Ahmed and Dakadeit joined me in gazing at the fire. Our dreams joined the smoke drifting vertically toward the stars. Simmering ethal branches answered each silent question that I could pose with vague promises and sharp threats. Ahmed spoke. "Tomorrow, we leave."

Without allowing a cricket chirp to interrupt, Dakadeit said, "Yes, I am ready."

◆

At dawn the army struck camp, complemented with one additional soldier in the ranks. She ignored me from the first dew-struck moment, and obeyed without comment each command from Tashmani or his sergeant. Once she smiled in my direction, but as I moved toward her, she scowled and jerked her camel into a trot.

After the initial shakedown march, we traveled at night, silently, with scouts far beyond the horizon and every trooper alert to the smell of smoke or fresh camel dung. Ahmed kept us east of any caravan route. We traveled over flat rocky plains, using the stars as guideposts. Our pace was slow and cautious. We had ample water in our goatskins and ate cold kuskussu at dawn and sunset. There was no hot tea.

Ghardia was only a day or so away when the camels began behaving strangely. Some few of our beasts began bounding off their feet like giant kangaroo rats. Nearly all began complaining in loud raucous moans that made their normal irritable behavior seem like that of docile lap dogs. Gazelle, normally furtive silhouettes on the horizon, dashed in panic-stricken circles through our line of march; there were desert fox who yipped and howled, day and night.

"It's the moon," the black Tuareg repeatedly remarked. We watched as the bronze disk crested the mountains and a bright red tit flared briefly from the bottom of the October moon. The alluring beauty of the moon destroyed our tongues and impaled our eyes. It kept overflowing into the night sky, until the stars drained every drop of moisture from the luminous disk and left only the desert of mountains and deep craters. The bedevilled night cranked the springs of our anxiety into the tight coils of dawn.

———◆———

Before us lay the long valley of Ghardia, with its endless march of dunes stretching into the distant western haze. Nearer to us, thin columns of smoke twisted and climbed into one amorphous cloud over the city's stout walls. In a placid muddy mass, the stain drifted gently to the south.

Without a hint of warning, I heard the shattering rumble of twenty
Maine thunderstorms and felt myself lifted by the eruption of sharp-
cresting waves surfing through solid rock. The camels lost footing;
men crumpled to the heaving ground, screaming in chorus with the
beasts. Pounding explosions and the buckling, bucking earth
continued for two lifetimes.

"An earthquake!" I screamed.

Men and camels sprawled artlessly on the rocky terrain. Supplies
lay torn from their bindings, creating small drifts around the fallen
pack animals. Cries of supplication to Allah howled from every
trooper.

"Look!" yelled Ahmed. Toward Ghardia a brown cyclopean-
shaped cloud bulged to enormous heights. From the lower roiling
depths, flashes of fire spurted. Muffled blasts of explosions sounded
as loud and rapid as the artillery barrage during the Battle of Saratoga.

"Praise Allah!" shouted Ahmed. He turned to Tashmani. "Tell the
men to line up in squads, right here, where they can see our mission."

Moments later, four lines of ten black Tuareg stood gaping at the
red-tinged smoke of Ghardia, a city of five thousand or more. The
royal palace had vanished, and municipal and commercial centers lay
shattered beyond recognition. Ahmed broke the silent gawking.
"Allah has sent a clear message to us. He has punished the perfidious
Arabs for their evil behavior." He waved an arm to direct our
attention. Look! Observe His might." We all turned from Ahmed and
watched the billowing smoke drift south.

"Allah is shouting that we must join Him to destroy the
treacherous Arab dogs. Tuareg warriors! We cannot refuse what Allah
demands!"

"Praise Allah! Praise Allah!" Ahmed's army cheered.

Our janissary captain held us captive with his eyes. "Listen, my
ferocious Tuareg. I also have a message, so listen well. The eagle
squad will guard the animals at this site and watch for our return. If

on our return we are pursued, you must attack! Kill the Arabs that harass us. Protect those Tuareg returning from Allah's mission."

Ahmed stepped closer to the eagle squad and lowered his voice. "Do not leave except to protect our return. All treasure that we collect will be divided on a share-alike basis, so you must not be tempted to leave while we are gone. The success of this mission depends equally on you, as with the other squads. Those are my orders." He looked sternly at the trooper in charge and shouted, "You are dismissed."

The disgruntled eagle squad followed their sergeant to the rear and began collecting scattered supplies and putting double hobbles on the trembling and strangely docile camels. The eagle squad moved about their tasks with the slightly veiled resentment of black slaves.

The remaining warriors waited for Ahmed's orders.

"We must move quickly while the Shamba are confused and frightened. There is one goal, and that is Sheik Brahim's palace and the stolen gold. Tashmani and Ja Mai Ne will lead the way through the city. Shoot only if attacked in force. Use swords and lances if resistance is offered by a few. Speed is our ally. Allah has given his voice for your support in this mission. Now, my wonderful warriors, we must put his commands into action."

The men shuffled and studied the pebbles at their feet. I was desperately trying to remember the route from our camp to the palace on that dreadful day. Where was the morning sun on my face on our trip to the palace? How did the slope of hills change under my feet on our hurried retreat from the palace?

Ahmed shouted, "Lion squad will follow Tashmani and Ja Mai Ne into the sheik's palace. Each warrior must find a pack animal, a camel or a mule, to carry the gold. The animals will be part of Allah's reward to you for punishing the Shamba."

"Captain," I shouted in return, "the palace is likely destroyed, and we will find the ruins atop the highest hill." I pointed at the squad. "Whatever your distraction, always move toward the highest hill."

"Good work, Ja Mai Ne. Now lead your warriors to the gold, buried or not." Ahmed al-Koita turned to the rest of his troops. "Tuareg, listen! No looting! You will receive gold to buy many camels. We must move quickly while all is confusion with the Shamba. The lions will race with Ja Mai Ne to the palace, but the ravens will stop as the hill to the palace rises sharply. The ravens must use swords and lances to silence any Arab pigs in the vicinity. When the lions come back down the hill, you will protect them on all sides."

The men shuffled in nervous energy, but all refrained from speaking. "I will stay with the elephant squad and move where I am needed," Ahmed said. "Now! To your camels! Allah be praised!"

—◆—

Even as we approached the town, the wrath of Allah was obvious. Rows of ancient palm trees lay like matchsticks on top of one another. Crevices deep enough to swallow a donkey gashed in jagged furrows through the oasis. Smoke followed wailing Arabs through the crumpled walls of Ghardia.

Our camels twitched and hesitated as we guided them through the first ruined streets. Parents were digging through rubble, calling on Allah to protect a child. Every building was completely devastated. There were no streets, but I led the way uphill by guiding my camel over the remnants of sun-dried bricks. Arabs, distracted by wounds and the loss of relatives, drifted ghostlike through the smoke and dust.

I kept sight of Tashmani only with some difficulty. Here and there a wild-eyed camel or mule was untethered by a member of our squad. Then, as the incline became greater, the sharp retort of rifle fire startled me. An angry buzz passed close to my ear, and I turned in my saddle to see the problem. The warrior immediately following me in line uttered a high-pitched scream of pain and fell to the ground. Amid the shattered remains of a building, a Tuareg warrior lay wounded.

My camel seemed anxious to quit the smoke and noise, but he kneeled quickly at my command. I ran to the pile of blue rags. My mind refused the first sight. No! It could not be. I looked again, and Dakadeit's beautiful face was twisted into a terrifying mask. Blood washed her robe a deeper blue. Blood washed over my hands and feet, into the dust. The deep-blue cloth kept sticking to her skin, preventing me from helping her. I pulled until suddenly Dakadeit's left arm lay separate from her body. It pulsed with a life of its own, squirming in isolated agony. Red rain kept falling and falling. My tongue filled with bile. My fingers lacked feeling and tingled with pain. I looked up into the brown smoke to plead a miracle, an intervention by Allah.

Dakadeit's eyes grew large and her breathing thin and rapid. She tried to speak. "Tash . . . mani . . ." Again she tried, shuddered through the length of her body, and lay still in the stink of death. I was entirely adrift in my grief. Such concepts as lost gold and humbled buildings held no meaning. My queen had been taken from me. The queen was lost to the Tuareg. All good sense was squandered in this scene of smoke and fire.

Two of the lion warriors sat astride their camels on either side of us. They held swords at the ready and looked away from my tears. Finally one said, "She is with Allah, Ja Mai Ne. It is his will. Now we must go."

I looked around for a place to bury my wife, or at least move her from further violence.

The two men kept repeating, "We must go. We must go."

A collapsed door leaned at an angle atop some rubble, creating a small cave. I retrieved the door, placed my wife atop her carriage, and hid her from sight. Such was the grave of Dakadeit, direct descendant of Queen Tin Hanan: a small cavity in a disintegrated building.

I felt nothing. I stood without seeing. Defiant waves rippled through my body, churning blood and bile as one. Smoke and dust and noise obscured me from the world. I willed myself to rise, to levitate above the killing, to move backward in time to the red tent, to Dakadeit.

"Go! Go at once," came the desperate screams.

Tashmani led me by hand and watched as I mounted my camel. He took the reins of my camel and clambered aboard his magnificent white beast. I barely noticed two black Tuareg wade through the rubble and hack down a handful of Arabs that appeared. We were near the site of the palace, and my attention became more focused. The lion squad wandered through brick and wood, trying to make some sense of Allah's grand design.

Beneath the dust I saw a rug with intricate designs of blue and red and a blond corner.

My memory clicked on a small cipher leading inevitably to the sum. The blond corner of the rug, buried in a fallen ceiling of mud bricks and palm tree timbers, gave me the orientation and necessary direction. On that previous visit to this place, when the floor and roof were one, I had made note of this distinctive rug. The acrid smell of charred flesh revealed two dead Shamba warriors, both facedown, crushed under a massive palm beam. A large pistol lay near the hand of one Arab, and I stooped to pick up the weapon. It was primed and ready to fire, as if the owner were prepared to fend off a visible enemy.

I pulled myself up against a still-erect door frame. Almost at the feet of dead guards lay ranks of neatly ordered chests, buried in the debris like boulders after a snowfall. No one, neither Tuareg nor Shamba, disturbed my solitude. I stumbled to the closest chest and cleared away bits of brick. It opened easily to show soft leather saddlebags molded one on another. The top pouch I held to judge the heft of gold. Satisfied, I replaced the gold, shut the lid, and began to check each buried treasure. The second and third chest mimicked the first. I looked up to see Tashmani watching my act of taking inventory. He stood rooted, curved sword in one hand, dagger in the other, two eyes suspended in the void of blue veil.

"You must die, Ja Mai Ne." There was no inflection to his voice; it was simply a stated fact.

"Why?" I could only give voice to my idiocy. This was my friend and teacher muttering nonsense about my death.

"The gold does not belong to the dey. The gold must serve the Tuareg and Allah."

Tashmani stepped toward me, through the shattered wood and brick, all the while raising his sword overhead in a slow, deliberate fashion. "May you find a quick death, my friend."

I lifted the stolen pistol from my side and fired. A crimson flower burst from Tashmani's chest; the sword flew upward and over his shoulder. A brave Tuareg warrior fell into the dust. In my left hand I held gold, in the other a gun. I dropped both and stood in dazed horror. My wife, my friend—what next, Allah? What next?

———

I remained a silent statue until I heard my name echo from ear to ear. "Jamie! Jamie!" The hellfire flared, and I discovered that Ahmed was shaking me, his nose almost on my nose.

"Jamie, what happened?"

"Dakadeit's dead."

"Yes. Tashmani. Tell me about Tashmani. They say you killed Tashmani."

"It must be that Tashmani was one of the seven—one of Bu Guttaya's seven assassins. He tried to kill me, Will, and instead I killed Tashmani."

Ahmed al-Koita turned from me to his waiting warriors. "Bring the pack animals—quickly!"

The troopers ignored me. I stood alone as the leather bags of gold were transferred from each wooden chest to a mélange of animals: piebald camels, a few mules, and even two donkeys. They were soon burdened and led from the palace debris.

Ahmed led me to my camel and watched as I mounted. He tapped the beast to a standing position. "Stay close to the Tuareg warrior in front of you." He clearly thought that I was still in a world far removed from Ghardia.

◆

The caravan of stolen camel, mule, and donkey descended from the heights of Sheik Brahim's palace. Rifle fire beat a steady drum upon my consciousness, and as we approached the remains of the city wall, curses in Arabic were drowned by miniature charges of two or three mounted Tuareg. Shots whined from behind exposed roots of palm trees, and then the desert enfolded us. Halfway between the oasis and the escarpment, the eagle squad thundered past with long rifles held high and whips flicking the neck of each camel to even greater speed. Gunfire chattered at our rear. The slope increased until, one by one, each animal thrashed through loose rock to scramble onto the flat plateau.

Ahmed was a whirlwind, as he directed one squad to establish a defence perimeter and the remnants of two other squads to combine the gold, water, and food supplies onto the best pack camels available. Within minutes the changes were made; camels and men were ready to leave. Two men were dispatched with instructions to the perimeter guards and to the eagles. The caravan moved out at a swift amble, due east—not south toward the Tuareg, or north toward the safety of Algiers. We went east toward the trackless Tademait Plateau and countless miles of table-flat terrain.

As we traveled away from the sun, small clusters of blue-robed warriors joined us until the final two—one slumped and flopping like a rag doll—made their appearance. Ahmed met with each addition, asked short questions, and listened attentively to the answers.

The wind increased in velocity. No sand hid in the recesses between the pebbles, and at Ahmed's command, we dismounted to walk on the lee side of our camel. He angled our line of travel to the left for an hour, and then an even sharper angle to the left. From dusk until the moon glared overhead, the caravan traveled to an oblique right. Eventually we used a constellation of four dim stars that formed a twisted cross to give us a consistent line of movement for our final change of direction.

There were now twenty-eight Tuareg warriors left from of the original forty-one—two of whom were severely wounded. The forty-first warrior, our queen, had an escort to heaven of twelve ferocious black Tuareg warriors. At dawn, Ahmed allowed the first break. Sentries were assigned, and water and dates were consumed. Men slumped beside inert camels. We were soon under way again.

At midafternoon on the third day of our flight, we stopped, and Ahmed called a meeting. Each squad sat in disciplined order before their captain.

"You are heroes in the eyes of Allah." He studied them as the wind whipped loose ends of robes and veils but did not move a single man. "Every whisper through the dunes and mountains will tell of your bravery. You are Tuareg warriors. Arabs will shake with fear when they speak of you, the black Tuareg.

"You are Tuareg by choice—freemen who have the power of bravery. You are warriors who are assured places in heaven, and you are men of wealth, because today each man will receive twenty weights of gold. Enough gold to purchase forty camels and cloth for ten families. It is yours."

None answered; none moved.

"Listen now, freemen, Tuareg warriors: Ja Mai Ne and I follow the north star to Algiers. For those warriors who accompany us to Laghouat there will be another five gold coins. If there are those here who would become janissary under my command and travel with us to Algiers, your twenty will become forty weights of gold. Think. Talk. Pray. I will seek your answers as the sun disappears."

CHAPTER THIRTY-TWO

January–February 1792

CEDAR TREES TWISTED IN WINDBLOWN torment; sleet whipped through branches and layers upon layers of clothes until a constant stream of water dribbled down my back and shoulders. I stewed in the discomfort of mind and body. Without a shade of doubt in my mind, the fourteen months spent chasing gold for the dey of Algiers had been wasted. Twice I was nearly killed, and I was perpetually caught between Tuareg and Turk and Arab in their violent subservience to various permutations of Allah's word. It seemed that all these desert pirates were bound together in an effort to destroy me with their idle concern for my life. The wind howled through this rock pile of memories. Icicles formed from the snot of my nose, and we had at least two more days slogging away atop the Atlas Mountains. I was content to let the djinni haunt my frozen daydreams. Visions of Alphonse taunted me with painful gestures of intimacy. Dakadeit and Tashmani were glib with unfulfilled promises.

My patient mount kept his head down and ploughed tenaciously into the blizzard. The mule nodded yes, yes, yes—agreeing that life made no sense at all and that good people die while the misbegotten live. There was no doubt in the creature's mind that promises grew with the alacrity of thistle weeds and then died slowly on the sharp spines of cactus. Good deeds seemed certain to punish. Everything in life remained unperturbed by effort or deed. The desert was always hot, and the miserable mountains were always cold.

I turned in my saddle to study six Tuareg warriors riding behind me. Each was stiff with layer upon layer of clothes and buried under the indignity of a coarse brown wool burnoose. Shriveled frozen gray masks replaced handsome black faces. They all rode small gray horses, trailing behind the remnants of Ahmed's army. A dozen heavily packed mules, each led by an armed Kabyle tribesman, came next, with the recently arrived detachment of janissary troopers at the end.

Ahmed and I rode side by side, guiding our horses down the slippery track.

"Three days more on the mountain, plus three on the lee side, and then we reach Algiers," Ahmed said.

"Six days until I meet my death angel." I refused to consider a reception to our return that would reward our efforts in any positive manner. The dey sent us to retrieve his all gold, and we failed to obey his command to the letter. The dey sent a squad of janissary troopers into the desert and only the captain returned. Nothing that we could give the dey would merit his approval. Nothing in my ledgers would give the dey or his banker much pleasure.

Ahmed al-Koita was not of my mind, and tried to turn sleet into sunshine. "Allah must be smiling on you, my frozen friend. The officer of the janissary told me that your friend Hassan is now the dey of Algiers."

We swerved onto a treeless stretch of road. Swift stinging shards of sleet pecked at every exposed spot of skin. Ahmed leaned toward me and shouted into the wind, "Lucky you! Maybe he'll give you a choice: first Christian secretary or most exalted Moslem secretary."

I barked a cough into my wool scarf.

The highway twisted into a dense thicket of cedar trees, and a soft windless respite embraced us. The horses became alert to the possibilities of a better life and shook off their drooping lethargy. My gelding eyed a likely patch of frost-chewed grass, and I reined him back on course.

I coughed and spoke for the first time since daybreak. "Have you received any news of negotiations for the release of American prisoners?"

"The sergeant didn't know much. He ranted a bit about lying American infidels—the usual bluster. I'd bet nothing has happened."

Two jays scolded in alternate fury as Ahmed continued. "It certainly doesn't matter with me. Whatever happens, ransom or no, I'm staying with the janissary. We've got most of the gold here on the mules, and maybe the dey will smile on me with a sack or two. Whatever happens, I should move up in the ranks a notch or two."

He moved his horse closer to mine and lowered his voice. "I'd never be rich in America. I'd never have a pot to piss in or anyone to empty it for me in America." He looked over at me and caught my eye. "We're both in the same boat, my friend. You'll never have it so good! Hassan Bashaw is a smart man. A powerful man who likes you."

When I didn't answer, he shrugged and continued conversing with himself. "You're great company today. Great company; I'd rather talk with a tree or into the mud."

Ahmed leaned over his horse and stared down at the mud. "Now there's something that stirs me—this mud." He gestured at the ground. "This black soft, gooey mud brings to mind Kitra's great soft breasts. I'm not lying. My pecker's so stiff I can hardly move." He sat on his horse in a shoulders-forward slouch, eyes shut and a skewed smile twisting his lips. "Kitra fits in all the right places, and I've got to find a way to bring her back to me."

"Hmph," I muttered. "Sounds like a worthy ambition: the exalted janissary officer married to a slave."

"Damn, hard to believe! First I perceive beauty in the mud, and now we have a bloody talking tree!"

Ahmed laughed at his great wit, and as his horse skittered into a little halfhearted dance, he pulled the Arab gelding back onto the trail. "You are correct; of course, my first wife needs to be the daughter of a large landowner."

"An old, rich landowner with a young, beautiful daughter and no other children," I suggested.

"Yes! He'll give me parcels of orchards and a string of fast horses."

"And the beauteous Kitra?"

"First the land and then Kitra." Ahmed gave a hardy slap to the rump of his horse. "There shouldn't be much of a problem—not after we unload these mules!"

He went on in this pompous fashion for some time, and when I didn't appear to listen or comment any further, he dropped back in the line to talk with the troopers. Good riddance. If this miserable trip had done anything, it solidified my intentions to gain the freedom of all the American prisoners. Not Will Melman, of course, but all the rest.

My mood and the weather improved slightly as we descended from the mountains. The rain stopped, and near midafternoon the sun replaced every cloud. Men discarded wool garments and began talking with arm-waving enthusiasm. The sun and moon were equidistant above opposite horizons when our guide shouted and pointed down the mountain. I rode to his side and stared. The distant city of Algiers sparkled in the clear winter air—a white diamond embraced by sapphire mist. I was nearly home.

<hr />

Dey Hassan Bashaw lounged against large fluffed pillows and accepted coffee from a white slave. Ahmed and I stood before him while he sipped and muttered and ignored us. He slowly emptied the cup. The coffeegee responded with alacrity and quickly served his master. The dey began speaking. His voice held the soft tones of feigned esteem. "I must intrude upon the time allotted for your report, so please humor me while I recount a short story of my own."

We both maintained our silent attention.

"It is a strange anecdote that began when Allah sent to me the son of Bachaga Messaoud Ben Sheik Brahim. Were you acquainted with the old sheik?"

"Yes sir," Ahmed said.

"His eldest son is currently leader of the Shamba. This man is my loyal servant, and he is the ruler of an extraordinary tribe of ferocious warriors. These Arabs send tribute to me with the punctuality of spring following winter. They flock to my side at the first call for assistance."

The cheeks of my buttocks clasped tightly, one to the other. I felt dust clogging my throat.

"My great ally, Sheik El Mouen, told me of a great earthquake destroying Ghardia. He recounted the terrible fate of his slaves and children. Tears coursed from his eyes as he described the disaster's magnitude. Buildings and lives were lost in a fury of violent tremors."

The dey maintained the perfect spell of silence before declaiming, "Then! Sheik El Mouen whispered to me of black slaves and a woman, dressed as Tuareg warriors, looting his wrecked palace. The sheik was courteous to me in every manner of his being and never hinted that the mighty dey held knowledge of such lowborn robbers. The sheik's relatives, however, were not as solicitous, and they screamed heinous allegations at my chamberlain, and threats of revenge to my advisors."

Dey Hassan Bashaw reclined against the pillows and studied distant thoughts. No one disturbed his reverie with sound or movement. "Allah demands compassion from all true believers," he said. "I have granted the Shamba tribe dispensation from tribute until the next Ramadan." He turned his eyes directly at me. "I have also promised the sheik fifty white slaves to help rebuild his palace. Sheik El Mouen promised undying gratitude if the levy could include literate men. Slaves capable of designing and building a structure that would honor the dey's loyal Shamba. Slaves capable of maintaining accurate records and balanced accounts were specifically noted as essential to the project."

I dropped my eyes and uttered silent profanities in four languages. Visions of Christian corporals and prison filth obscured the tiled floor.

"In company with Sheik El Mouen was the Sultan Agg-Abba of the Tazili Tuareg." Our dey once again used the immense power of silence. "When the fox and hen appear together it can only mean that the fox is well fed. Tell me, Christian slave. Tell me, former janissary captain. Which is the fox—Shamba or Tuareg?"

We both stood mute.

"The sultan's tale was worthy of a coffeehouse storyteller. He described a Frank who professed status in the dey's cabinet—a false Moslem who stole slaves and kidnapped his royal daughter. A monster that would destroy the natural order of Allah by making slaves equal to masters, and women equal to men."

The dey shook his head in disbelief. "An incredible story from our Tuareg ally—one that the sultan sensibly chose to diminish as an evil mirage. A confusion perpetrated by mountain djinni, or an amusement played by those who delight in creating trouble where there is none."

I moved neither finger nor tongue.

"You may be interested to know that the treasury of Algiers purchased ten white camels and forty black slaves for the sultan. His loyalty and friendship must be recognized, and his slaves replaced.

"Some of the sultan's blacks returned to the Tuareg. These audacious slaves carried stolen gold and rode on white camels. They wore veils of blue. Naturally, the Tuareg warriors could not tolerate renegade blacks in their midst, and the offending slaves were killed.

Some of the misbegotten blacks died slowly in the sand; others served to offer sport for lance and sword arms as a warning to all slaves. Allah demands obedience from slave to master. There are no exceptions to the word of God."

The dey's voice diminished in loudness and speed until his last statement was a slow whisper. I could hear the blue-backed flies buzzing in lazy circles amid the dust motes. After a long moment he cleared his voice and addressed Ahmed. "I have discussed the matter with your commander, and he is distraught over the failure of your mission. His rage at your incompetence exceeds my memory of the good man. Quartermaster Ahmet Blibita Mumdi and a full detachment of janissary destroyed. You will confine yourself to quarters at the barracks." His tough gravel voice finished the order. "Dismissed!"

It was my turn, and the dey wasted little time. "You left under a cloud, and you return in a storm. I am sorely tempted to make a gift of you to the amiable prince of Ghardia. There is no explanation for my compassion; you are my third Christian secretary, with your previous quarters. You may keep the first tavern and report tomorrow."

He waved me away, and I forced my legs to move toward the arched doorway. He spoke once again. "It is good for a young man to cherish a woman." A janissary guard smiled at the remark, and I continued my straight-backed retreat without breaking stride. The situation was bad, but it could have been worse.

CHAPTER THIRTY-THREE

February 1792

THE BAEGNIO APARTMENT RENDERED A mirror image of my life. Broken shards of glass described the transition from order to chaos. The quiet serenity created by Alphonse was now the domain of a laughing djinn. I stood at the open door trying to make sense of an incomprehensible spectacle. The last occupant had been ransomed the previous week, and at almost every step through the cluttered prison some person of my acquaintance repeated that fact to me. While unlocking the door leading to the roof, a poor starving fool yelled, "He's gone a week!" And as the heavy door swung open, the fool laughed a croaking mean laugh and yelled again, "A week. He's been gone a week."

Evidence of a celebration—nay, with testimony collected later from tavern gossips—an orgy! From doorsill to every corner of the apartment, broken bottles and crockery mounded as tiny atolls in a sea of fly-matted garbage. A cart of plague-dead slaves smelled sweet by comparison.

I retreated from the evil spectacle, returned to the prison courtyard, and engaged two black slaves to clean the filth. With studied petulance I used one of the few remaining silver coins to pay for the job. My tavern! My tavern! The records were gone, purged. Purloined. Nonexistent. My total inventory—every table and all money—had been stolen. The bath was filled with rusty, stagnant water and broken pipes. The stench and lassitude of the baegnio permeated every corner of my tavern, and with barely controlled rage I discharged every employee, cleared the customers (they were the lowest scum), and used the last of my money-belt horde to hire repairmen, plumbers, janitors, and guards. The apartment needed at least one more day of cleaning, and I slept that night in the empty tavern.

At dawn I reported to the dey's Moslem secretary, who barely looked up from sipping his coffee to shout, "You're not needed, infidel. Go away!"

I took the message as neither good nor bad news and hastened to see my friend Swedish Consul Peter Eric Skjoldebrand in his home. He welcomed me with a pensive expression and an invitation to break my fast with him.

Peter Eric was a Swede with dark complexion—a big man who held with his countrymen's propensity for a studied, taciturn personality. Although his walking pace was lumbering, his mind moved quickly and with a whimsically comical sense of humor.

He looked up from his coffee and pastry to say, "We have heard of your promotion from ambassador to third Christian secretary. Let me be the first to offer my condolences."

"Am I on my way to the burial grounds, my friend?"

"Sooner than you planned, but as we both know, all such matters rest with Allah."

I shrugged and concentrated on consuming four eggs and a rasher of bacon. Peter Eric sipped his coffee.

After cleaning the plate, I looked up and asked, "How go negotiations between my country and the dey?"

"I'd say they range from peculiar to perplexing," he answered.

"At certain odd times a person claiming both United States citizenship and consular status makes an appearance before our dey. The man claims money adequate for the release of prisoners, plus annual tribute for the safe passage of merchant ships, and then nothing happens."

"Nothing?"

"In the typical sequence, the illusive consul and promised ransom money disappear from the memory of the next negotiator, and the dey of Algiers becomes incensed at being trifled with."

"No surprise there," I said

Peter Eric continued. "I must admit that the behavior of your sovereign country appears carefully planned to keep all the captured American sailors as slaves and for you to remain in the dey's service into the next century."

"Is General Washington still president? Surely he wouldn't allow our reputation to be so tarnished."

"My dear young friend, your President Washington himself admits having no power. He proclaims his weakness an asset and denies any authority that may be given to him." Peter Eric shook his head and smiled sweetly at me. "Some more kippers? Eggs? Coffee? Possibly some kuskussu and mint tea?"

I gave him a well-practiced janissary glare and signaled the Spanish slave to heap more eggs and kippers onto my plate.

The Swedish consul continued. "Listen carefully, James. The Americans apparently imagine that every country is as muddle-minded as they and fervently believe that a few loudly shouted slogans will suffice as reality. Your esteemed leader makes pious statements about honoring treaties, yet we of the consular assembly cannot count a single instance of honor, and many of reprobation."

"Is there any hope of assistance from the French?"

"Ha! The French, your allies against the English, are most unhappy with the cavalier abandonment of signed agreements. Treaties negotiated after the victory at Yorktown, confirmed with the loving embraces of perpetual fraternity, are now ignored."

"My goodness! What are the French saying, Peter Eric? Can we Americans still serve together as friends?"

The Swedish ambassador stood from his chair to better make his point. "Every public pronouncement from Philadelphia and Paris claims mutual esteem, I'll admit that much. Your American politicians and merchants have, however, found it convenient to ignore longstanding debts to the French." Now a long finger pointed at my head. "The French claim treaty violations, and the Americans seem baffled by such slander. American merchant ships sail almost exclusively into English harbors, so, as far as the French are concerned, the enemy dominates American trade, while the ally languishes."

"Well," I said, "it is a certain fact that no one can tell an American merchant where he may sell his goods, and certainly no one can tell an American where he may purchase the slightest item."

Peter Eric returned to sitting in his chair and managed an eloquent shrug of his shoulders, all in the same movement. "Then, my friend, it should not surprise you that the French consul whispers damaging insinuations concerning all Americans to the dey of Algiers."

"Not after I've heard your interpretation of the state of affairs."

"To add sauce to the gander, it also seems to me that Hassan Bashaw is better informed of the contentions within your own Congress than is each envoy sent by the American secretary of state. In point of fact, my esteemed third Christian secretary, it is an incontestable fact that the dey of Algiers comprehends the significance of monetary appropriations made by the House of Representatives better than any envoy that has thus far approached him."

"Sir, I am the last person to contest my employer's intelligence or the multiplicity of his sources for information."

"Then you stand as the only American of my acquaintance to show him proper respect."

Peter Eric laughed quietly to himself and then looked at me with a benign smile. "I have served my country for nearly twenty years here in the mighty kingdom of Algiers. Boredom is my greatest enemy, so I must admit to you an eccentric form of entertainment: the theater."

"Do you frequent the coffeehouses for the storytellers?"

"Only for brief and occasional visits; my greatest pleasure is to watch the unscheduled performances of a most unusual comedy."

"Something un-American, I suspect."

"Indeed, it is an untitled farce featuring the itinerant American peace commissioner and the mighty dey of Algiers. I cheer as Hassan Bashaw renders his rendition of Barbarossa the Great, complete with curved sword carving the air and his outraged voice causing chandeliers to sway."

"All well practiced and universally appreciated, Peter. But what about his grand lines from Shakespeare's tragedies? Are they not worth comment?"

"I repeat each line before they are uttered and giggle with delight at my accuracy."

"Peter Eric, please do not play me for the country bumpkin. How does the dey gain secrets from the American government? Does he employ French spies?"

"Newspapers from Boston, New York, and Charleston are the most useful. The news is only a month old when copies of American newspapers arrive aboard European ships, and they all contain a detailed discussion of every bill before Congress. The loquacious editors from the *Boston Globe* attack Tories of the south, while incensed editors from the *Charleston Courier* describe the evil forms of legislation sponsored by the north. So there you have the sum total of the dey's spy system. Merely add a secretary or two with the ability translate English into a more respectable language, my naive friend, and we are finished."

"So, you will soon have me reading American newspapers for the edification of the dey of Algiers?"

"I'm certain that it will not be your only responsibility, my third secretary, but certainly an essential duty."

"Enough!" I said. "Too much good news is unsettling. Pray tell, my Swedish friend, what of the local news? How are my comrades in slavery managing?"

"Well, let's see. Of the twenty-five Americans captured in the summer of 1785, ten remain, plus you and Odabasi Ahmed al-Koita."

"Odabasi?"

"Yes, he is demoted from bolukbasi to odabasi—and lucky, at that. Ahmed failed on the recent expedition to Ghardia."

"I know that Ahmed is in trouble with his superior officers, but I also know he had convinced himself that the expedition was successful by every possible standard."

"The dey did lose some gold and a few slaves, and that is a matter of small concern. His very real concern is the possible loss of a committed ally, and because it was our friend Ahmed who organized and implemented the attack on that important ally, the dey's entire regency is threatened with disaster."

"We were both ignorant fools in that matter, without the slightest doubt."

"I'll repeat what you already know then. You and Ahmed have chosen to serve the dey of Algiers, and your master can be successful only from your efforts. You both must study each weakness of the dey and protect him. His survival is your salvation."

We sipped coffee and watched the servant remove the debris of our breakfast. I could feel the kippers and Peter Eric's advice sit as a lead weight in my stomach. He was correct in every manner of speaking. There could be no tentative allegiance to my master, the dey of Algiers. I must serve him with the same unabashed commitment that Captain Cathcart would receive, for the dey's failure to survive his enemies would most assuredly condemn me and all the American captives to a very painful death.

"Ahmed is an able young man," said Peter Eric. "He survived a difficult situation, and that fact counts in his favor. He is smart, and he is hungry for success—another two points in his favor. The coffeehouse philosophers predict a rapid climb through the ranks for Ahmed al-Koita."

"I'll do what I can to help his ascendency."

"By the by, there is similar agreement on your rapid ascent to first Christian secretary. Escribaño Grande!"

"Upon what evidence do you make that judgement?" I asked.

He smiled and wagged a finger with the air of a schoolteacher. "Remember the poet Milton when considering such questions. In Algiers it is always the 'airy tongues that syllable men's names.' So, my friend, there is nothing of substance, merely 'airy tongues.'"

"You and my uncle Stevens make a fine pair—both constantly improving my mind by telling me nothing. Save me from cunning teachers!"

Peter Eric nodded slowly up and down. "With a few more seasons, you'll change that prayer. I'm confident you will soon appreciate the likes of a good Swedish uncle." He gave me an expression of benign superiority and continued nodding, even as I stood to take my leave.

He coughed twice and continued. "In any event, are you interested in a status report of the American slaves?"

I regained my seat. "Yes."

"Now let's see. There were two other ships captured the same summer as yours. Am I correct?"

"Yes, Stevens was captain of the *Maria*; O'Brian and Coffin were the other two captains."

"Well now, both Captains O'Brian and Stevens continue to reside at my cottage northeast of the city gates."

"And what is the status of their health?"

"O'Brian is in vigorous health and spirit. He seems to gain in self-assurance with each passing month, and the Algerians hold him in high esteem as a sailmaker."

"A sailmaker, is it?"

"He is frequently called upon to supervise the repair and rigging of the dey's cruisers."

"And Captain Stevens—how does he fare?"

"Your captain is not much about. Cheap Spanish brandy and abundant self-pity restrict his status among the Algerians. He especially complains that you ignore his needs."

"My uncle is a drunken fool! I've paid his keep these past years, and my reward is vilification and maundering."

"That may be your perception of the facts, but he is also your captain, and you will be wise to pay your respects and meet his needs as you can."

"Agreed, as usual; what about the others?"

"Two of the mates under O'Brian, Robertson and Colville, were redeemed by friends. I believe the levy was eight hundred Algerian sequins. Six sailors, including your shipmate Sevillon Williams, have died of the plague."

"Captain Coffin was dead before I departed on our desert sojourn. Consumption, wasn't it?"

"Yes, and Omrod Williams remains in the madhouse. It is certain that he will not last much longer. The Arabs tease him by beating the metal bars and dangling food out of his reach. They urinate on the devil-infidel and scream with pleasure as he accepts their stream in his face."

We were both silent. The madhouse was full of demented souls whose frail existence rested upon charity prescribed by the Koran.

"Peter Eric, my one remaining tavern has been gutted. I must contact Miciah Baccri and secure some funds from my account. Can you arrange our meeting?"

"Save your time, my friend. Your money has vanished."

I sat in my chair, full of kippers and coffee, and tried to digest this new food with patient thought. Instead, I stood and yelled like a petulant child, "Impossible! I have his promise!"

"Your money was confiscated by the dey to pay for your mistakes. He told those who would listen that the camels for the Tuareg Sultan and a palace for the Shamba prince were purchased with your stolen savings."

"It's gone! The money's gone! Damn that Jew!"

"There was nothing Baccri could do. The dey knew your savings had been stolen from him and kept from him by your stealth and artifice. Baccri had neither moral nor legal grounds to protect your interests." The Swedish consul folded his hands on the empty table. "There you have it." His head began nodding again.

My capacity to endure another disappointment was surmounted by this last intelligence. Wads of cotton filled the void behind my eyeballs. Sound diminished until the parting phrases of Consul Skjoldebrand receded to an unintelligible whisper.

<hr />

That afternoon and evening I sat behind the barricaded doors of my tavern and sampled each container of peppered spirit. The first mouthful was difficult to manage past my tongue, but during the shadows of late afternoon the pleasant draughts tumbled effortlessly into my fathomless stomach. After each gurgling swallow of the now mellow liqueur, I chanted another line penned by Milton.

Under the whelming tide
Visit'st the bottom of the monstrous world.

Tides move in two directions, and before daybreak I was on my knees heaving the last tenacious waves of green bile onto the littered shore of my tavern. I recalled little of the nightmare. I remembered two or three times when a pounding on the door complemented those in my head. To both I mumbled, "Go away; go away."

CHAPTER THIRTY-FOUR

April 1792

THE DEY IGNORED ME DURING the first month of my return from the desert. I reported for work every morning at daybreak, and if American newspapers were available, I read the Arabic version to the exalted Moslem secretary until he ordered, "Go away—you're not needed!" I floated in the netherworld of uncertainty to drift from Peter Eric's office to a coffeehouse and back to the prison. There was no angry summons from the dey or painful confrontation with any of his minions. On one occasion, I met Ahmed in a quiet alley near the janissary barracks, and he seemed placed on the same level of purgatory. We were both isolated and ignored. Money equals power, and we had none.

I scrounged Algiers for some viable source of revenue and secured a position with the British surgeon Dr. Philip Werner. His records of both commercial transactions and medical services were chaotically spread through three stout wooden boxes in two separate rooms. I worked with diligent application to mitigate the twin problems presented: the need for an assemblage of clearly understood categories and the invention of a simple accounting system that could be easily maintained by the surgeon.

Near noon on each day I suspended my work for Dr. Werner and shared his food and company. We gossiped of Algiers and delicately affirmed the affinity, and needed friendship, of England with her former colony. He seemed to appreciate my efforts on his behalf and was an adequate student in learning the intricacies of double-entry record keeping.

Our last dinner together was marked by the consumption of a large turkey and two full bottles of Spanish red wine, all amid gentle discussions and some jollity. When I submitted my fee the next day, the doctor refused payment. He claimed me an audacious slave in charging criminal rates, and, further, the man declared that his generosity in allowing a slave into his home had been returned in a most unprincipled manner. The doctor loudly proclaimed that he would have an end to such perfidious behavior. He stomped his feet, waved his arms, and turned to leave me standing at his closed door without a single coin as compensation for my labor.

Sadly for Dr. Werner, the English were temporarily on the dey's list of despised people. My request for the dey to adjudicate the matter was not accepted. He refused a hearing of the dispute, yet Dr. Werner quickly paid his debt to me, the full arrearage, and vowed in loud croaking screams that he would never again deal with "American scoundrels or riffraff villains!"

The day following Dr. Philip Werner's payment of my reckoning, the demand for my genius as a bookkeeper exceeded the time available to render service. Although the dey had refused to publicly intercede on my behalf, the undeniable facts of Werner's capitulation to my demands were plain for all to see. When a few of the most important of the grandees offered substantial fees to me for trivial service, it became clear to one and all that my status at court would soon reward those who were my patrons. When the lesser grandees begged my services and paid my fees in advance of service rendered, my cash flow permitted the investments necessary to raise my tavern to efficient operation. I was able to offer distractions to the most reliable customers in the prison. And of course I refused entrance to the defective, poor, or violent.

During the day, my tavern served a cosmopolitan collection of Turks, Arabs, Europeans, and a few Jews, with a combination of good food, ample beverages, and the joyous bath. When the prison gates closed at sunset, the wealthy and educated slaves found the ambience of my resort credible. Business flourished, and my income increased without much thought on my part. I would not employ American sailors in my tavern, but I was able to provide meals for them at a couple of the lesser taverns. Of even greater importance, I believe, was my effort to encourage my compatriots with our constant goal of freedom for all American sailors. I tried to impart the knowledge that their freedom from slavery and my freedom from slavery were equal goals. I tried to educate them to the reality that my success as an esteemed employee of the dey of Algiers would render freedom for all Americans before any minions of General Washington's government could generate the requisite tolls demanded by the dey.

<hr>

As if the pendulum of financial luck had not swung far enough in my favor, Peter Eric Skjoldebrand advised me that my old friend, Ibn Hudaij, had a ship for sale, complete with a cargo of wine and cognac.

"Very interesting," I said, "but I have little available capital."

When Peter Eric fell silent, I added with detached curiosity, "What is his price?"

"He will take two thousand sequins, and I will lend you the full amount."

"That is most generous, Peter Eric, most generous. At what rate of interest?"

"No interest, and you may repay at your leisure."

"I'm speechless. Why would you do such a thing?"

"You know, of course, that my position as Sweden's consul prohibits my speculating in captured ships." There was a slight stammer in his voice. "You can serve as my proxy in this matter. I'm confident that the cargo can be sold to the various tavern keepers for five or six times the purchase price, thereby speeding your financial recovery and rendering a small profit for me."

We eyed each other—more as two roosters than clucking hens.

He continued with his speech. "It is also important for me to confirm the intimacy of our relationship. I can deal with information received in an expeditious fashion, and in the future you may see fit to warn me of problems that may affect my country or to help me into positions that might give some advantage to Sweden."

"A bribe then; your gift is a simple bribe." I managed a full quota of indignation in my voice. "I refuse your offer."

"Listen, James Cathcart. I know and appreciate your honesty. Your loyalty is first to the dey of Algiers, as it should be—"

"My loyalty, sir, is first to the United States of America. The dey is my employer, and he will receive the courtesy of my unrelieved attention." The display of anger seemed the correct tack to take, up to a point. "The truth is, Peter Eric, you are my friend, so be assured that I will respond to you as a friend. Friends, I'm told, help one another; therefore, I will always look for ways to assist you and expect that you will continue in helping all of the American sailors attain their freedom."

"My apologies, James. I spoke awkwardly and insinuated a character defect that is mine, not yours. I apologize."

"Accepted, most assuredly. I also realize that you are a most generous friend. In fact, a true friend." I paused for some mathematical calculations, and then said in a staid matter-of-fact voice, "Let me make a counteroffer. In exchange for the loan, which I gratefully accept, I will promise to repay the principal within sixty days at ten percent interest. Additionally, I will pay you twenty-five percent of the net profit."

"Agreed!" the Swede said with a big smile. "Here is my hand on the compact."

The dance was over. We had performed each step with grace and decorum, and now both actors were rewarded with immediate gain and future credit. Friendship is truly a remarkable gift.

◆

The profit from the sale of the Venetian ship went in many directions. I purchased two additional taverns and gave Ahmed six hundred Algerian sequins. My compliments went to important advisors of Hassan Bashaw, while Ahmed's compliments went to his janissary commanders. We purchased and presented our tribute with appropriate decorum, and ample bribes also went to the servants of these important men. I ordered clothes in the Turkish style from a Ragusian tailor, and he offered designs currently in favor by the grandees. Ahmed heard whispers of his impending promotion in rank and required two new sets of dress uniforms. The windfall profits disappeared very rapidly.

◆

Ahmed and I met almost daily at a coffeehouse near his barracks. On one bright warm morning, after three cups of coffee and two visits to the latrine, I explained to him my theories of mercantile success. "Buy cheap, sell dear, and control costs. Strike fair deals with customers, and restrict Americans from the inventory."

"You bloody nincompoop. Just because you're a good bootlicker doesn't make you a shrewd businessman. You know damn well that Peter Eric or Miciah Baccri will always set you up with the best deals."

"I'll ignore that pronouncement. What's troubling you? You're grouchy as a eunuch."

"I've been commissioned bolukbasi of the janissary."

"Congratulations—a quick promotion from odabasi." I looked more carefully. "I still see a frown. You should be wildly excited. Now a captain of the janissary, soon a general! Who knows? Maybe ruler of the world!"

"Shut your mouth, unclean beast." Ahmed motioned for a servant to bring another coffee. He took a long, deep inhale on his pipe; held the smoke for an interminable length of time; and finally spewed a slow, patient exhale up toward the cedar rafters. "The campaign is going poorly."

"You refer to your hunt for a wife?"

"I've paid good money to a marriage broker, and I get nothing in return. Merely excuses—more and more money paid, and more and more excuses. Tell me the truth, Jamie." Ahmed leaned forward and lowered his voice. "Am I too ugly or too poor?"

"Add too short," I teased.

He finally smiled. "You have an audience with the dey?"

"Yes, finally, I have a private meeting in his apartment. It's been over a year since our last meeting."

"We had the honor to appear in his presence on January 12, 1790—Christian calendar." Ahmed peered at me with his finest military stare.

"Yes, I have a vague recollection of that muster. So, fifteen months and my head is still properly connected. I wonder what he wants."

◆

The walk was a blur with no memory. The palace entrance, with frequent janissary guards and loitering supplicants, receded into the comfortable niche of distracted blindness. The maze of halls and arches and courtyards led interminably to the protected nest of the dey's apartment, and there, at last, the hanging cloth curtains and sumptuous divans provided relief from the austere brittleness of constant white marble.

The room smelled of Alphonse's musk.

As I approached dey Hassan Bashaw to humble myself and to kiss his hand, his changed appearance flared before me. Always, in my past experience, he had been a vigorous man, exhibiting wildly varied emotions and living life fully. Now he seemed an old man, his beard smeared white and head ringed with a mere fringe of gray hair. He spoke to the far corners of his apartment. "What trouble have you caused me lately, infidel?"

"Effendi, my responsibility and sole duty is to serve and to please you."

"You have a slippery tongue with no substance apparent. Do all Americans have the same parents? Do you all learn techniques of deceit as infants and practice them until death?"

He pointed a finger at me and drew it slowly across his throat, mimicking the motion of an execution sword. "Your descent into hell may be sooner than you wish, infidel dog, unless you practice the true believer's virtues of honesty and candor."

I knew this statement to be what the dey considered droll humor, and that any response had to be limited to a simple affirmation of improved effort. "I will do my very best, effendi."

It was Hassan Bashaw's obligation to direct a barrage of verbal insult and bluster toward me, and for me to give a compliant response. This strategy was designed to placate his enemies, divert spies, and relax the imams. It was a code easily deciphered by the observers of his court.

"Come, piglet, kiss my hand."

"Thank you, effendi. I do so with all my heart."

The initial ritual was complete, and now the question-answer game was put into motion." Tell me, my third Christian secretary, why should I not declare war on the Americans? They trifle with me at all times. Promises are made by their representatives and then ignored. My cruisers rot from lack of action, and the treasury drains like a tub with no plug. Your country claims poverty, yet American merchant ships are numerous as fleas and rich beyond belief. Prince Washington has no navy—none!—yet pretends the strength of England."

I maintained a studied silence.

"I am a patient man." The dey looked down from his study of the ceiling and gazed at me as if I had just arrived. "You are now my first Christian secretary. Take your tools in hand and write a letter to your prince."

"Yes, my lord."

"Tell Prince Washington that the ransom for his sailors is fifty thousand Spanish gold doubloons, a frigate of thirty-six guns, annual marine supplies worth ten thousand gold doubloons, and appropriate annual gifts to my family and advisors. You shall also tell him that this tribute will suffice to ensure safe passage for every American vessel and will liberate the entire lot of American slaves."

"Certainly, my lord."

"You will also stipulate in this letter that unless my terms are met—without deviation—within six months, I shall declare war upon the United States. There shall be peace with the Americans or peace with the Portuguese; it makes no difference to me. If it is the Portuguese who pay into the treasury and not the Americans, then my cruisers will fly through the Pillars of Hercules and destroy the American merchant fleet. I speak the truth!"

My promotion was made so lightly that I gave it little immediate thought and quickly assumed my station. I assured the dey that the terms to General Washington, so clearly outlined, were well within the parameters established for other small nations, such as Holland or Denmark. The dey indicated that I might finally be capable of some good judgement and bade me to come forward to kiss his hand. As I bent at the waist to do his bidding, he whispered.

"Do you have the one thousand sequins for the first secretary's position?"

"No," I answered.

"I will credit you for five hundred, but you must take the balance to my treasurer before Friday."

"Certainly," I whispered.

This exchange of information was accomplished through wide smiles and with the skill of two master ventriloquists.

The dey required secrecy in such matters. True enough, I had no ready cash to pay the dey his required five hundred sequins. The facts were clear: my funds were nearly all committed to long-term projects, but a loan seemed readily available from either Baccri or Skjoldebrand. I chose the Swede.

I found Peter Erik drinking coffee with a sea captain from his native country, and after the sea captain departed, I explained my dilemma in exact detail to the ambassador.

"Unprecedented! In my twenty years I've never observed such an episode." Peter Eric stood from the table and smiled at me. "I'll get the five hundred sequins right today," and he walked out of the coffeehouse into the busy street.

Within four hours all of the European consuls reported to me, or to one of my servants, that they also had never seen such charitable behavior by this or any previous dey. They came over to my table or stopped me in the street with their congratulations. They suggested plans for future meetings and bid their special greetings to the dey of Algiers. Their smiles to me were extraordinarily generous, and when I paid my gift of five hundred sequins to the dey's finance minister the next day, even the treasurer expressed his interest at my advancement. In fact, the entire court of secretaries and clerks—Moslem, Jewish, and Christian alike—all pressed gifts of money upon me or to my newly acquired servants.

I feared such grand success as a harbinger of disaster. It seemed that momentum was growing to find a road to freedom for me and all American captives, but the list of possible difficulties made any dreams for success a waste of time.

The dey's message to President George Washington I completed in Turk, Arabic, and English. The dey of Algiers personally sealed each document with a mighty chunk of red wax, and I sent them for delivery to the American ambassador in Lisbon as the most likely transfer port to the general. The entire task was completed six days after my original instructions.

We were both pleased with the beginning of my tenure as first Christian secretary to the dey of Algiers. Our mutual admiration grew with each passing day. He was the perfect ship's master. Every wind from breeze to gale he used to his advantage. There were no fantasies of excess in assigning responsibilities to his crew. A worm-eaten ship and coarse men survived deadly storms under the leadership of Hassan Bashaw. For my part, I worked hard to serve my captain well, and we quickly attained a well-run ship.

The dey spoke to me in either short furtive whispers or loud one-sided harangues. Of course he was required to direct his wrath at all Americans as a necessary strategy for the eventual negotiations for payment of their ransom, and since I stood before him as the closest and most obvious example of American subterfuge and deceit, I received the constant loud and public tongue lashings. The important people of Algiers always understood the purpose of such attacks upon me, and my status escalated in measurable terms. Small gifts from petitioners came to me with comfortable frequency. Court officials diminished their insults to my person and religion. My savings accumulated in Baccri's bank.

The most obvious affirmation of my improved social status came from the wealth accrued by my servants. Tradition requires that guests make a gift of money to servants of a host. The size of the gratuity measures the host's status, and my staff quickly became effective in providing answers or services for every wish the dey of Algiers channeled through my office.

CHAPTER THIRTY-FIVE

August 1792

THE AMERICAN MERCHANT FLEET REMAINED unmolested by Algerian pirates during the summer of 1792. The dey was distracted by the ebb and flow of European politics, but not infrequently he stopped a conversation with a consul or diplomat to shout at me. "The Americans! They trifle with me again! This is the end of my patience." No envoy came from America bearing the required tribute as stated in my letter to General Washington. No American minister dickered for the release of American slaves. The foreign consuls and court advisors all remarked on the outlaw behavior of the United States. They spoke to each other in small animated clusters scattered through the palace halls, always within hearing range of the dey or me. They constantly berated the Americans as uncivilized savages. "All must obey the necessary rules and conventions," they said. "What can you expect?" said the French consul, "There is no honor among those thieves."

The dey listened to the myriad complaints against my country and moved on to more pressing issues. During my early tenure as first Christian secretary, I was a minor participant in the Algerian rapprochement with Spain. Of the many infidel nations, Spain maintained a position at the apex of approbation for all Moslems. They had seen nearly one thousand years of war: a holy jihad of unending duration. Spain—the most Christian of nations—was indeed the Devil's most visible tool.

The dey studied a large map of North Africa while I stood at his shoulder. He appeared totally absorbed in his pursuit of knowledge, yet whispered to me from behind his mask of beard and moustache. "It appears, my infidel scribbler, that Oran is about to fall. The siege directed by my brother is nearly ended. He has the Christians drinking their own piss, so it will not be long."

"Congratulations, effendi. The Spanish are also likely enemies of my country."

The dey turned and looked at me as if I were a toad. A poisonous mushroom. "My brother, the bey of my western regency, has assembled twenty thousand Berber, Arabs, and Kabyle. This young twit of a brother has collected twenty thousand men, all trained from birth to fight against one another, yet now!" said Hassan Bashaw. "Now they are together and you smile. You deign to judge the success of my brother as a motive for our mutual celebration? Idiot! His success is my likely death, you fool! And yours, I might add!"

"But the Spanish, effendi—they must be driven from Oran."

"There are no Spaniards in Oran, you simpleton. Your earthquake—the same bolt from Allah that struck Ghardia—also leveled Oran and killed most of the Spanish infidels. Those who remain have no will for fighting. The remaining Spanish people are mostly starving women and bankrupt merchants. The infidel soldiers who survived Allah's fury scuttled back to their Spanish dens. Such is the worthy foe of my brave brother and his barbaric legions: women and children and peddlers."

The dey sat quietly for a long time. I remained silent, waiting for the inevitable question. "Advise me, my Christian secretary: Why is there such enthusiasm for such a corpse? How can my piddling little brother convince Arabs and Kabyle and Berber to join in common purpose to invade Oran? And of greater importance still, what posture of leadership should I assume in this matter? Give me an opinion, if you will."

Fortunately, I knew the correct answer to this conundrum. Hassan Bashaw was not a ruler who rushed into decisions. Every concern of the regency—every major crisis—met with a precise examination from his council of ministers. From that exalted forum the debate on each issue filtered down through the janissary officers until finally every permutation was discussed by the ship captains and grandees and important merchants. Whispers returned via the harems and baths to the dey's wives. In the end, Hassan Bashaw bravely made his independent and forceful decisions with little fear of contradiction.

My intimacy with Ahmed placed me in a position to judge the janissary temper. I also integrated information from the military with bits gleaned from other worthy informants. With Hassan Bashaw, I assumed the pose of a depositary of diverse sources of information. "The janissary, effendi, would support a treaty of peace with the Spanish. They feel little threat from the Spanish but a great concern for any coalition of our western tribes."

"My thought, exactly." Hassan Bashaw nodded. "The Rais and the merchants, of course, are equally adamant against such an agreement. `Death to the infidel!' they shout to me. The dey's cruisers have too long farmed Spanish blood and fortune for us to now act as eunuchs."

"It is a problem," I admitted.

"So it seems."

"Ha!" shouted the dey into my ear and to all those who were carefully listening to our discussion. "Arab and Berber together can never happen. Never! Allah would never permit such a deviation from nature. They were born to kill one another, not join for common purpose." The dey paced back and forth in front of the large map.

"If I can negotiate a treaty with Spain in the very near future, the old desert feuds will win out over a tired bone such as Oran."

"So it seems," I said.

The dey gave me his venomous smile. "Ahhh, as you must understand by now, my little piglet, we Turks can always beguile those desert bandits into serving their proper master."

"Of course, effendi. And what of the ship captains? It seems that both the ship captains and the merchants of Algiers are starving for new victims," I said.

The same deadly smile covered me like a noxious cloud. "Ahhh, do I see a ray of sunshine flowing from my Christian secretary. Are we both thinking that a morsel given to my captains and loyal merchants would cement my support in this regency?" My dey stared at me with narrowed eyes. "So, my good fellow, you must agree that the Americans must serve as fodder for my hungry friends. I'll give them the Americans, and that should make everyone happy. Isn't that so, First Christian Secretary? I'll throw a tasty morsel for all who follow the illustrious dey of Algiers, and all will be well in our city."

He gave a tired laugh, and I tried my best to maintain a dignified silence. My stomach gave a great heave of pain. How could it happen that my government had not responded to my letter in a timely fashion? Even a written response with an offer of lower ransom for the American sailors would have served to begin proper negotiations between dey and general. Now the path to freedom for me and all Americans had been torn from my grasp. Damn the dey and the general and me. All of us—blind fools.

In September 1791, the Spanish had signed a treaty agreement with their ancient enemy the Regency of Algiers. There was much grinding of teeth and profane oaths of "Infidels!" on both sides, yet the agreement was ratified by advisors of the Spanish king and officials serving Dey Hassan Bashaw. On the last day of February 1792, Bey el-Kebir, the esteemed and favored younger brother of Dey Hassan Bashaw, entered Oran. The few Spanish families remaining were unmolested by either janissary or Berber troops. Allah once again smiled with the pleasure of victory over the godless Christians. No blood from Moslem martyrs was necessary to drive the Christians from Oran. Only ink and false smiles were needed to purge the homeland from the last vestige of infidel control. Now all of Barbary was free from the insult of Christian authority. Never again would Spain find comfort for men or ships in the domain of Allah.

Hassan Bashaw did not involve me in the further negotiations with either Spain or Portugal. I observed the scurrying of ambassadors, and over the next months discussed the implications of each detail with Ahmed, Peter Eric, and, increasingly, Captain Richard O'Brian. As summer of 1792 drew to a close, six months after the dey's promise of action against my country, the ship captains and the merchants received their reward for supporting the dey in his quest for peace with the Spanish. The Algerian cruisers raced through the Straits of Gibraltar and began prowling the open Atlantic. From August through early October 1792, thirteen American ships with one hundred thirty men were captured. The ships and cargo were sold at fair prices to the merchants, and the sailors enslaved in the prison. Dey Hassan Bashaw smiled upon his constituents and listened carefully for the next whispers from his first Christian secretary.

The newly captured Americans suffered the twin scourges of slavery and the plague. Many died. We slaves were ignored by our countrymen. No one in our government gave any indication that they cared for our welfare. No ambassadors called; no ransom was discussed.

I arranged accommodations for the ship captains in homes of friendly foreign consuls. The mates and sailors were initially sent to the prison, and some were later sold to those who would buy them. Very quickly, in our small world of Algiers, the captains earned a deserved reputation as drunken louts. On each occasion that I reported an incident of injury or death caused by their swinish behavior, the dey questioned me on the merits of Christians in general and my countrymen in particular. I took them as rhetorical queries and maintained my silence. What else could I do?

During the winter of 1793-1794, six hundred European and American slaves endured the baegnio. Hassan Bashaw analyzed the warring nations of Europe and judged the carnage everlasting. In his mind, nothing could stop the bloodletting. He divined that European potentates and desert sheiks would always continue with their favorite vendettas, and none were likely to cause the dey of Algiers any protracted concern. He appraised the slave business as perpetually safe and profitable, and his cruisers now roamed with impunity and great profit.

Hassan Bashaw prospered, as did all those who patronized him. It seemed to me that my protector was a visionary on the same order as Thomas Jefferson. Both had the capacity to look far into the future and project abundant rewards from small beginnings. Neither felt limited by ethical constraints. Hassan Bashaw looked at my country and judged the United States more than a plum to be picked. His imagination invented a vast forest requiring constant pruning and care but producing a bountiful harvest of tall, straight ship masts; unending barrels of turpentine and of grain; tubs of salted fish; bales of cotton— and gold. He augured a partnership between the preeminent Barbary state and the outlaw republican nation. Only time was needed to organize such a contrivance. Time and good planning.

"First Christian Secretary," thundered Dey Hassan Bashaw. He filled the largest audience room of the palace with his presence. The cold winds of January 1793 fluttered the ornate wall draperies. His advisors and officers sat on pillows and huddled around small portable charcoal braziers. The chattering hubbub of voices trickled to a halt. I listened and held myself ready for his bidding.

"Your Excellency, what is your command?" I said.

"You will prepare a new list of my demands for your prince, General Washington."

"Yes, effendi. Shall I record them now?"

"Assuredly, infidel pig! Take your scribbler's tools, and write these terms in stone. I will not be trifled with again by the Americans."

I held pen in the air and indicated by gesture and posture that his words would gain immediate transcription.

"Two thirty-six-gun frigates. One million Spanish gold doubloons for the government treasury. For myself, they shall pay one half million Spanish gold doubloons." He gestured to those in attendance. "My officers and advisors shall receive two hundred thousand Spanish gold, and the American slaves may be redeemed from their owners with three hundred fifty thousand doubloons."

The entire court smiled, nodded, and proclaimed with loud whispers the wisdom and power of the dey. I scratched and sanded the terms and read them back to Hassan Bashaw for his approval.

"Yes, very good. Now you may add the conditions for peace and safe trade in our sea."

I nodded to indicate my ready pen, and he nodded in return.

"From this point forward, the Americans will send annual naval supplies to my court in the same quantity as currently given to me by Sweden, Holland, and Denmark. I require nothing more or less from the Americans than from these three small nations of no special importance."

The assembled court burst into cheers that continued until Hassan Bashaw held his hand toward them, and their silence allowed the dey his final word.

"You will complete the document with the usual threats and benevolent desire for good health, my first Christian secretary."

"Let justice be done!" and "May Allah provide!" echoed through the audience chamber and out into the arched hallway. The crowd dispersed, with many fleeing the cold, drafty room and others forming a long line in front of the dey. The court chamberlain spoke briefly with each petitioner and waved many away and out of the audience room. Others he directed to me or to various officers of the court. The remaining few he placed in rank order and allowed them a brief word with Dey Hassan Bashaw. Later in the day and through the early evening, I wrote the treaty in the formal language demanded by tradition. A week later I gave the document to a Portuguese ship captain for delivery to the American ambassador in Lisbon.

—————

Silent months melted into unsparing slavery and death. No word of comfort or relief came from the United States government. There was not even the small stipend—created from Alphonse's subterfuge with the Swedish cannon—for the ship captains. We Americans, alone of all Barbary slaves, languished without hope of redemption by our government. Some few were rescued through intervention by friends or relatives, but most Americans sank into the deep well of hopeless despair, and I was able to provide the basic necessities for those mates and sailors condemned to the prison.

Therefore, as our nation ignored their needs, I became their patron. Mates and sailors ate meals at my tavern without cost. Clothing I provided as needed, but very few performed jobs that earned remuneration during the evening hours. A few cobbled shoes or sewed buttons to generate income for their own special comforts.

The crowd of Americans commiserated among themselves with vindictive complaints and idle conversation. In spite of my best efforts to minimize their discomfort, none of my compatriots expressed the slightest hint of appreciation to me. They took my charity as their due and complained insufferably of their plight. At times I felt like a father to a massive family of ungrateful children. With my assumed obligations ever present, I expanded my tavern holdings to seven. Peter Eric Skjoldebrand and Miciah Baccri directed me toward a few successful speculations in the sale of wheat to the besieged French. Many of the gifts that I received from grateful patrons were sold in the bazaar. I must admit that, all in all, my financial obligations were satisfied, and a small surplus dribbled into Baccri's bank.

———◆———

When Alphonse whispered advice into my ear, I waited until after the last call to prayers and then wandered silently through the city. At some dark, quiet place with an unobstructed view of the heavens, I found a comfortable place to study the far-distant stars. My patient confidence always brought me success. "Yes, Alphonse, there it is— the new star. In the dark, beyond the least conspicuous of the constellations, a new star burns. Stay near that star, Alphonse. Someday I will join you. I will give you a wonderful gift. I will listen to your stories and watch the smile on your lips. Do not leave. Stay near that most fragile of all stars, and I will find you."

CHAPTER THIRTY-SIX

December 1794

A HMED SMOKED HIS SHORT PIPE with the patience of an old Arab merchant. He drank his coffee, listened to my prattle of intrigue at the palace, and grunted monosyllables to each description of incompetence. "What's the matter?" I asked.

"Nothing."

After a few moments, I queried, "How are negotiations proceeding with Lady Fatima?"

"Fine."

Conversations burst and collapsed all around us. Clinking crockery created a bright melody, street noises a steady cadence, with silence a dramatic interval. "Who is she working with now? That ship captain, Temeen? Is that the one? Temeen's daughter?"

"Will you shut up? You know damn well that she is a waste of my time and money." Ahmed pushed his head toward mine, with eyes that showed more white than normal. "This is the third time! The Temeen family marks the third failure!"

"I'm the infallible first Christian secretary; you must give me more information."

"Fatima tells me everything is going beautifully. The mother is willing, the daughter willing, then, poof, the father begins his bad dreams, and my matchmaker starts looking for another prospect." His nose was practically on mine. "What is this bloody crap?"

"I can only guess, my friend, but it appears that you are not what fathers want for their daughters, and, truthfully, I must concur with the good judgement on their part." I ducked Ahmed's punch. "Let us go to Lady Fatima's house and ask some questions."

Ahmed's matchmaker was not required to wear a veil in public. Her back twisted and humped to the left, forcing the posture of a perched vulture, and her moustache reduced mine to an adolescent's first effort. Bounteous hair-waving moles created a pattern of scenic wonder across her face. With eyes a milky-gray that constantly oozed a sticky yellow substance, her ugliness granted a freedom unknown by most women of Algiers. Even the most fanatic mullah looked aside as she passed in the marketplace. The passions of innocent men remained quiescent when confronted with a bare-faced Lady Fatima.

"There is this problem, First Christian Secretary: your friend has no family or recorded history. He is but a soldier, and who knows if the wind that brought him to our city will not catch him up again?" Fatima nodded as she spoke. "A sergeant's daughter, or possibly a poor and ignorant shopkeeper's daughter. Certainly he has no appeal to a family of wealth or ancient blood. How could a father have any happiness with a son-in-law who has no ancestors? No, no, no! It cannot happen. The colonel must change instructions to me or remain a bachelor."

"Tell me, Lady Fatima, is my friend's skin color, his race, a deterrent to a good match?"

"Certainly not, for Allah forbids such distinctions. That you should even ask such a question shows the depth of your ignorance, esteemed first Christian secretary. Family is everything, and he has no family. Where is the grandfather who can exult in the details of his pilgrimage to Mecca? Where is the father who will protect his son from insults, or the mother who can proclaim his virtues?"

"I try, Lady Fatima. I say to everyone at the bath that Colonel al-Koita is a man with Allah smiling upon him."

"Ahhh, First Christian Secretary, but where are the aunts and cousins who will repeat such truth? No one can listen only to a single friend, and an infidel at that." Lady Fatima made a slight gesture with her right hand, ordering both of us to move closer to her throne of soft pillows. "You Franks are ignorant beyond all hope of understanding." She ate three green figs and consumed a full cup of tea before continuing with her monologue. "It is an impossible task to infuse generations of tradition into your vacant heads. Just imagine the home of a respected citizen of this fair city—a true believer in the One God, Allah, and faithful to all instructions from the Koran. After Allah, a man must protect the honor of his family. Above all, he must ensure the sanctity of his women. Each home must create a barrier against the temptations and intrusions that stand as a constant threat to all women. The required sanctuary for modest women of the true faith is the harem."

"You judge the harem as a happy place, a secure and comfortable place, my lady?"

"It is only in the harem that innocent children and innocent women can survive the dangers that lurk behind every turn in the road. A father must chart a safe course for his daughters. He must guarantee a safe passage from the harem controlled by his wife to the harem offered by the chosen husband, and that is my job: to serve as a guide from one harem to the next. If I fail in this task, if I provide a husband who cannot protect a man's daughter, then my life is over."

"Tell us, Lady Fatima, what can two ignorant Franks do to help with your mission?"

Even as she poked a pinch of snuff at her bobbing head, Fatima managed an enigmatic smile at me. She sneezed, twice, and then turned to me. "It is said—I hear the words in many places—it is said that you exchange whispers with the dey. Can such lies be the truth? An ugly Christian, an infidel. Can such as you share one second of light with our benevolent uncle? Tell me these lies are not so."

I tried to match her smile and found myself bobbing to the self-same rhythm as Lady Fatima. Lady Fatima, the most renowned of all matchmakers in Algiers. Lady Fatima, grand chamberlain of all harems, custodian of all veiled secrets.

◆

Before the next new moon appeared, I arranged for Dey Hassan Bashaw, lord and commander of the janissary corps, to meet privately with Colonel Ahmed al-Koita in a small palace apartment. The servants were dismissed. There were no attendants and no advisors— merely two soldiers whispering over empty coffee cups. Hassan Bashaw himself assured me that no one overheard the conversation; such an impertinent intrusion would require harsh punishment. A beating with cudgels, or even death by flame.

The next day I met with Lady Fatima.

"Everyone is talking about the private meeting with our dey and Colonel al-Koita," she said.

"The dey assured me that the meeting was both private and secret."

"Of course it was," she said. "That is why my client is such a popular topic of conversation. I happened on a few chance encounters with wives of important court officers and illustrious grandees at the market. They were all matrons of eligible daughters, and today they were all busy as bees at my orange blossoms."

"Busy? In what manner were they so occupied with you, my dear lady?"

"They were seeking sweet answers. It was first one matron: 'Tell me, good lady, of this famous Colonel al-Koita . . .' and another: 'Can you visit our harem this next day . . . ?'"

"My goodness, this is an interesting dilemma, I must say."

"The third matron was absolutely without caution."

"Are we still speaking about the good colonel?"

"Certainly! The impetuous woman told me that her husband gives his blessing for their daughter's marriage."

"Marriage to Ahmed?"

"Certainly. Ahmed—your friend and the private authority on military matters to our dey."

"Oh," I said.

"You shouldn't keep such secrets from me, First Christian Secretary."

"Did you know that when Ahmed was a young child, his grandfather led the Malinke people to Mecca?"

"No!"

"Further, that while waiting in Cairo for transportation to Mecca, the gold spent in the bazaars of Cairo by the Malinke people doubled all prices within two days."

"No!"

From a bountiful harvest of young virgins, the lovely Fatima selected the eldest daughter of Ali el-Aziz as the softest, ripest peach. Her name was Atiyat, a sweet innocent protected by a large and powerful clan. A child of thirteen—so adored by her family that she was innocent of all threats beyond her father's harem. A wealthy household antedating the Turks—before Barbarossa, in fact! A heroic family with the necessary wisdom to survive the ebb and flow of war on the Iberian Peninsula, and eventually return to the true homeland with both respect and a fortune. A pastoral family holding the ingenious skill required to plant daughters in each patch of fertile soil.

"It is a good contract, my colonel," said Lady Fatima.

"Ahmed, you son-of-a-bee! You're rich! Look at this contract. A big house. Two orchards, a vineyard, and a horse."

"A horse, my lord?" Lady Fatima seemed to straighten the bends of her back. "A horse? My poor, ignorant infidel. This stallion is more famous than any prince from your heathen land." She shook her head. "He is as swift as the wind and sires colts in his exact image. He will produce more income than all the granted orchards and vineyards."

"My apologies, good lady," I said, bowing graciously. Both Ahmed and I smiled at my ignorance and his success.

She shook her head at me in rejection of my apology and turned to Ahmed. "Pay attention! Your marriage has been announced, and you now have many new obligations."

Ahmed suddenly appeared lighter in complexion; more northern Irish in hue than deep African. He was a very ugly white man. "What?" he said.

"Your wedding celebration is on the next Sabbath. In one week!"

"What do I do? Help me!"

"Look, my handsome general—relax," I said. "We'll get you through this campaign. Relax!"

Lady Fatima ignored my intrusion. "Today you will move into your house. I will find appropriate servants, but you must secure the presents."

"Presents?"

"It is simple, dear one. Tomorrow, send your bride silver jewelry with precious stones inlaid. On Sunday, send combs of ivory and brushes of the finest camel hair. Also on Sunday, do not forget her family! It is a very large family, and you must send trays of fruit and sweetmeats, down to the second cousins. To forget this important offering would lose you all respect."

My friend turned an ugly gray color, and I took pity upon him. "I've got the list, Ahmed. I'll have my dragoman chase down what you need, so don't worry a bit."

Ahmed smiled. In fact, his smile was of such blinding intensity that I nearly missed his departure. "Thanks," he shouted, as he disappeared from Lady Fatima's meeting room, "Let me know what's next."

I enjoyed working with Lady Fatima. She saw me as an ignorant bumpkin, but one who could be useful in providing services and money. She was as skilled in her vocation as was my first employer, José Garcia. Both looked to each small preliminary detail as a critical component of the final enterprise. He was content to work in calm isolation, and she demanded an audience. Ahmed camped at his favorite coffeehouse and followed each instruction delivered by my dragoman. In truth, his responsibilities were no more than that of an experienced corporal, while Lady Fatima was the acknowledged general. I became first Christian secretary for her campaign and carefully followed every command.

On Monday, Ali el-Aziz sent a groom's wedding outfit to Ahmed's new house. In the afternoon some of the bride's servants, with silk sashes across their shoulders, rode on donkeys through the wealthy neighbourhoods of Algiers. They were accompanied by men with booming kettledrums. The noisy army served to bestow invitations upon the women of each selected household to a bride's party.

On the following day, at the public bathhouse, Fatima orchestrated her first triumph. Even the dey's harem marked the rarity of such refinement. It was noon, Tuesday. Atiyat dazzled her guests in leading a chattering parade of women. They were preceded and followed by musicians and were attended by six men carrying eating utensils and linen. And then, by the water-carrier, by the perfume-carrier, and by dozens and dozens of maidservants—all in bright colors and flowing gowns.

The entire entourage traveled through the streets to a slow, measured beat. The bride walked under an apricot-colored silk canopy carried by four men with poles. Embroidered handkerchiefs fluttered over the bride from atop each pole. It was hot walking through the streets; therefore, a woman attendant walked backwards in front of Atiyat, waving a fan of black ostrich feathers. Women smiled beneath their veils and moved in graceful procession through the crowded streets. The entire bathhouse was taken over by the bridal group.

Later, Fatima sat with me—as two gossips in the harem—and described the constant music and entertainments. Somewhat delicately she listed each step of the ritual washing of the bride using rare oils and perfumes. The bride's features: "Her nose! Such a nose as hers can only proclaim wealth! It is the emblem of her father's status among the ancient grandees. Atiyat is honored with such an appendage. Her sons will be honored in the same fashion."

Lady Fatima reached for a soft, ripe fig. The dark sweet, fruity perfume permeated her small command post. She nibbled small bits, chewed slowly, and swallowed. "Ahmed will appreciate the true beauty of his wife after she has given him three or four sons. She is but a child. Skinny and long in the wrong places." Lady Fatima lifted her eyes to the ceiling and held out her hands in a gesture of supplication. "For the wealthy, Allah can change ugliness into fine beauty. For the poor, ugliness endures from birth to death. Thank you for my poverty, Lord. Thank you."

Fatima left off her small complaint to God and returned her attention to me. "Atiyat brings a large dowry to her marriage. It is only a matter of time. In a few years she will shine as a radiant beauty." Lady Fatima increased the bobbing motion of her body until it vibrated in ecstasy. "Such are the mysteries of Allah's plan."

On Wednesday I joined the men at a noisy party in Ahmed's new house. Gypsy girls danced with their faces unveiled. Music crashed in wailing fits against the large walls, and I watched the soldiers and male relatives of Atiyat. These respected men, calm and solemn in their customary duties, shouted obscenities, grabbed at the women, and behaved in a most undignified fashion. It was not pleasant for me to observe Turks and Moors—men who normally were responsible leaders of the community—acting in such a reprehensible manner.

When I described their loutish behavior to Fatima, she attacked me for not understanding how such women demanded the inevitable masculine response. "It is only natural! If a woman requires respect, she must stay in the harem. Honorable women stay in the harem. Teasing a man by showing the face or bare limbs can only lead to violence. The whores were fortunate to escape with their lives!"

After Fatima's anger at my stupidity diminished, she described the women's party, held on the same evening. "It is called Henna Night because the bride's hands and feet are stained with the orange paste." She told how Atiyat's mother smeared a gold piece with henna and tied it to her daughter's right hand. "It was a grand diversion. We sang and ate and bound strips of linen to Atiyat's hands and feet to keep the stain on all night. It will bring Ahmed great luck and many children to have such a pampered wife." Fatima smiled indulgently at me.

On Thursday my dragoman carried Ahmed's fifteen-year-old bride many presents of clothing. Lady Fatima reported that she immediately dressed in these fine robes and scarves. Her servants stuck sparkling diamonds on her forehead, cheeks, and chin, and the matron of honor brought Atiyat to her parents. The entire family— down to the most distant cousins—stood assembled in the main audience room. Atiyat Aziz kissed her father's hand. With loving care he tied a shawl around her waist, held her at arm's length, and smiled through his tears. With a flourish he brought out a sword and extended it a few inches over the floor. His daughter daintily skipped over the long pointed sword, and Ali el-Aziz said, "Bring forth offspring who will use this sword well." He recited three prayers to Allah while allowing tears to course past his famous nose. Every one of the relatives joined in the crying, some with loud wails celebrating the large tears. This was Atiyat's last day at home. She was no longer a child but a woman with great responsibilities. Tomorrow she would join Ahmed as his wife.

At dawn on Friday I followed the bride as she led a long noisy, joyous procession to Ahmed's new house. Cymbals celebrated the sun's emergence, and drums applauded the city's cool glory. Women peeked through second-story wooden shutters, and men stood against walls and in doorways to let us pass.

While Ahmed sat brooding in my cottage, worrying about making some inevitable mistake in protocol, Atiyat sat ensconced in a corner of the bridal chamber of her new home. She was surrounded by silken streamers and wedding gifts. He was surrounded by uneaten food and tepid coffee. Only his pipe provided solace to the churning of his stomach.

I traveled back and forth between the two dwellings as if I were some worried plover trying to manage nestlings that had somehow become separated. Each detail of the morning I reported to my confidantes, Ahmed and Lady Fatima, and they listened to the latest bulletin without comment or question. It took me some time to decipher the etiquette required for the display of wedding gifts. The richest articles were arranged at eye level, while the linen and lesser articles from neighbors or remote cousins hung near the ceiling. Jewels and precious gifts filled each small alcove of the bedroom. Every vacant space shimmered with garlands of silk flowers.

Throughout the day, beginning shortly after morning prayers, guests came to bring presents. Each new dab of humanity joined the original group, and the entire organism circulated in a changing, interwoven mass, inspecting, praising, and criticizing.

After the day's third prayer, I went with Ahmed and his janissary friends, accompanied by drums and music, first to our favorite coffeehouse and then in midafternoon to the mosque. We offered our special prayers to Allah, asking a blessing on this marriage, and then walked quietly through the narrow streets. The heat was oppressive.

Our band of men entered Ahmed's new house, and we were met by Atiyat's brothers and male cousins. The combined army of warriors escorted and jostled Ahmed to the door of his bridal chamber. A din of "The groom is coming!" parted the laughing, cheering crowd. Pushed by the men, tugged by the matron of honor, Ahmed met Atiyat. She stood before him staring at his chest. The room sank into a quiet void. The outside noises crushed into a gray silence. In a slow, deliberate sequence, Atiyat took Ahmed's hand and kissed it; then she removed her veil. The married couple looked upon each other for the first time. Atiyat quickly dropped her eyes to study her gold-threaded slippers. Ahmed held out a large unmounted sapphire for her examination—his "Face-See" gift to mark the propitious occasion. Tenderly, as if she might evaporate into a crumpled heap of dust, he embraced her, stepped back for another fleeting look, and left the room. Men and women cheered and quickly retreated from the wedding-night room.

Like two streams of ants marching to separate nests, the men adjourned to their quarters, while the women went into the harem reception room. Separated, the two sexes celebrated the wedding feast.

A huge mountain of wedding rice, tinted yellow with saffron, served as foundation for an endless formation of dishes, bowls, fruit, and carcasses. Servants filled every empty cup and bowl until darkness demanded the aid of lanterns. The muezzin called sweetly, with soft promises of glory to God. Every man silently deserted the food and laughter and followed Ahmed to the mosque for prayers. Silent lines of men walked through the dark streets. The wedding celebration was over. Ahmed and Atiyat were husband and wife.

I met with Lady Fatima on the next day. We sat together in her house and drank tea. Now and then we caught the other's eye and smiled. There was no need for conversation. Defeated generals require the buttress of hollow words, not the victors. After an hour or so of pleasant silence, I left her company and walked slowly back to the palace.

———

Atiyat's good luck emerged from the deficiencies of Ahmed's family. In most weddings of well-bred women, the bride moves into the household of the mother-in-law and is managed by the groom's mother in a most cruel fashion. Atiyat ruled her husband's realm without the countenance of a mother-in-law. Allah occasionally tolerated such allotments of accidental good fortune, and Ahmed's young wife used her luck to quickly establish a congenial and efficient home.

As her husband's best friend, I frequently met with Atiyat and surreptitiously studied her unfolding. At first she was a shy child, peering self-consciously at me from the shelter of her veil. Soon, however, I attained a status that Ahmed described as a "gelded brother-in-law," and Atiyat adopted me into her husband's family. Such a large nose! And also her ears and eyebrows. They seemed so fearsome and bold during our initial exchanges. Later, as we learned to look at the other, I accepted her abundant beauty. I saw only perfect roses and softly sculpted poems as adequate companions for her elegance. Her voice and her features merged into a seamless blend of loveliness.

We teased each other like siblings. We giggled in fond affection after Lady Fatima's daily visits. "What an odd family I possess!" Atiyat whispered to me. "You, an infidel Frank as brother, Lady Fatima as my mother-in-law, and a black slave for a husband. My, my!" She ruled her new domain with no threat of intervention. From the cocoon of her father's harem emerged a skilled and artful administrator of people. A wife. A sister. A loving daughter. With Atiyat, Allah was a kind and loving God. He made her beautiful in every conceivable form. Ahmed continued our weekly meetings with never a hint of second wives or concubines. Even after unending days of rain, with black mud churning in the wake of every man and beast, he spoke only of his duties with the janissary, and of Atiyat.

My dear friend advanced another rank in the janissary corps and over the next few years gained the reputation as a favored son of Allah. His father-in-law suggested investments that ripened with alacrity. The dey of Algiers favored him with special attention at reviews held on the palace parade grounds. His wisdom and wealth grew with each passing day.

It is said among the grandees of Algiers that whispers can be trusted as the truth, while shouts must be judged lies. Somehow this aphorism managed to gain frequent expression in the coffeehouses of Algiers. At the first mention of Ahmed al-Koita's name, there it was: "Whispers can be trusted . . ." When he appeared on the parade ground or was sighted walking through the bazaar, people said, "Whispers can be trusted as the truth, while shouts must be judged lies."

CHAPTER THIRTY-SEVEN

September 1795

JOSEPH DONALDSON JR., ESQ., PEACE AMBASSADOR from the United States of America, sailed into the port of Algiers on September 3, 1795. He arrived on a Ragusian brig commanded by my friend Captain Richard O'Brian. When the dey received word of Donaldson's arrival, I was designated a one-person welcoming committee.

"I'll not be trifled with again," said the dey. "Let the man know from the very beginning that he will pound rocks in the quarry if I'm trifled with again."

As my barge approached the brig, I could hear the gruff, angry shouts of an American. The clipped tones spilled over the gunnel and muttered toward shore.

"Who in hell are you?" demanded Ambassador Donaldson.

"I am James Cathcart, enslaved mate of the schooner *Maria* and first Christian secretary to Hassan Bashaw, dey of Algiers." Admittedly I was a bit taken aback by the hostile demeanor of my interlocutor, and put some edge to my own voice.

"You must be the bastard traitor I've heard about," he yelled. "And no Christian to boot, I'll bet."

"I assure you, Mister Ambassador, I am a loyal American, a Christian, and deeply committed to the success of your mission."

"Bah! Get me off this infernal ship. Nothing but rats aboard. Two-legged rats. Four-legged rats. Nothing but rats." He turned and limped toward the port rail.

O'Brian caught my eye, shrugged, and held his arms out in a silent statement of exasperation. I answered with a grim smile. The lower molars on both sides of my jaw began to ache.

The two of us supervised the rigging of a chair designed to lower Ambassador Donaldson from the brig onto my chartered barge. "Is he always such a barking dog?" I unconcerned if the ambassador heard me or not.

"Hard to say," said O'Brian. "We caught the tail end of a three-day blow, and that made for a rough crossing. It certainly gave Donaldson a hundred things to complain about."

"Still a good chop to the bay," I said.

Captain O'Brian turned from me to supervise the Sicilian sailors in their task. He pantomimed great care in handling the ropes and pulleys as Ambassador Donaldson was secured in his seat. Still, even with dedicated care on the part of the sailors, gusts of wind combined with erratic waves produce what seemed malicious sport as the sailors sang in concert with dips and halts of the bosun's chair.

"You black apes!" the ambassador yelled. His chair dangled from a yardarm, like bait over a waiting shark. The barge danced to different beats, and with a flailing thud, man and chair spilled into the arms of my waiting crew.

J. Donaldson Jr. howled in pain, and I climbed down from the ship to take command of the barge tiller. The ambassador from my country to the City and Port of Algiers was finally at his assigned post, and negotiations for the release of all American sailors was about to begin.

Our retinue proved a popular distraction to the idlers of Algiers. We walked from the quayside through the narrow cobbled streets, up the hill, and toward the house that I had rented for the ambassador. Children crowded about and pointed at his right leg, which was muffled in flannel and shod with a large velvet slipper. Arab merchants called insults and made pointed remarks concerning the infidel ambassador's sanity. Donaldson could not understand any language but English, of course, but the tone and intent were clear to any living person. "Are you already dead, Satan's messenger? Why are you wearing those ridiculous black clothes in the fall heat? Your hat, pig-foot—what is the use of such a three-pointed thing?"

His gout, the roughness of the pavement, the heat, and a walk that would tire a healthy man all conspired against my desire for a pleasant introduction to Algiers. The swirling, pressing crowds drove the surly Donaldson to finally begin swinging his crutch at the buzzing tormentors. A teenage boy dashed from the crowd and kicked the ambassador's good foot out from under him, causing the American to fall in a crumpled heap. The crowd rewarded the lad's heroic effort with cheers and promises of eternal heaven.

O'Brian and I lifted America's representative and protected him from further blows. Jeers and ludicrous nicknames followed us to the very door of Donaldson's handsome residence. The struggle to surmount a long flight of cold marble steps drove him to a final paroxysm of rage.

We lowered Ambassador Donaldson to a couch. He threw his hat to one side and his crutch to the other, all the while he screamed a string of pleas for relief from pain, mixed equally with vengeful profanities on all Moors.

At the height of the ambassador's ejaculations, Miciah Baccri entered the room and asked, "What is the matter?" The Jew had responded to my message for his immediate attendance at our conclave, and he now appeared in our midst visibly concerned and somewhat astonished with the behavior of Donaldson.

"Nothing at all," said O'Brian. "The ambassador is saying his prayers and giving God thanks for his safe arrival."

"His devotion is incredibly fervent," replied Baccri. The banker looked again at Donaldson, shrugged, and, respectful of all religious rites, sat in a chair until the penitent was quiet. In short order an excellent meal, prepared by the Venetian chef of my best tavern, arrived. It was near sunset, and with ample bottles of Spanish wine, fruit, and good service by my staff, his surly disposition mellowed to some small degree.

As coffee and port wine were served, Peter Eric arrived and joined in our discussion of previous American diplomatic efforts in Algeria. There was some small effort toward humor in describing John Lamb's first bumbling disaster in 1786, but Donaldson said, "Leave it off!"—and from that point we maintained a serious demeanor to our discussion. I made available my journal containing all negotiations since my arrival in 1785 and studied the ambassador whenever he talked.

He was not yet fifty years in age, but appeared a man of seventy. Excepting his profane language, Donaldson put me in mind of the sour Congregationalists who frequently perched along Boston's south shore. He wore plain black clothes and favored a hairless face to complement a bald head. His pope's nose protruded from bare pink flesh and conjured the vision of a newly plucked turkey ready for the oven. Donaldson spoke only English and had no interest in either word or custom of the Algerian. He asked no questions of our life as slaves. His sole concern was relief from pain. Relief from pain and food at ready reach. Here at last was our long-awaited ambassador, our ambassador for peace, and my doubts of his ability to fulfil his duty were abundant.

The next day was Friday, the Sabbath, but Hassan Bashaw

granted my request for an exception to the Koran's injunction against labor on such days. I had good cause to fear sabotage by our friends, the French, and felt anxious to begin our negotiations. The dey saw an impending coalition of merchants and ship captains as a threat to his plan for cooperation between Algerians and Americans, so he also was amenable to a quick hearing of the ambassador's proposal. Thus encouraged on both hands, at seven a.m. on Friday morning, Ambassador Donaldson presented his credentials to the dey of Algiers.

The dey moved stiffly about his throne and gazed briefly at Donaldson. "Does he have full power to negotiate?" he demanded.

"Effendi, I have just read his credentials, and it seems that he does have the necessary power. He is here to enter a treaty of peace between the great City and Territory of Algiers and the sovereign United States of America."

"Yes, but we have a peace not yet made, and there will be no trifling with me this time. None at all." The dey spoke Turkish, for it was his audience chamber and his audience of advisors that listened. "Tell the ignorant black crow that I will not be trifled with."

"Your Excellency, I have previously explained to you that no American ambassador has unlimited power, and that his instructions are further limited by President Washington and his advisors. Just as you would constrain an emissary from your court, so does President Washington limit his."

"I have been trifled with by these hypocrites for too many years. Peace will be costly," said the dey.

"If you ask more than they have to give, no peace is possible," I said. "If you ask within their limits, peace is possible this day."

"It is the Sabbath, and we will see about these affairs tomorrow," the dey replied. He waved his hand as a signal that the meeting with Ambassador Donaldson was terminated.

I came forward to kiss the dey's hand and complimented him on his prudence in moving quickly. When I turned and suggested to Ambassador Donaldson that he show his respect to the dey of Algiers by kissing his hand, the American ambassador harrumphed loudly, turned on his good foot, and gimped out of the palace audience room. I trailed behind him muttering newly discovered blasphemies.

In spite of the Prophet's injunction against working on the Sabbath, at nine a.m.—less than an hour after dismissing us—the dey sent a messenger to the ambassador's residence. The rolled parchment had one question scribbled in Turkish: "Does the ambassador have full power to conclude a treaty?"

I returned to the palace, muttering and complaining to myself about empty-headed masters, and repeated, "Yes, he does have full power to negotiate, but no power to conclude a treaty."

"Then take to him the terms that you made out by my order some months ago."

"Effendi, he will reject them." I let the silence of the dey's chamber roll for a long moment. Other than two guards at the outter door, we three were alone in the large room. "I think I know this man, and he will not stay long in this regency without some quick mark of success. If Your Excellency does not lower the demands to what has been paid by the very small nations, such as Denmark and Sweden, then Donaldson will leave and no one will profit."

"Silence, slave! Enough of your impertinence. I command you to instantly take those demands to your ambassador. Do you insult me with the invention that your country is less than Denmark? Bring me his answer this day."

As I approached the dey to kiss his hand, my foot slipped on the marble floor, and I fell.

"Can you not stand?" asked the dey.

"Yes, effendi, but the weight of Your Excellency's proposal made me stumble," I said.

The American ambassador's ugly intransigence drove us to scatter through the residence, Miciah Baccri found me slumped in a large soft chair, and I recounted the morning to him. He in turn informed me that after I left the audience room, the dey had laughed heartily at my excuse for stumbling and had repeated the comment endlessly to his ministers.

It was late morning when all rejoined our meeting with Donaldson, and his disposition was no sweeter. "Devil take you, Mr. Cathcart, and your monkey-faced dey, besides!" He sat in a stiff ladder-back chair with his gout-ridden foot elevated on a stool. "I rue the day Jefferson talked me into this miserable farce." Donaldson pointed his cane at me. "You, sir! Your lying letters got me here. Now! Now you must get me out of this heathen godforsaken place."

Both Skjoldebrand and O'Brian joined me in placating the old man, but he would have none of it. "Millions of dollars, frigates, and bribe money every year!" he shouted. "Jefferson is absolutely correct. We'll have no respect from penny-whistle tyrants until they have guns stuck up their black asses. We need a navy with good American sharpshooters to talk sense to these damn pirates!" He mumbled on in that vein for a few minutes until I interrupted.

"Ambassador, the dey left no alternative to me. We must return with a counteroffer, however small. In my last letter to you, I indicated that the dey would settle for something over one-half million Spanish dollars. We can at least begin with such an offer."

He refused to even consider extending the negotiations. The three of us pled our case with every argument except tears. The paint finally stuck in our favor when O'Brian said, "Look, Joe, what have we got to lose? Cathcart will take the risk upon himself. Give it a try."

We quickly agreed on $543,000 for peace and ransom for all the American sailors. I stood in the open door and bantered with Donaldson. "If I am burned, please send my ashes to the Philadelphia

Museum." He stared at me without answering, and I quipped, "As I am fond of your good company, sir, I will try my best to prevent a similar fate to your person."

Donaldson muttered, "Pshaw! Get on." I was told later by O'Brian that the ambassador's eyes became somewhat larger when Peter Eric remarked on the fate of the Venetian consul, and of Miciah Baccri's near incineration: The Venetian was stuffed into a cannon and exploded into small bits when negotiations between the two countries went awry. Baccri was described as staring intently at a large cauldron of bubbling oil before admitting the possibility of a debt cancellation to the dey.

My mood was elevated as the next step in the negotiations approached. The walk seemed shorter than before, and the children playing in the shade seemed full of good cheer. Not once did a donkey trailing an irascible master block my path.

The dey smiled at me as if I were a pampered dog and had just piddled on the palace floor. He maintained his look of sad contempt for possibly ten heartbeats and then erupted into a rage. "Infidel without shame! Pig-eater! Do you make a game of me, the dey of Algiers? What do you mean by bringing such proposals?"

"Please listen to me, Your Excellency. This document represents the ambassador's proposals, not mine. His powers are limited, and he can offer no more than what his government authorizes."

"You are a liar. All Americans are liars and triflers, and you are the worst! Your ambassador's powers are not limited, for the French consul informed me that Mr. Donaldson has carte blanche and can give what he pleases for peace. My own trusted consul to Paris has seen American newspapers citing his authority at eight hundred thousand. More can be had, I'm sure. Liars! Liars!" His face was near purple in color.

"Your Excellency may return my compliment to the French consul. Please understand that the counsel is an ignorant liar and an enemy of both the dey of Algiers and the United States of America. He hopes to advance his own cause at the expense of two nations who have reason to be friends."

"I've heard this all before from you, piglet. What is the substance of your claim when matched with that of the French? You claim him a liar, yet he has served faithfully in past agreements. You have called him a mercenary, yet it is the Americans who would travel our sea without paying their just due, not the French. The Americans ask to be treated as less than the Danes and Swedes, who have paid a fair tribute for our services. The Americans have paid nothing and promise nothing."

He was silent a few moments, studying my face. "How is it you stand before me? Are you my first Christian secretary or a running dog for the crippled vulture? This proposal is your work, not that of a man who only arrived in Algiers yesterday. Speak up!"

"I am an American, Your Excellency, and duty-bound to give my ambassador all the information that I possess. At the same time, I am a grateful servant of the dey. It was my hope, effendi that you would be pleased to observe that Your Excellency and your family were well considered in this proposed agreement."

"Read your proposal to me once again," he ordered. I complied and he asked, "Is that one hundred thousand dollars for me and fifty thousand for my family? Surely you mean sequins, not dollars."

"No sir, dollars; it is American dollars that are offered."

"Go out of my sight immediately! Thou dog without soul. American dollars. Ha! I would not wipe my bottom with such worthless paper. Gold! Spanish doubloons or Algerian sequins; nothing else will answer."

"May I presume, effendi, that if gold coin replaces paper dollars, that an amicable settlement can be attained between our sovereign countries?"

"Never presume to bring such trifling terms to me again," said

Hassan Bashaw. "You will find my displeasure diminished only through your pain." He pantomimed a beating of my bare feet and waved me off before I could kiss his hand.

On my way back to the ambassador's residence, the alleys were crowded with surly men pulling donkeys who struggled to bite the arms of innocent passersby. Children threw wet turds at me. Women dumped slops on my head from second-story windows. When I entered Mr. Donaldson's home—a dwelling rented from the dey of Algiers at my expense. A dwelling whose staff and furnishings were all paid for by me. After two cups of cool water, my tongue was flexible enough to begin speaking. Consul Skjoldebrand, Captain O'Brian, and the ambassador sat silently and listened as I reviewed each detail of the meeting. I kept my voice well modulated and refrained from interjecting a single opinion that might show my true feelings.

"It's as I expected," said Donaldson. "A fool's mission performed by a fool."

Red lights danced before my eyes. Suddenly I was standing before the ambassador, yelling and shaking my finger in his face. "Go!" I said. "Pack your bags, and I will arrange for you to leave on the next ship. You are worse than useless. You are a traitor to the Americans who have died here of plague and harsh treatment. A traitor to the war we fought and won!"

"Now, now," said Peter Eric. "Both of you listen to one who has served his country in Algiers for many years."

Donaldson and I let off staring at one another and turned to the Swedish consul. He spoke directly to the ambassador. "It is my judgement that you are closer to an agreement than might appear at this moment."

"It's the end," said Donaldson. "There was never a chance to finish an honorable peace."

"That may be so, but you need to exhaust every option. Another proposal needs to be formulated that will offer additional benefits to the dey."

"There is no more. Are you all deaf? I am not authorized to spend another penny on these heathen bastards."

"Mr. Donaldson," said Peter Eric, "you will never have such a good opportunity to establish peace with Algiers. With all the Barbary States, for that matter. Think of the worth in trade to the United States that such a treaty would bring about. This is your only chance to free American citizens from slavery and to give your merchants free rein in the Mediterranean. It is an opportunity that you cannot ignore."

We three marshaled arguments to an unyielding rock, and shortly after noon prayers, a messenger arrived, and I was again summoned to the dey.

This trip from ambassador's residence to the dey's palace was obscured by a heavy hot fog that poured from every orifice in my head. The thick mist prevented any opportunity for my comprehension of sight or sound. The smells from sewer drains guided me along the entire route.

"How can it be that my own slave is a lackey of the lame ambassador?" Contempt dripped in putrid ooze from his voice. "Do you and that Swedish infidel both conspire to make a fool of me?"

I could feel my shoulders sag, and there was no feeling beneath my Adam's apple. "Effendi . . .Your Excellency . . ." My voice faltered. The sand from three deserts clogged my throat. "I am in the worst of all possible positions. I mean to help both of my masters, and both accuse me of being partial to the other. I know my country wishes peace and that you deserve an honest consideration. I feel like a huckstering Jew, with both sides hiding concessions for fear of gains by the other." I finally looked up at him and saw that he was listening.

"Effendi, I stand before you with no authority to make another offer from my ambassador. As your ward, permit me to guess that Mr. Donaldson may have personal wealth of forty or fifty thousand dollars. In addition, I would risk all of my worth, perhaps $10,000, if I can convince the ambassador to add his own private property to the limit established by his government."

I concluded my speech with a heartfelt plea that I not be accused of partialities but be given some credit for trying to accommodate two difficult masters. The dey answered by directing me to sit down and write while he dictated proposal number three. The sum of the parts amounted to $982,000, which was a fall of one-third from his first demand.

"No! No! No! Not one more American cent," said Joseph Donaldson Jr., Esquire. "Go back and tell your pedergasting friend that he will not get a penny more from me." Donaldson glared at Baccri, Skjoldebrand, O'Brian, and me, in turn. "Not one more American penny and certainly nothing from my own paltry account. Nothing more for these heathen niggers. Nothing!"

"If I return with no improvement on your offer, Mr. Donaldson, you will be ordered out of the country. You will go home a failure, and I will receive five hundred bastinadoes on the soles of my feet."

"If I am ordered to leave this hellish place, it will be no loss to me," said Donaldson. "If you receive a bastinadoing, please have the consolation that you are serving your country."

"I resign! Serve as your own messenger boy. If you can't raise the total, you go tell the dey. I'm sure he will accept the information with good spirit and commend you as a shrewd negotiator."

I was piqued a good deal and knew that the dey had ordered me, and no one else, to return with any answer. Still, I wanted to mortify Donaldson for his obstinate behavior. Both Peter Eric and O'Brian tried to mediate between the two of us, and also to state clearly that they would not consider serving in the exchange of information between Donaldson and the dey.

I took another tack. "You may know, Mr. Ambassador, that for some years it has been within my power to purchase my own freedom. I have refrained from using that option because I felt a responsibility to help my fellow captives. It has long been my objective to achieve an honorable peace between the United States of America and the Regency of Algiers. Your intransigence encourages me to pay my ransom and leave you to suffer the bastinadoes that you hold so lightly. If I can provide any consolation for the prospect of five hundred blows on your bare feet, it is thought to be an excellent cure for the gout."

With that petulant attack, I turned and left the house. This time—the fourth time—I walked to the palace as in a sound sleep, for I saw nothing and remembered less.

CHAPTER THIRTY-EIGHT

September 1795

THE DEY RAGED AND THREATENED. He popped his eyes, waved his curved sword in my direction, and then collapsed on his cushions. After a few moments Hassan Bashaw made a slight movement of his hand, and I approached him with my head down. I felt more sadness than fear.

"Have we lost our chance, my first secretary?"

"In truth, Your Excellency, I don't know. The lame one is mad. Worse, he is ignorant beyond my comprehension."

A limp smile curled the dey's lips. His response was a slight whisper. "I am familiar with such advisors; they crash upon good sense like waves in a storm."

The dey subsided into himself, his malaise growing around us in a most palpable manner. Without permission I sat before him, cross-legged, within range to hear his whispered thoughts.

"If I send the lame one packing, then I must accede to my enemies and sign another treaty with Portugal. You will be then joined by many more American slaves, and I . . ." He lapsed into thought and then leaned toward me, a few inches separating our noses.

"My lame-minded countrymen see only the cruisers flying

through the gates of Hercules and returning with rich prize ships. They see our prisons overflowing with American slaves. That is the limit of their vision. They can't imagine America as a valuable ally. A worthy colleague in our many joint-ventures. Imagine, my first Christian secretary, two pirate nations joined for mutual benefit."

The dey leered at me, and I fought against responding.

"It is true, my neck-less infidel. Your ship captains are no different from mine—except the Americans are superior sailors. "Hypocrites! Triflers and hypocrites and liars. You Americans dash into ports without permission, picking the bones of nations at war. You steal from England and sell to France. That's your game now. Steal from England and sell to France.

"Smart. That's why I like you Americans. France has no fleet, England's fleet is hopelessly scattered, and the Americans move in like jackals. No! Like vultures! Silently, on huge wings, croaking 'Free ships, free goods.'

I maintained my silence.

"Here I sit, asking for a small pittance—a sum that is rightfully mine by right of conquest—and your little nation. A wild country with no military navy that has the affrontery to tell me that they will not pay their fair tribute to use my sea. They refuse my due, and a little lame man from a little faraway country has the audacity to insult the mighty dey of Algiers. They are very smart, indeed, those vultures."

He shook his head in a quiet slow wag, and again lapsed into a contemplative study.

———◆———

A Moslem secretary had been standing for a lengthy period of time in the archway to deliver a message, his head respectfully lowered. He issued a discrete cough from his throat.

The dey responded to the Moslem secretary. "Yes, I know who is waiting." Then he looked squarely at me. "Tell that crippled infidel dog that he will burn at the harbor gate if he contaminates Algiers with his presence tomorrow. The godless Americans have trifled with me beyond endurance. Swim if he must—or burn! I am finished with the matter." He waved a hand toward the Moslem secretary and stared at me. "Remove your putrid body from my sight. Now!"

I backed my way from the room in a low bow, retreated from the palace, and began walking the familiar streets. It was late afternoon. Farmers guided their unladed donkeys toward the city gates. Heavily veiled women scurried from the public bath or from visits to a friend's harem. Children scuttled about retrieving animal droppings. The smells of people, animals, and old buildings were comfortable to my nose. I was ignored by everyone.

On previous meetings at the ambassador's abode, I presumed to enter as if it were mine. After all, I paid the outrageous rent and provided both servants and provisions. On this occasion, though, I knocked, and a surprised O'Brian opened the door.

"Come right in, my good sir." With one hand still holding the knob, he bowed low and extended his free hand toward the study.

Without preamble, I walked up to the reclining Donaldson and said, "You must leave at daylight tomorrow or burn at the gate by nightfall."

He struggled to his elbows. "What?"

"Good evening, sir. Have a pleasant voyage." I turned and started toward the door so recently entered.

Skjoldebrand and O'Brian yelled, "Wait a bit! What happened?"

I continued out the still-open door, leaving them with mouths agape.

Two hours later O'Brian found me at my tavern. My original tavern. Alphonse's tavern. The bath, a goat meat stew, and a near full bottle of undiluted red Spanish wine worked toward improving my perception of American citizens. I was willing to listen. It was even possible that I would converse with my friend. What was the name of his long-ago captured ship? The *Dauphin*. Yes, I would speak with Captain Richard O'Brian of the brig *Dauphin*.

"The ambassador wants you back at his residence. He has some questions to ask," said Captain O'Brian.

"The ambassador can find someone else to provide assistance." I poured another measure of wine and waved the bottle in his direction. "Some for you?"

"No, thanks. I know that he's been a bastard, but you can't quit now. You can walk out on Donaldson, but not on the rest of us." He caught and held my eyes. "You and Will Melman—I mean Ahmed al-Koita—have found your way with the Algerian people. In a way, I have too. Every other American will die if they can't leave. If the plague doesn't manage it, then a rock or the madhouse will do them in. They haven't a chance unless you help."

"Captain O'Brian," I said, "for nearly ten years I've fed and clothed all the American sailors and their gratitude matches that of Donaldson's in every degree. They expect everything from me and give nothing in return. I see no reason to continue playing the fool."

He dropped his eyes and looked past me, down the bar. "I'll take a swallow or so, I guess."

We each drank our wine, silent in our thoughts. When the final swallow departed in smooth passage down my throat, I said, "Let's go and have another try at our ambassador."

O'Brian smiled through his remaining front three teeth, and together we left my comfortable tavern.

◆

Peter Eric began the negotiations. "Mr. Ambassador, as the Swedish consul, I have some idea how soon the United States would be reimbursed the sum paid for peace. The profits gained by conducting unimpeded trade throughout the Mediterranean will be enormous. Surely the American merchants with a vested interest could be taxed—on a voluntary basis if not by government fiat. The fact of potential profits to your citizens should be weight enough to bargain more liberally with the dey." He moved his chair closer to Donaldson. "There is also the matter of Portugal. If the dey again makes peace with Portugal, then the dey's cruisers will again sail the Atlantic unchallenged. What value do you place on the many vessels and citizens that will inevitably be captured by the pirates? Does the trivial difference that separates a peace with your two nations match either the real benefits of profit or the frightening costs of slavery?"

Donaldson seemed a little more flexible, but in what appeared to be a diversionary effort, he noted that the French consul had not made an appearance since his arrival.

I was not willing to mollify this man, yet I didn't yell and rant. My memories of the recent ministrations by the Mosby, and of the excellent provender consumed at my tavern, calmed my spirit. "Mr. Donaldson," I said. "It matters little what you were told in Philadelphia about the French. They are not your friends. Their every moment is spent in defeating your efforts to increase American trade in the Mediterranean. Whatever Consul Valliere may tell you, you may count it a lie. A distortion designed to thwart any intentions of peace with the Barbary state of Algiers and our nation."

"Pshaw. Secretary of State Jefferson was clear as a bell about the French. 'Seek them out,' he said. 'They are our one true friend. Our strong ally in the war.' That's what he said to me. His words, exactly."

"Well then," I said, "let's invite the French consul to tea. You are not one to mince your words. Just ask him, yes or no, did he tell the dey of Algiers that you, the American ambassador, have carte blanche in conducting all negotiations."

"A damned lie! Unseemly to even consider asking such an impertinent question. I'll have none of that," said Donaldson.

O'Brian spoke next. "It is a question of trust, Mr. Ambassador. I'm confident that I speak for all here present. If you allow Valliere any agency with the negotiations, then we will all withdraw immediately. Is that clear?"

"Perfectly clear, Captain O'Brian." Donaldson clenched his jaw and stared grimly at each of us in turn.

O'Brian resumed his struggle. "We must now take the second step toward mutual respect. Toward holding one another in mutual confidence. I will ask of you: What are the limits of your instructions? How much are you authorized to spend? We need to know."

After a few moments of silence, Ambassador Donaldson said, "I'm limited to $650,000. Including all expenses."

We three stared at him with outraged surprise. It was my turn to speak. "I know the last amount demanded by the dey, but I can guarantee peace for our nations and ransom for our merchant sailors at fifty or sixty thousand less than $900, 000. What do you say?"

The ambassador looked up from his couch. "Agreed," he said.

I called to my dragoman and sent him to retrieve Miciah Baccri for consultation and assistance. Donaldson struggled to sit upright, and he spoke to me with his normal bombastic voice. "None of that Jew. I'll have no Jew telling me how to spend American money."

I carried a stool over to the ambassador and sat beside him. There was no rancor in my voice or mind. In the matter of Jews, we Americans held with a common understanding. "Mr. Ambassador," I said. "There is no choice in the matter. I share with you the distaste for any dependence upon Jews. I share with you the concern for maintaining the honor of our fair country. Only Americans can serve without the threat of holding conflicting interests or subversive design. If any other choice were available, you would hear my enthusiastic recommendation for that alternative course."

Donaldson remained quiet and listened as I continued. "The dey and Baccri have a secret arrangement. All monetary transactions between the regency and foreign powers are managed by the Jew. It is a fact understood by all and acknowledged by none. There is no choice. If money is discussed, only the Jew can give us the true answers."

Donaldson studied my face and then nodded. "I understand," he said. "Harrumph." He then rolled over on his couch to face the wall. While we waited for Miciah Baccri, I began preparing the treaty. O'Brian disappeared to secure passage for the ambassador on a ship scheduled to sail the next morning. He also employed four Kabyle tribesmen to transport the ambassador's luggage, and gave them loud instructions. "Arrive at dawn. Nothing later will do. The American ambassador must flee for his life!"

With our scurrying around, the dey was certain to realize that we took his admonitions seriously. I wanted everyone in Algiers to believe that all negotiations between the dey and the American ambassador were finished. All hope for a treaty was abandoned, and only a chaotic escape remained.

Miciah Baccri entered the ambassador's study as if he were a bold black crow. He looked quickly around the room and saw only Donaldson and me. "What service may I render?" he asked.

"Miciah," I began, "what amount should the dey's first secretary of state receive to support our next treaty offer?"

"What will the new total be, my friend?"

"I judge that the dey will accept $585,000 if there is no vocal opposition from his cabinet. What is your perception of the situation?"

"You have asked at least two questions, First Christian Secretary. I will answer both to the best of my ability. First, we are in agreement that the dey is anxious to sign a treaty. I believe he fears an armed conflict with you Americans. He is well aware of your Thomas Jefferson's advocacy of a strong navy in support of the American merchant fleet. The dey would like to preempt a military threat and deal only with merchants and farmers."

"True enough," I said.

"Hidden between your two questions asked is a third: What will happen if Ambassador Donaldson leaves without a treaty? I judge that the Americans will rally to Jefferson, and he will be your next prince. The Algerian nation will then serve as a conveniently weak enemy to test the new frigates, and the Mediterranean will become an American sea."

"Humph! Little you know about American politics," said Donaldson. He stared at Baccri with his full arsenal of contempt. "You Jews think you're so damn almighty smart. Always with the answers. Never with the burden." He flopped back on the couch and stared at the ceiling.

"Yes, Mr. Ambassador, I am an ignorant man, attempting the impossible task of understanding a mysterious world." He was respectful in his manner, but refrained from any obsequious gestures. "I know a little of you, however. It is whispered that you have some standing as a broker of ship masts and keels; timber worthy of the finest ships—merchant or navy. I also know, from the *London Times*, that you lead the New York delegation in support of Jefferson's candidacy for president. I agree with you, Mr. Ambassador. It is little that I know. I stand before you as an ignorant, foolish Jew, presuming to offer some small assistance."

"Hmph," the ambassador responded.

Baccri turned to me. "The first secretary of state would be pleased with ten thousand dollars tonight and a similar amount in the treaty. Finally, I believe that the dey will accept the amount you mentioned."

"Could you deliver ten thousand tonight?" I asked.

"It is possible. The terms for me will be the principal amount, plus one thousand dollars for each month the total is unpaid."

"Robbery! Damned Jew robbery!" shouted Donaldson.

"Mr. Ambassador," I said, "the interest is neither exorbitant nor unfair. If, as you suggest, the total available for negotiations is over six hundred thousand dollars, the expense of the loan from Baccri will be miniscule."

"'Authorized,' you little beggar. The money is 'authorized,' not necessarily immediately available." Donaldson spoke to the ceiling, but his statement caused a distinct churning of my stomach.

"In any event," I said, "unless you can provide funds immediately, the sum must be borrowed. It is critical that we neutralize the dey's first secretary of state by making a gift of ten thousand dollars."

"Granted," said the voice from the ceiling.

Over the next few hours, I wrote the treaty. Peter Eric suggested equitable divisions of the sum and made a few helpful additions toward cleverly obfuscating our intentions. Donaldson deigned to sign and seal the final agreement, all the while groaning and complaining about the late hour and his painful leg. Baccri returned from his successful mission and smiled. The first secretary of state for the regency of Algiers was now ten thousand dollars wealthier, and he would pose no opposition to a treaty of peace between the regency and the United States.

During the dark hours after midnight, both O'Brian and Baccri agreed to accompany me to the palace in the morning. They also promised to remain completely silent during the negotiations.

I sent a messenger to the prison advising all Americans that their ambassador was leaving without a treaty. All letters for transit to the United States had to be ready for collection before sunrise. Everything seemed ready, and I retired for a short rest on a couch in the ambassador's study.

There was no sleep—merely a worrisome repose. Potential problems and forgotten contingencies plagued my mind with one imagined disaster following the other. My objective with packing and preparations for leaving was to create doubt in the dey's mind. Doubt that could as easily move against us as in our favor. The French consul, and likely others also, had diminished my ability to negotiate, and I felt that a ruse was necessary to accomplish our end. My wakefulness stemmed not from concern over diminished standards of integrity but from uncertainty: Would my diplomatic machinations prove successful, or not?

At seven a.m. on Saturday, September 5, 1795, I presented the fifth of our proposals to the dey of Algiers.

"Your Excellency, the American ambassador is standing ready to embark prior to the noon prayers. He has given instructions to me for a final desperate offer. The last proposal exceeded Ambassador Donaldson's instructions. He has nothing left with which to negotiate except his own personal wealth. In consideration of his wish for peace between our nations, and the desire to reconcile your captives with their families, the ambassador commits his entire fortune to the proceedings." I stopped speaking and presented the dey with a copy of our proposal.

He threw it aside and ordered me to read each item aloud. I followed his wishes. The dey waved his hand as if giving chase to an annoying fly. "It is nothing. Again you Americans trifle with me. Just this morning the dragoman of Consul Valliere assured me that the lame one had the power to negotiate an honorable treaty."

I turned to Baccri and O'Brian and stage-whispered, "Mark that lie." Stepping closer to Hassan Bashaw, I responded to him. "Your Excellency, it is my impression that the French consul's lies had been refuted. When Ambassador Donaldson disembarks in Spain, he will of course file a complaint at the court of France; but for what purpose? We all know the effort as a futile gesture and that the treaty before us is dead. My compatriots are doomed to perpetual slavery. Malicious, self-serving falsehoods by the French consul will prevent peace between two great nations."

The dey's voice sustained an urgent resonance. "Lies or not, the truth being that I have abated my demands by two-thirds of the original, while you twaddle with pennies. Tell your lame dog to embark as he pleases."

I stepped a few paces closer and lowered my voice. "Effendi, we have lost the opportunity for peace. May I humbly remind the mighty dey of Algiers of his promise to redeem the American slaves independent of a signed treaty?"

The dey exploded in a barrage of insults—predictions of my fate in hell and slashing of the air with his sword. His rage built to a crescendo as rapidly as a desert storm, and ended as quickly.

He finally settled among his pillows, drank a few sips of coffee, and inhaled a pinch of finely pulverized tobacco into his left nostril. He was ready to continue our negotiations.

"Effendi, the two nations that I hold dearest to my heart have been driven apart by a common enemy. My sadness is without limit. Two nations separated by a great ocean, with no history of rancor, are being forced to view each other as enemies. Each will now arm to the limit of their resources and destroy any opportunity to grow stronger together. Our enemies laugh while we must weep in despair."

At this moment O'Brian pulled at my coat to quiet the line of my argument. I twisted violently away from him and took two steps closer to the dey. He was a close observer of the exchange.

"I will not be silenced! You, sir, have treated me very well over these many years." The dey nodded his head vigorously in agreement with the observation of his beneficence. He waved his hand as permission for me to continue. "I must return your generous favors in kind. No selfish consideration can prevent me from warning you of the imposition thrown upon Your Excellency by the French consul. He is your enemy as he is ours. This is our last opportunity. America will never sue for peace again, but will return with armed ships beyond counting. If that awful conclusion is your choice, for the love of Allah, let the captives be redeemed. It has been ten years in slavery for us."

With that plea I rushed forward and fell on my knees to kiss the dey's hand. Contrary to my expectations, he placed his hand on my shoulder and then remained deeply in thought for some long moments.

He finally pushed me away, and I stood before him. "You are still a garrulous infidel; would that my horses raced as fast as your mouth." We studied each other for the appropriate next step. "Read the proposal again," he said. "Slowly. Line by line."

As I obeyed his instructions, the dey threw his hands up in mock surrender and said, "That is enough. Go and tell your ambassador that I accept his terms." He took another pinch of snuff and, instead of inhaling it, flicked it at my head. "But also tell him that his terms I esteem less than those tiny grains of tobacco. I act to pique the British, who are more our common enemy than the French."

I could not constrain my smile and felt an urge to jump and yell. The dey studied my features and calmly allowed time for most of the good feelings to leak away through the open windows. "You have good cause to celebrate this grand theft of my fortune," he said, "but stop for a moment. Recall the annuity of naval stores, previously promised by your country. It will now arrive with good speed. You must also instruct your countrymen on the etiquette of consular and biannual presents, paid in the same degree as do Holland, Sweden, and Denmark."

I gushed that I understood, kissed the dey's hand repeatedly, and paid him every compliment that my heart and mind could engender. O'Brian and I rushed in silent joy to the ambassador's residence and exploded with the news.

"Aye! So the heathen rat has agreed at last, has he?" said Ambassador Donaldson.

I ignored his stupidity and directed him to continue preparations to leave. The agreement had to be confirmed at the ten a.m. public audience. Also, our flag required a salute from twelve cannon to ratify the signatures. Hassan Bashaw or Joseph Donaldson could easily explode before the final act of protocol.

As certain as day following night, trouble replaced joy. Miciah Baccri had the presence of mind to remain in the palace after my jubilant retreat. He queried the dey's Moslem secretary to determine the exact reckoning of the naval stores due. When Baccri arrived at the ambassador's residence, he drew me aside. "Think carefully about this matter, First Christian Secretary. The annual obligation of naval stores will most likely exceed one hundred thousand dollars. Is it your intention to create a temporary diversion? A scheme to secure the release of American captives and give no regard for future peaceful relations between the two nations? What is your verdict?"

"No," I said. "This treaty must provide a profit for both nations." My stomach churned with acrobatic flips. I raced once more toward the palace, and in the quiet shade of an alley purged the accumulated bile of my stomach with a rush of clumpy vomit. The court chamberlain led me around a small file of petitioners waiting for the dey's attention. Hassan Bashaw listened carefully to my arguments for abrogating a portion of our agreement, and with a flippant wave of his hand permitted a codicil to the treaty limiting the annual dollar value of the marine supplies. After a mindless trip back to the ambassador's residence, I dashed about gathering people and documents. In truth, I felt like some hairy sheepdog trying to herd Donaldson, O'Brian, Consul Skjoldebrand, and Miciah Baccri toward the rescheduled eleven a.m. meeting. No one saw me stuff a silk American flag into my belt.

The meeting began promptly with my reading of the amended agreement—first in Turkish and then English. Both parties agreed to the terms and signed three copies. Peter Eric Skjoldebrand served as legal witness.

Three days! Just three days from the arrival of our ambassador to a treaty of freedom and peace! I felt flushed, and a strange tingle ran through my appendages. I approached the dey. Silently I handed to him our American flag.

He returned it to me saying, "You seem determined that your flag should be hoisted today." He put his hand on my shoulder. "Go—have it raised. I will not disappoint you."

I briefly left the reception room, giving necessary instructions to both a Moslem secretary and my dragoman. They left with the flag, smiling, confident of a generous gift from me.

When I returned, Captain O'Brian was serving as interpreter for Hassan Bashaw and Joseph Donaldson. Both were confident that God had created only one true language, and waited impatiently during the intervals of heathen gibberish. "Your countrymen are now free, Mr. Ambassador," said Dey Hassan Bashaw. "They may leave Algiers upon my receipt of your tribute. A warning! If any get drunk and insult a person of the true faith, they will be cruelly punished."

"Leave them in prison," Donaldson replied. "They'll stay out of trouble, and I won't be bothered."

The dey nodded in agreement, adding only that by staying in prison, they must continue to work in payment for their keep.

"Fair enough," said Donaldson.

O'Brian and I were aghast that after so many years free men had to continue as slaves. However, the treaty agreement was far too fragile to chance our intervention.

The remaining few minutes of the audience was spent by the dey praising my contributions as the primary negotiator for the treaty. "He is to be commended," said the dey to the ambassador. "At the very least, you must note his skill and dedication in a letter to your Prince Washington." The dey of Algiers permitted a small sour smile to America's ambassador. "This man Cathcart has served well as my first Christian secretary. He has also served you well in gaining important advantages for your country. No Americans before him understood the power of Allah's plan. None before him could perceive the advantages gained in your cooperating with this regency."

O'Brian's translation of the high praise drew no response from Joseph Donaldson Jr. Esq.

◆

The next ten days I spent transcribing copies of the treaty and securing presents for the dey and his cabinet. Our purchasing agent for the gifts was Miciah Baccri. From his relatives in Paris, Baccri secured favors appropriate for the dey. Every other benevolence—diamond rings, clocks, weapons, and fine linens, all the other gifts for ministers, advisors, senior civil servants—was purchased by the Jew from the dey of Algiers.

Hassan Bashaw thus found a market for his surplus trinkets, and Baccri bargained a generous price for his Algerian master. The American client accumulated an obligation that included the total cost of all goods, plus interest on all expenses, plus labor costs, plus earnest fees—the last being necessary to recognize the immediate lack of money available to the American ambassador. An extra earnest fee was tacked onto the original earnest fee in response to Ambassador Donaldson's inclination toward parsimonious behavior.

The details of one incident in particular circulated through the coffeehouses. The dey sent a peace present of a white stallion and a handsome German slave to Ambassador Donaldson. I advised Donaldson that a tip was necessary for the messenger.

"Give him a dollar," he said, "I have no change."

"Sir, twenty is the very least. You must not insult the dey with a dollar."

"'Tis more then he deserves," insisted the ambassador. "I'll not pay more."

I took ten sequins from my wallet and gave them, with my thanks, to the messenger. Donaldson observed the transaction and said, "Here. Here is the dollar I authorized." He held the coin with finger and thumb and pushed it tentatively in my direction.

"Keep your dollar. You'll need it to feed your new acquisitions." I managed a dramatic pause. "The gift should have greater merit than you suspect. Both may be let out for generous stud fees. All to your great advantage." The Ambassador laughed at me, and I departed for other tasks.

This period of time—the days and weeks following the ratification of my treaty—found me constantly at one task or another. Day or night, there was no difference. The details of our momentous treaty required many hours of patient dickering with clerks and ministers. The American sailors howled with rage at their continued imprisonment and claimed me responsible for their inevitable demise. Both masters—the dey and the ambassador—felt their needs paramount over all others. The clear commitment of the janissary to my diplomatic efforts demanded time, presents, and consultation with Ahmed. I had one other goal to achieve, and my failure to this end cost me the friendship of Captain Richard O'Brian.

We both wanted the honor of delivering our signed treaty to the American commissioner in Lisbon, Colonel Humphreys. Congress had in fact authorized Humphrey's power in mid 1793, but his dillydallying had caused the capture of ten additional American ships. Only he could disperse the funds agreed upon in the treaty. Only he could turn the gears of the US Congress toward final ratification of our efforts. Only he could make free men from slaves. It would be an honor, and a jot in all books of history, for a slave to serve as a messenger of freedom. A messenger to even such a venal person as Commissioner Humphreys.

When I discovered that O'Brian had petitioned Peter Eric and Miciah Baccri to approach the dey—and, then, for these two trusted associates to beg the dey's permission for the captain to carry the treaty—I exploded!

"You! You of all people know what I have put into this treaty. This treaty is *my* treaty! My effort made the treaty, and no one else's. I ask for nothing more than to complete the task—to deliver the evidence of my dedication and to receive my just recognition."

"James," said Captain O'Brian, "I am the logical one to carry the treaty. You are the logical one to stay here. Donaldson can't be trusted with even the smallest task. The dey will squash the deal unless you keep him happy."

"Donaldson is fine at doing nothing," I said, "and that is the sum total of his duty until the money is delivered. Only I am fully aware of the subtleties and protocol necessary to complete this transaction. Only I am able to answer the inevitable questions of detail that Colonel Humphreys is certain to ask. I am the one to serve!"

The debate raged until we were joined by both Skjoldebrand and Baccri and their weight was added to that of Captain O'Brian. They all assured me, over and over again, that I would receive just recognition for my efforts, but I was needed in Algiers. Captain O'Brian, as the senior-ranking captive, was the obvious choice to carry the dispatches and treaty.

On Friday, September 11, 1795, at two p.m., Captain Richard O'Brian departed aboard a Spanish brig. He had seen ten years, one month, and twelve days in captivity. Twenty days fewer than my term of enslavement.

CHAPTER THIRTY-NINE

January–May 1795

I REMEMBER THIS WAITING PERIOD as spent in a deep whirlpool. A single deep twist created by the furies of nature. There was no particular storm, for the sun reflected in a rainbow of colors from the wave-mist high over my head. The recollection is more that of a cork, a waterlogged cork, caught in a deep gyration, constantly shit upon by seagulls. Down, down I went, weighed ever deeper by a collation of salt water and shit.

First, O'Brian disappeared. The court knew where he was, but there was no direct correspondence between Algiers and Lisbon. Miciah Baccri fished among his relatives for information and reported that Colonel Humphreys had no money. It seemed that the United States Congress provided him with open letters of credit but no cash. Further, Miciah disclosed, the worthy colonel was enamored of a lovely Spanish banker's daughter and therefore unavailable to pursue exchanging the awkward paper credit of his office into tangible gold. To this task he had assigned Captain Richard O'Brian.

O'Brian! A pleasant man. Well regarded by his peers. My former friend was unqualified in the manners of court and ignorant of politics. This man O'Brian—word trickled through the capillaries of Jewish intelligence—was wandering from Lisbon to Madrid, and then from Paris to London, seeking aid and comfort for the American cause. Gold for paper was his simple plea.

Our bumpkin minister plenipotentiary had no vision of the world beyond the hard reality of ships, sails, and storms. He was a hen searching for the most ferocious fox. A lamb casting about for a diving eagle. Four more dedicated enemies of our fate would be difficult to imagine than Lisbon, Madrid, Paris, and (yes, indeed!) London. None wanted a stronger competitor. All wanted the United States to be a simple nation of farmers, with ships no larger than could be managed by one man and two oars. All four of these nations had committed gold and men to ripping one another apart, and were fully involved at that favorite task. To the capitals of these enemy nations drifted our hope for salvation from slavery—Captain Richard O'Brian.

Baccri and I sent messages through our own conduits, pleading that he deal with bankers or statesmen of Leghorn or Venice or any of the Hanseatic towns. I knew for a certainty that it would be a simple matter to negotiate letters of credit—even on my own name!—in any of these centers.

Hassan Bashaw raged.

After six months of wandering and pleading, O'Brian found Genoa, and he quickly raised nearly three hundred thousand dollars. With that amount in hand, and the balance quickly raised from other Italian bankers, he chartered a ship for Algiers.

Baccri knew of the financial details almost as they happened, and so did our enemies. French agents who had shadowed O'Brian in his excursions through Europe informed a cruiser from Tripoli of a fat goose, easily available, and it came to pass. The ship, gold, and O'Brian all ended in that most lawless of the Barbary States: Tripoli.

Hassan Bashaw raged.

In early November 1795, Donaldson was taken ill with the bilious colic. His disposition improved during this period of introspection into the nature of death, but reverted to normal with the restoration of gout as his sole complaint. He was nearly recovered, when on the twentieth of November, the American sailors and mates laid siege to his chambers.

"We're free men, you old hickory face!"

"Get us quarters in the town. Cap'ns ain't no better'n us."

"Enough of the plague and vermin. Get us beds and grub."

Their complaints and demands ran in that vein, and I served as their sympathetic advocate with the ambassador. He replied, in ill humor, that they should have patience and return to their prison.

"Bugger your patience, goat foot. The next rock I crack will be your head," and similar comments could be heard as they left the ambassador's residence.

—◆—

On New Year's Day, January 1, 1796, a siege was again laid upon Donaldson's house by the sailors and mates. On this occasion there was no budging them. The prison walls have seen the last American face, they promised.

Surprisingly, Roger Vaughn was their spokesman. He was quiet in his manner of presenting each argument but firm in his convictions. "Mr. Donaldson, sir. This house, in a manner of speaking, is American property. Since we mates and men are free by right of your own signed hand, we choose to reside here. With you as company if you wish, but we won't be returning to any prison."

"Now, see here!" With great expression of pain, Donaldson lifted himself from the couch. "You have no right!" he said. "Get out!"

The sailors ignored his command and began spreading through the house. They ate fresh fruit and vegetables in the kitchen. Laughed and spat and drank from bottles of wine and brandy in the makeshift office.

Donaldson waved his cane at them and bellowed again. "Get out!" When he struck a sailor on the shoulder, the gaunt swabbie turned to the American ambassador, grabbed the walking stick, and broke it over his knee. As an afterthought, the seaman gave a gentle shove to the ambassador and toppled him to the floor.

Donaldson's shouts brought servants, and soon the prison guardians arrived. They beat the sailors with the flat side of their swords and with long, stout sticks. I was in the palace when news of the insurrection came to the dey, and he immediately ordered all of the rebels chained, two by two, and sent to the harbor to load heavy rocks.

With the trials and tribulations created by Donaldson, and with the burden of my own self-pity to keep me isolated from good friends, I managed to neglect any contact with Ahmed. He remedied the situation with a note directing me to meet him at our favorite coffeehouse. He was smiling when I met him, and quickly released a list of his current triumphs for my pleasure.

"My estate is flourishing beyond my wildest expectations," he gushed. "I'm now a general and a father!"

"Father!" I cried. "You are a father!"

"So I've been told by the child's mother. It will be a few months before the evidence is before us, but I've been promised a son."

"You'd be better served by a daughter. Sons grow to an age, and then disappear from your protection; pray to Allah for a daughter to comfort your old age."

Ahmed nodded toward the coffeegee for a refill of our cups, then waited until we were alone again. "I've been in recent conversation with an emissary of the Turkish sultan."

"Allah's emissary to the world."

"So to speak. He's certainly my commander of the janissary."

"Will you share this celestial conversation with an unworthy infidel?"

My friend in life smiled and drained his cup. "The emissary said that I'm the single leader of the janissary here in Algiers, and I will likely assume even higher responsibilities in my older age."

We sat smiling at the other for a long moment. "Will, I will miss you when I leave this beautiful place." A small constriction of my throat gave us another long pause. "Maybe a son is better, after all—someone who will follow in your steps and serve his people."

"Allah will decide, my friend, so give it no further thought."

"Allah will not impede my memories of our adventures, Ahmed, but may he love and protect you far, far into your old age."

Ahmed was pleased. He was also pressed toward many duties, and although he protested that my company was central to what he most desired, I took my leave.

◆

Later, while I was eating some pasta covered with olive oil and herbs and anticipating the hot, mindless depth of the bath, a contingent of American sailors roared into my tavern and surrounded me. Each in turn cursed me and called me a traitor and coward. These very men were recipients of my charity. They ate my food, wore my clothes, and received any protection that I could muster. When they began to threaten me with physical violence, I was forced to call upon my tavern guards and the Christian corporals for assistance.

◆

Just when every moment of my life seemed dedicated to black deeds, Peter Eric suggested a captured Genoese brig as a meritorious investment. A crew from Ibn Hudaij's cruiser had recently sailed the prize into harbor loaded with a cargo of supplies and passengers bound for Mecca. The holy season was close upon us, and the demand for quick passage by the pilgrims, plus a good quantity of wheat in the hold, combined to elicit a promise of likely profit.

Quietly, without creating suspicion or depressing prices, I was able to sell six taverns and then reinvest my money in the brig. Hassan Bashaw was silent about my enterprise, and my gift of an eighth interest in the ship to the first secretary of state permitted my ship to undertake an uneventful and profitable trip to Egypt. As part of my arrangements, I was able to parole an American to serve as captain, and he dutifully followed my instructions in securing both passengers and freight to Alexandria. He then chartered the ship to Tarabulus with a cargo of flax. In this fashion of selling needed goods for a high price, and buying surplus products in the same port at a low price, my captain worked his way through six Turkish ports before returning to Algiers.

"I'm an old man." said Hassan Bashaw.

He looked old. His whiskers were listless, and the fingers of each hand shook with a slight tremor. Ahmed and I stood before him, marveling at his sedate response to the volatile situation.

"I'll have none of your running away." The dey spoke to me in soft tones, but there was no mistaking the intensity of his command. "You got me into this swamp of broken promises, and you will see it through until the end. Liars and incompetent fools. There is no treaty and no freedom for you until I have the gold securely in my palace." Hassan Bashaw turned from me to Ahmed al-Koita. "You must act quickly if this treaty is to be completed. I am promoting you by one rank. What is that now? General? Yes? Can't have anything less for the job."

He motioned General Ahmed al-Koita closer and handed him a square leather dispatch case. "Give this to my little brother, the bey of

Tripoli, and stand by his side while it is read. It simply says that he must give up the ship, gold, and O'Brian, or suffer a war."

He paused, and with a weak smile said to me, "The French are clever in their ways, are they not? Friends into enemies, with only the provocateur to benefit." He nodded with palsied wariness. "It is as you warned.

"Now, General al-Koita, after the bey has read the dispatch and displayed his tantrum, you will order the gold and O'Brian to my court, posthaste. Maintain the dignity of our regency and insist upon this order, by my command."

"Yes, my lord."

"Now then, when O'Brian stands at your side, tell him, in English, to make a very superficial count of the gold and then take his leave of Tripoli. You may sell your camels and return to Algiers aboard his ship."

"I have my orders and I will obey, Your Excellency." Ahmed looked splendid in his uniform. His black skin glowed with strength.

"My fastest messenger can reach Tripoli in twelve days," the dey told his general. "Possibly a janissary troop can urge their camels with the same lack of caution."

"It shall be done, Your Excellency."

The dey nodded to dismiss us. We both kissed his hand, in turn, and backed away from the apartment.

Ahmed and his squad of troopers traversed the mountains, wadi, and desert—from Algiers to Tripoli—in eleven days. It was forty additional days before O'Brian, the gold, and the ship arrived in Algiers.

When O'Brian returned with the gold to free the captive Americans, there was no joy and no celebration. Some of us marked nearly eleven years burying friends and losing teeth. Now the Mediterranean was open to our merchants, and we were free.

I was free.

With the fact of liberation attested to by treaty and gold, a gloom settled upon each free man. I was not exempt from the malaise. Even though my isolation was complete, I still listened and watched. The Americans stood together in drunken ignorance, waving their arms and shouting at me whenever they spotted me in the baegnio or in their ceaseless wanderings around the harbor. I served as their lightning rod for lives misspent and shortened. I was the Jew who had squandered their every penny. The nigger lover who ignored his compatriots in favor of pirates. The leech of their blood.

Through the spring of 1796, small bands of Americans found passage home on merchant ships bound to Boston or New York, yet for no specific reason that I could name, I remained. Ahmed and I still met in the coffeehouse and talked of his plans. I was silent of mine, and after a few rebuffs, he made no further inquiries.

The matter of naval supplies from the United States remained a niggling concern to the dey. By gaining completion of this part of the treaty, Algiers would be independent of the northern nations—Denmark, Sweden, and Holland. With ship masts, planking, and tar available from the United States, the dey could manipulate the annual tribute due from European countries to his great advantage. War or tribute, it mattered little to the dey, and he knew that his ship captains were anxious to spread their sails. The picture of an American alliance, with ample profit for both nations, remained, but the intensity of his desire for this dream was greatly diminished.

In mid-April the dey informed me that he had no confidence in the United States fulfilling the treaty, but as a last resort he would send me with a letter to my prince.

"I am a free man, Your Excellency, and no longer in your charge."

"In what manner are you free, my escribaño grande? Your feet are certainly free to carry you where they will. I question if your heart—or stomach, possibly!—remains free of my bond. It is a question, then: Will you serve as my commissioner to your country?"

"Most assuredly, effendi. It is my honor to serve you for this final task."

In the next few days I sold my brig and purchased an Italian three-mast polacca ship. O'Brian, alas, still remained in Algiers and generously agreed to supervise the change from lateen to square sails, as most seafaring men judged the Atlantic Ocean best weathered with square rigging.

My departure gift from the dey was a painting of my portrait by the court artist. Hassan Bashaw provided me with a captain's uniform consisting of purple jacket, outlined with gold trim, and a pale-green vest. Large shoulder epaulets marked my rank for the picture. He viewed the completed miniature painting and remarked, "Here is permanent evidence of American slaves starving under the heel of evil Moors!"

We both laughed.

Even a most considerate artist had been unable to hide ample evidence of good food and my sedentary avocation. We laughed in sad recognition of our parting.

"Tell your prince that he has nine months to complete the terms of our treaty. If we have not received the naval supplies by then, I will void the agreement and send out the cruisers."

His shoulders and chest settled inward, and he waved me away. "May Allah protect us both, my infidel friend."

"May Allah bring us together once again," I responded.

"It may be his design to return you to my service. We shall see. We shall see."

I kissed my patron's hand for the last time and left the palace. At the next dawn I took leave of the important grandees, the officers of the realm, and Ahmed al-Koita.

"You're making a mistake, Jamie," Ahmed told me. "You have

nothing but enemies in the United States. Stay here in Algiers; you can count on at least two friends."

"I can't, Ahmed. I need to go home."

"I'll miss you, Jamie," said Ahmed al-Koita.

"I'll miss you, Will Melman."

After receiving my dispatches and orders from Captain Barlow, I sailed at the meridian, after nearly eleven years a slave. The eighth of May, 1796, captain and master of my ship, the *Independence*.

Glossary

Baegnio Prison

Bashaw Title designating high military rank in the Ottoman Empire.

Berber One of several North African tribes.

bey Turkish title of respect, and provincial governor in Algeria.

caliph The secular and religious head of a Moslem state.

City of Mopti Currently named Jenne

coffeegee A servant responsible for making and pouring coffee.

dey Title given to governor of Algeria prior to 1830. Also, a title taken by rulers of Tripoli and Tunis.

djinn A mysterious spirit of the desert with power of good or evil. djinni, pl.

dragoman A servant with equivalent status as a British butler.

effendi Title of respect.

Frank	A North African title for all Europeans.
grandee	An eminent or high-ranking personage.
gran porte	Ruler of the Ottoman Empire.
imam	Prayer leader and Moslem scholar.
Imam	One of the leaders considered by the Shiites to be a successor of Mohammed.
jihad	Moslem holy war against infidels.
Jiliba River	Currently named Niger River.
Kabyle	One of several North African tribes.
kel rela	Nobility of Tuareg.
kuskussu	Essential component of North African meals. Varies according to ingredients available, with one constant: fine-grained semolina. Usually seasoned with cayenne or chili peppers.
metulem	A Tuareg greeting.
mole	A dock created from packed earth and rocks.
Moor	People of mixed Berber and Arab lineage.

mosaby Young man (or boy) who serves older men.

muezzin One who calls the Moslem faithful to prayer.

mullah Title for Moslem religious teacher or leader.

rais Leader or captain.

saeltia Two-masted vessel, lateen-rigged sail, larger and more sea worthy than a xebec.

sbirro Crier for prison.

sheik A leader of an Arab family, village, or tribe.

subaltern Lowest military rank for an officer.

Tuareg Nomadic tribes who occupy western and central Sahara. An individual of the Tuareg tribe.

vikilharche Captain of the port of Algiers.

wadi Gully or riverbed that remains dry except during rare rainy seasons.

xebec A small, three-masted Mediterranean vessel, usually with triangular sails in a lateen rigging.

Selected Bibliography

The Conquest of Morocco, Douglas Porch, Alfred Knopf, New York, 1983

Arabic Thought 1798-1939, Albert Hourani, Oxford Press, London, 1962

The Diplomatic Relations of the Barbary Powers 1776-1816, Ray W. Irwin, Russell & Russell, New York, 1970

The Surest Path: The Political Treatise of Nineteenth Century Muslim Statesmen, Editor Leon C. Brown, Cambridge, 1967.

The History of the Maghreb, Abdallah Laroui, Princeton, 1977.

The Shores of the Black Ships, John Marriner, London, 1971.

The US and North Africa, Charles F Gallagher, Harvard, 1963.

The Barbary Slaves, Stephen Clissold, London, 1977.

America and the Mediterranean World 1776–1882, James Field, Princeton, 1969.

Barbary Legend: War, Trade and Piracy in North Africa, 1415–1830, Godfrey Fisher, Oxford, 1957.

Memoirs

Cathcart, James Leander, *The Captives*, compiled by Mrs. J. B. Newkirk, LaPort Indiana, 1901.

Cathcart, James Leander, *Tripoli: First War with the US*, compiled by Mrs. J. B. Newkirk, 1901.

American Captives in Tripoli, Dr. James Cowdery's Journal, Boston, 1806.

A Journal of the Captivity and Suffering of John Foss, Newburyport, 1798.

History of the Captivity and Suffering of Mrs. M Martin, Who was Six Years a Captive in Algiers, Boston, 1807.

Horrors of Slavery: Or the American Tars in Tripoli, William Ray, Troy, 1808.

Biographies

Life of the Late General William Eaton, Charles Prentis, Brookfield, 1813.

Our Navy and the Barbary Corsairs, Gardner W Allen, Cambridge, 1905.

The Story of the Barbary Corsairs, Stanley Lane-Poole, New York, 1902.

Everyday Life in Ottoman Turkey, Raphaela Lewis, GP Putnam's Sons, New York, 1971.